A Cast of
Falcons

The Dr Nell Ward Mystery Series

A Cast of Falcons

Sarah Yarwood-Lovett

First published in Great Britain in 2022 by

embla
books

Bonnier Books UK Limited
4th Floor, Victoria House, Bloomsbury Square, London, WC1B 4DA
Owned by Bonnier Books
Sveavägen 56, Stockholm, Sweden

A CIP catalogue record for this book is available from the British Library.

ISBN: 9781471415340

This book is typeset using Atomik ePublisher

Embla Books is an imprint of Bonnier Books UK
www.bonnierbooks.co.uk

For Ian.
This book is about finding your animal and following your heart, so of course this one's for you. You're the most golden person I know, and my Partner in Crime in every sense.

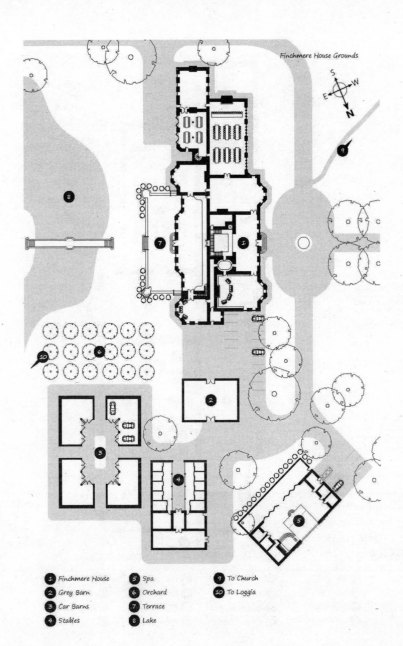

Finchmere House Grounds

1. Finchmere House
2. Grey Barn
3. Car Barns
4. Stables
5. Spa
6. Orchard
7. Terrace
8. Lake
9. To Church
10. To Loggia

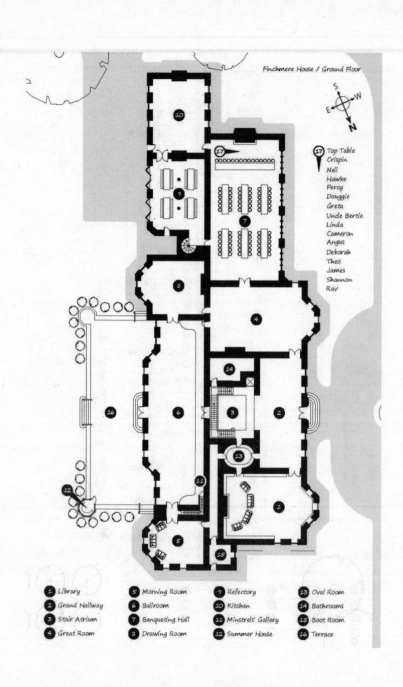

Finchmere House / Ground Floor

17 Top Table
Crispin
Nell
Hawke
Percy
Douggie
Greta
Uncle Bertie
Linda
Cameron
Angus
Deborah
Theo
James
Shannon
Rav

1 Library
2 Grand Hallway
3 Stair Atrium
4 Great Room
5 Morning Room
6 Ballroom
7 Banqueting Hall
8 Drawing Room
9 Refectory
10 Kitchen
11 Minstrels' Gallery
12 Summer House
13 Oval Room
14 Bathrooms
15 Boot Room
16 Terrace

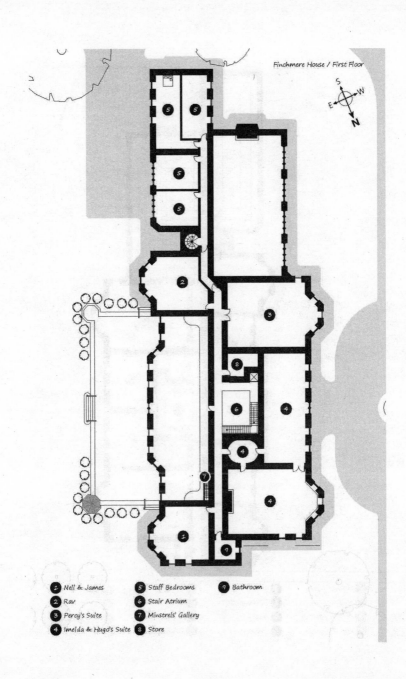

Finchmere House / First Floor

1 Nell & James
2 Rav
3 Percy's Suite
4 Imelda & Hugo's Suite
5 Staff Bedrooms
6 Stair Atrium
7 Minstrels' Gallery
8 Store
9 Bathroom

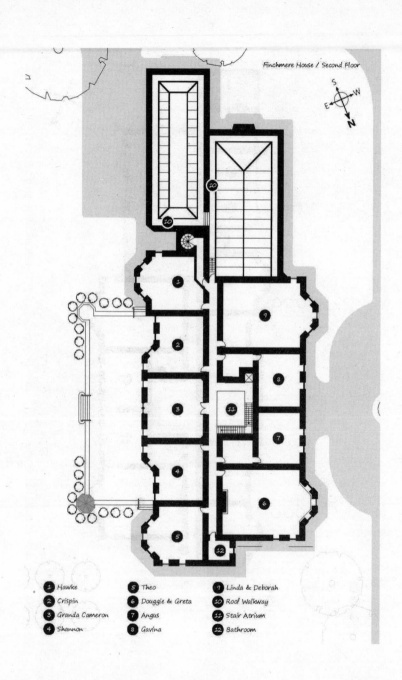

Finchmere House / Second Floor

1 Hawke
2 Crispin
3 Granda Cameron
4 Shannon
5 Theo
6 Douggie & Greta
7 Angus
8 Gavina
9 Linda & Deborah
10 Roof Walkway
11 Stair Atrium
12 Bathroom

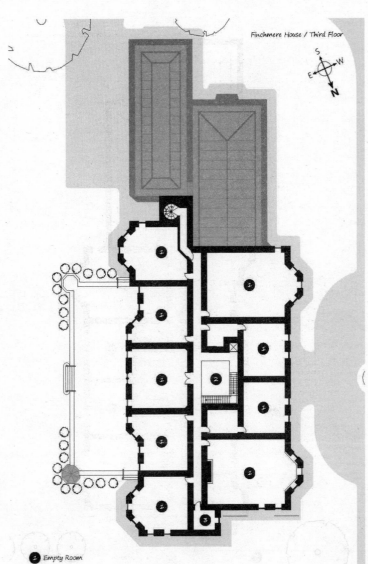

Finchmere House / Third Floor

1 Empty Room
2 Stair Atrium
3 Store Room

Chapter 1

Arthur held the gun to the side of his head, his hand shaking. Taking a deep, shuddering breath, he released the safety catch, his eyes screwed shut as he braced himself to squeeze the trigger.

Nerves jangling, he dropped the gun and jumped as it landed on the desk with a clatter. His jittery gaze swung to the office door. Locked, like the windows. There could be no shred of suspicion on those he loved.

He sloshed whisky into the tumbler. His fourth. Not that it mattered. Nothing mattered now. Gulping, Arthur felt the liquid trickle down his chin. He spluttered, choking on the fumes flaming the back of his throat and nose. *Well, one way was as good as another.* Maniacal laughter threatened to erupt.

Maybe mania was a response to his intense shame. He'd burned up with it. Yet he forced himself to read the newspaper article again. No escaping it. His family were better off without him, without the disgrace he'd caused. He couldn't put them in the position of having to decide whether to stand by him, or not. And he couldn't face their disappointed loyalty, or their desertion. He'd put them through enough.

With a surge of emotion, Arthur snatched up his note and added, *I love you. I love you all too much. I'm sorry.* He placed it at the corner of the desk, where he hoped his blood wouldn't reach it.

Enough now. A calm fell over him, like watching himself from the outside.

With ritualistic deliberation, he checked the safety catch, drew the gun up like a salute and settled the barrel against his skin. He took a breath – his last breath – his lungs filling, his heartbeat steady, but pain metastasising inside him. Staring at the photo of his family, Arthur pulled the trigger.

Five years later

Saturday 13th March – 3 p.m.

'There's no point being upset about it, Nell – my parents can't make it now. Granda's too ill. They can't leave him.'

'Oh, Percy.' Rotating twenty feet up in the air, Nell leaned back in her climbing harness as she stared at her best friend's face on the screen. Not the most ideal moment to FaceTime. But she couldn't ignore Percy's calls. 'Surely, if ever there was a sign to give up on rushing this wedding, this is it? First you couldn't host it from Glencoille Castle; now your folks won't even be here? This is a *huge* deal.'

Despite trying to do the right thing by Percy, Nell inwardly groaned, as her mind raced. The wedding was in three hours. It wouldn't be simply a matter of recalling all those gilt-edged invitations, asking almost a hundred Scottish clanspeople, eminent guests and political associates to the wedding of Lady Persephone MacKenzie to Mr Hawke McAnstruther. This would mean having to herd up expectant guests, all in their wedding finery, who'd have travelled from far and wide to be there. *But it would be OK, surely? Illness couldn't be helped. People would understand.*

In the corner of her phone's screen, Nell noticed that a pained frown pinched between her brown eyes, so she made her expression more sympathetic. With her free hand, she smoothed her pixie-cut chestnut hair, which was sticking up on end from the exertion of the climb. She was already frowning again. To be fair, it was more to do with the harness digging into her thighs than the unravelling of Percy's society wedding.

The irony was, it wasn't even supposed to be a wedding. Things had escalated somewhat over the past couple of weeks. *Originally*, Nell had been invited to Glencoille for Percy's engagement party, complete with a week crammed full of outdoor-adventure activities. But, with news of Hawke's mother, Linda, having that awful terminal diagnosis, the engagement party had morphed into a wedding. Then, as Percy was finalising plans, Glencoille Castle's roof had sprung a leak, and merrymakers ceilidh-ing around buckets in the ballroom wasn't something the insurance could accommodate.

When Percy – her freckled face devoid of its usual spark and drenched in disappointment – had told her that she'd had to find another venue or cancel the whole thing, Nell had found herself offering to host the wedding at Finchmere. And she'd pulled in every favour possible to give Percy a wonderful day. *But now . . . what?*

'It's fine, Nell, really. All I need you to do now is rearrange the seating plan.'

That was typical Percy. She could magic up mischief and tempt everyone along with her, and she could spin drama out of thin air, but she'd always wave away a real calamity with minimal fuss. Nell studied her friend's face for signs of what she really wanted. But there was no hint of regret, just steely resignation. Percy's typical bravado.

'Percy, whatever you want to do is fine by me. Honestly.' Nell shifted her weight, as she dangled amongst the dusty beams of light slanting through the open slats at the top of the old barn's clock tower. The view reminded her that she wasn't hanging on the line for the good of her health, but that she actually had a job to do. But it could wait. Percy needed time to decide what she really wanted.

'Oh, God, easy for you to say, Nell. But, you see, someone has gone to a huge amount of effort on my behalf. Use of Finchmere's family chapel, a banquet, band, fire-dancers, a full-on drone swarm light-spectacular, a mountain of a cake, the whole place spilling over with flowers by six designer florists. Plus, family and close friends staying in the house, with a week of activities planned. *And* even putting up all the other guests overnight in Finchmere's hotel, or in hand-picked places in the local area. And all in a stupidly short time.'

Nell stuck her tongue out. 'Well, you're one cool customer. I didn't think you'd noticed.'

She was relieved to see a hint of a smile. Then Percy shrugged, making her fiery curls quiver. 'Even if we could postpone most of the guests, with Uncle Bertie coming, y'know . . . show must go on.'

'Oh, come on . . .' Nell bit her lip. She knew Percy wouldn't buy it if she tried to deny that sorting out the security for Percy's godfather, the Duke of Aveshire, had been a pain. But these were Percy's *parents*, who were usually the life and soul of the party. 'Are you absolutely sure? They'll be so upset, Perce.'

Nell spotted a flicker of doubt on Percy's face, quickly hidden with her typical plucky grin. It didn't reach her eyes. 'I know. Me too. But we just can't cancel this late. I'm headed up the aisle in *three hours*, Nell!'

'Nothing is impossible, Perce. I'll take care of it.' Well, she was appropriating credit there. As if to remind her of who was doing the real work, Nell's phone buzzed with texts flashing over Percy's face: questions from the harassed event manager.

'Can we just carry on as planned, Nell? Will you make these final few arrangements for me? Please?'

'Fine.' Nell nodded, though it didn't feel fine. 'But I do need to know if Hawke needs his own room to get ready in.'

'Oh, come on, Nell. Of course Hawke and I need to get ready separately. It's romantic! Besides, my frock's taking up my entire room.'

Nell didn't doubt that, even on short notice, Percy had something spectacular up her sleeve. Now they were in their thirties, the past couple of years had been a never-ending wedding circuit of springs and summers at increasingly glamorous country piles. And Percy wasn't the type to be outdone.

'And if it's not too much to ask . . . I'm out and about, at the stables on your lovely estate. Can I persuade you to add a good country hack to the week's programme of activities?'

'Already done. I *have* met you, you know? I know what you like to do.'

'OK, sorry. I've just got in the habit of having to point things like that out to Hawke.'

Nell kept a tactful silence. Then she managed to say, 'Sure. Well, I'm looking forward to meeting him, and to getting to know him over the week.'

The five days of celebrations also meant that Nell's parents would have a chance to get back from their own friends' wedding (apparently, when you were on your fourth husband in your mid-sixties, the wedding circuit upgraded to a villa on Lake Como), in time to share some of Percy's extended nuptials. She had seemed more disappointed at Nell's folks missing the wedding than she did about her own.

'But I don't see any point in reallocating your parents' room. I'm sure if they can make it, they'll move heaven and earth to be here. And we can clear their table settings, but I'll save spaces for them at the top table. Just in case.'

As she imagined the rearrangements, Nell asked, 'What about Theo and Angus?' These two close family friends were always at their gatherings. Despite living in Switzerland, suave businessman Theo had known Percy's mum, Greta, since they'd gone to uni together, and always turned up to support her charity events and join celebratory occasions. And Angus, Glencoille's sheriff, was like a brother to Douggie, Percy's dad: the two men had been best friends all their lives. Growing up, Nell and Percy had all but lived at each other's places during school holidays. Both of their estates had frequent visitors, but this close group was more like family to Percy – and to Nell.

'I don't think they'll come if my folks can't make it.'

The disappointment Nell heard in Percy's voice matched the thud of her own. But then she caught sight of Rav looking up at her, as he stood in the dimly lit barn, twenty feet below. He was being endlessly patient, considering she'd got him to come early and help with this task before the ceremony. Now she was interrupting their hurried work to chat. While he belayed her rope, he couldn't pointedly check his watch. But as Rav shook his always-unruly dark wavy hair out of his brown eyes – which so attentively watched her every move to make sure he'd catch her if she slipped – Nell knew they'd be rolling at the badly timed call.

After final assurances to Percy, Nell ended the call and then texted her event manager with the update, before wiggling her phone back into her pocket – all while twisting high in the air.

The harness squeezed her thighs, and the leg that had done all the hard work, rappelling up in the slingshot, throbbed after the twenty-foot ascent. But here she was, dangling beside a barn-owl box that Rav had hauled up over the barn's truss and which was about the size of an oven. All she had to do now was wrangle the box onto the platform that had once housed the tower's long-disused clock mechanism.

Grabbing the corners of the wooden box, she pushed it upwards until an edge jammed against the platform. Taking a deep breath, she shoved as hard as she could to deliver the box up and onto the shelf, until a third of it teetered on the ledge.

In mid-air, she had nothing to brace against. Nothing at all to rely on but the biting harness and her biceps which, until now, she'd *believed* were reasonably toned. Sweat stung her eyes as she heaved again, shoving the box as hard as she could onto the platform, until it shivered backwards and nestled into position. Now she had to get a few inches higher. Grasping the knots of her climbing rope, Nell slid them up, lifting her right foot inside the slingshot. Stepping down hard pushed her up, level with the box.

'How does that look?' she called down to Rav, as she spun in the harness. The entrance to the box lined up with the missing weatherboards of the opposite wall, which led out to the rough grassland of the orchard, linked by hedgerows to the farmland beyond, offering perfect foraging habitat.

'Spot on.'

It was good to be working with him again, enjoying their easy rapport, intuiting what the other was doing. She'd missed that.

Swaying, Nell reached out to grip the platform and pulled herself in closer. 'If they take to it, I can watch them coming and going from the summer house. Like a luxury hide.'

Stretching her other hand inside the box, she felt for the two cameras, already set to motion detection: one, infrared, which she angled to cover activity inside the box; the other she clipped to the outside of the box to cover the barn and record adults flying in – and perhaps, eventually, owlets fledging. Nell unfurled the cameras' cables and let them dangle fifteen feet downwards, tapping against the barn's stout jowl post. The recorders were at the ends of the cables, so she could change SD cards and batteries without disturbing any future nests. Or going through this rigmarole every time.

Reaching in, she spread out the layer of fine sawdust chippings across the base of the box; then she took the spool of garden twine from her thigh pocket, unwound and cut the length needed, and lashed the box into position.

'Done?' Rav called from below.

'Nearly. I'm—ow!' She'd caught her finger in the knot, so massaged her whitened, grooved fingertip: it pinched, but nothing like the harness threatening to cut off circulation in both her thighs. Hurrying, she tied the knot and checked that the box was secure. 'Done!'

With her leg cramping, she inched her way down the rappel line. When she finally reached the ground, her foot got tangled in the loop and she staggered against Rav.

His muscular climber's arms shot around her, steadying her with strong tenderness as her cheek grazed his.

'You OK?' He studied her, his eyes full of concern.

She tested her foot, as Rav held her.

'Nell? Sweetheart?' James's voice, calling from outside the barn, made them both jump.

As Rav let go of Nell, she staggered, half-spiralling on the line she was tethered to, fumbling with the carabiners for release from the tight harness. 'In here! Putting the owl box up.'

James walked in, squinting in the dim light, a wide smile on his face. 'Don't you have enough to do today, then?' But his grin faltered at the sight of Rav, his shrewd blue eyes appraising them both. As Rav moved away to gather up the ropes, Nell shimmied out of the harness, avoiding her boyfriend's detective-level scrutiny. The last time he'd looked at her like that, he'd arrested her for murder. And she hadn't felt as guilty then as she did now. *Not that I have anything to feel guilty about . . .*

Raising her gaze to meet his, she explained, 'We couldn't leave it any later to install the box. It's already late for nesting season. Another few days and we don't stand a chance of it being used.'

James arched his eyebrow at Rav. 'Lucky you thought to bring your climbing gear. To a wedding. Can't imagine that would occur to many people.' Even though his tone was jocular, and his grin disarming, Nell caught a slight edge to his voice and frowned. *He wasn't jealous, was he?*

Rav, however, was either amazingly unruffled by, or totally oblivious to, the hint of interrogation, as he grinned and coiled the ropes into his backpack. 'It's always in the car. I'm prepared for a glamorous heist and a multibillion pay-off, but somehow it's only ever for birds or bats.'

It was true that Rav's kit – for climbing and anything else they needed for their ecological surveys – lived in his car. But he didn't mention that Nell had asked him to get there early to help out.

And, somehow, that made Nell squirm guiltily again.

Saturday 13th March – 3 p.m.

Hawke McAnstruther snaked his hand through the hot tub's foaming water and tugged the tie of Shannon Lanner's bikini. She sipped her champagne then set her crystal flute on the marble surround of Finchmere's spa, leaning back as he kissed her and slid his thigh between her legs.

Shannon's olive skin had the same expensive Mustique-tan – soaked up on superyachts not sunbeds – as the haughty girls who'd joined his school when it went co-ed. Once untouchable, unattainable; until now. At thirty-five, he was gaining some financial ground on those girls who'd rejected him back then – now he'd worked out how to diversify his portfolio. The maths was part of the foreplay. Take Shannon: she may have a protected trust fund, but her family business – a string of restaurants, one with a Michelin star and all overseen single-handedly by her mother since Shannon's father died – was now under strain and easy prey to a business guru like him. Whereas Percy and her folks were a different game altogether; his royal flush – if he played his cards right.

Unravelling Shannon's strappy bikini top, he hurled it across the spa. It snagged, spider-like, on granite rocks, before the waterfall swept it into the infinity pool. He would have let the flowing water lead his eye to the vast atrium window, with its epic vista of rolling downland – if he didn't have a better view right in front of him.

Shannon didn't twist away or squeal, 'What if someone walks in on us?' even though Finchmere House heaved with staff. And Percy (his fiancée and Shannon's cousin) would be on the prowl by now. Devilment gleamed in Shannon's eye; he felt the curve of her wicked smile with his tongue. But, behind them, cutting through the bubbles and the soft classical music, his phone buzzed for the fourth time.

Breaking away from the kiss, she challenged, 'Percy wondering where you are?'

'Probably.' He kissed her. 'But I'm busy right now.'

Sliding her hand inside his shorts, caressing his buttock, she whispered, 'Yes. You are.' The possessive pierce of her talons in his flesh fired heat through him. He pulled her to him, biting her lip.

Twelve minutes later, neither of them hurried to get back into their swimsuits. Shannon must spend as long in the gym, and as much money on skincare and waxing, as he did. Stretching, he checked his phone. 'Ah. Percy wants to make sure I've ignored any messages from Douggie.'

Percy's father had been coming up with excuse after excuse to delay the engagement announcement and then the wedding. And his opposition to Hawke *and* his relationship with Percy had only grown along with Percy's resolve to rebel. It had been great sport from Hawke's ringside seat. Especially as Douggie's bluster had initially been betrayed by his shocking poker face: trembling cheeks, nervous swallow, neck turning puce. As Douggie had become more desperate, his threats had become more overt – and now he was showing his hand. Even so, Hawke knew it wouldn't make any difference. *Because we both know I'm the one with the ace up my sleeve.*

Hawke could see that the more Percy's family pushed her to change her mind, the more she dug her heels in. But, while Shannon's high-risk, unpredictable game-playing made him hot under the collar, Percy was the choice prize. The fact that she was truly high-stakes sport *and* all too easy to tempt into trouble was impossible to resist. Letting the jets work on his lower back, Hawke sighed. 'In a few hours, I'll be in line to inherit Glencoille Castle and its few thousand acres.' He swooped Shannon's jet-black curtain of hair over her shoulder, improving the view. '*Then*, you'll have to call me Lord.'

'Not quite.' Shannon arched an eyebrow. 'Granda Cameron isn't dead yet. *Then* it's Douggie and Greta's, who, OK, are custodians already. *Then* it's Percy's. Would have been mine, too. By rights, *you'd* be calling *me* Lady.'

As her lip curled, Hawke chuckled. 'You really are a jealous little viper in the nest, aren't you? Nothing like the disinherited to know the order of succession inside out.'

'It's wasted on Percy. But she'll still get everything. All because my idiot mother renounced her half of the estate – in the name of love, for God's sake.'

He cupped her breast. 'How *do* you cope, slumming it in your Thames-side penthouse?'

She swivelled in the water, slid a long, lithe leg across his lap and sat astride him. 'By taking what I can get. And if it's Percy's – or Nell's, for that matter – so much the better.'

Chapter 2

'Go on, then.' James gestured up at the owl box, his blue eyes fixed on Nell's. 'Tell me what I'm supposed to be noticing.' A hint of a smile made his eyes gleam.

Nell smiled back at him. *Have I just been projecting?* Despite being in the early days of dating, James had already confided that his previous partner had cheated on him, and Nell worried that her closeness with Rav, as ecology colleagues and friends, would prod that bruise.

But there wasn't anything to worry about; she and Rav weren't as close as they used to be. Nell had once thought there could be more than friendship between them, but when Rav had found out about her background, before she'd mustered the courage to tell him, he'd seen her lack of openness as a lack of trust. And they hadn't seen each other much since Nell had started dating James – not even at work. Yet, despite the new footing their relationship was on, Nell couldn't help occasionally wondering what Rav had been about to say at the Finchmere ball, two months ago, before he was interrupted by James, who'd finally made his own feelings about her clear.

Nell had been flattered by James's enthusiasm, and they'd grown close while he prepared for the murder case. He'd never questioned her background, even though it was a surprise to him during his investigation. She loved his ambition, his difficult career choice, his inner grit. And his sexy, piercing blue eyes.

She took James's hand, glad that he wanted to know about her ecological project. 'We know barn owls are perching in here, see?' She gestured around the barn. Dust motes danced in the dim slanted light slicing through the windows.

Rav kept his distance, lashing the camera cables to the jowl post on the other side of the wide barn.

James squinted. 'OK, what clues are you seeing that I'm not?'

'Those white splashes over the trusses?'

'Isn't that paint?'

'Looks like it, but no. It's owl droppings. And with the brown-and-cream feather snagged on the lintel over the door . . . And these,' Nell gestured at a line of two-inch-long black-grey pellets under the cross-beam, 'show us that this is where they perch to regurgitate the fur and bone of their prey. The darker they are, the fresher they are, so I know this is a current favourite spot.'

Nell heard her inner nerd emerging. No normal person would sound this enthusiastic about owl vomit. But James tugged her hand. 'You think they'll nest?'

'Hope so.' She returned the twine to its shelf, beside the garden pegs, and then, as they walked outside, she hooked the chain with its No Entry sign across the doorway.

After shivering in the fusty barn, Nell blinked in the bright sunshine. The afternoon held the fresh, zesty optimism of spring: of buds about to burst into life, trees hazing with zingy green leaves, and the verdant sweeping lawns fronting Finchmere House filling the air with the sweet scent of cut grass. Daffodils gilded the far banks and haloed the trunks of the copper beeches along the driveway leading out to the lane. Birds darted between the trees, then hid amongst the blushing creamy cups of magnolias near the house, before taking refuge in the dense wisteria – yet to bloom – climbing Finchmere's façade. Around them, the skies trilled and twittered with the melodies of birdsong.

'Well, Percy's got a beautiful day for a wedding,' James said. 'And this is such a stunning place.'

But cheerful though the birdsong sounded, the warbling harmonies trumpeted discord, claiming territories and warning of challenge. And both Nell and Rav snapped round when the chirruping song of a wren became a staccato tutting.

'Ah, he's upset about that magpie,' Rav pointed, as the pied bird fluttered too close to the wren's nest for comfort. The tiny bird hopped along the branches of the magnolia, firing out more indignant, protective tuts until the magpie strutted off.

Nell realised that James hadn't noticed where they were looking; he hadn't tuned into the eco-drama. Concerned he'd feel left out, she took his hand. 'Let's get a drink. Tell me about your day.'

She hesitated, half-turning to Rav. 'Thanks for helping... Would—'

But, luckily, Rav seemed to intuit the reason for her indecision. His glance flitted from James to Nell, and he gave her that easy smile. 'I'd better go and grab a shower and change, ready for the big event.'

James nodded, turned and walked on, and Nell smiled gratefully at Rav, who took a small, flat parcel out of his backpack. With a wink, he tucked it into the top of her rucksack, which she'd slung over one arm. He leaned in to whisper, 'Small gift, for the host.'

Before Nell could say thanks, he shot off towards his car, beyond the smart stables, and past the pristine garages housing her father's classic-car collection.

As she hurried to catch up with James, Nell noticed that Rav was looking across the orchard, frothing with blossom, to the summer house at the corner of the terrace. Rav glanced over his shoulder, checking how the summerhouse lined up with the gap in the weatherboard, and caught Nell watching him. He gave her a double thumbs-up and turned around.

James was heading round, via the back of the house, to the terrace, rather than using the shortcut across the courtyard and into the house via the boot room. She'd given him the standard tour of the premises, and all their nooks and crannies (most recently conducted for Hawke's mother, her partner and the best man, although Nell still hadn't met Hawke himself), but maybe James felt more at ease using the proper entrances. Nell caught up with him at the steps, leading up from the formal rose garden – topiary-hemmed, neatly pruned and ready to flower – to the ballroom.

She slipped her hand in his as they dodged staff stringing up webs of lights along the espaliered apple trees, ribboning blooms across the walls, and the wisteria cladding the stone walls of the house. As they reached the door to the ballroom, they nearly collided with Percy.

'Nell! Oh! And James! Have you seen Hawke?' Percy's wild, red hair escaped her hairband as she scanned beyond the formal rose gardens to the lake, meandering southwards, where squabbling mallards guarded their nests in the reeds and dabbled around lily pads. 'He unpacked, went to explore and that's the last I've seen of him. I need to check something with him.'

Nell shook her head. 'I didn't realise he was here. Might he have gone for a walk in the woods?' She squinted across the gardens, northwards, past swathes of buttercup-bright aconites under luscious pink camelias, to the emerald, mossy woodland, misted with spring-green buds. Primroses, crocuses and snakes-head fritillaries peppered the downland stretching towards the white stone loggia, nestled against the hill.

'Maybe. Shannon arrived soon after us and offered to show him round the grounds.' Percy rolled her eyes theatrically. 'Shouldn't have invited her. Moment of weakness.'

'She *is* family, Percy.'

'Don't remind me.' She wrinkled her nose, then glanced around. 'I thought I'd check the garden, then maybe the spa?' She started to head down the terrace steps, but a background drone suddenly became the intense thwacking and high-pitched whine of a helicopter coming in to land.

Checking the time on her phone, Nell frowned. The duke was over an hour early. From all corners of the house, security personnel ran forward. Sprinting with them to the front of the house, Nell knew they must be wondering about the last-minute change to the schedule.

James and Percy kept up with her, and they halted at the sight of the helicopter, hovering low over the vast lawn, making the grass shimmer like a green sea. With touchdown, Percy's copper curls whipped around her face as the helicopter's blades whirred to a whining halt. Stepping closer, Nell's mind raced to work out where she could ensconce a demanding and elderly guest. *Oh, bloody perfect. I still need to get changed, make sure the tables are reset, and some guests haven't even arrived yet . . .*

But a flame-haired bear of a man – Douggie – burst from the door and strode towards them.

Nell's heart lifted. *Percy's parents had made it!* Then, with growing dismay, she realised that Douggie's gait wasn't showing the set determination of someone who'd rearranged a parent's care to ensure they could make their daughter's wedding; it was a grim march into battle. Behind him, Greta, willowy and auburn-haired, appeared to weave and stagger a little on her feet. Dread slithered in Nell's stomach. *Greta's . . . drunk?* A slim man, perma-tanned and ageless but probably in his fifties – *Theo* – dashed to Greta's side and took her arm. *What the . . . ?*

'Oh . . . *bollocks.*' Percy's good humour was replaced with a scowl of disbelief.

Nell shot her a bewildered look, as Percy turned and marched back to the house, swearing again under her breath.

But Douggie had her in his sights. 'Percy! Hey! What the bloody *hell* do you think you're doing?'

As the family stormed inside, Nell rushed to keep up with her friend. 'Your father poses a very good question, Percy,' she hissed. 'What's going on?' They crossed the parqueted hall, heading up to the suite that Percy had claimed they wouldn't need. 'I thought they were indisposed.'

And the family had arrived en masse. Nell side-eyed Granda Cameron, distinctly hale and hearty – *not* on his deathbed, as Percy had implied – whose wheelchair was being pushed by Angus towards the Butler's lift. *Bloody hell.* If Angus and Theo were turning up like this – for what . . . a confrontation? – then whatever was going on, it was serious.

Beside her, Percy's silence wasn't one of calmness or of someone frantically trying to work out how to wriggle out of trouble. It was like a swelling river, surging against a dam, ready to burst. Nell sensed that behind closed doors, the eruption of Douggie vs Percy would be epic.

James had watched these reactions, and now caught Nell's hand and squeezed it. She levelled a grim gaze at him in answer to his silent question. *No, no, I'm not OK. How can I be, if my best friend isn't?* On the first-floor landing, she tilted her head along the hallway and James nodded, let go of her hand and tactfully headed to their room, while Nell continued upstairs with Percy.

As they reached the second floor, the lift doors opened and Angus steered a complaining Cameron along the galleried landing to the hallway to Douggie and Greta's suite. Nell wasn't sure if Angus's presence was a good sign: if anyone knew how to reason with Douggie, it was Angus, putting his sheriff-honed mediation skills to good use. But he wouldn't be here for a minor issue, and he didn't look in a conciliatory mood. With his dark beard and hair trimmed to a uniform stubble, and a gimlet-eyed, stoic expression, he was a forbidding sight.

Once they were all assembled inside their suite, Douggie wheeled round, his face crimson from holding back. 'You know full well I'd never interfere without good reason. But this . . . this *lad*,' Douggie spat the word like a cobra spitting venom, 'he's no good. You can't go through with this, Percy. We,' he gestured at Greta, white-faced against the wall, 'won't allow it.'

Nell's jaw dropped. Since she and Percy had been little, Douggie and Greta had been open about their good luck that, despite being pushed together by their plotting, political parents, they'd turned out to be compatible. But they'd made a point of raising Percy to make her own choices and, true to their word, they'd loved her ex, Hamish, a student doctor struggling with university fees. *Mind you, he never did propose. Would they have reacted like this if he had? And given their awkwardly recent break-up – which Percy had been unusually tight-lipped about – are Douggie and Greta worried that Hawke's a rebound?*

Douggie rubbed his autumnal hedge of a beard and glanced at Greta, as she sank onto the Louis XIV chaise longue. He strode over and took her shaking hands between his two huge paws. He nodded at his wife, then turned. 'We mean it, Percy. If you marry that man, we will disinherit you.'

Chapter 3

Saturday 13th March – 4 p.m.

Nell reeled. *What the hell?* Like her, Percy, had been trained since birth to take on her estate, and they'd both established new businesses, new ways for their properties to grow and be self-supporting. Over the last two years, Percy had made Glencoille a destination for adventure activities, with a first-class reputation and healthy profit margin. She guarded her responsibilities fiercely, not even allowing anyone else to cull the deer herd, in case they were a poor shot. Percy *was* Glencoille.

Percy's pale face blanched. But her jaw set. 'I can't believe you'd say that, after everything—'

'We're not just saying it.' Douggie's broad, caber-tossing shoulders set. 'We'll do it. Lawyers are meeting us here tomorrow afternoon. It's your choice.' He swallowed hard, tugging at his shirt collar.

'*Choice?*' Her chin jut mirrored her father's. 'It's an ultimatum!'

Her parents, Granda Cameron, Angus, and even Theo, were lined up in a wall of stony disapproval. Nell reached for Percy's hand and squeezed it. But Percy pulled away. A split-second glance between them told Nell it was her cue to leave.

She nodded and left the room, leaning against the door as she closed it. *What the hell has Percy been doing? And what am I supposed to do now?* She heard the band warming up, the pattering of feet on polished parquet as finishing touches were made before the estate filled up with people expecting a celebratory ceremony, banquet and entertainment. *God, am I back to finding an excuse to cancel? Or should I try to smooth over the cracks and carry on as planned? What would Percy want? And how could she ever forgive her parents for a threat like this?*

With leaden feet, Nell headed to the galleried landing, downstairs and along the hall to her own room. Only then did she realise she was still clutching her rucksack.

Beyond the closed door to her en suite, she heard the water of the shower stop and James call out, 'So, what's happening?'

'Honestly? I'm not sure.' Nell pulled out Rav's gift and unwrapped the tissue paper. A T-shirt. A Western-style, sepia photo of her, riddled with bullet holes, below the caption: Cookingdean's Most Wanted. A reminder of Rav declaring himself her partner in crime when she was a murder suspect, before the awkwardness had grown between them. But he'd helped in the barn when she'd asked, and they'd fallen back into that ease of working together. Maybe Rav was trying to show her that they could get their friendship back on track.

But, as James emerged from the en suite, she shoved the T-shirt under her pillow and turned, breathless, to see him towelling his wet hair. Another towel was slung low around his lean abs. Despite the concerns whirling in her head, Nell was momentarily distracted.

A slow, knowing smile spread across his face as she came closer, and he pulled her to him and kissed her, his damp chest pressing against her. He pulled away to look at her, stroking her cheek. 'You still look worried.'

She chewed her lip. 'I am. Percy's folks have threatened to disinherit her if she marries Hawke. God knows why. And God knows what I should do now.' She shrugged hopelessly.

'Wow.' James stared at her. 'Disinherited? Is that, you know, a usual threat if you have an estate? Or—'

'No, James. That's the most awful thing her parents could say. And it's not about money. It's about Percy being brought up to know everything about her home and responsibilities so she can take it on and run it successfully. I know she leans into the party scene, but she's just as happy fixing fences or crawling through mud with her gillie, watching out for the deer.'

'So she won't go through with the wedding then,' James said. 'If that's all true, she won't risk it, will she? She can postpone and try to talk her parents round. It's the least nuclear option.'

'Which almost certainly makes it, by definition, the option she *won't* choose.'

'That's just bullheaded. And stupid.'

'Yeah, well, Percy can be contrary at the best of times. But at the moment she's being especially stubborn.' Nell undressed. 'And I'm the host, so I'd better be prepared for anything.' She dashed to the bathroom. 'I'll be quick.'

Ten minutes later – thankful for a pixie cut that dried fast and the smudgy eyeliner that suited her better than precise lines – Nell clutched the bodice of her gown, and asked James to help.

'God, you're gorgeous.' He trailed his finger up her naked back, zipped the gown and turned her in his arms. 'I'm so bloody lucky.' She thought he'd kiss her, but he shot her a rueful look. 'I know you want to get going . . .' As he paused, she heard the unmistakeable *thwomp* of another helicopter.

'Oh God. *This* one has to be Uncle Bertie. We'd better hurry. I need to greet him and I want to check on Percy first.'

Nell darted across the galleried landing overlooking the hall landing to Percy's room and knocked on the door. 'I've said all I'm going to say!' was yelled from within.

'To me?' Nell asked.

In a couple of seconds the door opened, and Percy stuck her head into the gap. 'Give a girl a chance, I'm trying to scrub up in here.'

'For a wedding?' Nell asked. She was suddenly struck by the loneliness of it all. Percy had always been riotously popular, yet no school or uni friends were sharing her excitement, getting ready with her, giggly and heady from champagne on empty stomachs. Percy was so determined to go through with this, she must either really be smitten with Hawke or desperate to get Hamish out of her system once and for all.

At Percy's nod, Nell confirmed, 'It's on, then?'

'Of course. And you'd better move your arse or we'll both be late.'

Nell joined James on the landing. 'Well, we're on.'

As they rushed towards the stairs he shot her a knowing glance. 'OK, then. If Percy hasn't told you anything about Hawke, what have you dug up online?' James asked.

Nell shot him a wry smile. 'Ha. I've had to turn into a right cyberstalker.'

James's blue eyes gleamed. 'Good. Let's compare notes.' He slipped his arm round her waist, his head close to hers.

'Honestly, I don't know what to think. Seems successful, with six casinos and luxury hotels. Did you see his Instagram?'

'All those stylised shots of decadent nightlife? Far too cool for school.' James eyed her warily.

'Pff. More like a total player. Trying to be Monaco, but really more Las Vegas. About a decade ago.'

The tug of his lips told her he agreed. 'But why are her folks so set against him?'

Nell shrugged as they walked down the stairs. '*That* is the multimillion-pound question.'

Saturday 13th March – 5.30 p.m.

Rav messed up his dark wavy hair in front of the bedroom mirror. Nell had once said she liked it like that. *What am I doing? She's with James now. She's just a friend.* Still, he wished he wasn't staying down the hall from their room. It was too close for comfort.

The daily – no, *hourly* – regret burned: during the one argument he'd ever had with Nell, he'd said they were just friends. And then he'd compounded his stupidity by leaving straight afterwards to spend time in India, bringing his family trip forward without telling Nell. He'd thought they were close, and he'd been certain she felt the same way, so he hadn't contacted her while he nursed the wound caused by the knowledge that she hadn't trusted him enough to share her background with him.

When he'd finally summoned the courage and was about to tell her how he really felt at the ball here two months ago, it was already too late. She was with James.

So now he and Nell were locked into friendship. He wasn't sure what was worse – seeing her with someone else, or not seeing her at all. *God, I'm a bloody idiot.* He'd wasted all that time, *and* his chance to be with her. *Have I hurt her and ruined our chances?* The thought made him feel sick.

So, of course, when he'd hurried along the hall to the stairs, wanting to be early for the ceremony, he found himself trailing behind Nell and James. Like some sad stalker. *Perfect.*

Oh, God. She looks stunning. An amethyst gown hugged her waist, rich purple streaking into the long lilac-and-white chiffon skirt. Bare, kissable shoulders, a trail of freckles leading his eye downwards until her dress interrupted . . . *Ugh. Is it possible to be just friends?* He couldn't help it: he was constantly searching for any sign, a spark in her beautiful amber-flecked eyes, that she still felt something for him.

Though he hated to admit it, Nell and James, who was done up in full police dress uniform, made a great-looking couple. James had a lot going for him. Handsome, clearly ambitious and a good detective.

Rav took a moment, gazing over the balustrading of the galleried landing to the hall below. It was lined with expectant-looking staff. Glittering chandeliers slanted light on the panelled walls and made the parquet floor gleam.

Gathering himself, he smoothed his tux. The Savile Row made-to-measure was a contrast to the hoodies and combats that he and Nell usually wore for work – and it was a gift from his friend and colleague, Sylvia, who had considerably more style than him. And Nell seemed to like it the last time he'd worn it.

Bracing himself, he caught them up, affecting an easy-going, 'Hi. You've both scrubbed up OK.'

'Oh!' Nell's head jerked round. The slightest tug of her eyebrows rocketed worry through him. She was upset about something. Him? Or had he interrupted something? 'So have you.' A fleeting smile tugged the corner of her mouth, but didn't settle. She was tense, too.

As they reached the hall, a member of staff had coats ready, while another offered sweet-scented gardenia buttonholes. An older woman in a smart suit – housekeeper? Event manager? – murmured to Nell, 'The Duke of Aveshire's here, freshening up in his suite. But guests are already gathering in the church, so you can go over and we'll make sure someone accompanies him.' She hesitated. 'And, just so you're aware, the security team have identified an intruder in the grounds.'

Rav's head jerked up, but Nell just groaned and whispered, 'Press?'

'Probably. The team are dealing with it.'

'Thanks, Mrs F.'

Jesus. Rav couldn't believe how casual Nell was about it. It was like she and him were the same species, but living in totally different ecosystems. He checked James for his reaction, but he was busy talking to the waiter who'd passed him his coat. Rav's concern was interrupted by another waiter offering a nip of Glencoille whisky against the crisp evening air, and a lantern for the return journey from the chapel. The drink burned Rav's throat, shooting warmth through him, as he took his coat and shrugged into it.

Through the open door, the tree-lined driveway led his eye across the downland, bronzing in the evening light. Outside, the winding path to the family chapel carved between grass banks smothered with golden daffodils, the air sweet with narcissus. Rows of flaming torches lit their way to the distant, squat church aglow with lights.

Two women were loitering by the first torches, and they turned at the sound of footsteps.

'Nell, honey! Is it OK to head over?' A statuesque black woman with a buzz cut, New York accent and cheekbones like skyscrapers beamed at them. Her canary-yellow cocktail dress was fringed, 1920s style.

'Of course. Would you and Linda like to walk over with us, or are you waiting for Hawke?'

The woman turned to her blonde companion, who was wrapped in a tight cerise raw-silk dress. Linda, Hawke's mother, must be about a decade older than she appeared: with sleek hair, suspiciously unlined face and startlingly white teeth, it was clear she invested in her preservation. 'I think Hawke's already there. With Crispin,' said Linda. 'So we'd love to join you. Haven't they got the most glorious evening for it?'

'Oh yes, it's beautiful.' Nell fell into step with the women. 'Linda and Deborah, this is my partner, James. And my good friend, Rav. And this is Linda, mother of the groom, and her partner Deborah.'

Deborah immediately linked her arm through Rav's. 'Awesome to meet you, Rav. Are you a friend of the family? You have to give me all the goss about Percy. Can you believe we haven't met her yet?'

Rav hesitated. He was sure Nell had told him that the reason for the rushed wedding was Linda's terminal illness. But he needn't mention it. 'Percy's . . .' He searched for the right words, then met

Deborah's eye with a grin. 'Well, I don't think life will ever be dull with her in it. But I haven't met Hawke. What's he like?'

Deborah glanced at Linda, who was now engrossed in conversation with Nell and James. 'Well, Linda adores him. She's made sure he's had the best of everything, so he's had a better start than most.' She shot Rav a disarming conspiratorial grin. 'But I think there's something to be said for having to work for something, find your inner grit. Know what I mean? When things come too easy, you don't know the value of anything.' Deborah's casual shrug made her sound more philosophical than pointed.

'Maybe Percy will be good for him, then?' From what he knew of her, Rav thought she'd be like Nell: wanting to be valued for what she did rather than what she had. But the view was a sharp reminder that what both women had was pretty extraordinary. Nell's estate was something else: a slice of downland stretching further than the eye could see, even on a clear evening like this. Acres being rewilded were dotted with shaggy longhorn cattle. In the distance, her family's motor-racing circuit was on the other side of the River Nye, slicing through the undulating hills. How had Nell been able to hide all this from him, in the beginning of their friendship? It still stung.

'You never know, do you?' Deborah held his gaze for a second and Rav had to remind himself she wasn't reading his mind but answering his unguarded remark. Her brown eyes were sceptical. 'Either that or double the trouble.' She arched an eyebrow. 'So I hope you're right, honey.'

Chapter 4

Saturday 13th March – 5.45 p.m.

As they walked to the church, Nell was happy to let Linda speak, and so was Linda, who clearly had the knack of spinning out a conversation, even though she didn't know anyone at the wedding. She hadn't even met her future daughter-in-law yet, let alone the rest of her family.

James was listening out for clues about Hawke as attentively as Nell was.

'Of course, Hawke always has done a lot of charity work. So it was natural that Greta would choose to host one of her events at our, well, *Hawke's* luxury hotels.' Linda's roving, assessing eyes took in the extent of Finchmere's acres, pound signs practically spinning in their hazel depths. Nell had a feeling that, in company, Linda would be looking over her shoulder for the next social conquest.

'Ah yes. You set up the family business, didn't you?'

'Yes, me and the late hubby. God rest him. Hawke had the idea to add casinos.' Linda sniffed. 'Not my first choice, I admit. But he's keen on diversifying, and he has good instincts. I gather Percy works hard to look after her estate. I think Hawke is just the same.'

'Well, that bodes well,' Nell said, lightly, wanting to reduce the tension. Probably the last thing Linda needed, with her health prognosis, was to get upset. She was bearing up incredibly well after what Percy had said about her ravaging treatment.

The sounds of the organ drifted from along the path as they approached the thirteenth-century church. Nell let the others go in ahead of her, on the pretext of checking that Percy's bridal bouquet was awaiting her in the vestibule, but really to cast her eye around to see which members of the family had arrived, and what the atmosphere was like.

Inside, the nave was already packed with guests. A man who *had* to be Hawke moved along pews, shaking hands in greeting. Nell studied him intently: blond, with the same assessing eyes as his mother. Beside him, a tall, broad-shouldered man of about the same age offered gentle handshakes, moving in Hawke's wake with understated charm, conferring compliments to the groom and setting up jokes so that Hawke could secure the punchline.

One half of an unwilling twosome, but too tactful to say so, Rav sat with James in the second pew. James looked great in his impressive dress uniform, perfect shave, trimmed hair, shining brass buttons. He oozed authority as he studied the order of service. Beside him, Rav, in his Saville Row made-to-measure tux, and with his untameable hair, leaned back and scanned the crowd. Catching Nell's eye, he smiled warmly at her, and she had to turn away, remembering how he could melt her with that smile.

She concentrated on introducing Linda and Deborah to the guests, having memorised names, extended family, work, hobbies and charity endeavours, so she could create a conversational hook between anyone.

But Linda was a natural. With the laser focus of a seasoned social climber, she created her own connections, homed in on any intriguing details, and asked edgy questions with a sly, conspiratorial wink. Likewise, Deborah disarmed with her warmth and instant camaraderie. When the two women reached their places at the front, Nell felt no guilt at leaving them to it so she could introduce herself to the groom.

'Hawke? Pleased to meet you. I'm Nell. Percy's best friend.'

'Ah! The famous Nell, our *heroine*. We meet at last.' Hawke's lips twitched into a smile. 'I gather you've arranged all this for us. Not a bad effort for short notice.'

'You're welcome.' Nell was aware he hadn't thanked her. But he should have, and his gracelessness put her hackles up. Hawke had a line of luxury hotels and could have easily hosted his own wedding, if Percy's parents couldn't or – given their reaction on arrival – had refused to. Uncertainty rolled in Nell's stomach. *Why hadn't Percy been honest about that with me?* Mustering a smile, she turned to Hawke's friend.

'And you must be the best man?'

'That's me.' The smooth sidekick smiled, making his grey eyes crinkle. His handshake was indeed gentle. 'I'm Crispin—' Glimpsing something in the far doorway over Nell's shoulder, he stopped and nudged Hawke. 'I think we're on, mate.'

But, glancing back at the door, Nell saw Crispin do a double-take. She whipped round, expecting to see Percy – but it was Percy's cousin, Shannon, slinking into the chapel on the arm of Uncle Bertie, whose dress uniform was rigid with medals. Faces turned, and there was a collective gasp as the guests took in her dress. Her white, Grecian-style gown plunged to her navel, anchored by a metal belt of gold twists, the chiffon skirts swirling dangerously around her. *Typical Shannon: she's gone all out to rival the bride.* And Shannon was basking in the attention like a cat in sunshine.

It was chilly in the chapel, and while marvelling at the absence of goose pimples on Shannon's tanned flesh, Nell smiled at her companion. 'Uncle Bertie. Percy will be so pleased you're here.' She kissed the Duke's cheek, then turned to James. 'This is my partner, DI James Clark.'

'Ah. An officer of the law. Excellent,' Uncle Bertie barked like a brigadier addressing his ranks, cut-glass accent at the volume of someone who both never had their word questioned and was compensating for growing deaf. 'You'll get along with Angus, Glencoille's sheriff, no doubt.'

James nodded politely, shaking the Duke's hand.

'And this is my friend, Dr Aravindan Kashyap. We work together.'

'Call me Rav. Nice to meet you.'

'Excellent. We need more ecologists.' Nodding, he turned to Nell. 'Right. Where do you want me?'

At Nell's suggestion, he settled beside Linda and Deborah. Linda looked like it was Christmas.

Shannon leaned in to bestow insincere air kisses either side of Nell's face. 'Goodness, Nell, this is more like a funeral. You really need to liven things up. Good thing I'm here!' She eyed Hawke up under her dark lashes. 'Well, don't you look gorgeous. In your suit.'

Nell frowned as Hawke bit back a smile. But then Shannon squealed. 'Crispy? No *way*! What brings you to the party? Please don't tell me you're a broken-hearted ex of Percy's?'

'I'm the best man.' As for Hawke, he set Shannon up with the punchline, waiting with one eyebrow arched.

She obliged, lowering her voice. 'You'll have to let me be the judge of that. *Again.*' She ruffled his brown hair and let her hand trail along his shoulder.

Well, of course Shannon knows both the groom and the best man, and has slept with one of them. Somehow managing not to roll her eyes, Nell finally sat down, settling between James and Rav.

Shannon's eyes widened. 'Well, well. *Two* men, Nell? Is this your second attempt at shaking off your good-girl image?'

Nell tried to unclench her jaw. She wasn't going to give Shannon the satisfaction of baiting her. 'Shannon, this is Rav; and this is my partner, James. Rav and James, this is trouble.'

'Oh, don't forewarn them, Nell.' Shannon pouted. 'That spoils all the fun.' Her air kisses lingered, then she smoothed her glossy black hair as her eyes flicked over James. 'What's your rank?'

'Detective inspector.'

Nell noticed the pride in his voice, and then Rav's look of surprise as he side-eyed her. She felt her cheeks burn, embarrassed that her association with James might have had something to do with his recent elevation from DS to DI. James was a good detective. But since they'd been dating, Chief Constable Trent had developed a sudden interest in improving James's golf game. And promotion had followed soon after.

But Shannon was delighted. '*Well.* Inspect me any time, Detective.' She shot him a cat-got-the-cream smile and lowered her voice. 'And it's your lucky night, gorgeous. You've got me for dinner.'

Trust Shannon to scope out the seating plan ahead of time.

A flustered James was saved by everyone meerkatting at the sound of footsteps in the doorway. *Oh God.* Nell drew in a tense breath. Douggie and Greta *had* come.

Stern-faced until they'd stepped over the threshold, when a lifetime of training kicked in and they exuded bonhomie, Percy's parents moved forward, graciously accepting congratulations on their way to their pew. Theo and Angus were close behind, the latter tucking Granda Cameron in his wheelchair at the end of the pew, before sitting beside Greta and Douggie.

Shocked that they'd turned up, Nell wondered if Percy really would go through with it. Had she reached a truce with her folks? Or were Greta and Doogie counting on her jilting Hawke at the altar and determined to have a front-row seat for that?

Time drew on. Murmured conversations became torturous as the organist moved on to yet another cantata. Nell's eyes slid to Douggie, whose gaze was locked with Angus's. The two men exchanged a slight shrug, worry shadowing their faces.

At last, the organist stopped and there was a hushed silence, as all heads turned hopefully to the open chapel doors and the exquisite view of the grounds beyond, dotted with the flickering flames of the torches.

A rousing drumbeat began, like rolling thunder, building until haunting bagpipes joined in. Nell, with her gaze fixed on the church entrance, recognised the tune. 'Ya Bassa.' Battle and die. *Oh, Percy.* As the Gaelic war song reached fever pitch, Nell first heard the distant whinny and galloping hooves, and then saw her own white mare come into view, streaking across the hill, through the low, golden evening light, and then along the flame-lined path towards them. Percy was astride Pegasus, her scarlet wedding dress and veil streaming out behind her.

As she dismounted at the door and strode into the church, the sight of her in a blood-red gown extracted gasps. The satin bodice, all exquisite origami and sharp angles, wasped her waist, while the fullest, shimmering skirt billowed around her, almost taking up the length of the aisle. A long, red veil frothed from her copper curls and – *oh God* – she was wearing the Glencoille tiara. Nell saw Greta's eyes widen as she registered it, then narrow at Granda Cameron. Percy couldn't have accessed the bank's safe for the family heirloom without permission. *Is Granda in cahoots? What does that mean?*

From one hand, Percy's extravagant pure-white bouquet of lacecap hydrangeas, lilies and orchids trailed to the floor. Her other, swinging, hand still held her riding crop. Nell frowned, but realised that Percy was carrying it for effect, not for the horse. As Percy reached her groom, on the very last beat of the drum, she whacked him playfully on his bottom. Hawke caught the crop, pulled her close and bent her backwards in a long, lingering kiss.

Douggie and Greta sank in their pew, eyes downcast. They remained like that throughout the vows while, through the chapel's mullioned windows, the sky was streaked with peach and then rose and finally vermillion. Nell had planned the ceremony with the precise awareness of sunset times handily ingrained from years of bat surveys. The sight of the glowing sun sinking behind downland was stunning – and would have been perfectly romantic, *if* the groom *hadn't* been enemy number one with the bride's parents.

Finally, the vicar asked, 'Should anyone present know of any reason that this couple should not be joined in holy matrimony, speak now or forever hold your peace.'

There was a second or two of tense silence.

Then, Greta's voice rang out. 'Yes, I do!' Her hand shot up in the air.

As the congregation gasped, Percy whipped round, her eyes blazing with outrage at her mother.

Nell's stomach dropped. *No . . . no . . . no . . . A family row's one thing; but they'll never get over a public showdown like this.* Greta was taut with tension, and Linda stared at her in horror, before her eyes flicked nervously over the guests. But Hawke simply folded his arms, a smile playing on his lips. His amusement thumped dread through Nell.

Douggie laid a restraining hand on Greta's arm and she pressed her lips together, her face etched with worry. Then her shoulders dropped as the fight seemed to ebb from her, and Nell finally released the breath she'd been holding. But her relief was short-lived.

Greta shoved her husband's hand away and swayed to her feet, ignoring the murmurings around her. '*Someone* has to say it.'

Chapter 5

Saturday 13th March – 6.15 p.m.

Voices buzzed as Greta stood, trembling like an aspen leaf.

Nell's gaze switched to Percy, whose warrior-like bridal stance was crumbling as she stared at her mother, wide-eyed and tearful. In contrast, Hawke beside her looked almost bored.

Douggie stood up beside his wife, wrapping an arm around her, but she elbowed him away and the silent congregation froze.

Angus was gesturing at Douggie to do something. *Anything*. But Greta was not to be silenced.

'We're all thinking it,' Greta glared at the men like their refusal to speak up was a betrayal. 'Percy's not—'

Theo rose quickly and elegantly to his feet, and took Greta's hand, his gentle smile quietening her long enough for him to turn and raise his deep French-accented voice. 'Ah, Percy, she is not an easy choice, no? All of us here, we know and love her. But she is more than a free spirit, this one. She is a firebrand. Ask her to do something, and this we know: she will do the opposite.'

A smattering of uneasy chuckles echoed around the pews.

'But look beyond her headstrong ways and you will find a generous, kind, intelligent, vivacious young woman. And no mother,' Theo squeezed Greta's hand, 'would think any young man was good enough for her. Indeed, any mother would be wise to question whether this man could match up. Or even to ask if he knows fully what he is taking on!'

He gave a theatrical Gallic shrug, as he added to Greta, 'Maybe this is what you were about to ask?'

Relieved laughter rippled around the congregation, dissolving the tension.

For a few seconds, Greta stared wilfully at Theo, then at Douggie and Angus, but then her body sagged and she sank back into her seat.

Angus puffed out a sigh, raising his eyebrows at Douggie. But across the aisle, Linda stared at Greta, head tilted, those assessing eyes narrowing as she took everything in.

Saturday 13th March – 7 p.m.

With the ceremony finally over, a brave-faced Percy seemed determined that the party mood would prevail, despite Greta's attempt to derail the wedding. She led guests back to Finchmere House, whose symmetrical stone façade was now emblazoned with her family crest in projected light, and out to the terrace.

There, staff circulated with lavish canapés and drinks, as guests milled, enjoying refreshments and music from the band. Daring fire-dancers performed breathtakingly dangerous feats on a platform over the mirror-smooth lake, which reflected the blaze, eliciting gasps from the high-society crowd. Firepits glowed around the water's edge, inviting guests to join a Highland-whisky discovery tour. Overhead, a drone light-display mimicked fireworks to the dramatic music, finally forming a heart with Hawke's and Percy's names ribboned through it.

Meanwhile, a couple of journalists from *Hello!* had set up in an area of the hall to interview the bride and groom. Percy and Hawke, along with guests, posed for pictures against a backdrop of the hall's dramatic staircase, with its elaborate floral displays, spiked with purple thistles. Nell had been infuriated at the journalists' addition to the guest list, but the wedding exclusive had been Hawke's idea apparently, and Percy wouldn't hear a word against him. So Nell gritted her teeth and smiled.

When the Master of Ceremonies invited guests through to the banqueting hall, Nell hung back with the family, before filing in and taking her seat.

From the top table, she overlooked the sumptuous hall. Soft candlelight glowed from elaborate candelabras along the seven tables, all swathed with snow-white linen and glittering with silverware. Rows of expectant guests, in impressive uniforms and colourful gowns, craned their heads as the door opened and the Master of Ceremonies announced, 'My lords, ladies and gentlemen, may I introduce your bride and groom, Lady Persephone Doineann MacKenzie and Mr Hawke McAnstruther.'

To cheers and applause, Percy and Hawke walked under the sapling oaks arching up to the vaulted ceiling. A stroke of luck that the arboretum had delivered the oaks destined for planting in the East Glen a week early, just as Nell was finding it impossible to enlist yet another florist to decorate the hall.

She'd taken liberties with the seating plan to sit next to Hawke, so she could observe him at close quarters, and perhaps even get to know him a little over dinner. Ever unconventional, Percy couldn't have cared less. Neither could anyone else. Etiquette tended to be followed by those who weren't comfortable breaking rules, and the MacKenzies were never averse to that.

Sizing Hawke up, Nell again took in his conventionally handsome looks, his exceptional grooming – natural-looking highlights, expensively moisturised skin, gym-toned physique and a manicure that was better than hers. But then, she did spend her life crawling through bushes, so that wasn't hard. And Hawke had opted for McAnstruther tartan trews, rather than a kilt. *Clever, demonstrating clan roots without attempting to upstage Douggie and Angus in the kilt stakes.*

His confidence was striking as he smiled languorously at Nell, clearly expecting her to find him irresistible. And though she found his arrogance off-putting, she was determined to play the consummate hostess. Besides, he was married to Percy now, so she had to at least *try* to get on with him.

She took a deep breath. 'Congratulations, Hawke.' She gave as warm a smile as she could muster.

'Ah, are you one of the few who actually mean that?'

'If you make Percy happy, and if you're good for her, then, yes, I mean it.'

Hawke chuckled and began his starter: smoked-salmon terrine with citrus velouté. 'I'm likely to disappoint you then. I hope I'm very bad for her.'

Nell didn't smile, so Hawke nudged her. 'Oh, lighten up.'

Needled at being told how to behave, in her own home, by someone without the manners to thank her for hosting his entire wedding, Nell simply replied, 'I hope today has lived up to expectations.'

'Oh, exceeded them. Completely.' He leaned in again and she smelled the acrid breath of someone who'd been drinking since breakfast. 'As have you.'

Bloody nerve! I wish you'd lived up to mine. Even a little bit.

'Well, Percy hasn't had a chance to fill me in yet. So I'm catching up with all the stories about the proposal and how you met . . .' She forced herself to smile.

'Oh, Greta held a charity event at one of my hotels in November. I was my usual charming self. But Percy and her friends ran into some trouble; then Percy met her knight in shining armour – *moi*. And that was it. Head over heels.'

'Ah, love at first sight for you, then?'

'No, not me! Her!'

'Chivalrous indeed.' Nell ate, amazed that she could manage cordial small-talk with this man.

'I jest.' Hawke nudged her and used the gesture to linger in Nell's personal space a moment too long. 'I'm a very lucky man.'

Trying not to recoil, Nell used the excuse of sipping her water to turn away. *If Percy's prepared to lose everything for him, there must be something to like. And why did she need rescuing? I didn't think Perce and I had secrets. But she wasn't exactly honest about getting me to host all this, was she?*

Hiding her flutter of unease with another sip of water, Nell felt Hawke study her. She tried to crinkle her eyes as she smiled. 'So did you know the family well already? Since Greta hosted an event at one of your venues?'

'Not really. Her people arranged it with my people. But after I came to Percy's rescue, she invited me to Glencoille for the weekend and,' he splayed his hands, 'romance blossomed. After we spent Christmas together, I basically moved in. So I know the family well by now.'

If he's been living with them for the past three months, why did

Greta and Douggie leave it until the eleventh hour to talk to Percy? 'How do you get on with them?'

Hawke chuckled. 'The *real* question is, how do *they* get on with *me?* Parents can't expect to hold on to offspring once they're married, can they? But, as the best friend, *you're* a different game entirely. Do *you* play nice, Nell?' His gaze lingered on her face and lips, dropped briefly to her chest, and met her eyes again with a lazy half-smile.

Ugh. What a . . . 'No, Hawke. I don't play games.'

At the arrival of the fish course – East Lothian lobster – Nell turned away from Hawke to talk to Crispin. At the other end of the table, she glimpsed Shannon leaning attentively towards James. Recalling Shannon's comment in the church, Nell eyed Crispin. 'How do you know Shannon?' she asked, framing it as small talk.

'Oh. She turned up at a polo match I was playing at.' He grinned at Nell. 'Came for the men in their polo whites, stayed for the after-party. Do you play? Percy rode in on a magnificent beast – I assume she's yours?'

'Yes, Pegasus is mine, but I only ride; I don't play polo. I'm not a fan of using spurs.'

'Oh, agreed, I don't use them. Can't abide the idea of hurting something in the name of sport.'

Nell realised that meant Crispin was a skilled rider. 'Did you meet Hawke at polo, too?'

'Sort of.' Crispin chuckled. 'He won't thank me for telling you, but when we met at school, he couldn't ride. Desperate to be in the polo team, break into the set, you know. Felt like an outsider. So I taught him. I thought if he was that keen to learn, he'd be a pretty committed member of the team rather than the few who mooch about until it's time to pop the champers. He did have some spectacular falls, though, so I'm amazed he survived. He gave me this for my trouble. Just an accident, during a game.' He pointed at his nose, crooked from a break. Distinctive enough to mar his good looks, or add to them, depending on taste.

Nell wondered about his fling with Shannon. She might flirt like crazy, but she was selective about who she actually seduced.

'Then Hawke and I went to uni together.' Crispin cut into her thoughts. 'We both had similar family businesses, in hospitality, and both did MBAs. I had a scout around your place this morning. You've diversified nicely. Keeping the National Trust from the door.'

Nell frowned, thoughts crystallising. 'What do you do in hospitality?'

'Peale's Prestige Hotels.' He shot Nell a wry look over his wine glass. 'Heard of us?'

She flushed. 'Oh, Crispin.'

'Yes, it's what we all dread, isn't it? But we're getting by, selling off the family silver. And the Holbeins.'

She'd vaguely heard about the failure of the business and the family estate being sold. Crispin's father, Lord Peale, Earl of Tercelford, might have been old money, but the family had no current currency. *Ah, does that explain Shannon's short-lived interest?* Chasing a title until she realised the coffers were dry? Only then did Nell notice that Crispin's tux was exquisite quality but a classic cut, a smidge tight across the chest, the sleeves a little too short. Details that eagle-eyed Shannon would never miss.

'You seem to have adapted.'

'Can't expect to keep it, can we? Better to think of it as entirely transient, but not depend on it. I can't complain. I've had an amazing start in life, good education, essential life skills—'

'Like polo.'

'Like polo.' The grin made his eyes sparkle. 'Different for Mother, though.'

'Yes, I can imagine. How is she?'

'Oh, terrible. Certain she's a social pariah. And distraught since Pa died.' At Nell's sympathetic face, he added, 'It's fine. A while ago now. Of course, Hawke was a brick, having gone through it.'

He leaned forward a little to look at Hawke, and Nell followed his gaze. The groom was waggling his eyebrows at Percy along the table, until she couldn't hold in her laughter and had to look away.

'I know he seems like a right tw . . . *wit*, but he's harmless, really. I admire his ambition, his drive.'

Nell kept her disagreement to herself, and leaned back as their plates were whisked away and replaced with the main course,

Glencoille venison. Changing the subject, she then asked, 'Where did you go today?'

'Oh, the hotel, the racetrack . . . then I took a walk along the river. That weir is earning its keep. Have you had any outrageous demands from the Environment Agency?'

'Not many. But I'm on their side. I'm an ecologist.'

'Oh, dear Lord. Enthusiast or professional?'

'Both.' Nell grinned. 'But what about Hawke? Do you know how he and Percy met?' She was hungry for more details but wasn't going to give Hawke the satisfaction of asking, when he'd been deliberately obtuse.

'Charity gala, wasn't it?' Crispin nodded at the waiter offering wine and Nell tried talking to Hawke again, mustering a smile.

'Where will you and Percy live now you're married?' she asked, wondering how her friend felt about moving out of Glencoille. Unlike her, Percy had never moved out and got a job. But then, her estate was twice the size, at nearly 20,000 acres to Finchmere's 10,000, with much more to manage, especially since Percy had established her outdoor-adventure business across Glencoille's wild Highlands.

'We'll live at Glencoille. Obviously.'

'Oh?' *He couldn't be this oblivious, surely?* 'Wouldn't you prefer your own place?'

Hawke sat back, chewing. 'Do you know that when you try to be diplomatic, the tip of your nose turns pink? And I bet you blush when you lie. It's adorable. But it's a damning tell.' He swigged his wine. 'Pays to notice in my line of work.'

'OK, then,' Nell shrugged. 'I can't imagine it's much fun for you or Percy to know that the family aren't behind your marriage. But why do they feel like that?'

'Oh, a direct question! Bold move. *Brava.* Now I see why you and Percy make such good friends.' He took his time, taking a long draught of wine, another mouthful of food, keeping Nell waiting for his answer. She decided not to let the tactic work and began to turn back to Crispin.

The chatter around her increased in volume, in proportion to the amount of wine consumed, rippling with laughter and merrymaking.

Along the table, Shannon was squeezing Rav's bicep. *What the hell?* Averting her heated gaze, Nell sipped her water. Then she felt James's eyes on her, and raised her head, smiled at him. His brow creased, asking if she was OK. She nodded.

Hawke needled her again. 'And another thing I've learned since running casinos is that everyone has a secret.'

Heat flushed Nell's face. She hoped the candlelight would hide her blushes. 'Really?' She made her tone bored, not baited, and didn't turn to face him.

Spearing a tender, pink morsel of venison, Hawke said, 'You, for example. I bet you'd be a tough nut to crack. A challenge.' For a nanosecond, his eyes narrowed, sharpening his vulpine features. Then one corner of his mouth slid upwards. 'Where are *your* weak spots?'

'Leveraging weak points sounds like manipulation.' Nell kept her voice even, as he goaded her.

Hawke chuckled. 'Not at all. In any business, finding and pressing those buttons is how you motivate staff into optimal performance. And a family business is challenging enough at the best of times. It's just good management.' He swirled his wine as if he'd delivered a killer line at a TED talk.

A vision of a fox nosing into a chicken coop flashed through Nell's mind. If he'd been sniffing out family secrets, no wonder he'd ignited Douggie's fury.

'Oh dear. Disapproval. I told you, I'm impervious. You can't be thin-skinned when you run casinos, with people blaming you for their ruin. Percy's the same. Apple doesn't fall far from the tree, eh?'

Nell sipped her water again. *Is he talking about Percy's family now? What's he getting at?*

Leaning in, Hawke's tone grew confidential. 'Intriguing, though, how Percy relies on you. You're the voice of reason? The angel amongst us?' He paused as empty plates were cleared, replaced with dessert, and then leaned in again, his voice low and silken. 'No one would ever guess a *devil* lurks beneath, eh?'

As Hawke attacked his chocolate delice, Nell's cheeks flamed, her heart hammering like a hummingbird's. *He knows about the tape?* She controlled her reaction, returning his amused smile with one of her own, while the waiter tidied her immaculate place setting. 'I have my moments. Like most people, I imagine.' Fighting to stay calm, she took another sip of water.

'Your secret's safe with me, Nell.' Under the table, his hand sliding up her thigh was hot, clammy, through the chiffon of her dress. 'I've always preferred dev—arrrgh!'

His pained cry, as Nell stabbed him with her dessert fork, was thankfully drowned in the chatter around them. He ripped his hand from her leg to rub his wound.

'If you play with devils,' Nell fought to keep her voice steady, 'watch out for pitchforks.'

Chapter 6

Saturday 13th March – 8 p.m.

Rav had noticed Nell shooting Shannon hostile looks from the other end of the table. Whether it was the attention that Percy's cousin had been paying James or just animosity towards an obvious troublemaker – if that dress was anything to go by – he couldn't be sure. But Shannon had now turned her spotlight on him, bombarding him with a never-ending stream of chit-chat.

'Hawke's mother, Linda, only came out a few months after his father died. And boom! Gets together with Deborah. Hawke had no idea. Can you imagine? But Hawke *is* an upgrade on Percy's ex; Hamish didn't exactly ooze charisma. And Greta's not just merry. She's fallen off a twenty-year wagon. OK, now I've shared all my juicy news, you have to tell me yours. So, what's the deal with you and Nell?'

Discomfort prickled but he gave a casual shrug, determined not to give Shannon even more fuel for gossip. And with James only inches away from them, he didn't want him to get the wrong idea, either.

'We're friends.' Ugh, he hated saying it. 'And we work together at the same ecological consultancy.' God, how would he manage as colleagues when his contract resumed next week? Hearing about her weekends with James on Monday mornings, trying to keep a professional distance on all their nocturnal surveys . . .

Along the table, he spotted Hawke lean lecherously towards Nell and then recoil, shock scorched across his face. *What the hell . . . ?* Rav tried to catch Nell's eye, to see if she was OK, but she had already engrossed herself in conversation with Crispin.

'Uh-huh.' As Shannon's eyes flicked between Rav and Nell, they narrowed, as calculating as a cat's.

As the meal ended, without any speeches – *something to be thankful for or a bad sign?* – Rav followed the other guests, merry on good food and drink, into the great room. Despite the grand name, and its vast size, it contained a cosy assortment of sofas, grouped for people to relax and chat, with a glamorous curving Art Deco macassar-ebony bar at the far end, near the door to the ballroom. From there, Rav heard the boisterous tunes of the band's first reel.

He was about to go over and speak to Nell, at least to check what had happened at dinner, when James appeared beside her and they linked arms as she steered him away from the crowds, towards the door to the hall. But then Nell turned, eyes scanning until they found Rav, and she beckoned him over. 'We have to meet the family properly. And then – *please* – can we hit the bar?'

Rav smiled gratefully. It was only when they approached the library that he remembered the last time they'd been in that room. *Oh, man.* He'd got it badly wrong at the ball: about to ask her out when she was already dating James.

As they passed the photographer in the hall, his journalist colleague eulogised, 'Lady Eleanor Beaumont? Heavens, you look *glam-mazing* – who are you wearing? You *must* let us take a few snaps! It would be *criminal* for you to look that *fabulous* and not be immortalised in our pages.' As he gestured at the camera, Nell relented and smiled.

While the photographer snapped away in silence, the journalist asked, 'And which of these handsome men are you with tonight?' He fired notes into his phone, barely needing to glance at the screen.

'Me!' James said, and Rav noted a spike of annoyance. 'She's with *me.*' He threaded his arm through Nell's and joined her for a photograph.

'Ah, the dashing military man. Fuelling all our fantasies. What rank, darling?' James's protests of being police, and a DI at that, were met with, 'Ooh, well done you!' a wink and then, 'Thanks, hun!' as the journalist turned to Rav.

'And who are you accompanying tonight?' He glanced around, in case he needed to usher someone else into shot.

'No one.' Rav gave an easy smile. *Just label my picture 'big fat gooseberry' in the national press. Great.*

'Oh, be still my beating heart!' The journalist fanned himself. 'He looks like the next incarnation of Bond and he's single. This is double-oh-*dangerous*!'

Rav wasn't used to being flirted with by blokes and didn't know how to respond. 'Uh. Thanks.'

'And I think we're crediting Savile Row, am I right? Gieves & Hawkes, from that ravishing cut... So right to go for made-to-measure, babes, when you measure up like *that*.' He winked.

'Uh, thanks, yeah.'

Grinning, Nell prodded him and they walked towards the library, as a wealth of socialites posed for the photographer, close-up ready.

As they were leaving the hall, Rav heard the journalist rhapsodise, 'Oh. My. Days. You are *perfection* in Prada, looking *gorge* in Gucci...'

Rav braced himself as they entered the library, forcing a smile as he heard Nell introduce him. From the fireside armchairs, Uncle Bertie, Douggie and Angus – in kilts and cropped Prince Charlie jackets – looked up, nodded at James and Rav, and then returned to muttering and swirling their whiskies.

Awkward memories aside, the library was fascinating: crammed with relics and all the estate history, a rolling ladder ensured that every book lining the panelled walls was within reach. Cabinets held all sorts of curiosities. And wallowy armchairs and sofas around the flickering fireplace invited you to curl up.

'Cameron, this is my good friend and colleague, Dr Aravindan Kashyap.'

The elderly man seated in the wheelchair beside the wide fireplace adjusted the MacKenzie tartan rug across his lap and, though his lip curled, made no acknowledgement.

Maybe he hadn't heard? 'Call me Rav,' he enunciated, smiling and offering a handshake.

Cameron raised a green-ridged hand, twisted with arthritis, with obvious reluctance. It looked painful, and Rav felt a stab of sympathy – which was short-lived, as Cameron conversely greeted James with an enthusiastic handshake. *Right*. A slither of warning put Rav on hyperalert: it wasn't the first time he'd been subjected to this type of treatment.

He watched closely as Greta, with no hint of her outburst in the chapel, introduced Deborah and Linda.

'This is Hawke's mother, Linda McAnstruther. I understand Hawke gets his business nous from her.' The smile on Cameron's lips died as Greta continued, 'And her friend Deborah Grey—'

'Partner,' Deborah corrected.

'Sorry, partner. Joining us from New York, where she consults for McKinsey. And a business acquaintance of Theo's.'

Rav's radar was on the money: Cameron ignored Deborah and turned to Theo. *Ah, this was the man who'd talked Greta down during the wedding.* He was effortlessly cool, looking like he'd just stepped off his yacht on the French Riviera.

Glossing over Cameron's reactions, Greta spoke to Deborah. 'Theo and I are old friends. Since our university days. How funny that you both invest in tech start-ups. Are you allies or rivals?'

'Depends on the day.' Theo gave an elegant shrug.

'Depends on the *deal*, honey,' Deborah laughed. 'We go back a long way, don't we, Theo? What a small world! Can you believe it?'

While Greta looked a touch put out, Theo greeted Linda with a kiss on each cheek. 'It is so wonderful to meet you at last, when I have heard so much about you from Deborah. I must know how your hospitality academy is doing. And I hope to see pictures of your own happy day, eh?'

Deborah beamed her dazzling smile. 'How sweet of you to remember. Just last month.' She nudged Linda's arm. 'Show him, honey.'

Linda reached into her clutch bag for her phone and scrolled, looking for photos of their wedding, not noticing Cameron's scowl as he gestured at the drinks cabinet.

When Shannon brought him over a drink, Cameron grunted. 'I see your mother didnae turn up.' Rav realised that Cameron was asking Shannon about his own daughter, but his tone dripped acid.

'No, Granda. Some trouble with work. She had to stay in London.'

'Pff. Messin' aboot wi' her restaurant. That girl has no idea aboot responsibility. D'you realise she hasnae been to see me since your father's funeral? Even if she was ashamed of the circumstances, she still had her duty to do. Tell her if she carries on like this not to bother.'

'Well, I'm here, Granda. And I'm a MacKenzie at heart, you know.'

'Pff. You're another useless female spelling the end of our line. All any of my bairns had to do was have a male heir.' He lifted his drink to take a sip, and Shannon turned away, clenching her jaw.

'No irony in a crusty old homophobe having a penis fixation,' she muttered, and catching Nell's eye, they both had to bite back the first smiles – albeit wry and regretful ones – that Rav had seen them share all evening. Then Shannon turned to Theo and brushed imaginary dust from his shoulder.

'Theo, you plus Versace is just not fair on all the other men. Where's your conscience?' She leaned in to look at the photos he was viewing, and he tilted the phone so she could see.

Shannon arched an eyebrow. 'Oh, the New York Public Library – very high-end. And are you both rocking Vivienne Westwood frocks? I love the rebel vibe.'

Deborah grinned. 'It was kinda our way of showing that we were doing what we wanted, not what was expected anymore.'

Theo raised his glass in a toast to her and Linda. 'To *amour*.' He arched an eyebrow at Nell. 'And I see that, at last, the flames of love melt the heart of our dear Nell, yes?'

Gleeful at making Nell blush, Theo nudged her teasingly, but Rav felt for her. He knew how fiercely Nell guarded her privacy. For a second, her eyes met his, and he bit down on an unexpected pang at the intimacy in their look; but Nell only trusted him as a friend. Good old, reliable Rav.

He turned away, to the curio cabinets lining the walls, and tried to study the artefacts: shed antler tines; shells; a small dagger (similar to the *sgian dubhs* tucked into Angus's and Douggie's socks) with a swatch of Douggie's tartan at the hilt; a collection of impressive fossils; a peregrine falcon – ancient and balding.

The odd collection was a decent distraction. But not enough to overcome the regret he felt, his discomfort at even being here. He pushed his hand through his hair. He was here for Nell, wasn't he? Who had enough on her plate without him adding any emotional complications.

But he couldn't spend the night here. No way. *Maybe when the party winds up, and guests start to leave . . .* Yes, that would be fine. He'd leave at midnight.

Just three hours of torture to go . . .

'Friends, hmmm?' Shannon's whisper blazed his neck, laced with scents of amber and oud. 'You can't expect her to notice if you don't do anything to provoke her attention.'

Chapter 7

Saturday 13th March – 9 p.m.

James spun. The room, glittering with the rich colours of gowns, streaked around him, a dizzying kaleidoscope against the band's rousing reel, and the clapping and whooping. Hands grabbed him, swung him in all directions, galloped him for miles along the ballroom. Finally, the familiar shape of Nell and the sound of the accordion's long chord heralded the end – and, somehow, he was still alive.

He dragged Nell to the wall, puffing. 'I need a breather. I thought there'd be . . . you know, one of those people telling you what to do. No idea what's going on. I'm basically dance-floor roadkill.' He shot an envious glance at Rav and Shannon. Rav didn't know the steps any better than James did, but he clearly had rhythm and the confidence to improvise.

'OK. Let's get a drink.' Nell smiled at him.

The band's rhythmic music vibrated through his chest and it took a while to navigate past the chaotic dancing. Guests whirled past. Deborah and Theo were step-perfect, even holding a conversation. Crispin looked like he was born to it, dancing each reel with a new partner. Linda danced with Bertie, beaming as she matched her steps with the Duke's. Only Douggie and Greta were notably absent, and James guessed that at any other party, they'd be the last dancers standing.

He and Nell moved into the mirrored Art Deco bar, where the dancing and whooping faded into the hubbub of conversation, laughter and tinkling of glasses, against the background melody of the band. As they perched on the plush stools, James heard the gaggle of guests next to them exchanging scandalised gossip.

'I mean, you don't stand up in church to protest your daughter's marriage for no good reason, do you?'

'Well, *I* heard she *had* to rush things. That, or she'd have to be very . . . *generous* with her bridal couture.'

'Classic entrapment.'

'You'd think they'd have hosted it themselves at Glencoille, if they approved of the match.'

'No, well, *roof repairs*, dear. That old chestnut. Either a rather draining bill – or a rather tired excuse.'

'Greta and Douggie always have lived on the edge.' A tinkly laugh. 'I mean, *financially*.'

'Well, then, maybe a rich husband is just what the family needs—'

The speculation halted as Nell pointedly cleared her throat and raised her hand to the bartender, and the gossiping group darted twitchy glances in her direction. She turned and stared them down. 'I do hope you're enjoying my best friend's wedding. I know she was very selective with the guest list, so it must have meant a lot to her that you could come.'

Twittering nervously about how lovely everything was, the guests sidled away. Nell glanced at James and gave a long exhale. 'That's all I've heard all night. Twenty million theories about why Percy's doomed.'

James sipped his neat Glencoille whisky, holding Nell's eye contact.

'Yes, all right, I know we agree with them. But we *care* about her,' Nell said. 'For everyone else, it's just scandal to chew over. And I just know some of the gossip will end up in print. How can it not, with Hawke inviting journos here?' She downed her Bellini and asked for another.

Noticing Percy making a beeline for them, James nudged Nell. 'The problem of being with the most glamorous host in the universe is that she's always in demand,' he said, trying to cheer Nell up. He tilted his head towards Percy as she greeted them.

'Ahh, James. I saw you giving it your best shot out there.' Percy grinned. 'Try doing it in heels and massive skirts. I am *exhausted*!' Percy hefted her ruby-red gown. 'What was I thinking? Are you having a good time, though?' When he nodded, Percy leaned towards Nell. 'What did you make of Hawke at dinner?'

James read Nell's hesitation, the long breath she took before replying. She obviously didn't like Hawke, yet had to be diplomatic.

And Percy realised something was up. She prodded Nell. 'What?'

'Oh, I'm getting a sense of who he is,' she said lightly. 'How did you two meet?'

Percy instantly blushed. She met Nell's eyes with a slight jut of her chin. 'Let's just say, he put himself out to help me. He's just genuinely kind.' She grinned. 'As well as drop-dead gorgeous, successful, witty, sexy as all hell—'

Nell's eyes dropped to her lap for a split second and she chewed her lip. James frowned. But Nell raised her head and smiled, only to meet Percy's faltering expression.

'What is it, Nell?' Percy's eyebrows were raised, her expression forlorn.

To James's trained eye, Nell's body language leaked giveaways with every movement. Her smile was too wide, too forced, as she gave a shrug that wasn't quite relaxed enough to convince. 'I just hoped you'd share the story.' She held Percy's gaze for a long moment. Then her lips drew into a line of regret. Her gaze twitched to the party over Percy's shoulder. Another forced smile. 'But maybe now isn't the time. The evening's going . . . well, isn't it?'

'What . . . what did Hawke say?' Percy touched Nell's arm. 'Tell me.'

At the slight shake of Nell's head, Percy took a deep breath, folded her arms. *That chin jut again.* James now knew that was a sure sign that Percy would get her own way. One way or another.

Nell shook her head. 'It's nothing, Perce.' She sighed. 'Just that Hawke was sure you wouldn't share the story.' Her lips clamped again, and again she tried to disguise her discomfort with a shrug. 'You're entitled to your privacy. Just that it sounded . . . odd. And I don't like the thought that you can't confide in me, *trust* me.' As Percy opened her mouth to protest, Nell nodded. 'I know. Now's not the time. I-I just want you to know I'm in your corner, Perce.'

James heard concern in her tone, but Percy swatted her friend. 'Oh, Nell. Nothing to worry about. We haven't exactly had much time for heart-to-hearts lately. But I'm the open book out of the two of us!'

Nell's slight wince, just a faint squint around her eyes, showed James that Percy's words had inadvertently wounded. She tilted her head at Percy. 'Are you the same with Hawke?'

'What do you mean?' Percy's good-natured grin died on her lips. 'Of course!'

Nell nodded, bit her lip, and Percy's eyes narrowed.

'Because he knew an awful lot more about me than I know about him.' Beside him, James felt Nell's body tense.

'Well, yes, I've told him loads about you! Of course I would!'

Nell took another deep breath and James sensed her groping for something diplomatic to say. 'Then I look forward to getting to know him just as well.' But her tone was slightly too clipped.

'You can't leave it like that, Nell. If something's up, just tell me.'

'Fine.' A breath exploded from Nell. 'How does he know one of my deepest secrets, Percy? How do I barely know the first thing about him, but he knows . . . *that*?' Her breathing was rapid.

Jesus. James knew that meant her tape. *How the . . . ?*

'What are you talking about?' Percy frowned. 'Don't tell me you've set against him, too? Don't you think I've got enough to deal with, warring with my parents?'

James saw Nell's temple throb, but she clamped her lips again, as if holding in a comment or maybe changing tack, and said, 'Come on, Percy. Your folks wouldn't threaten to disinherit you over nothing. They *love* you. This is *killing* them.'

Percy's forehead creased with tension, but she managed to sound calm. 'My parents should have got their facts straight before they started with their threats,' she said. 'Same goes for you, Nell. I thought you were on my side.'

'Oh, Percy . . .' Nell looked pained. 'I *am*, that's—' But Percy had swept off in a swirl of scarlet.

Nell groaned. 'Brilliant.'

James squeezed her hand, noticing that Angus, who was sitting nearby, had looked up from his drink, his eyebrows raised in enquiry.

With his sheriff's instinct fired, Angus moved closer, folded his bulky arms and waited. The seams of his jacket strained as he took the stance of a man used to using his brawn as an impassable wall.

'I think I'm starting to understand how Hawke's been making trouble.' Nell's face flamed and James, seeing that whatever she had to say was difficult, wanted to reach for her hand. But he gave her space. 'Put it this way: Hawke made it clear he knows about my tape.'

Even thought he'd guessed, James felt a jolt of shock at the confirmation. *That was under an injunction.* Even when his investigation had unearthed it, merely bringing it up in front of Nell's lawyer had nearly cost him his job. If Hawke was digging like this, it wasn't a matter of a few idle Google searches. It was impossible to find. And Nell wanted to keep it that way.

Angus's eyes glinted like flint about to spark a fire.

'He's only known me five minutes. I can't be his only research subject.' She held his gaze. 'Is he digging up trouble for the family, Angus? He was practically bragging about it over dinner.'

James hugged Nell to his side, scanning the room. Greta and Douggie circulated with convincing smiles. But James prickled with the same foreboding he had before a fight erupted in a pub, or a peaceful protest spiralled into a riot. All he could do was stay alert. And try to keep Nell out of harm's way.

Angus sucked his breath. 'The *bastard.*' He clenched his fist, temple vein pulsing. 'If he won't shut his mouth, someone'll shut it for him.'

Chapter 8

Saturday 13th March – 10 p.m.

Rav disentangled himself from Shannon. She'd insisted on a dance, but one was enough. From the way she kept checking over his shoulder, Rav had the feeling she was trying to make someone else jealous, and he was just a pawn.

Maybe he was on edge because of the undercurrent of tension. The celebrations were strained, with guests, avid as vipers for gossip, continually scrutinising the family for tiny giveaways in body language.

The women were spectacular at the subterfuge. In public, Shannon and Percy were perfectly cordial, and Greta greeted each guest warmly, every inch the proud mother in a remarkable U-turn from her performance during the ceremony. In her antique-gold gown, with an impressive owl-egg-sized purple jewel in the glittering necklace around her neck, she hadn't stinted on grandeur for the occasion. Shannon had seen him admiring it and, with the confidence of a seasoned valuer, had whispered, 'Musgravite, darling, one of the rarest gemstones in the world. Can't buy them anymore, at least not that size or quality – one has to inherit them.' She'd rolled her eyes at that. 'Like everything.'

By contrast, the men were hopeless. Well, Theo was a smooth operator, but as Rav walked into the great room, scanning for Nell, he spotted Angus muttering to Douggie, their stances expanded like wolves about to attack: hackles up, chest puffed, biceps tensed. Crispin was faring slightly better, partnering Deborah and Linda for dances with great charm and good humour, but Rav was sure that was because the best man was oblivious. His search took him past the bar. *Ah, here she is—*

Great. With James's arm around her, the two of them having a cosy moment.

Rav veered away and walked straight out to the hall.

Despite being embroiled in the family conflict, Nell had put on a convincing face, dancing over the cracks. Yet another reminder of how easily she could hide things. He hated it. But he had to try to understand it. After all, what else was she supposed to do, while she was hosting Percy's wedding? She was caught between her best friend and her warring family, with a houseful of guests as audience to every interaction.

Skirting away from the photographer, Rav headed towards the bathroom under the stairs, beside the Butler's lift. But two people were already lurking in the shadows, talking in hushed tones. He halted and backed away, using a vast floral tower, voluptuous with hydrangeas and studded with thistles, as a barrier.

'Look, I've just had a phone call. And it's confirmed. *Now* will you believe me?' he heard Deborah whisper to Linda. 'For *God's* sake, what's it gonna *take*?'

'Don't you think poor Hawke has a hard enough time? Do you really have to get on his case, too? Tonight, of all nights?'

'"*Poor Hawke?*" Gimme strength . . .' Deborah's velvet voice rose an octave. 'You're in denial about that boy, honey. It's no good. For him – or for you.'

Rav squeezed himself backwards, into the foliage, as Deborah walked out into the main hall.

'Hey!' Linda stalked after Deborah, swerving the photographer who was packing up his kit and ready to leave, then hissing, 'When I want your advice about my son, I'll ask for it. Until then, just leave him alone.'

Saturday 13th March – 11 p.m.

James marvelled at how such a massive room could become so bustling and vibrant. People-watching from the bar was great sport. The responses to the gift bags definitely split the crowd. They contained Hawke's £1,000 platinum chip to play at any of his casinos, a gift voucher for a deluxe overnight stay at one of his hotels – complete with three-course meal and spa treatment of choice – a flight of highland whiskies, a voucher for one of Percy's *Wild Adventures* at Glencoille and a signature spa massage oil. Those guests who, he guessed, were from old money smiled politely and then misplaced their bags, whereas the new-money crowd – slightly shinier and more appraising – dived in, examined everything and squirreled the contents away carefully, even purloining an extra bag when an abandoned one was found.

The opportunity to sit back and watch also gave James the chance to take in the artwork on the wall. Two charcoals and two oil paintings were arranged to catch the eye. He was admiring a vast moody seascape, the dynamic brushwork apparent in the glistening oils, when Shannon slid up to his elbow with a cocktail.

'What takes your eye, then, Detective?'

'This is terrific.' He pointed at the seascape.

'Oh, yes? Know anything about art?' She sipped her drink.

'Well, I know what I like.'

She eyed him over her glass. 'I should hope so.'

'Feels like this one has got a bit more to it, let's say, than those charcoal sketches. More talent.'

Her cheeks dimpled as she held the grin back, so he knew he'd made a blunder.

'This, Detective, is a fake. The original, you're right, is breathtaking, but *this* is not it. The original's languishing in a bank vault because it costs too much to insure. At least, that's what Nell's father claimed, when I spotted it wasn't the real thing and asked. Personally, I wouldn't be surprised if that was a cover story, and they were caught out. Like you.'

She turned to the sketches, and so did he, hiding his embarrassment.

'Whereas this,' she gestured at one of the charcoal scribbles, 'is a preparatory sketch for a painting.' She tilted her head, inviting him to guess, but he had enough sense to stay quiet. 'By Claude Monet. I think it's stunning. It really captures his use of light, his bold lines. But no one ever looks twice at it. Because everyone here is an idiot.'

James pursed his lips, then realised he must look like his boss, Val, when she sized someone up.

'What?' Shannon looked uncomfortable at the scrutiny.

'Well, you make out that you're all about shock and appearances. But it's just a front, isn't it?'

Shannon narrowed her eyes. 'Don't try to compensate with psychology because your observational skills have failed you. *Detective.*' She drained her glass and pushed it across the bar before stalking off.

James acknowledged the burn, but also recognised this was Shannon's MO. He watched her threading her way across the room and felt a flare of gratification when she glanced back.

As he scanned the crowd, James saw Douggie walking over to the bar. Though James was relieved that he looked a little happier, a little lighter, he also knew that the only thing that would make Percy's father happy would be a quick annulment of her marriage. James doubted he'd managed to negotiate that. *So what's he up to?* He watched as Douggie leaned against the bar and raised his hand at the barman, who reached under the counter and produced a special Glencoille-crested glass, filling it with a measure of whisky, a squirt of soda water and a chunk of ice. He handed it to Douggie, who turned and headed back to his father.

Cameron seemed to be scolding Percy, his stabbing finger almost colliding with her drink, making her nearly spill it, before Hawke appeared to come to the rescue, leaning in and taking Percy's champagne off her. To stop it soaking her dress, James assumed. But, no; Hawke downed her drink himself, making Percy swat him and Cameron chuckle.

Well, something's finally pleased the old man. Seems like winding up Percy earns you brownie points.

But Percy seemed to give as good as she got: when Douggie offered the crested glass to his father, she grabbed it instead, sticking her tongue out at her grandfather. She gestured at the door and James guessed that Cameron was retiring with a nightcap. Sure enough, Hawke handed Percy's now-empty champagne flute to a waiter then steered Cameron through the hall, in Percy's wake.

As Douggie watched them leave, his shoulders dropped, relief rolling off him.

Was he pleased that his father had left the party? Or that his daughter and new son-in-law had?

Saturday 13th March – 11.15 p.m.

As soon as the duke left, Nell knew the party would ramp up a gear, then die a death.

The band played their most rambunctious numbers, and guests swirled about in delighted chaos. James looked more confused than ever but, at least while they were dancing, she didn't have to listen to gossip, and he'd seemed to realise that.

He'd had some understanding of what was expected of him and the role she'd had to play tonight. He'd discreetly squeezed her hand whenever a guest fired off a cutting remark, and made smooth conversation, giving her his unspoken support. And he was doing better than he thought at the dancing. At least, his ability to laugh at his missteps had made Nell relax a little, and having to improvise around his unanticipated moves had kept her, literally, on her toes.

At midnight, a spectacular drone display was set to swelling orchestral music. The lights formed into the famous Glencoille monarch and stalked across the water of the lake, then scattered into fluttering hearts, before fusing again as a vast eagle soaring over the gathering.

The staff offering drinks murmured about the last arranged transport departing, to encourage the remaining stragglers to make a move.

Finally, the last guest left, leaving only family members and those who were staying at the estate, and Nell heaved a sigh. She'd just wanted to get through the night. With no drama, no disaster. With Greta nearly stopping the show, and then all the gossip on top of the family's argument with Percy, it hadn't been ideal. But it hadn't been the explosion it could have been.

Even so, she brimmed with regret. For arguing with Percy, and because of her instinctive dislike of Hawke *and* her conviction that her friend had made a huge mistake.

As she perched on the sofa next to James, Nell hoped to see Percy, before she went up to bed, to try to make amends. Her gaze drifted over to the great room's bar, where Rav stood looking over at her. He seemed twitchy, like he wanted to speak to her, but was making no move to do so. She was about to go over, on the pretext of getting her and James a drink, when Shannon and Hawke appeared, gliding over to the bar together. As Shannon poured them both some champagne, Hawke undid his bow tie and took his jacket off, folding it over the back of a bar stool. The suggestion of Hawke and Shannon settling in for drinks seemed to be Rav's cue to leave the bar and head towards Nell and James. But halfway over, he paused, turning his attention to the landscape painting on the wall, and the sketches next to it.

Is he genuinely interested in art, or is he avoiding being alone with me and James? Nell sighed. She felt drained. And she'd been reading ulterior motives into people's actions and comments all night. Her eyes roamed around the room again, and she spied Douggie and Angus, striding in from the hall, their faces grim.

What now? Nell sat up, a million awful thoughts streaking through her mind.

'What's all this about Hawke shootin' his mouth off?' Douggie hissed as he got close.

'What?' Nell grappled with the unexpected question.

Angus gestured impatiently. 'You said he'd been bragging over dinner about making trouble for the family.'

'Aye, so what did he say?' Douggie demanded.

'Nothing,' she said. 'Well, nothing *specific*. Just . . . hints.'

'Hints?' Douggie turned on Angus. '*Hints* was enough for you to get Greta all fired up? *Agin*? God, man. What were you *thinking*?'

'It's trouble enough,' Angus reasoned. 'He's playing games, isn't he?'

Douggie huffed. 'That's not news, is it? I can't have Greta being upset over hints that he's got trouble in mind.' He paced restlessly towards the fireplace, and Angus trailed after him. Eventually, the men sat down, and Theo joined them, just as Percy whirled through the room, having seen off the last guests.

'Goodnight, all,' she said, with possibly a fake yawn, before picking up her billowing skirts and turning to leave.

Nell jumped up. 'Percy, hang on,' she called. 'I need to speak to you.'

As Percy hesitated, James tactfully settled back on the sofa, suddenly engrossed in checking his phone.

Percy turned to Nell, her eyebrows lifting mournfully. 'What is it?'

'I . . .' Nell moved over to her and lowered her voice. 'I want to apologise. You've got enough on your plate. Let's not argue.'

Percy side-eyed her, before her features softened and she let out a sigh. 'Fine,' she said. 'How could I survive if my family *and* my best friend all hated my husband?'

Despite the gentle bravado, Nell saw distress in Percy's eyes, and her heart lurched.

'Oh, Perce . . .' She took Percy's hand, aching to tell her that Hawke was nowhere near good enough for her; that he was a letch and she should disentangle herself from him as quickly as possible. But now wasn't the time. Percy had to be prepared to listen, and she was still fighting for him. 'Just remember your worth, Percy. And make sure he deserves you.'

Percy at least gave her a half-smile – until she caught sight of something over Nell's shoulder that made her groan. Nell turned to see Greta walking in from the ballroom with Linda and Deborah.

'*Great*. I was hoping to sneak off to bed without having to speak to Ma.'

Percy had barely acknowledged her mother since her outburst in the church, and Douggie had kept Greta occupied over the evening, making sure that he, or Angus or Theo, was with her. *To prevent any more confrontations or to stop her drinking? Or both?* But now, Linda's appraising gaze darted from Greta to Percy and she steered her group over to Nell. Opposite her, Percy drew a resigned breath, and James rose, pocketing his phone.

'Thank you for a wonderful evening,' Linda glanced between Percy, Greta and Nell, clearly uncertain who should take credit.

Nell noticed Greta's gaze wandering, in an attempt to detach herself from the remark, and the event.

'We're looking forward to the horse riding tomorrow, aren't we, Deborah?' Linda nudged her, filling the silence.

Nell smiled. 'I'm glad. We should have good weather and there'll be a picnic by the Nye—'

Suddenly, Greta's expression darkened, her eyes fixed on something across the room and her body tensed, like a stalking wildcat. Following her gaze past Linda and Deborah, Nell had a millisecond to spot what Greta had seen: Hawke's hand trailing over Shannon's bottom. And . . . was she imagining it, or was Hawke staring over Shannon's shoulder, directly at Greta? Was he *goading* her? Shannon seemed oblivious as she leaned into his embrace, took a strawberry from the bar's plate of garnishes, dunked it slowly in Hawke's champagne and slid it provocatively between her glossed lips.

Greta was already storming over to them, puce and furious. 'You good-for-nothing *snake*.' She put all her rage, all her force into the slap, sending Hawke almost prone across the bar, his drink flying. Shannon staggered backwards.

Linda shrieked and Deborah gaped in disbelief. Rav twisted round from his position in front of the paintings.

But James sprinted across the room, planting himself between Greta and her son-in-law, who was gathering himself. Douggie had hurried over, and grabbed Greta's arms and pulled her away.

Hawke just smirked. Nell couldn't believe it. He cupped the livid handprint blotching his pale cheek, his terse laugh ringing out around the room. 'Well. So much for family relations. That'll cost you your Christmas cards. And visiting rights with your grandkids.'

Eyes blazing, Greta turned and snarled, 'You're not good enough for my daughter. You don't have to keep proving it. But don't think you've won. She can still divorce you.'

'Mother!' Percy exploded across the room to face Greta down. 'Haven't you done enough?'

Hadn't Percy seen what Hawke was doing? Great, this will be another reason for Percy and Greta to be at odds. And Hawke loves it. Glancing at Hawke, whose lips were twitching in insolent amusement, hatred scorched through Nell. *He'd cuckooed his way into this family and now he was tearing it apart for entertainment? I could kick him in the—*

'Oh, I've won.' Hawke swaggered closer to Greta. 'Just remember, *you* made her choose. Between you and everything you have. Or me.' He splayed his hands. 'And she's chosen.'

'You conniving little—' Greta's fury was cut off as Douggie, and now Angus, grabbed an arm each and pulled her back to where Theo stood. Nell watched as they released her, and Theo enfolded her in a firm embrace.

Douggie still looked incandescent, and Angus steadied him, his brows raised in mournful loyalty like a faithful Labrador, as he held on to his arm.

With ice-calm dignity, Linda glided to Hawke's side and squared up to the family, like a gazelle staring down a pride of lions. 'What does my son mean, you've asked your daughter to choose?'

Her defiant glare bounced between the family and its allies, who'd fallen silent, then she nodded. 'I see. Don't think our family is good enough for yours, is that it? That's rich. We've made ourselves an honest living. Done well for ourselves by our own talent and hard work. But your ancestors killed and land-grabbed their way into titles – and *you're* just the same, brawling at your own parties – yet *you* think *you're* the high and mighty ones?' She took Hawke's arm. 'Come along, my dear. Let's get some air.'

As Linda propelled Hawke into the ballroom and out to the terrace, Deborah lingered to scan the room. Nell saw her lock eyes with Theo, before she slunk outside to join Linda.

'Perce?' She looked incensed, and Nell clasped her arm. 'Are you OK?'

Percy's lips drew into a grim line as she shook her head. 'How can I be? I thought if we were married, they'd take things seriously, and be more reasonable. But it's a nightmare.' She side-eyed Shannon, who was blotting spilt champagne off her skirt.

Nell agreed it was a nightmare, but Percy was blaming her family, while Nell believed the blame lay with her new husband. *Ugh. Why the hell had Percy rushed into this with such a slimeball?*

As she bit back any unhelpful replies, she heard Percy's father muttering, 'Would you mind helping Greta upstairs, Theo?'

As Theo steered Greta out, Douggie grumbled to Angus, 'This has to be resolved one way or another. And sooner, rather than later.'

'Aye. And you want to be a bit more circumspect,' Angus told him, wary as a guard dog. 'If things get any more acrimonious, you're as good as giving Linda all the ammunition in the world to leak scandal to the press.' Angus nodded at Nell. 'You see how it is, lass? This is no game.' He dropped his voice, gesturing towards Percy. 'Make her see sense, eh?'

Chapter 9

James took stock of the aftermath.

Cleaned up and leaning against the bar, Shannon was still rigid with bravado. But at least she was keeping quiet.

Percy appraised her cousin surreptitiously, then turned to Nell. 'Do you know why Ma hit him? I mean, I know she doesn't like him, but I never thought she'd behave like that.'

'Yes. Didn't you see?' At Percy's frown, Nell winced, then mouthed, 'The bottom squeeze,' as she side-eyed Shannon.

Percy sagged, rubbing her forehead. Her eyes screwed shut like she was in agony, warding off something awful. Then she nodded slowly. 'Of course.' A short, hollow laugh. 'Of course.'

'I'm so sorry, Perce.' James heard the anguish in Nell's voice at her best friend's pain.

Percy shot a look of disgust and betrayal at Shannon, who met her gaze, with the audacious confidence of a jungle cat, before straightening up and swaying a little on her six-inch heels. She was drunker than she'd appeared and lurched sideways, nearly toppling over.

'Uh-oh . . .' James lunged to catch her and was overwhelmed by scents of amber perfume, sharp champagne and earthy whisky. He knew vulnerability masked with bravado when he saw it.

But Percy was oblivious. 'It's always the same with you, isn't it, Shannon?' she said. 'If something isn't yours, you have to take it anyway.'

Shannon laughed, 'Poor Percy. You think he loves *you*?' She drawled, 'You're the meal ticket, you *idiot*. And I'm . . . I'm his *lit-tle* tempting dessert.' Her voice slurred through her triumphant smile.

'OK, ladies, time to call it a night.' James tried to help her to stand without him needing to hold her up.

'Oh, God.' Nell looked at James, then at Rav. 'Somebody needs to help her get upstairs.'

'Uh . . . Don't look at me,' Rav protested. 'There's no way I'm taking her to bed.'

'No, I should hope not,' Nell said, and James noted her arch tone.

Shannon drew herself up, looking past them at Crispin, as he wandered in from the ballroom. 'Crispy? You'll be my hero. Take me up?'

Crispin looked warily at her. 'What's going on?'

'An exercise in diplomacy,' Nell said.

'Right.' He nodded as Shannon seized his arm, leaning heavily and murmuring into his neck as he walked her to the hall.

Percy maintained her proud façade until Shannon left. Then she turned a distraught face to Nell. 'Hawke's been making a total fool of me, hasn't he?'

'Mmmhmmm.' Nell clearly had something to add but was trying to hold it back.

Percy's eyes narrowed slightly. 'What?' she asked, her voice trembling.

Nell grimaced. James could see she wished she'd been more circumspect.

'What?' Percy repeated, staring at her. 'What else? Tell me.' At Nell's head shake, Percy pressed, '*Tell* me, Nell. I deserve to know the full picture, and it can't get any worse, can it?'

Nell gazed at Percy for a moment, then nodded. 'Yes, you're right, you do deserve to know the full picture.' She exhaled heavily. 'I'll be blunt, Percy, because it's not my place to apologise for this. But . . . Hawke groped me earlier.'

Percy gasped. 'Seriously?'

James felt his blood start to boil. *What the . . . ? When? What exactly did he do?*

'Was that over dinner?' Rav asked, his face clouding.

'Yes.'

But before James could say anything, Percy pushed past them, her face thunderous.

'Perce? Where are you going?' Nell tried to catch hold of her arm, but Percy shook her off.

As she strode to the door, James heard her snarl, 'To deal with my husband.'

Upstairs, in their suite, Nell felt the tension from the disastrous day expand in her chest. After Percy had stormed off, Rav – distinctly stone-faced – wasn't far behind her, leaving Nell feeling dazed with the fallout.

James had led her upstairs, but now she couldn't stay still and paced restlessly in front of the fireplace.

'What a total creep.' She shuddered. 'I can't believe my best friend just married him.'

Looking at her with concern, James asked, 'Are you OK? After what happened at dinner? Do you want to make a complaint?'

Nell turned to him. 'I didn't even think of that. Yes, honestly. But it would hurt Percy horribly. I can't, can I? Not when she's married to him. Quite honestly, what I'd like—'

But she was cut short by a scream that pierced the air.

Stopping dead, Nell stared at James.

The screaming didn't stop.

Together, they raced out of the room, to the hallway, towards the stairs and the commotion.

Nell grabbed the banister of the open stairwell and peered down to the hall, one floor below. The view took a moment to process.

Mrs Faulkner, the housekeeper, stood with her hands over her face, shaking and crying. Crispin was kneeling beside something . . . no . . . some*one*.

A crumpled body lay sprawled on the hall floor.

Chapter 10

Nell flew down the stairs towards them, and saw that Crispin's face was white, a dropped drink at his feet, shattered glass in a bronze puddle.

Nell's eyes took in the body on the floor: *Hawke*.

He lay face-down, eerily lifeless, his legs bent in the wrong directions, broken, like a dropped marionette. His blond hair was matted with blood, which was also leaching across the wooden floor, seeping into the whorls of the woodgrain.

As Nell kneeled beside him, a hot iron odour filled her nostrils, meeting the acid rising in her throat. She fought the urge to recoil from the sight of Hawke's dislocated jaw, twisted sideways, ripped from his face.

Instinctively, Nell reached for a pulse, knowing it was pointless. She felt sick as her fingers, pressing against the twisted neck, felt nothing. Nell swallowed hard and turned away from the awful view: pale, slack skin collapsed over broken bones had peeled back from the eye socket, exposing lurid pink muscle. The eyeball protruded, tethered by its optic nerve, squashed against Hawke's ruined cheek.

Crispin pushed himself to his feet, swaying and then staggering through the main door. Mrs F watched him go, then turned sharply at James's voice. But James was on the phone. Calling a colleague.

Oh God. Nell stared at him but he was stern-faced, guarding the body. No, guarding the *scene. Jesus. Does he think this was . . . deliberate?*

Nell swallowed. 'The police will be here soon,' she told Mrs Faulkner. 'And I imagine there will be questions.'

Mrs Faulkner nodded, valiantly composed. 'I'll gather everyone somewhere and get a room ready for the police. Better put the kettle on.' She left with a brisk nod.

While James was still on the phone, Nell ducked outside to find Crispin. He was bent double, leaning on his fists against the wall, dry-heaving. His convulsions subsided into gulps for air.

'Come inside,' she said softly. She put an arm around his shoulders, and steered him in through the hall and into the great room.

From the hall, she heard James command, 'Stop. Use the back stairs.'

But the running footsteps and the rising scream told her that James had been ignored. Hurrying into the hall, she saw Linda reach the bottom of the stairs, approaching Hawke's body while trembling and shaking her head. 'No . . . *no, no, no, no* . . .'

Hawke's mother sank to the floor, keening like a wounded animal, and Nell stood frozen with the horror of it all, just as Douggie strode in, then stopped dead as he took in the scene.

'Jesus Christ,' he muttered, then lifted his eyes to catch sight of Nell, who shook her head. Shocked, they watched as Linda, vivid red blood soaking into the cerise silk of her dress, held Hawke's head in her hands, rocking with hysterical sobs.

Nell darted a look at James. If this *was* a murder scene, then Linda was royally messing up any forensics. James ought to tell her to stop, but was clearly biting back instructions.

When Deborah arrived a minute later, it was a relief. She, of all people, could persuade Linda to step away from her son. But as Deborah approached Linda, eyes wide with horror, she was met with quivering hostility.

'Leave us alone.' Linda's voice was the low growl of a lioness defending a cub. 'I know you're not sorry. So don't even bother pretending.'

Deborah recoiled like she'd been burned, staring at Linda, opened-mouthed.

James spotted Angus descending the main staircase, and called out. 'Use the back stairs, please!'

Angus ignored him and looked over at Douggie. 'What the hell happened?'

'A . . . horrible accident,' Douggie said, his voice flat.

Angus winced at the sight of Hawke. 'Must have been blind drunk,' he said. 'He fell from upstairs?'

Nell and James locked eyes, as Mrs Faulkner appeared with a tray of brandies. When she offered one to Crispin, he took it with shaking hands, had one sip and grimaced.

'Sorry, I'm . . . going to be sick again.' He staggered around Hawke, Linda and Deborah, and across the hall to the bathroom.

Fractious at the chaos, James gestured at Hawke's body. 'Could I ask you all to move away, please, into the great room. The police will be here soon.'

The thought of the police's imminent arrival made Nell uneasy. *Where the hell was Percy? Or Rav, for that matter?* They'd both exited earlier, at the same time, both in bad moods . . .

'Come on, Lindy. Here, have some of this.' Deborah tried again, offering Linda some brandy.

'What do I want with that!' Linda lashed out, sending the glass shooting out of Deborah's hand and smashing on the floor, shards scattering and liquid puddling around them. Crouching patiently, Deborah gathered up the broken pieces. But her heels skidded from under her on the spilt brandy and she lost balance.

'Dammit!' She righted herself but cradled one hand, oozing with blood.

'Oh, are you kidding me?' James shook his head at Nell in exasperated disbelief. As one, they moved in. Nell led Deborah to the ladies' bathroom, while James kneeled beside Linda.

'Have you got any glass in those cuts?' Nell asked, after Deborah had rinsed her hands. She took the first-aid box out of a cupboard and opened it on the counter.

'A couple of Band-Aids should do it,' Deborah said, as she examined her wounds under the lights.

Nell stuck one plaster gently across Deborah's left hand and another, more awkwardly, over the knuckles of her right hand. 'Linda's clearly in shock,' she said. 'I'm sure she doesn't blame you. The whole situation is awful.'

Deborah smiled sadly. 'Actually, she's not wrong. I wouldn't have wished any harm on her son, but there was no love lost between Hawke and me.'

Had Deborah seen Hawke for the stirrer he was? Or the philanderer. Or both. She could hardly ask. Well . . . not *yet*. They returned to the hall, where Nell saw that James had taken Linda through to the great room and Mrs Faulkner was cleaning up the broken glass.

Something upstairs caught Nell's eye. A flash of red. She blinked and squinted through the balustrade. It had to be Percy. As James resumed his guarding position, Nell darted through the great room and banqueting hall, to the back stairs. Sprinting up the stone spiral steps, then along the first-floor hall, she half-expected to collide with Percy. But Nell saw and heard no one – until she reached Percy's room.

The door was ajar. Nell could only make out muffled voices, words spilling in shock, like a torrent, before being cut off with gasps. Greta's voice. 'You realise what this means . . . don't you? What if there's police . . . What will they . . . ?'

'They'll see it was an accident.'

Percy's firm assurance made Greta's sobs subside – but fear slithered in Nell's stomach.

Chapter 11

Sunday 14th March – 1.25 a.m.

James was having no success trying to corral the family. But this was one thing he could do for Nell: control the horror, do all the right things because . . . Well, if Hawke had fallen, it was a rather convenient coincidence. No, he just *knew* this was going to explode into a murder case. And probably a sensationalised one, at that – *which Nell would hate.*

So any evidence he could preserve, the more clean-cut he could make this case, the better.

But members of the family were determined to ignore him. Totally oblivious to the implications.

He stared around at the company. *Or were they?*

Pushing open Percy's door, Nell heard the approaching sound of a car engine, wheels crunching over gravel, blue lights pulsing through the window.

Greta gripped Percy. 'The police are here.'

Nell swallowed, her throat dry. 'I should . . . We . . . should . . . Are you . . . ?' she thumbed in the direction of the hall.

As Nell took the lift downstairs, with Percy and Greta beside her in brittle silence, her heart plummeted as fast as the descent. She tried to prepare to face the police, but she was frantic at the thought of the people she cared about the most being questioned. Arriving in the hall, a nudge at her side made her jump. James squeezed her hand, shooting reassuring warmth through her. But it was fleeting.

Greta recoiled from the scene, and Douggie gathered her and Percy away from Hawke, ushering them into the great room, then turned to James.

'James, lad,' he wheezed. 'This lot, these police. They'll be your lot, won't they?' Glancing at the front door, he drew James away. 'Look, Greta's in a fragile state. Whatever's happened here tonight, I need you to keep her well out of it.'

As James protested, Douggie shook his head. 'She won't remember a thing, son. Take it from me. Don't put her through any unnecessary stress. She can't take it, lad.' He clapped a large paw on James's shoulder. 'I'm counting on you.'

Outside, the car doors slammed and gravel crunched under purposeful footsteps.

Nell recognised DCI Val Johnson. She nodded at Nell, her grey bob swaying, owlish face taking in the scene. But her shoulders were tense, her lips in a tight line. *Because James is here as a guest? Or . . . Ah.*

Nell answered her own question, as Chief Constable Trent walked in through the doorway, and all over Val's authority. Nell shot her a knowing glance. Last year, when Val had questioned her as a murder suspect, Nell had sensed tense undercurrents in Val and Trent's working relationship. And, considering Trent's affiliations with Nell's MP mother – working on reform bills and being a frequent fixture at her fundraising balls – it was inevitable he'd want to intervene on this house call.

Val took a deep breath. 'DI James Clark, good to see you. I trust you've preserved the scene—'

Trent interrupted, turning to Nell and smoothing his uniform. 'Lady Eleanor. You must be assured that we will do everything to ensure that this matter is investigated quickly. And discreetly.' He glanced around. 'Your . . . mother?'

'Is away. With Dad. And at the moment, we . . .' Nell drew a breath. 'We have no reason to think this is anything other than a horrible accident.'

Val's eyes narrowed, her head tilting, making heat flame Nell's face.

Trent nodded. 'Of course. A tragedy. Which we will deal with, with every sensitivity. You may rely upon that.'

'We'll have to follow proper procedure,' Val asserted. 'As you'll understand, Nell.'

'Just protocol,' Trent fussed. 'We'll expedite things to minimise any inconvenience.'

As Val raised her eyes to the ceiling, James stepped forward. 'I've done my best to preserve the scene, ma'am.' Nell noticed Trent wince at the word 'scene' and then glower at James, who added, 'Unfortunately, most people have walked through it.' He sighed. 'It all happened very quickly.'

'Right.' Val didn't hide her exasperation.

James gestured at Hawke's body, 'But I can give you a full account.'

'Excellent,' Val said crisply and Nell felt indignant on James's behalf. He'd been off duty and they'd all had a few drinks. Val could hardly expect him to be on high-alert mode.

'I'll do what I can to get us off to a quick start.' Despite Val's disapproval, James was trying to sound brisk and professional, and both of his superior officers nodded.

Mrs Faulkner came forward and gestured through to the great room. 'I've set aside the morning room for you,' she told Val and Trent. 'Through there, and through the ballroom. I'll bring a tray of strong coffee.'

'Thank you.' Val smiled, then took a plastic-wrapped packet from her bag. She opened it and pulled the white suit over her pinstriped one, then pulled the blue booties on over her sensible shoes. Trent looked horrified as she passed him a packet of his own.

'I, er . . . I—'

'I thought you wanted to assist, sir? You can consider it *protocol*, if it helps.'

But Trent shook his head. 'You . . . er . . . You get on here. I'll make a start on the questioning.'

Val pursed her lips again. Reaching into her bag, she pulled out an iPad. 'Statement pro formas are on there. It saves time if you create a file and add each person's statement to the folder as you go.'

As Trent stared at the iPad, James cleared his throat. 'Perhaps I could give my account first, sir. Then I could make notes while you speak to guests in turn.'

Trent drew a reluctant breath at the breach of process, but James pushed his advantage. 'I won't interfere in any questions. I'll simply scribe – you can check the accounts are faithful.'

'Oh, very well.'

Val snapped on her gloves, staring at Trent. She side-eyed James, who looked pleased at his intervention. Then her eyes slid to Nell. Val's questioning gaze made Nell squirm. Behind her, she felt Douggie's presence, looming.

'Lord Douglas MacKenzie,' he introduced himself. 'Hawke had, of course, been drinking. Most of us were in a fairly merry state, celebrating my daughter's wedding—'

'Here? Today?' Trent gaped at Douggie, then at Nell. He pointed at the corpse. 'Well, yes. Tragedy indeed.'

'Hawke must have stumbled going up the stairs to his room on the second floor, fallen over the balustrade,' Douggie said.

Val glanced up at the waist-high balustrading and arched an eyebrow.

'As you can appreciate, this . . . accident has been a terrible tragedy for us all,' Douggie added.

'Really?' Linda, in her blood-soaked dress, glowered from the doorway into the great room. 'A tragedy? For *you*? You bloody hypocrite!' Her face flushed and her cheeks trembled as Val tilted her head, her investigative radar twitching.

Great.

'Sweetie, come and sit down.' Deborah dragged Linda back into the great room and Nell caught her fading murmur, 'You'll have your chance to speak to them.'

Douggie grimaced. 'Hawke's mother. She's in shock.'

Val made no attempt to respond and, in the ensuing silence, they heard the rumble of another vehicle arriving.

Douggie frowned.

'That'll be the pathologist,' Val explained. 'Or SOCO: scenes of crime officers.'

Douggie looked taken aback. 'This isn't a crime scene—'

'So, if you'd wait in there, sir,' Val interrupted, 'Chief Constable Trent will call you through for your statements, one by one. In the order you arrived after the . . . accident?' Val waited for Trent and Douggie to go into the great room, then turned to check the stairs, looking at the position of the body and angle of the fall.

A stream of colleagues joined her, all suited and booted, masked and gloved, and carrying stout metal cases. One SOCO laid out metal plates on the floor, as another took photos. A third unclipped their case and removed some sample bottles.

Val murmured something about seizing bloodstained clothes to one forensic officer, who then tiptoed into the great room and whispered to Linda. Mrs F directed them both to the back stairs.

The woman Nell assumed was the pathologist waited as photos of the body were taken from every angle, then kneeled on the plate beside Hawke's head. She examined his shattered cheek, then looked up, frowning, and called to the SOCO on the stairs, 'Measure the height of the landings, would you, for my calculations? I'll need all the options to compare against the damage and impact to his face and body.' Nell blanched and backed into the great room.

In contrast to the organised activity of the hall, the silence of the great room swamped her. The clock in the corner ticked through twelve agonising minutes. Douggie sat beside Greta, holding her hand. Deborah, Theo and Angus looked despondent. Shannon had curled up beside a still-shocked-looking Crispin. But Percy was ramrod straight – probably more to do with her corseted bodice than inner grit, although her jaw was set, chin up, determination crackling off her. Mrs Faulkner brought in yet another tray of hot drinks, then added extra logs to the fire, which was burning low in the grate. The flames grew, casting warmth on the sombre party.

At last, James walked in from the ballroom. 'Crispin? Mrs Faulkner? You were first on the scene.'

Mrs Faulkner and Crispin stood, and James beckoned them through. Nell followed them, expecting to have to excuse herself. But no one took any notice. She hurried across the wide ballroom and pressed her ear to the oak double-doors into the morning room. The voices beyond were muffled, but Nell could just about make out their words.

'Ailsa Faulkner, housekeeper.'

'Crispin Peale, Hawke's best man.' Nell heard his voice crack. 'Good mates since school.'

'The extra staff left at midnight. I'd cleared the kitchen and most guests had left, so I checked the library and great room – must've been about 12.30.'

James cleared his throat. 'Would you send me the full guest list? And also the list of staff?'

'Yes, of course. I'll do that as soon as you've finished with me. At 12.30 a.m., the family friends staying here were still in the great room, so I left, organised a few things in the kitchen, and returned to the great room at about 1 a.m. to finish up,' Mrs Faulkner said. 'Some minutes later, Crispin came in, looking for some brandy at the bar for a nightcap. I offered to get one for him and went to the bar to pour it. He'd gone into the hall—'

'I went to use the bathroom,' Crispin said. 'But I didn't get that far when Mrs Faulkner came out with my drink.'

'Yes, I followed him and handed him the glass when . . . when . . .' Her voice trailed off shakily. 'Hawke . . . landed . . . right *next* to us.' Nell strained to hear; her voice was almost a whisper. 'I'm afraid I screamed.'

'And you corroborate that account?' Trent asked Crispin.

'Yes,' Crispin said. 'I-I jumped out of my skin. I dropped my glass. Then I realised what it was and I couldn't . . . I just—'

'I didn't clear it up,' Mrs Faulkner said. 'Crispin's drink, I mean. It was too close to-to the young man. I couldn't mop it up without disturbing him and I knew I couldn't do that.' A pause. 'In case it's important for your . . . *tests*. Another drink was dropped later on. By the wall. I *did* clear that up. I didn't want the spillage to cause another accident . . .'

'Very sensible.' At Trent's validation, Nell could imagine James trying to hide his annoyance at the scene being contaminated. 'How long were you in the hall for?'

'Just . . . well, it couldn't have been more than a minute,' Crispin said.

'Did you see or hear anything?' Trent asked.

'No, not that I recall.'

'No, nor me,' Mrs Faulkner added.

'You didn't see anyone going upstairs? Or hear steps on the stairs? A stumble?'

'No, nothing.'

'Or hear voices, perhaps? Or sounds of a struggle?'

Nell's stomach knotted.

'No, I . . . No, I didn't hear anything like that.' Crispin sounded surprised.

'Anything else you can add?' Trent asked.

A silent pause made Nell back away from the door. She was standing a respectable distance from it when it opened, and a white-faced Crispin and worried-looking Mrs Faulkner emerged.

Nell slipped in. James's head snapped up, a wry half-smile at the speed of her arrival, and Nell felt her cheeks flush. James's smile briefly grew and he bit it back, studying the iPad.

The lemon-and-white morning room was usually cheerful and welcoming, catching the early sun, but now Nell shivered on the small sofa. Trent was leaning on the Davenport writing desk, sipping Italian coffee from the centuries-old Wedgwood Beaumont-crested bone china. He looked quite at home, while James was hunched over the iPad balanced on his knee.

Nell leaned forward. 'As you know, my full name's Lady Eleanor Ward-Beaumont. Or Dr Nell Ward. I'm Percy's best friend. I organised Percy and Hawke's wedding here today. And I'm currently in a relationship with DI James Clark.'

She saw James wince. Maybe she shouldn't have said it now, when it might be included in her statement. But, as Trent leaned forward to pour himself more coffee from the silver coffee pot, James mouthed, '*Currently?*' at her, pulling a comedic indignant face.

Now it was Nell's turn to suck in the smile. 'We, DI Clark and I, were in my room on the first floor,' she said. 'We heard a scream, so we ran out. It was clear the sounds came from the hall downstairs, so I paused on the way to look over the landing banister to see what had happened. I saw Hawke had fallen, and Crispin and Mrs

Faulkner were beside him. I suppose that would have been just after 1 a.m.'

'That's exactly my recollection. And the time was 1.15,' James confirmed.

'Did you hear anything beforehand or see anything on the way down?' Trent asked.

Nell shook her head.

'You were hosting a wedding today, I gather. So how many staff were here at the time of the accident?'

'We had some extra teams today to prepare for the event. They're known to us, either drafted in from the estate's hotel or from agencies we've used before. Everyone's vetted very carefully. By the time of the accident, the extra teams had left, leaving only our three full-time staff, who live in: Mrs Faulkner, Chef Bayer and Mr Murray, the estate manager.'

'Who arrived at the scene next?' Trent asked.

'Linda McAnstruther,' Nell said. 'Hawke's mother.'

James glanced at Trent. 'She's getting changed out of those bloodstained clothes, sir, so that we could bag them and take them to the station. And, as the deceased's mother, she may appreciate some respite. We could talk to her when she feels ready.'

Trent nodded and dismissed Nell. James shot her a small smile before she left.

Back in the great room, Nell saw that Linda had returned, and gently touched her arm. 'They said you could talk to them another time, Linda, if you'd prefer it—'

Linda cut her off by rising to her feet. 'No. I'll see them now.' She stalked past Nell, who exchanged a glance with Douggie. His arm was tightly wrapped around a worryingly pale Greta.

No one else looked up. Nell crept into the hall, which was eerily empty now that the officers had finished their initial investigations. Hawke's body had been taken away, but the sickly, metallic tang of his blood still lingered in the air. A small numbered tag marked the dark pool on the floor. Nell grimaced.

Taking a deep breath, she ducked under the tape and tiptoed

upstairs, between the markers on the banister and balustrade. On the first-floor landing, by the door leading to the ballroom's minstrels' gallery, Nell glanced around – and then nearly jumped out of her skin.

'Nell,' a familiar voice whispered.

Chapter 12

Sunday 14th March – 2.45 a.m.

Rav stepped out of the shadows along the hallway. 'Sorry! Didn't mean to startle you,' he said. Nell looked terrified, though, and he had a split-second urge to hug her, before she whacked him on the arm.

'Where the bloody *hell* have you been? I've been . . . worried.' She whacked him again.

'Sorry. I-I . . .' He raked his hair. 'I couldn't come down.' He could feel his chest rising rapidly as he stared at Nell.

'What's the matter?' Nell looked at him.

'Oh . . .' He raked his hair again. 'Him assaulting you. It's beyond . . . Totally unacceptable. And that's bad enough, but on his wedding day? Poor Percy.' He blinked. 'I just needed some air.'

'Right.' He felt the weight of Nell's scrutiny.

'And I could just see James reading all sorts into the situation,' Rav heard himself rambling. 'And you know better than me how trigger-happy James is at arresting people on spurious grounds.' He winced. That was a low blow, reminding Nell that James had arrested her last summer. He folded his arms, but Nell's eyes had homed in on his knuckles, which had some specks of dried blood on them that he'd not yet washed off.

'What's that?' she gestured at his hands, and he saw her face flash with alarm.

'Nothing.' But he knew he looked sheepish. 'I bashed my hand against the door in the dark, that's all.' He gave a lame shrug. 'Shouldn't have had that last whisky at the bar. Nothing to worry about.'

Nell's concerned eyes studied him. 'Well, I will worry, won't I.'

'There's no need.' But he couldn't help the warmth that spread through him at the thought that she cared. *As a friend*, he reminded himself.

A short, tense silence built between them, and finally Nell said, 'They're interviewing people downstairs. I'm going to eavesdrop.'

Rav pretended to be scandalised. 'Nell!'

'Yeah, yeah. Come on.' She tiptoed along the galleried landing, pressed open a door concealed in the panelling and dragged him inside. 'We can listen to the interviews through here.'

With his jaw dropping in stunned silence, he followed her in, onto the minstrels' gallery, overlooking the ballroom. Closing the door behind them, she led him to the far end, and down the hidden staircase in the wall between the ballroom and the morning room. Rav stepped carefully in the gloom, on the uneven, narrow stairs. Nell sat on a step and Rav sat beside her, keeping as quiet as possible, listening through the wall to the police questioning Linda and trying not to notice Nell's perfume: jasmine and orange blossom.

'I was in my room, changing for bed,' Linda said. 'But I had the worst feeling. I just knew something . . . something *awful* was . . .' They heard her heart-wrenching sobs, until she tried to speak again. 'And . . . then I heard someone scream, and I, well, I had to put something on, so I was all fingers and thumbs . . . I dashed straight downstairs. I couldn't believe . . .' Linda blew her nose. 'I know you think I'm just upset but – *please* – listen. Greta argued with Hawke. She . . . *attacked* him. And if she'd do that in front of all of us, who knows what she's capable of in private?'

Trent said something that Rav didn't catch.

'Greta strongly disapproved of the wedding. I heard that she even threatened to disinherit her own daughter.' Linda's voice was tremulous. 'She was angry. Really angry. She slapped my darling Hawke's face hard enough to leave a handprint across his cheek. You'll probably see it. In the . . . post . . .' The word 'mortem' was lost in more wails. As her sobs subsided, she added, in a steelier tone, 'And her daughter's just as bad. Percy came out onto the terrace to finish what her mother started.'

Nell sat up straighter.

'With Hawke?' Trent asked. 'What happened?'

'I don't know.' Linda sobbed again. 'Hawke said he had to talk to *his wife*. And he sent *me* away. That was the last thing he ever said to me.'

Beside Rav, Nell cupped her hands over her mouth. He wished he could think of something reassuring to say.

It took a few minutes for Linda's crying to subside, and Trent murmured something in a kind tone as she was dismissed.

They heard a crisp summary from James. 'Douggie arrived at the scene from the great room. At the time, he seemed composed but worried.' The door creaked and, after murmured questions, Douggie confirmed, 'I'd been in the kitchen, having a coffee.'

'Anyone with you? Staff?' Trent asked.

'Chef Bayer and Mr Murray, the estate manager, were having a nightcap in the refectory. They'd've been out of earshot of the accident. I only heard the scream because I'd realised it was past one in the morning, so I'd been heading back to bed. I was tired; I was going to use the lift.' To a mumbled question from Trent, he said, 'No, no. Well, there had been a few disagreements earlier in the evening. But everything had died down. And then, at the . . . *time*, I didn't hear any disturbance other than the scream.'

After a pause, James said, 'Deborah also came in from the great room. Expect some contaminants in the forensics from her cutting herself in the vicinity of the body.'

Deborah herself was factual and impersonal. 'I'm Deborah Grey, Linda's partner. I'd taken a bourbon to the terrace and was reading emails on my phone. I didn't realise the time. An email came in just as the scream made me jump, so I know it was at 1.15. I dropped my phone down the terrace steps, so I had to find it, then I rushed straight inside. I couldn't believe it. Poor Lindy . . .'

After the door clicked shut with Deborah's exit, James said, 'Angus arrived next. From down the stairs. Yes, the main ones.' He sounded distinctly unimpressed. 'His body language was very defensive.'

Angus's unmistakable boom soon added, 'I'd been cleaning my teeth. For a moment, I wasn't sure if I had imagined the noise over the running water. But, being sheriff, well, you know how it is, as *men of the law*. You always check, don't you? And there it was. A terrible accident. Terrible, just terrible.'

After a moment, James gave his next summary. 'Theo came in next, also down the main stairs. Quite composed, but appeared shocked at the scene.'

Theo himself sounded about as contrite as Angus had for corrupting the scene, his Gallic shrug apparent in his words. 'I am Theo Fox. I live in Switzerland,' he began, 'but I came here like everyone else, for what we expected to be a week of celebration. I'm a long-standing friend of the family. Anyway . . . I heard the scream from my room. I was about to shower before bed, but the noise . . .' They heard a heavy intake of breath. 'I quickly dressed again and then came down to see what was happening. I couldn't believe my eyes when I saw him.'

'So far, so innocent.' Rav turned to Nell, who was pale with concentration, but nodded. And then the next interview began, and he felt her tense.

It was Percy.

'Lady Persephone, my condolences on the loss of your new husband,' Trent began. 'This must be a terrible shock. If you prefer, we can postpone this discussion.'

'It's fine,' Percy replied, tightly. Nell grimaced. The defensive edge to Percy's voice flagged clearly that it wasn't fine.

Trent murmured some questions.

'I'd been in my room. I don't know the time. I didn't see or hear anything.' Percy's tone was defiant.

'Can you confirm where your room is?' Trent asked.

'First floor,' Percy said.

'May I ask why you and your new husband had different rooms?'

Rav heard Nell's intake of breath. 'They've already been snooping in our rooms?' she whispered, clearly recalling the last time the police had invaded her privacy.

'You've searched our rooms?' Percy unknowingly echoed Nell's concern. Rav noticed her accent deepen. *She must guard her privacy as fiercely as Nell. But the police should have asked permission, surely, or got a warrant to search?*

'Only Hawke's, to collect anything that may be useful. It's just procedure,' James reassured her.

'Uh-huh.' Percy held a short silence. 'It was so that we could get ready separately before the wedding.' The obvious comment about bad luck was left unsaid, hanging in the air.

Nell glanced at Rav. Her face was shadowed in the gloomy stairwell, but he could guess what she was thinking. That Percy had more than enough motive to kill Hawke. He tried to put himself in her shoes: she'd been prepared to give up everything for a man who'd been having an affair with her cousin; a man who'd thought nothing of groping *Nell* under the table on his wedding day.

Part of Rav envied Percy's courage, her rebelliousness. In his family, his sister Aanya was the rebel, while he was the peacekeeper: his ideal niche. And it didn't hurt that it meant he was always the golden boy, and never in the wrong. But maybe it made him a bit too conformist.

He snuck a sideways look at Nell.

Sometimes . . . sometimes he wanted to go after what he wanted, not what was expected of him.

Chapter 13

Sunday 14th March – 4.30 a.m.

Nell sensed that Rav wanted to say something. His closeness was suddenly very apparent. His thigh nudged hers as they perched side by side on the step. He stretched his legs out, crossing his ankles – the movement casual, but also making sure he avoided accidentally touching her. Something about the gesture made her feel bereft. She knew it was a ridiculous overreaction, and more likely a response to the horrific situation and how her best friend must be feeling. Now she was a widow.

And she only felt worse when she heard James say, 'Lady MacKenzie – Greta – is rather drunk and distressed, sir. We may not get much out of her tonight.'

'Hmmm . . .' Trent sighed. 'She's not the only one who's distressed. And since we took a statement from the victim's mother, we really need to follow up with Greta MacKenzie tonight.'

'Right . . .' James hesitated. 'These interviews are voluntary, sir. Nobody is under caution, or even obliged to talk to us. Yet. This is just an unexplained death – at the moment.'

'No, but a single missing statement in a file will raise questions,' said Trent. 'And it would actually be unfair on Lady MacKenzie. Ask her in, DI Clark.'

Nell grimaced at Rav.

A few minutes later, Greta had been ushered in and Trent wasted no time in firing the first question at her.

'Lady Mackenzie, can you give us your account of the evening?'

A stubborn silence was met by coaxing from James.

'This isn't formal questioning,' he said gently. 'We're only gathering statements, to give us a picture of what happened. Anything you can tell us could help.'

The question was rephrased a few more times, but the answer was the same: silence.

Finally, the sound of the door alerted them to the next interview. 'Shannon Lanner, Percy's cousin.' Her voice was shaky. 'The *poor* relation. No castle and no title for me. I was a little . . . worse for wear last night so I've no idea of the time when Crispin kindly helped me to bed.' She paused. 'We used to have a thing, but he was just being nice . . . He didn't stay. So, I was in my room. Second floor. Alone. The noise woke me up. I was a bit . . . woozy. When I went to see what was happening, I couldn't be sure I wasn't having a nightmare.'

As Shannon was dismissed, Nell caught Val's voice, and stiffened with indignation.

'They're at it again!' Nell hissed. 'Val was in the *hall* when I came in here, yet she hadn't gone through the great room to go into the morning room. So she's been having a right old snoop about! Just like at my place before!'

Rav raised his eyebrows at her. She knew he was thinking about how outraged she had been, all those months ago, when James had questioned her, and used the opportunity to poke around her house. He echoed her sentiments – both then and now. 'Bloody liberty.'

'We can ask the family to vacate the premises now we've taken statements,' Val said.

'Oh, that's just brilliant,' Nell fumed. 'They'd better not kick us out in the middle of the night.'

'Is that really necessary?' Trent asked.

'Well, it *is* protocol,' Val said, pointedly, a distinct hint of sarcasm in her voice.

'You're absolutely right, ma'am,' James said. 'Strictly speaking, we *should* move them all out, protect the scene. But the scene's been compromised anyway. And, bear in mind, if they go home, that would be Scotland for four suspects, Switzerland for one, New York for another . . . Asking them to stay at a hotel will become an admin nightmare. And anyway, the obvious choice is Finchmere Hotel, a couple of fields away, which is part of this estate.' He paused, as if allowing the inconveniences to take root, before adding, 'This is a huge house. We can isolate the scene. Could it be an option to simply cordon it off, and get a police guard on the stairs, landing and Hawke's room?'

'Indeed, preventing any unnecessary inconvenience,' Trent agreed.

'Well, it *would* keep them all in one place,' Val reasoned. 'Where *you* are also staying, as a guest, James. And while you're obviously not a suspect, you still can't officially be part of this case. So I'll lead, and you'll have no access to files. But we know we can trust you with our progress updates. As *we'll* trust *you* for any . . . intel. Anything that comes out in an unguarded moment. Understood?'

'Very good, ma'am.'

Nell gaped.

Rav shrugged, whispering, 'He's a *detective*, Nell, what did you think he was going to do?' He jerked his head. 'Come on.'

They crept back to the hall. Standing just inside the door to the great room, Nell saw that Douggie had wrapped Greta into a hug. But Greta held herself stiffly, with an air of defiance.

Linda glowered from across the room, perched tensely on the edge of an armchair. She clearly believed attack was the best form of defence; she held herself with the taut readiness of a coiled snake about to strike.

The only one who'd changed for bed, Shannon was shivering in a pink camisole and candy-striped boxers. No, she was crying. *Ugly-crying.* Lips stretched downwards in miserable anguish, snot and saliva dribbling. *Bloody hell.* Had Shannon really cared about him? *That creep? Seriously?*

As Trent, Val and James walked in, the company looked up, expectant.

'Thanks all, for your cooperation,' Val said. 'We can leave you for now. James has negotiated that, rather than making you vacate the house, you can stay here. But this is on the proviso that you all observe the cordon across the main stairs, and use the lift and the back stairs instead. Agreed?'

Once everyone in the room had nodded, so did she. 'Good.'

As Trent bid them good evening, James did a double take at Rav. 'Where have you been? You'll need to give a police statement.'

Rav raised his hands, attempting an apologetic expression. 'Fine. But I slept through the whole thing. Nell just came to find me, knocked on my door, woke me up.'

Swallowing, Nell stared at Rav. He shrugged at her, like he knew she'd have his back.

'That right, Nell?' James asked.

'Um . . . Yes.'

'You went to his room?' James's gaze flicked from Nell to Rav.

'Yes. But I used the lift.' Nell knew she was a terrible liar. Her words sounded breathless, even if it would have been perfectly reasonable to check where Rav had got to.

James's manner was brusque. 'I see. So do you have anything else to add to your statement?'

'Only that I was sleeping,' Rav said.

James sighed again and went out to the hall, shutting the door as Val and Trent drove away.

As Rav scanned the room, he noted that the detectives or SOCOs must have taken Hawke's jacket from the bar. His musings were interrupted by Linda charging over to Greta and Douggie.

'I doubt you gave the detectives the full picture,' Linda snarled at Percy's parents, 'But *I* did.' She stalked towards them. '*I* know – you've had it in for my boy and one of you' – Linda's accusing finger pointed at Theo, Douggie and Angus, who were clustered around Greta – 'one of you *killed* him.'

'Linda!' Nell scrambled to stand between her and Percy's family. 'We don't know that anything like that happened. I'm so sorry for your loss. But this won't help—'

'Yeah, you're all in it together, aren't you?' Linda hissed at her. 'Of course you are . . .'

Even in the midst of her grief, Shannon's lips twitched, watching the scene like it was sport. But, beside her, Crispin leaned forward, looking worried.

Laying a hand on Linda's arm, Deborah said, 'Come on, honey.' But Linda shook her off.

'You all think you're better than him? My son was an honest, hard-working, successful man. He earned everything he had. And he's – he *was* – worth a million of any of you!'

'The guy didn't have an ounce of integrity in him!' Greta gave a short laugh. 'Yet you think he was some kind of saint! Yea Gods! It's like you didn't even know him!'

'I knew *everything* about him. You can't live *and* work with someone and not know them inside out. And he was a damn sight more respectable than all of you put together! I wish he'd never met your bloody daughter!'

As Greta lunged forward, Douggie pulled her back. 'Enough. Nothing good will come of this. Let's get you to bed.' It still took all three of them – Douggie, Theo and Angus – to bundle Greta into the lift.

Linda turned her frustrated wrath onto James. 'They'll pay you off. Or use their influence to wiggle off the hook. Like worms. And that's what they are. They act all high and mighty, but they're just worms. I'm going to drag all their dirty secrets into the daylight. And I'm going to hound you until you get justice for my son.'

Chapter 14

Sunday 14th March – 4.45 a.m.

Once James had managed to calm Linda down and most people had retreated, again, to bed, Nell went off to find Percy.

She was in her suite, staring out of the window into the darkness. Nell folded her into a long hug. But she seemed too shocked to speak, and she was freezing.

Running to the kitchen, Nell prepared a hot-water bottle, then dashed to the cordoned-off hall to say goodnight to James, who had set himself up as nightwatchman while they awaited the permanent police guard. Taking the lift to her room, she grabbed the T-shirt from under her pillow and hurried to Percy's room. Her friend had already changed into an oversized T-shirt, emblazoned with 'Balliol College', her body wracking with sobs.

Nell tucked the bottle by her feet and wiped her damp hair from her face, then curled up around her. The sobs eventually subsided into shudders, and finally Percy fell into a fitful sleep.

Extracting herself gently, Nell changed into her own T-shirt and, as Percy had flung out an arm across the bed, tried to get comfortable on the chaise longue.

Sunday 14th March – 5.30 a.m.

Nell hadn't realised she'd dozed. Yet a noise had stirred her awake. In the darkness of Percy's bedroom, she held her breath, straining to hear. She uncurled from the chaise longue, grabbed a dressing gown and crept to the door.

As she passed Percy's bed, Nell realised it looked suspiciously ... flat. Fear slithered.

Muffled noises from downstairs spurred her on to the landing. Looking down onto the hall, distorted shadows, cast from the external house lights, slanted across the walls and over the stain on the floor. She shuddered. Something about the silence felt ominous. Weighty.

James wasn't there.

She sneaked down the stairs, past the markers and tape in the hall, prickling with unease.

The library door was ajar. Nell crept in. Heavy brocade curtains filtered the grey predawn light as Nell picked her way around the fortress of sofas, peeping over the high backs.

The smell hit her first. Rich iron, echoes of the hall where Hawke had lain. High, sweet, dreadful. Spiking instinctive fear.

A shape slumped on the sofa. Nell edged forward, drawn to it, despite her senses deterring her. The dying embers of the fire gave the room an eerie glow, illuminating the person's feet in dark shoes, oddly akimbo, the body in gloomy shadow. Their head hung too far back, the artificial sitting position disturbing. A dark stain around their neck had cascaded down their front. In the flickering firelight, the scene was Halloween-ish. Nell punched the light switch.

The repellent images revealed by the dazzling bright light shocked her senses.

A gurgling wheeze escaped from Linda. Her hand twitched as her terrified eyes met Nell's.

Blood bubbled in her butchered neck, her severed oesophagus stark white between ruby ribbons of muscle. Linda was pinned with the dagger like an exhibit, as crimson gore poured down her chest.

Nell ripped off her dressing gown. 'HELP!' Her roar was full of ferocious urgency. 'HELP! LIBRARY!'

Recoiling from the vile, vivid wound, Nell used a cushion to prop Linda's head up. Then she slid the fingers of her other hand over the slippery trachea, trying to match the severed ends, hoping it would help to restore her airway. Blood spurted over Nell's hands, arms, face. *Jesus. Her artery's ruptured.*

Once she'd got Linda's head at the right angle, she wadded the dressing gown against her neck, pressing hard. The gown sponged up Linda's blood as Nell scrabbled, one-handed, for her phone in the dressing-gown pocket. It slipped in her bloody hand. She righted it on her lap and tapped 999.

Running feet approached. Heels clicking on parquet. Nell glanced up to see Deborah rush in, then freeze, eyes wide, before her shocked scream escaped.

'Can you . . . ?' Nell shakily passed her the phone, just as the operator answered.

Deborah's breathing was ragged. 'Ambulance. And police. Quickly.' Deborah stabbed the speakerphone icon with a trembling finger. 'They need the address.'

Nell supplied it and was asked to describe the injury. Avoiding Deborah's frantic eyes on her, she said, 'Her throat's been cut. The artery's ruptured. And she's been stabbed in the chest. With a dagger.'

Deborah gasped. She tried to reach to stroke Linda's hair, but Nell wouldn't give way – she had to keep pressure on the wound. Instead, Deborah squeezed Linda's hand, murmuring, 'It's gonna be OK, Lindy. Help's coming. Just sit tight, honey.'

The operator asked a series of questions in a voice that was calming yet agonisingly slow: is the patient breathing and conscious? Can you estimate the amount of blood loss? Deborah answered while Nell tried to clamp Linda's wound. *God, how long was bleed-out time? How long would the ambulance take?*

'Can you wrap something around the knife?' the operator asked. 'Don't take it out, but try to stem the bleeding?'

Looking around the room, Deborah fluttered, unsure what to use.

'Cushion.' Nell nodded at one on the sofa. 'Use the cover.'

With panicky, clumsy fingers, Deborah unzipped the cover, pulled out the cushion and wrapped the material gently around the knife. The russet silk cover was instantly soaked.

As Nell kept pressure on Linda's throat, blood bubbled up through the material, hot scarlet rivers running through Nell's fingers. *God there was so much blood . . .*

Wincing, Deborah clamped the knife steady and pressed down. She managed to turn a bright smile to Linda. 'They won't be long, my darling.'

'Who did this, Linda?' Nell asked.

Linda's mouth moved. Nell watched her lips purse weakly. Her eyes were fixed in the grip of terror.

'Try again, Linda. Who did this?'

But Linda looked too weak to respond.

Blue lights streamed through the gap in the curtains, pulsing a cold, shuddering tide across the room. The effect made Linda's already grey face look ghoulish. Deborah rallied, forcing a bright tone. 'Honey! They're here. You're gonna be OK.'

An awful rattle heaved from Linda's chest and a surge of hot blood streamed through Nell's hands. Linda's whole body sagged and her eyes glazed.

'No, no, no, no . . .' Deborah's murmurs became desperate sobs. She ran to the door. 'In here! Please!'

Nell backed away, shaking, as the paramedic took over. Someone wrapped her in a silver blanket. She turned, conscious for the first time of blood caked thickly all over her hands, up her arms, smeared across her T-shirt.

Deborah was sobbing. 'I didn't believe Lindy. I told her Hawke's fall was an accident . . .' She swallowed. 'But she was right. And now she's . . .' As she shook her head, she squeezed her eyes shut.

The activity around her jolted Nell out of the blur. This was her chance, her only chance, to take in the scene. Nausea burned but she cast her scientific surveyor's gaze around the room, taking in every detail, seeking evidence for what had happened.

It didn't look like there had been much of a struggle. Furniture and furnishings were in place, unrumpled. The cabinet that the dagger had been taken from was closed.

Linda's gaping, awful wound was branded on her memory. The cut was deepest on Linda's right side. Her bright scarlet blood showed that the attacker had sliced her windpipe, then her carotid artery, tapering off to the left side of Linda's neck, where the wound was shallower. And there were no defensive wounds on Linda's arms. So either she'd been sleeping and held down while a right-handed person attacked from the front, or a left-handed assailant had attacked her from behind the sofa. Had Linda felt safe with them? Or had they struck while she dozed?

Once Linda's throat and windpipe were slashed, she couldn't have called for help. Nell shuddered. *Poor woman*. Even so, after severing an artery, the killer would probably be a bloody mess; their clothing must have been cleaned, or disposed of, somehow.

Bleed-out time of an artery was what, a few minutes? She must have found Linda just moments after the killer had . . . Nell's brain rejected the spike of danger. *Who has a motive? God, it's horribly obvious*. Greta, of course. And therefore Douggie. And Angus, and Theo. Possibly Percy. *Where the hell is she?* Nell closed her eyes, resisting the tide of suspicion rolling in.

Deborah's voice made her jump. 'I can see how hard you tried to save her. I-I was useless. If I'd believed her, she might still . . .'

'No, I'm sorry, Deborah. I just . . . I can't believe this. You're guests in my home – I can't believe . . .' Nell's body jittered, as adrenaline drained from her, her teeth chattering with the cold. She tugged the blanket around her.

The sound of gravel crunching, as a car pulled up, forced Nell to drag herself to the hall and meet Val. She recognised DS Ashley Hollis with her. 'Thanks . . . for coming out.'

Val's eyes widened as she took in Nell's bloodied state. 'You better take me through.'

Hurriedly, Val pulled on her protective gear, just as James hurtled into the hall, coffee sloshing from the mug he clutched.

Despite the alarm on his face, he looked wrung out. 'What the . . . ?' He gaped at Nell, and instinctively moved towards her to gather her into a hug but stopped himself, glancing at Val. 'What the hell's happened, Nell? Are you hurt?'

She shook her head. 'No. I'll show you . . . In the library.' Nell shuddered. 'With the dagger.'

Val shot Nell a wry look, gallows humour not failing her. 'So where's our Miss Scarlett got to?'

If she was talking about Percy, that's what Nell wanted to know, too. So she kept quiet. But she wondered if the gentle joke was a sign that Val saw her as almost one of the team.

'More to the point,' Val glared at James, as he pulled on the suit that Ashley had given him, 'where did *you* get to?'

'I was only gone a moment.' James hopped as he pulled on a bootie. 'I felt myself drifting off so,' he hurried to keep up as they walked into the library, 'I thought a second or two to brew a strong coffee and a quick bit of fresh air in the garden would be better than me falling asl—*Jesus*.'

They stood in the doorway, leaving room for the paramedics. Deborah was staring at the crew, clearly shell-shocked.

'Ms Grey.' Val walked over to her. 'I'm sorry for your loss, Deborah.' She turned to her colleague. 'This is DS Ashley Hollis – she's a family liaison officer, and she'll be here as a support for you and to keep you updated as we investigate.'

As Ashley nodded, a corkscrew of her Afro fell over one eye. Her smile at Deborah was kind, full of concern. 'You're Linda's wife? I'm sorry for your loss.' She steered Deborah out towards the hall, and Nell saw a SOCO waiting. The suggestion of forensic examination of the scene focused her mind and she turned to Val.

'The dagger was in the cabinet there.' Nell pointed. 'Unlocked. And we'd all been in here after dinner. Anyone could have seen it.'

Val studied the contents of the cabinet. 'That's an interesting collection of . . .' she glanced at Nell, '*artefacts*.'

'Just ecological things I found or had an interest in, growing up.' She watched Val's indifferent gaze slide over the display of shells, skulls and specimens.

'Ecology is an odd profession, isn't it?' Val said amiably. She turned and cast her studious eye over Linda. With no hint of irony, she continued, 'Judging by the blood spatter, the assailant must have severed the carotid artery on her left side, with the end of the cut.' The spray of blood had fountained up the back of the sofa and cascaded out in front of Linda. It didn't look like the pattern on the sofa cushions beside Linda's head had been interrupted. Most of the blood had pumped straight out. Nell shuddered.

'She must have been dead when you found her.'

Nell shook her head.

'Jesus,' James said again. He seemed more shocked than Nell felt. He gazed at her.

But Val's eyes lit up. 'Did you hear or see anyone? Any indication who'd been in here? Or did Linda give you a sign?'

'No. I asked her and I think she tried to mouth a name. But it was too late. And I didn't see or hear anyone.'

'Could they have still been in the room?'

Nell shook her head. White-suited forensic officers filed into the room, opening cases, their gazes taking in the surroundings. One waited beside Nell. Val nodded at her. 'This is Gwen, she'll take clippings from your nails, a DNA sample and your clothes.'

The forensic officer set out a series of labelled bags. She unwrapped a sterile nail clipper and reached her latex-gloved hands out. Nell held her hands steady as each nail was cut and the trimmings placed in the bag. The sight of her fingers was alien. Linda's drying, crimson blood had caked around her cuticles and in her knuckles.

As Gwen sealed and labelled the bag, Nell said, 'My DNA results are already on file, if that will save you time and expense.'

'Oh?' Gwen's casual tone didn't curtail the gleam in her alert brown eyes. 'How so?'

'I was involved in a murder investigation at Cookingdean.' Nell held Gwen's gaze, as it inevitably dropped to her T-shirt. She knew that even though she was covered in blood, none would have disguised Rav's caption, 'Cookingdean's Most Wanted'.

'How useful. Then I just need the helpfully labelled T-shirt, please.'

Nell nodded. She pointed upstairs. 'I presume I can . . . in my room?'

'Sure.'

Nell was disconcerted when Gwen followed her. And even more by the congregation in the half of the hall that wasn't cordoned off. Everyone stood in knotted, tense clusters. James must have gathered them all up for questioning. Already self-conscious in the T-shirt and boxers she'd slept in, Nell recoiled from the gasps breaking out as the assembled company noticed the claret bloodstains smeared up her arms and face.

Rav leaped up. 'Nell?' He reached for her, but Gwen blocked him with a white-suited arm.

Nell shook her head, pointing upstairs. 'I have to . . . I'll be down in a bit.'

As she walked past the throng with her police escort, contagious suspicion crackled: uneasy glances passed between Douggie, Angus and Theo; Crispin's and Shannon's jaws dropped. Greta and Deborah bookended the group, both distraught.

But Percy was still missing.

Nell headed upstairs via the lift, avoiding the taped-off stairs. She didn't argue when Gwen followed her into her room. She took off the T-shirt and boxers, folded them, and dropped them in the bag that Gwen held out.

'Is it OK if I shower now?' Nell asked. She didn't care that she was naked. A woman bleeding out underneath your hands had a way of making usual concerns seem petty.

'Of course. Once you're ready, will you come downstairs to give your statement? We'll wait.'

'Thanks,' Nell said. She watched Gwen leave, then walked into the bathroom. As she set the shower running, she heard the bedroom door open and close softly.

Panic and paranoia surged.

Was the killer coming for her?

Now, her nakedness *did* make her feel vulnerable. She scanned the room for something, anything, her vision black-edged and tilting with the cocktail of fear and adrenaline. She couldn't cover herself up *and* defend herself, so her shaking hands snatched up a can of deodorant and grabbed the lighter beside the candles. She held them out before her, pointing them both at the door: one thumb pressed against the spark-wheel, and her other hand's index finger on the can's plunger.

Chapter 15

Sunday 14th March – 6 a.m.

The soft knock on the bathroom door made her hold her breath; tense, silent, shaking. Then the voice – James – 'Nell? You OK?'

Releasing her held breath made her sag like a ragdoll. 'Come . . . come in.' Nell lowered her arms.

James took what she was clutching gently from her. 'OK, Jason Bourne. Let's put the improvised flamethrower over here, out of the way.'

She shivered, teeth chattering as he reached for the bath towel and wrapped her in it, hugging her to him.

'Don't you need to help? With the investigation?'

James shook his head. 'I can be a detective in a minute. Right now, I'm all yours.' His arms clasped round her, his chin resting on her head. Nell felt his jaw clenching.

Clinging to him, she gripped his broad shoulders, her face pressed into his neck. 'Oh, James. It was horrible. Her throat was slit. Wide open.' She shuddered. 'I'll . . . I'll never forget that awful look in her eyes.'

'I'm so sorry, Nell. I don't know how that happened in the short time I . . .' His voice cracked. 'God. I'm sorry.'

'Does it give us a timeline, though? If you know you were only gone a short while?'

James shook his head. 'I didn't check my watch. *Idiot*. I just jerked awake and knew I had to get something to stay that way. If I had stayed put, you'd never . . .' His shoulders hunched with tension.

'I just wish I could have saved her.'

'It would have taken a miracle, Nell. Honestly. I'm just glad whoever did it didn't hang around.' James squeezed her tighter and planted fierce kisses in her hair. He steered her towards the shower. Nell didn't think an ocean could wash this off her. She stood firm, then hesitated.

'I'll get myself cleaned up.' She needed privacy but she didn't want to be totally alone. 'But . . . would you . . . would you wait in the bedroom?'

'Sure.' He hesitated, then left, closing the bathroom door softly behind him.

Nell grabbed a nail brush and got in the shower, gasping under the scalding water. Squeezing all her shower gel onto the brush, she scrubbed her hands and nails, arms and body until her flesh stung and the sweet jasmine lather finally blotted out the metal smell of blood.

Around her feet, the water swirled crimson, then pink, then clear.

Sunday 14th March – 6.15 a.m.

Rav waited in the hall for Nell to come downstairs. Seeing her covered in blood, having to hand her clothes over to forensic officers, brought back memories of the last time they'd had a brush with a murderer. She'd been cool under pressure, but that's when they'd had their argument. Too many emotions had boiled to the surface. He wasn't going to make the same mistake again and assume she was OK just because she was good at putting on a brave face.

Nell had looked ghost-white when she'd passed him in the hall. He wanted to make sure he'd be there for her when she came down. He'd given his statement to Val first, but seconds felt like hours.

So, he'd sat there, watching the police coming and going, murmuring and organising how they'd process the scene, how they'd take another round of statements, and how they'd take DNA samples from everyone.

Percy had slunk in, her face gaunt with worry. He'd shot her a sympathetic half-smile. Her attempt to return it looked more like a grimace. But, as she perched on the antique chair in the hall, he noticed that, however exhausted she was, her eyes followed the detectives' every move, listening to all their conversations.

Around him, the house guests simmered with the same single

question that they didn't dare ask. *Who could have done something like . . . that?* They'd followed the directions of the detectives almost in a dazed state. Everyone was keen to label Hawke's fall as an accident. Because if it wasn't, they were either dealing with a multiple murderer or multiple murder*ers*.

When Nell finally appeared in the hall from the lift, Rav's heart jumped, even though James was close behind her.

'Nell.' She still looked shell-shocked. And so, so pale. Him saying her name must have summoned the company from the great room and suddenly, around Rav, the stunned fug became a clamour of questions. Greta, Douggie, Angus – even Theo – clustered around her, all talking at once, asking how she was and what was going on.

While a couple of people tried to comfort Deborah and offer sympathy, Crispin and Shannon joined the rest of the fray encircling Nell, asking stupid questions.

Nell's bewildered face scanned the throng. 'I-I don't have any answers. I'll . . . ask. Where's Val?'

'Morning room.' Deborah pointed. She'd changed into leggings and an oversized Harvard hoodie, but she was still shivering.

Nell nodded, then slipped through to the great room, followed by the other guests, who hung back as she walked through the ballroom. With James. Rav itched to follow. *But I can't . . . can I?*

Minutes crawled by like years. The company fell silent again, huddled around the fire.

Finally, they heard footsteps, and Val peered around the door. 'Any of you seen Nell?'

Rav's heart lurched. 'She was coming to see you. With James.'

Val frowned. 'Well, James is with us. No Nell, yet, though.'

'What?' Fear lanced through Rav. He reasoned that she couldn't be in danger; everyone was here. He clamped down on the rising terror. *Where would she go?*

Suddenly, with total certainty, he knew where Nell would be. And if she needed time alone, he would protect that.

Val eyed him in steady silence, then said, 'If you *happen* to see her, we do need her to come and give her statement. As soon as she's ready.'

Once Val returned to the morning room, Rav took the opportunity to slip through the banqueting hall to the kitchen. Mrs Faulkner was preparing yet another tray of tea and coffee.

'Don't suppose you have a flask?' Rav asked.

Mrs Faulkner pointed to a cupboard and passed him the jug of coffee she'd just made. He poured some into the flask while she wrapped home-made shortbread, sprinkled with sugar, in a napkin for him. Her small smile as she refilled the kettle and put it on to boil suggested she was on to him. 'The back door here takes you out to the garden.'

Rav hurried outside, shivering in the dawn air as he crossed the terrace towards the wisteria-covered summer house, which overlooked the rose garden. He tiptoed closer to look through the windows but, with the early cerise glow of sunrise glinting on the glass, he couldn't see inside. So he knocked, then opened the door a crack.

Her shocked face jerked up as he walked in, then her shoulders sank with her long exhale. She was huddled under a blanket, knees pulled in. Judging by her red eyes, she'd been crying.

He teetered on the threshold. 'Could you use some company?' He offered the flask and the bundle of biscuits. 'Or I can just leave you with these? No obligation.'

Her tremulous smile encouraged him to take a step inside. Nell nodded at the space beside her, and he sat down, poured a steaming cup of coffee and passed it to her. She hugged the plastic cup. Her hands shook and he instinctively wrapped his around them. Her fingers were ice-cold.

'Don't blame you for escaping.' He smiled gently.

She tried to smile back. 'I just needed to get out of the house. I can't believe what just happened.' She gulped back a sob. 'So . . . so *violent*. Linda was a guest, in my home. And someone here did *that* to her.'

'You're not responsible, Nell.'

'How can I not be? I didn't stop Percy pressing ahead with this wedding. When it was clearly a bad idea. I just accepted her excuses to rush it, to have it here. Percy's always been impulsive and I should have known better. If I had just tried to talk to her, maybe she'd have broken off the engagement. And Hawke and Linda wouldn't . . .'

Tears started to roll down Nell's cheeks and Rav carefully took her coffee from her, letting her sob into his shoulder. He felt his T-shirt grow damp, then soaked, as he sat in silence with his arm around her. But he was too aware of her body pressing against him, her face in his neck, her scent. He had a sudden urge to gather her up in his arms, but held steady, careful to keep the hug platonic.

But when she eventually sat up, wiping her face on the sleeve of her hoodie, mumbling, 'Sorry', he felt a physical loss. He swayed towards her, and had to force himself to sit back, to maintain a distance. He passed her the cup again. 'Drink this. It'll warm you up. And have the biscuits. Sugar's supposed to be good for shock.'

Nell sipped the coffee and nibbled the biscuits, staring out of the window. She ignored the formal gardens and stared towards the orchard – over the lacey apple blossom and candyfloss wisps of cherry – to the grey barn, with its ornamental, redundant clock tower. Rav watched her as colour returned to her cheeks and tension ebbed from her shoulders. He topped up the coffee and gestured at the window, encouraging the distraction. 'Seen anything?'

She shook her head. 'I hoped to. Being around dawn. But no signs yet.'

'You can't seriously be expecting the box to be used this year, though. It's too late, isn't it? They'll have started checking out nesting sites in January – February at the latest, surely?'

Nell shook her head. 'This pair had a site. In an old oak tree, in the woods near the weir. But a pair of kestrels moved in on their territory and evicted them. First, the kestrels blocked the owls in the nest by sitting at the entrance with their wings spread. Then, when the owls tried to escape, the kestrels dive-bombed them again and again, until they surrendered. Forced out. It was brutal.'

'Jeez. Talk about turf wars.'

'So now they're homeless and looking for a new nest. Since they perch in the barn, I hoped they'd take to a box in there.'

As if on cue, a blood-curdling screech made them jump, then focus on the habitats around the barn. Against the pink-streaked sky, a ghostly shape skimmed the hedge. Nell gripped Rav's hand as she watched the barn owl land on a fence post. Bright-white chest with honey-gold wings. The head rotated, until the inquisitive heart-shaped face stared right at them.

Nell gasped. 'That's the male! Checking things out.'

The owl's body heaved and bobbed as he let out another hissing shriek. Then he flew towards the barn, straight through the gap in the weatherboard. Seconds later, another screech pierced the silence.

'Oh wow,' breathed Rav. 'I reckon that's a call to a mate. That he's found somewhere to nest.'

From the woodland, a second shriek came in reply. Rav and Nell gaped, locking eyes, before Rav nudged her to look out of the window. She turned in time to see a second, more speckled, barn owl – the female – glide past, straight into the barn.

'I think we just witnessed moving-in day,' Rav whispered. 'Imagine if you hadn't given them an alternative site, and they missed a year of breeding.' He nudged her. 'You make a difference, to a lot of things. To a lot of . . . people.'

Chapter 16

Sunday 14th March – 6.45 a.m.

Nell appreciated Rav's kind words, and the distraction of the owls helped. Talking about something they both cared about, and which was unrelated to the murder was . . . settling. Taking a breath, she was about to speak, when voices outside made them both freeze.

'I just can't believe that the last things we said to one another were so . . .' Deborah's voice was thick with anguish. 'I wish . . . I wish I hadn't been so hard on her. But I couldn't get her to listen. I started blaming her for the whole mess Hawke had got himself into. That she was as bad as him if she knew and didn't *do* something.' Her words cracked into sobs. 'And now I'll never be able to say sorry.'

'Oh, Deborah, you did what you thought was right at the time.' It was Theo, in his hushed, gentle accent. 'You had Linda's interests at heart.'

Nell and Rav exchanged a wince, sinking low on the bench, out of sight. Nell realised that Theo was Deborah's only acquaintance, or maybe friend, in the house now. So it was natural she'd turn to him. *But won't he feel his loyalties divided between her and the family?* With an unsettling shiver, Nell wondered if Theo really was Deborah's ally.

'She didn't want to hear it, though.' Deborah gulped. 'What was I thinking? I mean, we both knew she'd been bolstering his margins. And I'm not talking a few cents, here. I'm talking major cash injections. I thought, at first, I could make some suggestions, help him turn around his mismanagement. But then I got my assistant's email, with her research on Hawke. And that changed everything.'

'Did Linda know about that?'

'Oh yeah.' Deborah took a shuddering breath. 'Telling her about what I'd found out, that's when . . . when things got real bad. I thought

100

it would be a shock. But it was obvious she knew. In hindsight, I shoulda known. She still co-owns the business.'

Inside the summer house, Nell frowned at Rav.

There was a pause before Theo spoke. Then he said, carefully, 'Do you think her involvement may have been greater? More than simply knowing of it? More than complicity?'

Deborah's sigh was audible. 'I truly hope Lindy didn't do business like that. Running down other enterprises for a cheaper takeover. I've seen people who operate like that, and I've also seen the impact that has on the workers, on the business owners. It's inhumane.'

'Linda built her business very quickly.' Theo's tone was measured. 'From small B & Bs to a national chain of eight luxury hotels in a few years. Expensive real estate in expensive places. You think he learned his trade from her?'

'If you'd have asked me yesterday, I'd have sworn no. But today . . . Well, like you say, at best she was complicit. And I have to hand it to Hawke: he targeted businesses to expand his offering. Spas, boutique hotels – hooked a couple of top chefs after trashing the establishment side of their restaurants. You know, the guy had a *plan*. All of them small, privately owned companies. And all of them driven into oblivion.'

'Nice guy,' Theo said.

'I'm just reeling, I guess,' Deborah said. 'First that, then the fact that Lindy *knew*, then . . . then . . .'

'It's been a terrible shock. You must be kind to yourself. We can go in and—'

'Oh, boy. Mrs Faulkner is a doll but if she offers me another fix-all cup of tea or coffee, I'm gonna flip. Out.' Their voices faded away, in the direction of the terrace and the house.

Rav gave a long exhale. 'Bloody hell. The more I know about Hawke, the more—'

Nell cut him off. 'Well, you know what that means, don't you? Percy's family weren't the only ones with a motive to . . .' She mimed a shove. 'And Linda and Deborah's relationship was clearly on rockier ground than anyone knew . . .' She raised hopeful eyebrows at Rav.

He nodded. 'So? Are you ready to go in? You'll have to make a statement.'

Tension clenched her stomach. 'I will. But . . . not just yet.'

'How about a walk?' he asked. 'Show me the prime real-estate the kestrels ousted our barn owls from.' Relief rolled through Nell at the suggestion to get outside and *move*. It was just what she needed. She clambered to her feet. 'Yes, it's a good walk. You'll like it. And it's not far, so afterwards I can . . .' She swallowed. She couldn't say it, but she knew the walk would give her time to calm down; calm enough to give a coherent account to Val.

Walking across the garden, Nell inhaled deep lungfuls of clean, bracing air, purging the stench of blood that had clung to her ever since . . . She swung her arms wide, feeling her shoulders crunch, then loosen. As she headed towards the loggia and the woodland, her stride lengthened, her sluggish body waking up.

'I'm starting to feel a bit better.' *Is that just the walk? Or is that Rav?* He always knew what to say, what to do.

She took another deep breath of the dewy morning air. There was something comforting about the smells of a forest. Rich, woody notes punctuated by revealing scents: mulchy wafts of fungus, musky whiffs of fox, the high, clean scent of nearby water.

She knew Rav would notice the same things. His gaze followed the fox's track through brambles quivering with hidden, nesting song thrushes and wrens singing over each other to declare their territories, warning others not to infringe. He spotted the cracks in tree trunks where bats might roost, his eyes flitting along branches for signs; and he registered the bright sunspots of primroses that indicated this woodland was ancient. Their silence was more than companionable; it let the countryside speak for itself.

In the apricot dawn light, they trekked uphill as the worn earth footpath, laced with tree roots, met the river carving through the valley. The swirling water thundering over the weir and the air ringing with melodic bursts of birdsong were the sounds of the universe carrying on like everything was normal.

The muddy riverside path attracted her attention, but she resisted kneeling to check if one of her favourite residents was around. She glanced at the rocks across the watercourse and the bank. The largest boulder was always a good spot, and today it didn't disappoint. Black spraint, right on the top. She paused, as if needing a breather, and waited to see if Rav noticed.

Immediately, he checked the rock. 'Hey, Nell, I think this spraint has fish bones in.' He sniffed it like a wine connoisseur. 'Definite hints of jasmine tea.' Scanning the path first, he then kneeled carefully so he didn't trample any evidence, squinting at a small, star-like paw print. Five short streaks indicated toes. 'Is this what I think it is?' He was whispering. It always paid to be quiet.

He looked up and she nodded. Spotting a ripple in the water, she gasped, then pointed.

'Oh, no *way*.' Rav stood beside her, staring at the V-shaped wake in the river from the small brown head and the long, undulating body as it headed to the far edge.

The otter scampered out from the water and up onto the far bank, sniffed around a rock, and then jumped on to it.

'I didn't think there were many down this way.'

'No, well, it's taken a while. We built the fish ladder into the weir five years ago.' She jerked her head towards the shallow, underwater steps structure that allowed the fish to bypass the weir unscathed. 'And two years ago we naturalised the riverbanks. And the fish stocks improved, and then, we spotted this chap. He made everyone's day!'

'I bet. It can't be easy to find food when the river's this high, though.'

'I think he crosses the river using these rocks, and maybe hunts from them.' The otter paused to investigate a tree trunk, then bounded along the path under the bridge.

She turned to Rav, hands on hips. 'Well, you've passed one test. How about the other one?'

Grinning, he glanced around, homing in on the veteran oak. His eyes ran over the gnarled branches, focusing on the collared cavity formed from a removed limb. But he didn't walk towards it; he moved backwards, into the undergrowth, watching, listening. Nell joined him, waiting in the cover of the understorey, holding her breath.

A faint, hissy *klee-ee* sounded from the tree.

Pleased with his detection skills, Rav's comic smug smile stretched into delight as a bobbing head appeared at the entrance. They gasped as the kestrel hopped up onto the edge of the hole, surveying the landscape. To Nell, the interloper's fluttering wing stretch had a hint of smug swagger.

'Well, he knows he owns the place,' Rav whispered.

'Yeah, doesn't he!'

Without warning, a silent white shape shot past. The barn owl – talons stretched out before him – struck the kestrel. With indignant squawks, the kestrel lurched sideways, feathers flying, then toppled backwards into the cavity. Frantic *klee-ee, klee-ee* calls of both kestrels clamoured, as the owl soared away.

Nell and Rav gaped, then choked back laughter.

'Wow!' Rav winced. 'Now *that's* a family feud! Falconidae vs Tytonidae. Talk about two households—'

'Pff, don't you dare say, "both alike in dignity". Hardly. One's *literally* a housebreaker.'

'Hey, I can't help it. I'm *enraptored*.'

Nell groaned at the terrible pun, but she felt a pang. She never felt this natural with James. She didn't have that itch to be somewhere else, with some*one* else.

Nell shook herself, making it look like a shiver. She didn't need any complications right now, not after all the things that had happened in the last few hours. Good friends *would* know what to say. No point making something out of nothing.

Needing to put physical distance between them, Nell wandered around the edge of the copse, towards the river. After the wet winter, it was in full flood, and roared under the wooden bridge and over the weir crest, churning down the laddered waterfall. At the edge of the bridge, she watched the water eddying below her in a hypnotic, whirling torrent.

A rustle behind her startled her and made her twist round. A man was marching towards her, bulky and menacing, hunched into the collar of his black overcoat.

Heart racing, she backed towards the river, a scream rising in her throat. But then familiarity flickered.

'H-Hamish? Bloody hell! You scared me to death!'

The misery on his face morphed into hostility and Nell recoiled.

'What is it?' she managed to say.

He huffed a hot cloud of frustration into the icy air and moved close, thrusting his face near hers. 'Oh, I'm just dandy, Nell. For a man you've just stabbed in the back. I thought we were friends, and here you are hosting *her* wedding to . . . to . . .'

Rav dashed over, looking alarmed, which made Hamish snarl, and then turn and stomp across the bridge, head low.

'What's going on?' Rav asked. 'Who was that?'

'Hamish.' Nell gave a long exhale.

'Percy's ex? What's he doing here?'

Nell took a deep breath. 'Well, there's only one reason I can think of,' she said, looking anxiously at Hamish's retreating figure. 'And given what's happened . . . that's not good, is it?'

Sunday 14th March – 7.45 a.m.

'Linda's killer, whoever that is, had left the scene of the crime only minutes before you found her, judging by the state of the blood and her wounds,' said Val, glancing down at her notes. 'You saw nothing? Heard nothing?'

Nell, who'd been answering Val's questions for a good twenty minutes, shook her head. Rav saw James, who was sitting next to her, squeeze her hand as she sat, her face drained of colour.

Rav glanced away. Nell looked so vulnerable, but she was trying to be stoic as she described the gruesome scene. Seconds away from a brutal and bold murderer. No wonder she was so on edge. He wished it was him beside her, able to take care of her. But that was never going to happen now.

'Hang on . . .' Nell's voice pulled him out of his thoughts. 'The security team did report an intruder, around the time of the wedding.' She turned to James. 'We assumed it was the press, but . . . should I ask them to pass on their report?'

'Definitely,' James said, but Rav saw a flash of annoyance in his eyes, probably because Nell hadn't told him this before.

Then it hit him. Since *Hamish* was here . . . could he be the intruder? Rav eyed Nell to see if she had the same thought, but she was too busy tapping out an email on her phone.

Val turned to James. 'Good. I've got statements and DNA and fingerprints from all the family. I'll head to the station and get things processed.' She tilted her head.

Rav noticed James's slight nod in reply. They were under constant surveillance now. He wasn't sure if that was reassuring or not. Folding his arms, he tried not to feel defensive. But, as everyone stood and walked through to the hall, he followed them. *I'm just seeing them out*, he told himself. *Not trying to listen in*. But he had to swerve Mrs Faulkner, who hurried past with a laden breakfast tray, heading towards the lift.

Val eyed it. 'For a minute there, Mrs F, I thought this was another of your reviving coffee trays.'

'There's coffee out in the refectory. Along with breakfast, laid out on the sideboard. You and the team would be welcome to help yourselves if you'd like.'

'Oh, thanks.' Val frowned. 'Then who's that for?'

'Lord MacKenzie. Meaning Cameron . . . MacKenzie.'

'*Who?*'

'Percy's grandfather.'

Val turned an exasperated glare to James. 'So when I thought I had got statements from everyone in the house, there's someone here I don't even *know* about?'

James looked annoyed, but with himself this time.

Nell followed Mrs Faulkner to the lift, so Rav did, too. Right now, he didn't want to let Nell out of his sight.

'I saw Cameron head to bed early on the night of the wedding, at about 11 p.m.,' he heard James explain. 'He's in his nineties and wheelchair-bound. So I don't see him as a realistic suspect.'

'Oh, good.'

James's head jerked round at her tone. 'What do you mean?'

'Well, I didn't realise we could save ourselves the time and expense of an investigation,' Val said archly. 'Go on, tell me who *is* a realistic suspect? Or, better still, the murderer? Save us all some time.'

Rav couldn't help but be amused by Val's sarcastic tone.

As the lift doors opened, Nell got in with Val, James and Mrs F. So Rav squeezed in, too.

'Um, we don't require an audience to question Cameron MacKenzie,' Val said.

'No, but the questioning might be easier with an introduction,' Nell said. 'Given he'll be in bed and probably feel at a disadvantage. Which will make him even more cantankerous.'

The lift doors opened, and Rav watched Val and James follow Mrs F and Nell along the hall.

Balancing the tray on one hand, Mrs Faulkner opened the door to Cameron's room. With a gasp, she stopped dead.

The tray slid out of her hands and clattered to the floor.

Chapter 17

Sunday 14th March – 8 a.m.

Pandemonium broke out: James rushed in and Val blocked the door. Nell craned her head from the doorway. Cameron was leaning over the edge of the bed, his face a purplish red.

James stopped short of the bed, observing from a distance. *He thinks it's another crime scene.* Nell's stomach dropped.

Mrs Faulkner's sobs were shocked half-gasps. 'I'm so . . . sorry. About the mess.' She pointed at the dropped tray, broken crockery, spilt drinks and food.

Nell squeezed her hand. 'It doesn't matter.' She steered her past Val to a seat, just as Douggie and Percy flew upstairs.

'Wait,' Val ordered, blocking their way. She shook her head at Douggie, conveying the bad news with a sombre look.

'What happened?' Douggie demanded. He was breathless, but Nell thought he sounded . . . almost relieved? Then a guilty expression flitted over his face.

'I'm very sorry to tell you, sir, but your father's—' Val began.

'No . . .' Douggie rubbed his face. 'Aye. Well . . .' he said quietly. 'At his age, it's to be expected.' He gestured inside. 'I'd like to . . .'

'We can't let you in,' Val asserted. 'Because we don't know the circumstances of his death.'

'He was in his nineties. With heart issues and poor health.' Percy's chin jutted. 'It doesn't take a rocket scientist . . .'

Nell shot her a warning look.

James pocketed his phone and moved round Val to talk to Douggie and Percy. 'Dr Saunders is on her way,' he said. 'And though it may well be old age, we have to be sure. Until then, you can't get any closer, Percy. Too much has happened. I'm sorry for your loss but we—'

Percy shook her head. 'Sorry for my loss? He was a bigoted old bas—'

'Percy!' Douggie looked horrified.

'Well, he was,' she said. 'Especially to you, Dad. You couldn't do anything right.'

Douggie swallowed. 'My Da had a tough upbringing. Tougher than anything you can imagine. He had his shortcomings, I'll nae deny it. But considering all things . . . He was a good man.' He rubbed his face. 'Anyway, the solicitor's coming down this afternoon.' He shot a look at Percy, as if thinking of the threat he'd made upon his arrival, which was redundant now. 'So we can set our affairs in order straightaway. I'll call them with this . . . news. So come along, now, lass. Family meeting.'

Percy didn't move. 'Do we have to get into all of that now? Surely it can wait?'

Turning on the stairs, Douggie stared at her. 'No, lass. This isn't about some sticks of furniture. This is my estate. And my responsibilities. Not least to all the folk who work there and depend on it running smoothly for their livelihood. Take one minute and think about all the others who are affected by all this, eh?'

Percy didn't stir. Douggie's face furrowed with a frown. '*Move.*'

At the low growl, Percy unfolded her arms and stomped down the stairs. But as she passed Nell, a frisson of reprisal flitted over her face.

With the foreboding that her friend had got herself into more trouble, Nell leaned against the wall. *What the hell is Percy up to now?*

Sunday 14th March – 9 a.m.

James went to the refectory for a coffee, imagining the faces of his imminently arriving SOCO colleagues called out to deal with a third body.

He sat heavily, stirring his drink and looking towards the vast glass doors out to the garden. When Nell had first shown him around, the architecture nerd in him had loved that this extension was an obvious addition, probably built about the same time as the spa: all chunky oak frames and glass, framing a glorious view of the lake and woodland beyond.

It felt like years ago.

Now, appreciating the view seemed frivolous. His mind was occupied with how he'd regain his lost ground with Val. She was much quicker to criticise him since his promotion. *Is that just expectations of the high rank? Or does she disagree with Trent?* The insecurity gnawed at his confidence.

And around the house, he was constantly alert for the slightest lead, reading suspicion into every nuance of body language, fearful for Nell, and wondering if his own role, as investigator, put him in danger, too.

Where is Nell? He'd hoped to find her in here. He'd hung around, in case she came in, at least for coffee. *Ugh. I bet she's off with* him *again.* Like she had been when he and Val had been waiting for her, to take her statement. Of course, detectives had nothing better to do than dangle about while witnesses went on nature walks.

At the far end of the refectory, also ignoring the view, Percy and her family were in deep conversation. They glanced over warily. James shook his head at the unspoken question. He wouldn't have anything concrete to share with the family until SOCO had finished processing Cameron's room and the post-mortem had been completed.

Based on the initial signs of rigor mortis in the face but not the body, Dr Saunders had placed time of death at around seven to eight hours ago. Between 1 a.m. and 2 a.m. Hawke's death had been at 1.15 a.m. Had someone used that distraction to run in, maybe wake Cameron on the pretext of telling him about Hawke, and then . . . ? He made a mental note to check who was late to the hall.

The statements everyone had given for Hawke's death showed that no one in the house had an alibi leading up to that time. And once they'd been gathered up, the questioning had gone on until about 4 a.m. After that, everyone had claimed to be in bed, while Linda was being butchered.

With an apologetic nod to the MacKenzies, repeated pressing of the coffee-machine buttons and attention directed to his phone, he was careful to give the impression that he had no intention of overhearing Douggie and Greta's conversation with Percy. While, of course, he listened and studied their body language intently.

'Solicitor can come at 4.30 p.m. to read the will. So that'll be . . .' Douggie squeezed his eyes shut. 'That'll at least be one good thing.'

'I know, love.' Greta squeezed his arm. 'At last.'

Beside her, Percy seemed to be shrinking in her seat, holding her cup of coffee in front of her face. Grief? Relief? Guilt? No, more sorrowful. Almost . . . *regret*?

But Greta hadn't seemed to notice. She patted Douggie's arm. 'Do you think . . . ?'

Douggie shook his head.

'Could all be very different now, you know.' Her eyes slid to Theo, who sat along the table with Angus. *All still thick as thieves.*

But Theo glanced at Angus and they both shook their heads. '*Non, ma chérie.*' Theo raised his palms. 'Things are not that simple.'

As Greta stared at him, chin trembling, Angus agreed. 'Aye, you need to think about things. From all angles, Greta. Not just your own.'

Sunday 14th March – 9.15 a.m.

After James had phoned SOCO from Cameron's room, and headed downstairs to meet them, Nell had grilled Mrs F in the kitchen for any detail of the room, anything she'd spotted about Cameron. But Nell had observed more from her awkward angle than the housekeeper had through her shock.

Rav had stuck to her side like a shadow. Nell glanced at him. It was a comfort. When he was around, it wasn't just that she felt safer – she could actually relax.

His stomach growled and Rav looked apologetic.

Nell suddenly registered that they were surrounded by the aromas of a cooked breakfast. 'Oh God. I didn't even think about food.' She pulled Rav towards the refectory. She might not be hungry, but he clearly was. And probably not mentioning it because he thought she couldn't face it.

But she nearly U-turned in the doorway, as faces looked up from the table. *Wow. Everyone.*

Shannon and Crispin were huddled together. They were both

reading their phones, turning to each other and muttering. Crispin looked worried and upset, whereas Shannon seemed engrossed.

James was sitting next to Percy, studying his iPad. When he looked up and saw her, he smiled – looked relieved, in fact. But then his gaze caught Rav behind her, and his smile faded to irritation.

Douggie, Greta, Angus and Theo formed their usual quartet. But there wasn't the usual tight sense of accord. Angus and Douggie looked . . . acrimonious. A cafetière and a pile of buttery toast sat, untouched, before Greta, and there was some distance between her and Theo. Then Nell noticed Deborah, who was sitting on Theo's other side, as he murmured something to her.

Between reading and tapping her phone, Deborah replied to Theo, hugging her coffee but not drinking it, and shooting occasional, wary glances at the family. She gave a tense smile to Nell.

'Hey, Nell, where's good for a walk?' she asked. 'I-I could use some fresh air.'

'Up to Nye weir is nice. Head across the garden, to the loggia and into the woodland, then follow the path along the river. It's my running route, so it's a good distance for a walk. Bit of a climb up the hill but the view from the bridge is worth it.'

'Thanks. Sounds good,' said Deborah, rising from her seat as Nell turned to the sideboard. She was starving, she realised, and helped herself to some kedgeree.

Rav came up and nudged her. 'I thought you hated running?'

She turned to his teasing grin like a flower turning to the sun. 'I do. But next time we're surveying and we face off a farmer with a shotgun, I at least want to be able to outrun them!' She referred to a site they'd worked on, where the tenant farmer was understandably unhappy about the land being compulsorily purchased for the road-widening scheme.

'Hope you're training in your site boots, then. Or waders!' His joke died on his lips as James joined them to make another coffee.

'What are you two laughing about?' James asked, as the coffee machine gurgled.

'Nothing,' said Nell and Rav together, before she added, 'Just a work joke. Probably not very funny.'

She was trying to put him at his ease, but it seemed to have the opposite effect, because James's expression grew pinched as they all stood in an awkward silence.

Shooting James a sidelong glance, Nell suddenly felt weighed down. *What am I doing? It shouldn't be this much hard work.*

Avoiding eye contact, Nell made a show of checking the morning's post on the silver salver, beside the pastries and porridge – two letters for her mother, nothing for her – and sat at the table. When James sat down next to her, she realised that, despite this being his umpteenth joltingly strong coffee, he looked like he could sleep standing up.

Here he was, working tirelessly to solve this, and she'd been mooning about with Rav. She felt a stab of ingratitude and squeezed his hand.

Sunday 14th March – 9.45 a.m.

After James headed off to the station, and Nell had taken Percy off for a walk, Rav was left behind, drinking his coffee.

Greta paused to speak to him, as she headed out with Douggie and Angus. 'How are you, laddie?'

'OK. Considering.' He gave her a smile. Though her face was tight with worry, Greta was calmer – well, she was *sober* now. But she was kind. Thoughtful. She noticed subtle things. Like him, feeling awkward at being abandoned, not knowing what to do with himself.

'And Nell?' She sighed. 'This is horrible for everyone, but this is her *home*. It must be awful for her. Are Imelda and Hugo on their way?'

Rav took a second to realise she meant Nell's parents. 'Oh. I don't know.'

'Yea Gods! They'll want to know, lad! If she hasn't called them, perhaps suggest it, eh? It might bring Nell some comfort if they're here.' She patted his arm and followed the men out, who were deep in conversation, their heads together.

Rav knew Greta had a point. And he wasn't going to pass up a reason to speak to Nell. Ever since their dawn walk, after she'd found Linda, the tug to be with her had grown. He knew it was futile, that she was with James now, but he found himself thinking about

113

whisking her away from all this horror. Right now, he wanted to walk up the weir, claiming to be exploring. But he told himself not to follow Nell and Percy, if they needed to talk.

Instead, he wondered about heading over to the rewilded areas, to see what Nell had been up to there. He was just about to get up and head out when Crispin and Shannon moved to sit beside him.

Shannon's phone dinged. She ignored it.

'Has James given any indication how long . . . *things* will take?' Crispin's tone was low, as if keen not to offend Deborah. But she was at the other end of the table, sitting with Theo, the two of them engrossed in something on Deborah's phone.

Rav's heart suddenly hammered. He hadn't thought beyond making sure Nell was OK. And she'd want to solve this. All the time he was here, he could help. *Assuming she wants to sift through her close friend's family and their motives . . .*

He shrugged at Crispin. 'Until the investigation's complete, I guess,' he said quietly. 'Why? Are you in a hurry to leave? Hadn't you planned to stay anyway, since there was a week of activities lined up?'

Shannon's phone dinged again. She still didn't check it.

Crispin sighed. 'Well, yes, I *had*, obviously. But now, well . . . And staying is a little . . . awkward.' There were another two dings from Shannon's phone, which again she ignored.

Rav nodded. 'My condolences. Losing a mate like that must be horrific. I don't blame you for not wanting to hang around.'

Crispin nodded sombrely, as Shannon's phone dinged yet again.

'Do you need to get that?' Rav asked her, with a hint of impatience.

Shannon tossed her hair back. 'Endless social-media notifications,' she said, in a bored tone. '*Hello!* have just published their feature on the wedding online, so I'm trending.' She sighed. 'It's all so draining.'

Rav saw Crispin's mouth tense into a tight line.

'Wait, they published already? Weren't they supposed to wait for editorial approval?' Rav asked.

Shannon shrugged. 'Depends what Hawke agreed with them.'

'But . . . but . . . don't they know? How can the *party* be in print when we're dealing with . . . *everything*?'

'Bad taste, isn't it?' Crispin's tension was clear in his voice.

'But they won't know until the deaths hit national press,' Shannon reasoned. 'Which, admittedly, won't be long.'

'What do you mean, "won't be long"?' Rav spluttered.

'Darling, we've had police crawling all over the house half the night and morning. There's always a leak.'

'Can't you . . . give people NDAs? Or something?'

'Oh, be practical. It's far too late for that. And can you see those detectives being kept from the bodies while they sign NDAs?'

'No, but . . .' He ploughed his hand through his hair. *Nell will hate this.*

'So we're stuck here, all under one roof, with press about to go berserk.' Crispin grimaced.

'It's not all bad, Crispin,' Shannon teased through the steam of her lemon and hot water. 'You get a few more days with me.' She eyed Rav. 'And I'll bet you aren't averse to spending more time with Nell, either,' she said. 'Perfect opportunity to seduce her away from her blue-eyed detective, huh?' When Rav didn't react, she prodded him. 'Admit it. I've seen the way you look at her.'

Rav's face flamed but he tried to keep his cool. 'No, Shannon, we're not all hell-bent on destroying other people's relationships,' he said, though guilt made his words sharper than he intended, and her expression flashed from provocative to petulant in a split second. Rav almost expected her to hiss like a cat, disgruntled because *you wouldn't play its games.*

'Don't give me that, Rav. I see you. You'd be right in Nell's sensible M&S granny pants if she gave you half a chance, whether she was with our delectable detective or not.'

As Rav gritted his teeth in annoyance, Shannon slid closer to him, flooding his senses with her overpowering scent, her eyes too knowing. 'The only difference between you and me, darling, is opportunity.'

He had to hand it to her: she knew a good line to make an exit on, and before Rav could give any kind of retort, she'd risen and swept from the room, with Crispin in her wake like a trained puppy.

As Rav sat alone, contemplating Shannon's too-astute comments, he caught Deborah's eye. Probably clocking his hangdog expression, she smiled and then got up and moved over to him.

'I wouldn't usually interfere, honey,' she said, sinking down beside him, 'but I couldn't help overhearing Shannon's . . . *performance*. And all this tragedy lately . . .' She waved a graceful hand, her fingers fluttering to her lips as she swallowed. 'Well, it puts life into hard focus, you know?'

Rav looked at her warily. 'I don't . . .' he began to say, but his words faded as Theo joined them, sitting down next to Deborah.

'Lindy and me . . .' She blew out a long breath. 'We had barely any time.' She shook her head, tears brimming. 'What we did have was . . . *perfect*.' Her smile trembled. 'Well, a few disagreements notwithstanding.' She drew a deep breath. 'But we both took too long to admit what we really wanted. *Who* we really wanted. And then . . .' She shook her head. 'Life can be cruel. And it's far too short, honey. If you think you've found your "one", then you need to tell her.'

A swell of emotion surged up through Rav's chest. He managed a small smile but his thoughts were whirling. Nell had made her choice.

God, he must look like such a loser.

He looked up again, expecting to see pity. But Theo's eyes met his with a deep understanding that somehow steadied him.

Deborah's phone flashed with an email subject line: *McAnstruther Casinos*. She snatched it up and read the message, shooting an apologetic glance at Rav.

'Sorry, honey. Work. You know how it is.'

Nodding, and emboldened by Deborah's confidences, Rav asked, 'What will happen to Hawke's businesses, Deborah? Will you take control of them?'

Deborah gave a short laugh. 'Oh, definitely not me! It's a long way from what I do, and what Linda and her late husband, Tom, started. They grew it all from one bed and breakfast, until they created their line of boutique hotels.'

Rav raised his eyebrows. 'Wow.' Deborah was smoothly feeding him her and Linda's marketing spiel – *not* the private concerns he'd heard her confide to Theo outside the summer house.

'Tom had the nous but Linda had the drive, the ambition,' Deborah went on. 'She wanted to create something for Hawke's future. And together they gave him *all* the opportunities – expensive private education, a great social network.' She sighed. 'And I have to hand it to him, he sure knew how to make the best of his connections.' She looked sideways at Rav. 'But that's the *only* good thing I can say about him.'

Rav stayed silent, willing Deborah to say more. She leaned back. 'Maybe I'm being unfair. The kid lost his father. And I think that made Linda overcompensate . . . indulge him. She just can't . . . *couldn't* . . . see any faults in her son. And lemme tell you, honey, how he conducted his business was only one of them.'

Rav watched her as she gave an elegant shrug. She wasn't shy about criticising Hawke. But she was every inch the devoted widow. *Is that out of loyalty to Linda? No point in besmirching her life's work now she's dead. Or is she covering up any trace of motive for killing her?*

Chapter 18

Sunday 14th March – 9.45 a.m.

Nell and Percy trudged through the kitchen garden. For the past few minutes Percy had been giving her the third degree about her love life, which was not the plan as far as Nell was concerned. The plan had been for her to ask the questions.

'Oh, come on,' Percy said. 'You're supposedly with James, but Rav has been following you around like a lovesick pup—'

'He's my *friend*, Percy. And you've confused "lovesick puppy" with concern for my wellbeing,' Nell said. 'Three people have died within twenty-four hours, in my home. It's nice that Rav's considered how horrible that's been.'

It was quite convincing, but still Nell's cheeks flamed.

Percy registered her friend's blush with raised eyebrows. 'I know you inside out, Nell. So don't bother lying to me. How long are you going to keep the two of them dangling?'

Nell focused on the orderly vegetable beds, yet to sprout. The turned soil was delineated with neat rows of green garden twine, wound around wooden pegs driven into the ground beside neat, etched wooden labels.

'Speaking of love lives, what happened with you and Hamish?' They crunched across the gravelled courtyard and, for a moment, Nell wondered if Percy hadn't heard. As they threaded through the formal garden, she kept a patient silence.

'I'm not talking about it, Nell.' Percy's gaze was turned away when she finally spoke, her head lifted, jaw jutting. But Nell saw her chin trembling.

'OK, I'll let it drop. But just answer this. Would you want to see him again?'

A grim laugh exploded from Percy's lips. 'Nell, you're bloody priceless.'

Nell paused, but Percy strode on into the wood. Following, Nell stepped carefully over tree roots which were as tangled as her thoughts, and then between bright sunbursts of amber crocuses and lemon primroses. Ducking under the low arching branches of alders, bearded with verdant moss, she climbed the hill until her puffs of breath clouded in the chill air.

The distant, white-painted stone loggia nestled on the woodland edge. It overlooked the gardens and the lake, with a view of downland stretching into the next county. As children, she and Percy had made dens here. As teenagers, it had been their bolthole to play music and gossip in assured privacy.

The last time they'd been here, Percy had confided in Nell how serious her relationship with Hamish was becoming, the plans she'd had for Glencoille, based on conversations with him, and her hope to marry him. Hamish had come here, too, talking about his plans to finish his work abroad, and Percy hadn't baulked at the idea of waiting. She'd said it would give her time to get her own businesses established. She had glowed with confidence and purpose.

Nostalgic sadness engulfed Nell like a tidal wave.

'Linda dying makes everything worse,' Percy said. 'Especially after she and Ma were at each other's throats like a pair of wildcats.'

Nell glanced at her. 'Where were you, Perce ... when Linda died?' she said carefully.

Percy shook her head.

'I know you got up, Perce. Your bed was empty. What were you doing?'

The chin jut was more defiant this time. 'What you *should* know is that you're not the detective here, Nell. It's none of your bloody business.'

'Oh, don't be like that, Perce. I'm on your side, remember?'

'Are you, Nell? With your boyfriend investigating my family? *Questioning* everyone?'

Nell was about to retort, but Percy pushed past her and charged up the loggia steps – but she didn't turn around, she didn't sit on the top step, their customary spot. She halted.

Sensing something awful, Nell crept forward.

Percy crouched, picked something up, then turned. She held up a delicate flame lily, its red-orange petals only slightly faded. The rare flower Percy adored – the flower that Hamish exclusively always gave her.

'He's been here.' She turned her stricken face to Nell. 'Did you *know*?'

Nell couldn't deny it, not that she had time to.

'Did you invite him here?' Percy backed away from Nell and down the steps, shaking her head. 'Don't you dare *ever* tell me you're on my side again.'

Sunday 14th March – 10.15 a.m.

In the police station car park, James hesitated before entering the path lab. Under the circumstances, he wouldn't be able to access the reports; he'd leave an audit trail and risk a disciplinary. But there was nothing wrong with a friendly chat, was there? He took a mistimed deep breath and the heavy, sweet chemical stench of aldehydes punched him in the gut as he walked in.

Dr Saunders didn't even look up. 'I'm going as fast as I can. I'm on the second body of the day and it's not even lunchtime.'

'Thanks, Doc. Just wanted to come in and see how it's going.'

Her head jerked up at James's voice. 'Oh, I see. You wanted me to give you the headlines so far. Nice try. But even if I was bribe-able, I still have tests to do. I never deal in half-arsed information.' Her scalpel sliced expertly, and deft hands removed the liver with such dexterity, such respect, that the gesture looked almost tender. Its weight was noted by her assistant, who recorded the information with equal care.

Peering at the organ, Dr Saunders nodded at her assistant. 'Some evidence of cirrhosis.'

James knew the process couldn't be hurried, and saw that his impatience would irritate. Dr Saunders wouldn't speak until she had something of worth to say. 'OK, I'll leave them all in your careful hands, Doc.'

Across the car park, he ducked into the station building, hoping someone on the team would be ready for a coffee break. And maybe a chat. Just about work in general. Just to be a good, thoughtful colleague. *I'm allowed to hope.* He *needed* something to go on. Some insight, some way to solve this case as quickly as possible. Nell and Rav would be playing at detectives – he knew they wouldn't be able to resist it. And they probably wouldn't be all that great at hiding it, either. With the killer under the same roof. His stomach churned. *If I don't get a lead to go on soon . . .* Well, he didn't even want to think about that.

The incident room buzzed. DC Hesha Patel typed with ferocious precision as she uploaded file after file of data being emailed in from the officers interviewing the extended guest- and staff-lists; other officers ran in, dropped files off and darted out again; and DC Ed Baker pinned information to the board with determined efficiency. James had only ever seen Ed move this fast when someone had brought in bacon sarnies after an all-nighter.

Val stood back, reviewing the information. She arched an eyebrow. 'Can't stay away, then, James?'

He aimed to give her a supportive smile. 'Just want to be able to help the team. Where I can.'

The incident board bore photos of their suspects, and James's stomach lurched to see Nell's picture up there for a second case, with everyone's whereabouts listed for each murder victim.

Val raised her hands, exasperated. 'It's impossible to narrow this down. Hardly anyone has an alibi. During both Cameron's and Hawke's murders, everyone claims to have been in their rooms, except for Douggie in the kitchen, Deborah on the terrace and Crispin in the hall with Mrs Faulkner. At the time Linda was killed, everyone claims to have been in bed.'

She pinned a floor plan of Finchmere House to the board, showing the rooms, main stairs, lift and back stairs. 'And with all these handy routes to get around the place, I'd say pretty much everyone has opportunity.'

Ed leaned against a table, folding his arms. 'We've searched the place for any bloodstained clothes.' At James's expectant look, he shook his head. 'Mrs Faulkner hasn't found any. She didn't hear anyone having an early-morning shower after Linda's murder, either, but that was a long shot, since it's pretty unlikely she *would* hear in a house that size.'

'Well, I'll keep my eyes peeled around the house. And we can keep up the search teams.'

He peered at the awful photo of Linda's wound, the dagger embedded in her right shoulder. No wonder Nell had been so soaked in her blood. 'A left-handed person slitting her throat from behind the sofa might only have had some blood spatter on their arms and hands, maybe cuffs if they were wearing long sleeves. But a right-handed person attacking from the front would be covered. Either would have stabbed her on the right side to avoid the spurting blood.'

The smell of coffee wafted in as DS Ashley Hollis came in bearing a tray of crucial caffeine, making the team around James take a welcome pause.

'None for me?' James joked.

The remark fell flat. James had expected a friendly grin or a, 'Hey, sure, good to see you – let's compare notes!' At worst a, 'Well, you know where the kitchen is.' But the taut glower, from Ashley, was totally unexpected. They'd arrived at Pendlebury together from college – more than just peers, they'd always been friends.

Ashley pursed her lips. 'Of course, Detective Inspector.'

Ah.

As Ashley wheeled around to return to the kitchen, James followed.

'Hey, I was only joking. I can make my own. How's it going? Got any leads?'

'You're not in charge of this case. Unless you think none of the rules apply to you, now?'

'Ash?' James turned his palms up. 'What's going on?'

Ashley grabbed a cup from the draining board, slopped coffee from the percolator and held it out. 'Here you go, *sir*.' Her fake smile was acid.

'Tell me what's wrong, Ash. This isn't like you.' As their resident psychological expert, Ashley was typically a family liaison officer, and also straight-talking and funny, with valuable insights.

'OK.' She folded her arms. 'You realise you and I were both up for this promotion, don't you? And look who got it. The one who plays golf with the chief. Because your girlfriend's got connections.'

Ouch. From Ashley, that really stung. The nagging insecurity pinched again. *Does Val think the same?* 'You don't think I earned it, Ash?' He forced himself to meet her eyes, but she gave a short laugh.

'I think you're a decent detective, James. I wouldn't take that away from you. But I don't think you're a whole rank better than I am. And I didn't even get a look in. And look at you now. Here, to find out what you can. When you shouldn't be. Like you're above all the rules.'

He didn't know what to say to that. They looked at each other: her burning with defiance, him squirming with guilt. Then she turned and walked back to the incident room.

Following, he met Val's expectant gaze. 'So, James, got anything for us?'

'The MacKenzies' solicitor will be down at 4.30 p.m. to read the will. I'll sit in and report back.'

Val nodded. 'Anything else?'

He nodded at the incident board. 'I've been thinking about motives.'

Val tilted her head, so he continued.

'For Hawke, we know that Percy's parents were opposed to her marriage to him. By extension, Angus and Theo were against it.' James folded his arms, frowning. 'They're long-standing friends: Angus and Douggie since they were boys; Greta's known Theo since uni. He sponsors a lot of her charity events. And she's battled alcoholism, so I wonder if Theo's also her sponsor?'

'What's he been drinking?'

'Haven't noticed.' Out of the corner of his eye, James saw Ashley huff a sigh. 'I'll keep an eye on that.'

'What about motives for killing Linda?' Ed asked.

'The family's desperation to rid themselves of Hawke might have extended to Linda,' James reasoned. 'Linda wasn't going to keep quiet about the rows they'd had. And we know families like that guard their privacy.' His mind flashed to Nell's tape, to her revelation that Hawke knew about it, and Angus's reaction. 'And Hawke was the type to dig up dirt, presumably to use it for leverage.'

'Oh?' Val perked up. 'What? And how?'

'Nothing concrete yet.'

Val's eyes narrowed. 'I'm not buying that, James. Spill.'

As James hesitated, Val guessed. 'Are we talking about Greta? She's been totally uncooperative so far. Which is only marking her out as our prime suspect. Open rows with both victims, less inhibited because she was drunk and, with all that, unwilling to give a statement.'

James's eyes flicked to the board, at the star beside Greta's name. And also Rav's, who'd claimed to be asleep. With a sigh, James admitted, 'Hawke knew about Nell's tape.' His team were familiar with it; they'd uncovered it during their previous investigation involving Nell.

'Was Hawke blackmailing her about it?' Val asked.

'Not that I'm aware of.'

'Was she concerned that he knew?'

'Of course.'

'Don't you think Nell would be pretty devastated that a man like that had just married her best friend?'

'I'd be furious,' Ashley said cheerfully.

'Oh, come on.' James rolled his eyes at Val. 'My point is, if he's got something like that on Nell – which has a superinjunction against it – he could easily have something else on some*one* else.'

'I'll ask you again, then. What – and who?'

James shifted his weight. 'I don't know. Yet.'

'Hmmm . . .' Val turned to the board and, against Nell's name, wrote, 'Motive: tape; best friend's marriage.'

'For God's sake, Val!' James protested.

But Val ignored him as she drew on the board.

'I know that you and Nell are each other's alibi, James. My point is, when someone upsets or does wrong by someone you care about – like Percy for Nell, or . . . others amongst this party – your actions can be more extreme than if you were only standing up for yourself.'

When James glanced at the board, he saw that Val had drawn an arrow to Rav's name.

'He's the chivalrous type, isn't he?' Val mused. 'From what I've seen of him lately, as well as during the last investigation they were both involved in, I can see him defending Nell's honour. He doesn't so much hold a candle for Nell; it's more like a floodlight.' She arched an eyebrow at him. 'Wouldn't you say, James?'

Chapter 19

Sunday 14th March – 10.30 a.m.

Not daring to follow Percy in full flounce, Nell trudged through the orchard and the confetti of petals on the tufty grass, past the garages and to the barn. There, Rav loitered by the doorway. He was studying his phone, frowning. He looked up as she approached and pocketed his phone hastily. His smile seemed forced, but then he jerked his head towards the chain with its No Entry sign. Nell stayed silent, listening, her eyes locked on his, her heart fluttering.

A sharp, insistent squeak from inside the barn made a smile spread across her face.

'Both still in there; so, the male returned after his drive-by warning to the interloper,' Rav grinned. 'Bodes well, doesn't it!'

Nell unclipped the chain and tiptoed in. Faint rays slanted in through the doorway, highlighting the oak frame of the barn, soaring up to the clock tower. Her eyes adjusted to the low light as she peered up at the large wooden box.

In complete unison, they bowed their heads, studying the floor below the box and underneath the length of the cross-beam. Nothing was there.

'Huh, that's funny.'

'Isn't it,' Nell agreed. She scanned the rest of the floor. 'Ah. We're not crazy, look!' She pointed at several dark-grey owl pellets, strewn against the wall.

'Yes, some over here, too.' Rav pointed at more pellets that were scattered against the opposite wall and into the corner.

Nell turned to Rav, frowning quizzically.

He shrugged. 'Someone might have swept up . . .'

'No way. Everyone knows it's strictly out of bounds. Including guests.' As Nell studied the floor, she backed into the wooden shelf. It clattered to the ground and she set it back on its home-made supports, the noise making her shoot a guilty glance at the owl box.

'Let's leave them in peace, before you trash the joint.' Rav rolled his eyes, grinning.

'What were you looking at? On your phone?' Nell asked as she re-clipped the chain across the doorway.

'Oh.' He exhaled. 'The party story has been published online.'

Nell's eyes widened. 'Already?'

'Yeah, and that's not all. Hawke's and Linda's deaths have also been reported in the news. So the online party photos are being touted on another website as a last hurrah. Like some macabre last-moments montage.'

'Oh, *God*.'

'Don't worry. I put Shannon on the case. I had a feeling she'd know how to handle the situation.'

'Uh-huh.' Nell arched an eyebrow.

Rav ignored it. 'She called *Hello!*. They're going to take action on the photos being hijacked. And they're going to take down their article out of respect.'

Sighing in relief, Nell said, 'That's good. I'll have to find her and say thanks.' Nell tried to muster a gracious smile. She had a feeling she failed, but Rav tactfully moved the conversation along.

'So how did you get on? How was Percy?'

'Oh, awful. She knows that Hamish was here.'

'You told her you saw him?'

She shook her head. 'No, he hasn't only been hanging around the weir. He's come to the *house*.'

'He called in? When?'

'No, he left a flower for Percy at the loggia.'

Rav frowned. 'Well . . . how can you be sure it was him? A flower is a flower, isn't—'

'Hamish only ever gave Percy flame lilies.' She raised her eyebrows.

'Wow. That's . . . yeah. Unusual.'

Nell shoved him. 'So that's how she knows.'

'Unless . . .' Rav said. 'Someone else knew that, and they're messing with her mind?'

Nell shook her head. 'I might've thought that. But since I know he's in the area, I'm certain it was a message from him.'

'But . . . what's he saying, then? That he's not over her? You don't think—'

Nell held up her hand.

'Don't. I've had all the thoughts, and none of them are good, are they?'

She led him through the boot room, where Mr Murray's heavy overcoats for gardening in all weathers hung over his row of boots and Hunter wellies. She noticed that a few guests had left muddy shoes there, after walking in the garden, to avoid wearing them through the house. As they cut through the oval room, the sight of the police tape across the library doorway stopped her short. It was like she could smell the blood again, see Linda's desperate, rolling eyes. She took a breath and headed through the great room to the drawing room.

This was the room the family used the most. To Nell, it always felt homely and *safe*, with muted, *Country Living* tones making it relaxing. The luxurious velvety L-shaped sofa was arranged for people to enjoy both the large TV on the far wall and the roaring fire under the impressive marble mantelpiece. Beside the fireplace, a wingback chair was settled in a reading nook. The coffee table was piled with books and magazines, revealing the family's interest in classic cars, antiques, science, business and, unsurprisingly, ecology; and *Private Eye* magazine was an insight into Nell's mother's political views and sense of humour.

They settled on the sofa. Nell prised off her trainers and wiggled her toes at the fire. Rav sat next to her, stretching an arm out, his T-shirt sleeve taut around his biceps.

'Hamish is a *good guy*,' Nell said, after a minute. 'He brought out all the best in Percy. You only saw her with Hawke, who was . . . ugh, a slimeball enabler. The total opposite.'

Rav frowned. 'Then wouldn't it have killed him? To see the woman he loved being taken in like that? Might've been enough to make him murderous?' He met Nell's gaze. 'We all have our limits.'

Nell gave Rav a questioning look, then decided he meant nothing by his last remark. And the light and shadow cast over his face from the flickering flames in the grate made his expression unreadable. But his solid closeness, his matter-of-factness about deep, unshakable love drew Nell towards him. She had to force herself not to lean too close against him. Instead, she drew her knees up, hugging them, putting a barrier between her and temptation.

'Do you think we're just looking for one murderer?' Nell whispered.

Rav shrugged. 'Maybe two? Or *three*?'

'You think Cameron was murdered, too?'

'Don't you?'

'Well. He *was* ninety-odd. And it'd been a big night. And a pretty stressful one for the family. He came down with the cavalry – Percy's parents, Angus and Theo – in the helicopter, so he would've known about all the issues, even if . . . Oh—'

'What?'

'If Percy was hiding the fact she was getting married from her folks, so it was a fait accompli in the face of their disapproval, then Cameron *had* to have known in advance. Because Percy was wearing the Glencoille tiara. He'd have needed to give her access to it. So he either didn't know Percy was doing it in secret or he was pro the marriage, and anti-Douggie and Greta's resistance to it, and in on Percy's deception. Either way . . .'

He nodded. 'Either way it doesn't look great for the family, if there was back-stabbing like that going on. And I guess it can be relatively easy to make someone that age look like they've had a heart attack.'

'What about the others, though? Totally different MOs. *If* Hawke was pushed and didn't fall.'

'Come on, Nell. We know Hawke didn't fall. Maybe the same person killed his mother. Maybe just someone being opportunistic. Whether they were walking upstairs with Hawke, or saw Linda in the library, with the dagger right there in the cabinet – both situations reek of someone with an axe to grind taking a chance, don't they?'

'Maybe.' Nell bit her lip. 'Percy's folks are the obvious culprits all round, aren't they?'

Rav shrugged. 'Greta is the obvious prime suspect. Argued with

Hawke and declared war with Linda. And perhaps, with Douggie inheriting, she's about the only one with a motive to kill all three. But with that foursome, I have the feeling that if one of them has a motive, they all do. They're a tight-knit bunch, aren't they?' He glanced at her, looking like he was about to say something but then thought better of it.

'Douggie and Angus are always conspiring, but they're definitely behaving like they think something's up.' She looked at Rav, chewing her lip. She didn't want to admit her thoughts, but they had to consider all angles, didn't they? She took a deep breath. 'Honestly, I think . . . I think they've either got something to hide or they're protecting someone who does. And they were acting like that before the police even got here.'

'Maybe the answer's simple? Greta was drunk. And OK, she might manage as a functioning alcoholic. But it wasn't an ordinary night, was it? Maybe she was too drunk to remember anything, and that's why she couldn't give a statement.'

'You think that's the only reason why Douggie and Angus are so worried about her?' She shrugged. 'I'll be honest, I can imagine any one of them shoving Hawke down the stairs. I'd have been tempted myself. But doing that to Linda . . .' *Surely Percy's folks couldn't have . . .*

'It would take a lot of strength, though . . .' Rav's defence of Greta trailed off. 'Actually, it wouldn't. It would take an opportunity and a rash moment of anger. And Greta couldn't exactly claim not to fall foul of her temper after everyone witnessed her slapping Hawke.'

Nell realised she must have looked stricken, because Rav smoothly changed focus. 'OK, what about the others? Crispin was Hawke's best man. Not who I'd expect for someone like Hawke to have as a best mate. I'm guessing he hasn't got all the dirt on Hawke. Nothing to let slip in the speeches.'

'Oh?' Nell leaned forward. 'Yeah, you may have a point there.'

'But what if they fell out? They've both had flings with Shannon. Maybe Crispin still has a soft spot for her and thought she was being used by Hawke.'

'And what if he knew Linda, too? They must have met before, since he and Hawke go back to school days.'

'Feasible,' Rav said. 'Then there's Shannon. What if it was more than an affair? What if they were really in love? And he married Percy to get the inheritance, utterly rinse her in the divorce and run off with Shannon?'

'*Jesus!*' Outrage flashed through Nell. She huffed. 'I wouldn't put it past Hawke, from what I knew about him. Or Shannon. She's always been hell-bent on destroying or going after anything Percy has. Makes you wonder what poison she dripped in Crispin's ear when he took her up.'

'Then, the alternative option: what if Hawke *didn't* want to carry on the affair after marrying Percy? And if he rejected her, well . . .' He raised his eyebrows. 'Hell hath no fury . . .'

Nell wanted to agree with him, but she couldn't. 'I'm not sure Shannon would show her hand like that. Her revenge would be emotional indifference.'

'Nah.' Rav shook his head, looking mystified at Nell's lack of understanding. '*Pretending* to be emotionally indifferent, maybe. But that's not the same at all. Add that to the fact that she's a woman who likes to get what she wants, and I don't think much would stop her. She's not exactly bothered about taking the amoral option, is she?'

Nell wondered if he was right. The unease tingling through her body told her she couldn't deny it.

'Either way, their affair is a mighty strong motive for Percy. Who went looking for him.' Rav sighed. 'I can imagine the police having a field day with that.'

Oh God. Is that why Percy's so wary of James? Nell felt sick. 'Oh come on. I know how it looks, but honestly . . . Percy is not capable of murder. Anyone who's known her for five minutes knows that she's too soft-hearted. Mischief, drama – sure. But she'd never hurt anyone.'

'OK,' said Rav. 'Then who else might have motive?'

Nell looked up at him, grateful he'd moved the conversation along again. 'Deborah's revelations about Hawke's business were very . . . revealing.'

'That must be what I heard her and Linda arguing about during the ceilidh.'

'What? *Before* Hawke . . .'

Rav nodded. 'I mean, she sounded *appalled* about Hawke, and I'd bet anything he wouldn't listen to her.'

'No, there's no way he'd have listened to advice. He was a right know-it-all smug git.' Nell shuddered at the memory of their conversation during the banquet.

'Well, imagine if Deborah had spoken to him, and if she was treated to his special brand of smugdom? More than enough to . . .' He mimed a shove. 'And if she was *also* shocked about Linda's reaction . . .'

'Especially if it would damage their business together . . .'

'Yeah. I think it's possible that she'd . . . And she'd inherit everything then, wouldn't she? If Linda co-owned the business, Hawke's share would revert to her, and then – probably – everything of Linda's would be left to Deborah.'

Nell frowned. 'But Deborah sounded so upset.'

'No, she sounded *guilty*. But about their last words being an argument . . . or something else?'

Nell nodded. 'OK, you may have something there.'

'And it wasn't exactly a surprise to Theo, either.'

'So Deborah must have confided in him about it before.'

'And what if that sent Theo down a path of no return? He wouldn't want Hawke's dodgy business deals reflecting on the family, would he?'

'Oh, please don't bring it round to Percy's folks again.'

Rav winced. 'Sorry. Well, what if Hawke's businesses somehow had a bearing on some of Theo's? He invests in various ventures, right? What if one of the businesses that Hawke ruined was one that Theo – or Deborah – had backed?'

'Hmmmm . . .' Nell nodded. 'That's not unlikely. Let's investigate.' She took her iPhone out of her pocket. 'I'll take general searches, since I've already poked around Hawke's social media. Why don't you look at Companies House and more specific business interests?'

'On it,' Rav said, prodding his phone to life.

Nell couldn't help her flutter of delight at working with Rav again. But . . . shouldn't it be her and James working together? It wasn't his fault he wasn't here. But, even if he was, he probably wouldn't be able to share details of the case anyway. Still, she had a feeling

James wouldn't like it. But what was she supposed to do? *Not* try to find something to help? *Ridiculous* . . .

A creak outside the door, from the direction of the ballroom, made them both jump and look at each other in horror at being overheard. Nell dashed over and opened the double door a crack, but no one was there. She opened the door wider, and the vast marble-floored space was empty. As her breathing grew rapid, she registered there was no defining scent on the air, no lingering amber perfume of Shannon, or Douggie's sandalwood. No retreating footsteps with clues of the owner in the sound of the footfall. No signs at all of who'd been listening.

It could have been anyone.

Chapter 20

Sunday 14th March – 11.45 a.m.

James made a round of coffees, hoping his hastily bought Hobnobs might help to thaw Ashley out a little. He didn't really want to leave on a sour note with her. But his reasons for staying were wearing thin. Ashley didn't even look up from her desk.

'Any news from Trent?' James asked her.

'Nope.' She remained engrossed in her computer. 'He's gone to London to take the statement from the duke. But he'll take all day about it and he probably won't even upload the file. Not that we're expecting anything useful from it. Albert left before all the action happened. This is just Trent taking an opportunity to hobnob.' Then she did turn towards him. She shot a scathing glance at his choice of biscuits, then at him, before turning back to her screen again.

Val took a coffee and, as she sipped it, James hurriedly justified why he was still there. 'The report from the security team has just come in. Nell must have given them my email address rather than yours. And I saw that the press is on the case with the deaths. And some photos have been published online. I thought it might be helpful for the investigation if I can get them?'

At Val's nod, he fired off a text to Nell, asking for the photographer's contact details. Then he sent another one, in a less officious, more affectionate tone. Then added two kisses.

When he looked up, Val was pursing her lips at being kept waiting. 'All done there? So? This security report?'

James opened it on his iPad, eager to see if this was the glimmer of hope Nell was relying on to steer the investigation away from the family. Val had another sip of her coffee, and then gave in, took a biscuit and dunked it.

But, as James read, his heart dropped. 'Oh, bloody hell.'

Val's head jerked up, biscuit wobbling, 'What?' She didn't notice when half her Hobnob plopped into her coffee.

'OK, so the report sets out the technical details of the team's deployment and positions around the house – special requirements for the duke's arrival. His helicopter landed, he freshened up, then he went to the chapel accompanied by Shannon. They glimpsed the intruder just before the start of the wedding ceremony, at 5.35 p.m., lost track of him for sixteen minutes, then located him near the chapel at 5.51 p.m.'

'Description?' Val fished for her Hobnob.

'Likely male, tall, in a black overcoat and black woolly hat,' said James. 'He was holding something which they couldn't identify, which caused concern for obvious reasons. They pursued him, chasing him across the grounds, towards the gardens and the loggia, into woodland. That's where they lost him. The security team regrouped, assigned a sub-team to watch the area between the woodland and the house, but saw nothing further until the duke left.' He glanced up. 'And that's when the security team left. So . . .'

'So if the intruder had any malintent, he'd have had an opportunity once the house was unguarded. And that's exactly when the murders occurred . . .' She frowned. 'Even so, the place is riddled with security measures. I've seen the alarms—'

'Yeah, that's the issue.' James sighed. 'No one could get in without knowing the codes. But Nell is quite open with the codes to any family guests—'

'So the intruder is someone the family knows. Or has at least been a guest.'

Great. So now instead of setting Nell's mind at rest, I'll have to ask who else she knows – who else she considers a friend – who might be capable of this.

Sunday 14th March – 12 p.m.

When Nell beckoned to Rav from the doorway of the drawing room, saying, 'Come on, let's get out of here,' he hesitated. So much for thinking he should back off; he couldn't refuse. He crossed the room to her and whispered, 'Where, though? We're not supposed to leave.'

'Yeah. So, technically we're not going to leave the estate. But that does give us a few options.'

'Like?'

'Like Finchmere Hotel. For lunch. James can hardly blame us for not wanting to eat, canteen-style, with a murderer, can he? He might even think it's sensible.' They reached the hall and Nell called the lift. 'Give me five to get changed.'

Rav noted that Nell had singled out James, rather than generalising about the police. It wasn't exactly a criticism, but maybe all was not completely idyllic in their relationship. The flicker of hope was snuffed with guilt as he waited in the hall.

To distract himself, he stared at the balustrade, thinking about the angles and Hawke's injury. He had to have fallen from the second floor, but if he was pushed, that was risky. Most of the guests had rooms there. The killer would have needed to be quick on their feet to hide, or dash downstairs. His gaze followed the stairs upwards to the third floor. Had someone lured him up there? On the pretext of a private conversation?

The sight of Nell emerging from the lift in jeans and jumper and walking boots, her hair still damp and cutely ruffled, pulled him out of his thoughts.

'Let's walk over and have lunch in the Orangery,' she said, her eyes straying to his hand, which rummaged in his pocket for his wallet. 'We'll have it on the family account. We've been up most of the night, and it's Sunday, so we'll have the roast and all the trimmings. And definitely dessert.'

'Sounds good.' Curiosity about seeing the hotel in Nell's estate won over the argument of paying and Rav nodded, following as she led him across the garden, retracing their earlier steps to the woodland.

Remembering Greta's words, he asked, 'Have you told your parents about all this yet?'

'No, I haven't.' Sighing, she took out her phone, pausing to type – then retype – a text. She read it and pressed send. Then she turned her phone off.

'Nell! They'll want to talk to you, to make sure you're OK!'

'Yeah, well, there's only so many times I can keep going over everything.'

'I get it. But turn your phone on so you can speak to them if they call. They'll be worried.'

Pulling a face, Nell turned her phone back on. It rang immediately and, rolling her eyes, she answered it while she and Rav walked on.

'Yes, I'm fine, Mum. Yes, horrific, but . . . James and his colleagues are on it; they're doing a great job.' There was a pause. 'Percy's . . . Well, she's bearing up, considering . . .' Nell frowned at the next question. 'You really don't have to come back . . . really . . . no, *really*. Right.' She pursed her lips. 'Uh-huh. OK. *Fine*. Yes. Sure.' She pocketed her phone. 'Right, so they're leaving their friends' wedding immediately to rush back to a house with a murderer in it. Happy?'

With sanctimonious certainty that he'd given sound advice, Rav didn't hide his amusement at her indignation. 'Well, what did you expect them to do? It's their estate, after all.'

'Yes, all right, don't be a smart-arse.' Nell's nose crinkled, and Rav's grin widened.

They walked up the hill through the woods to the river. As they reached the weir, Nell glanced across the bridge, biting her lip, and Rav knew what she was thinking.

'Hamish?'

'Yes.' Her eyebrows flashed in surprise. 'Mind reader.'

'How long were he and Percy together?'

She frowned. 'Oh, it must have been about two or so years. They met at another one of Greta's events. They weren't an obvious couple. You'd never pair them up in a million years. Yet, for Percy, it was fireworks. Smitten from the start.'

'Wow. Same for him?'

'Totally. Completely devoted. They were adorable together. I think the attraction was that they were just such opposites. They both had what the other needed. Do you know what I mean?'

A wave of heat, at Nell's words and her unguarded expression, flashed over him. 'Got a pretty good idea, yes.'

Nell's gaze became questioning, but she continued. 'Percy had just graduated and she was wallowing around, not knowing what to do with herself. She worked on the estate, and did some half-hearted volunteering, but nothing gave her a sense of *purpose*.' Nell paused to climb over a stile, automatically checking if any posts were wobbly.

'So, how did Hamish change that?' Rav asked.

'Well, Hamish had such passion for his profession. When he gave a talk at an event that Percy helped Greta organise, I think she was bowled over by how dynamic he was, his sheer drive for what he was doing. His motivation, his belief in the power of change . . . Well, it was infectious.' She gave a comic grimace. 'Probably bad choice of words, given he's a virologist.'

'Sounds like a regular hero,' said Rav. 'Is he from a similar background to Percy?'

Nell shook her head. 'He didn't talk about his family or his upbringing much, but I got the impression it was tough. Not much money, one parent died before Hamish went to university. I think a lot of his drive stemmed from that; it made him determined to succeed in life. He was very studious, got into Balliol on a scholarship, deeply committed to his work.'

'So that talk he gave . . . It must have been pretty inspirational to enthral a firecracker like Percy?'

'It was,' said Nell. 'Hamish was back from a three-year stint in Sierra Leone, working with Doctors Without Borders, MSF, on the Ebola virus at a paediatric clinic.' She frowned. 'Freetown, I think. His training programme was in desperate need of funding. He wasn't a natural speaker; I remember how nervous he was, but he was so passionate, and his first-hand experiences were just so, well, *powerful*. He moved everyone in the room, most of all Percy. She went up to speak to him afterwards and, from that moment, they were inseparable.'

They fell into a contemplative silence. Rav guessed that Nell was mourning what might have been between Percy and Hamish, while he was thinking about what could be. He lengthened his stride up the hill, aiming to reach the kissing gate first. He held it closed, so Nell could tuck herself into the enclosure, and grinned at her.

When he didn't release the gate, Nell smiled. For a heartbeat they locked eyes, but then she leaned away from him to soak up the view of the rolling green fields through the woodland's tangle of branches. 'Percy was good for Hamish, too,' she said. 'She drew him out of his shell, brought out his fun side. And he channelled her fireball energy for good. They were just *right* for each other.'

'They're lucky they found each other. Let's hope all's not lost.' He held Nell's gaze, and tension crackled between them. He stepped back and let the gate swing open.

As Nell walked on, talking, Rav shot her a sidelong glance. *She must have felt it. Is she babbling now, to hide it?*

'Percy just ... *blossomed*. She had all these great ideas for new business enterprises on the estate. She was good at the grand plans; Hamish was good at the detail. So she ended up with really well-researched, well-put-together business proposals to establish adventure activities.' She glanced at Rav. 'You'd love it. Rock climbing and abseiling on Mount Coille; sailing and fishing on the loch. Nature tours. She got them up and running, profitable and gaining a great reputation.'

'Sounds amazing. All that in under two years?'

Nell nodded. 'Yeah, not bad going.'

'So, what happened?' As woodland thinned out to rolling fields, Rav glimpsed the distant whitewashed Georgian hotel. 'How did it all go wrong?'

'Hamish left in July for another six-month stint. The plan was that he'd come home in December, find a job and, well, honestly, I think everyone thought they'd get married.' She frowned. 'But then everything went quiet, and Percy stopped talking about him. Last Christmas, and all of Hogmanay, she kept herself to herself, and then there was the murder trial, so I couldn't see as much of her ... I lost track of what was happening with them.'

Rav's strides matched Nell's, as hers lengthened downhill.

'I'm convinced Percy still loves him, though. Hamish must have hurt her badly in some way that she didn't want to talk about, and then Hawke came into her life. He must have made some serious moves on her in January to get her to say yes to his proposal in February.' Her face hardened. 'Hawke was clearly a rebound. And his MO was to take advantage of someone's vulnerability, wasn't it?'

Rav wanted to squeeze Nell's hand or wrap an arm around her. She was so fiercely protective, yet underneath that shield, so hurt on Percy's behalf. Around them, the fields graded into Finchmere Hotel's mown lawns. Planted borders brimmed with dusky-pink hellebores, lush pink camellias amongst glossy leaves and tiny white stars of daphne filling the air with heady scent.

'Hawke's moves must have been pretty compelling,' he agreed, 'for Percy to risk alienating her family . . . being disinherited.' He shook his head. 'Greta, Douggie, Cameron . . . they're a formidable bunch. They remind me of my folks, in some ways.'

'Oh?' Nell looked at him. 'Has your mother tried to matchmake you with anyone recently?'

'Oh yeah,' Rav shrugged. 'Every week. At least.'

Nell looked like she didn't know if he was joking or not. 'You once said it was up to you to find your own partner.'

Remembering the conversation they'd had all those months ago, at her place, he shot her a heated look. He'd wondered then – hoped – it would lead somewhere.

'True. But I couldn't do what Percy's done. Making a stand against your whole family is a massive deal, isn't it? When they have your best interests at heart, I mean, and they love you. If you have that in a family, you're lucky, I reckon. And, let's be fair, her folks were *right* about Hawke. She should have listened, or at least believed them.'

'So, if your parents disapproved of someone you'd fallen in love with, you wouldn't stand up for that person, and for yourself?' Nell asked.

Rav held his breath. The conversation was getting dangerously close to the bone.

'I'd . . . hope I wouldn't have to,' he said. 'I'd hope that the *right* person for me will like my folks and get on with them, and vice versa.'

'Oh. Well, let's *hope* you find the perfect person, then.' Nell's voice was clipped. Wincing inwardly, he followed her to the terrace, threading between tables and chairs, and then into the vaulted-ceilinged, timber-framed Orangery. Citrus trees in ornate pots formed natural screens, fragrant with orange blossom, giving each linen-swathed table a leafy, private snug. She didn't meet his eyes as she sat down, fussing with the linen napkin and spreading it on her lap. But she was flushed. From the brisk walk and crisp air, or . . .

Gustav, their waiter appeared with menus and water. Nell ordered the roast lamb with all the trimmings – and 'extra Yorkies and gravy, too, please, Gustav' – and Rav did the same, along with a coffee. He needed the caffeine. After the broken night's sleep and the tumultuous events of the weekend, his body clock felt all over the place. It wasn't an unfamiliar sensation for an ecologist: he was used to predawn surveys mixing with daytime office work and nocturnal surveys merging into the next predawn visit. Nell combatted the fuzzy, hungry haze with caffeine and carbs. He consciously kept to protein, especially if surveys interfered with going to the gym or climbing. Judging by the way Nell occasionally glanced at his biceps, it was imperative to Rav that he maintained his physique.

'Oh God, yes please. Pints of coffee,' Nell agreed now and smiled, with those cute dimples and the amber flecks gleaming in her dark eyes. With Deborah's advice flashing into his thoughts, Rav had a sudden urge to lean over the table and take her hand.

An echoing crash thundered from the bar.

'What the—' Nell craned to see what the drama was about, through a cluster of people waiting for drinks. Rav glimpsed an arm flailing at one of the barmen.

Nell pushed her chair back, rose and walked over, and Rav followed her.

Rivers of wine and champagne were dripping from the copper-topped bar, puddling on the floor amongst smashed glass, while the barman attempted to calm a tall, clearly drunk man, who was windmilling his arms and sending other guests skittering away. The barman backed off, holding his hands up in surrender.

'Oh God,' Nell whispered. '*Hamish.*'

Before Rav could register his surprise, Nell had darted over and taken Hamish's hand. She had to duck, as his other arm thrashed out again.

'Hamish!' she hissed. 'Calm down.'

At his name, Hamish swayed to a standstill. He peered at Nell, and his face creased in anger.

'Idon'evenwanna*speak*toyou.'

'I know. And I know why.' Nell gestured at the mess. 'You don't get this drunk, this unhappy, if you're over someone, do you?'

Hamish groaned and doubled over the bar like she'd winded him with a sucker punch.

Nell tiptoed closer, rested her hand on his back.

He shrugged her off, like a wounded animal lashing out, and hissed, 'Jus*leave*me*alone*!'

Nell backed off, then tried again. 'Let's go somewhere quieter, Hamish, and I can get you a coffee and we can talk, OK?'

'Whatbloodygood'sthatgonnado?'

'It might help. Let's try.'

Hamish hung his head, shaking it miserably. As Nell waited, his shoulders rose and fell with a deep sigh. Then, without looking up, he nodded.

'Give me a hand, here, Merl. Let's head out to the corner on the terrace,' Nell said, and the barman shot round, holding Hamish's other side, steering him through the French windows.

While one of the waiting staff shot into action, sweeping glass and mopping up the alcohol, the female maître d' moved from table to table with apologies and vouchers, and Rav followed Nell, Merl and Hamish outside. Just as he reached the terrace, however, he saw James striding towards them, stopping short opposite Nell.

James did a double-take at the sight of Nell. 'Did they call you out, too?'

'What?' Her bewildered expression answered the question.

So what the hell is she doing here, then? After he'd got her and the family special dispensation to *not* have to be ousted from the house while they investigated. *God, this family's determined to not respect the process.* He'd thought he could at least count on Nell . . .

So he should give her the benefit of the doubt. 'I was on my way back to Finchmere when I got a call about a disturbance at the hotel,' he said. 'You OK?'

'Oh. Yes. Fine.' She looked fraught, though, her eyes darting around nervously.

Then James spotted Rav coming through the restaurant doors, and his hackles went up.

'What are you doing here?' he asked Rav, his tone sharper than intended.

Nell answered for Rav, her face flaming. 'We came here for lunch. We knew we couldn't leave the estate. So I thought just nipping over here would be a change of scene. But still, you know, *allowed*.'

Oh. Very cosy. Basically, a date. 'Uh-huh.'

'It was Hamish,' Rav cut in. 'Who caused the disturbance. Percy's ex. He's here.'

James turned in the direction Rav pointed and saw a dishevelled-looking man sitting, with his head in his hands.

'Anyone hurt? Anything damaged?' James asked.

'No. Nothing serious,' Nell said, blushing slightly.

Fair enough. This was her place, her choice to make a complaint about that or not. She obviously wanted to downplay the situation.

'So, Percy's ex has turned up here, to what was supposed to be her wedding?' said James, frowning. 'Is that a bit weird?' *Could he be their intruder?*

Nell bit her lip. 'He's . . . not really over her.'

James nodded. Jealousy, revenge, unrequited love, possessiveness . . . the motive potential was stacking up. He walked to Hamish and hunkered beside him. 'You OK, mate? I'm James. You're Hamish, I gather?'

Groaning, Hamish mumbled, 'Oh . . . youknoweverything.'

'I know you're Percy's ex. But that's all. Anything else I should know?'

Hamish shook his head miserably. 'Jus' . . . I've . . . messedevery-thingup.'

'In what way?'

Hamish's face contorted. 'Theworst . . . theworstway.'

James felt for him. Having your other half leave you for some idiot was something he could definitely relate to. And he knew only too well how corrosive jealousy could be. He glanced over at Nell, who was watching the two of them. Standing next to her, Rav looked awkward. James felt like an idiot for being so distrustful. It was more to do with his baggage than with Nell, which wasn't fair on her. He should count himself lucky.

Another groan from Hamish brought him back to the matter in hand.

'OK, Hamish, man to man. Is this heartbreak, or something else?'

'It'stheend!' Hamish buried his face in his hands and sobbed. 'Theendofeverything.'

James sighed. 'We'll need to get you sober, mate. Where are you staying?'

'I can give him a room here, if that's easier?' Nell offered. She glanced up as Merl came out and laid Hamish's belongings on a chair. He also set down a mug of steaming coffee, and left them to it.

'Yes, if you could, that would help.' James smiled at her and she held his gaze for a second. Embarrassment, at being such an idiot, burned. It wasn't unreasonable for her to check in on part of her business; it was still part of her estate. She'd essentially just crossed her garden to get here. He felt his face soften, and she smiled back.

Then James registered what Merl had brought out: a folded black overcoat and a dark hat. *Uh-huh.*

'I'll need a full statement from him. As soon as he's sobered up,' he said, back in official mode.

He saw Nell's face drain of colour, then turn and look at Rav, who smiled reassuringly at her.

And the seed of doubt took root again in James's mind.

Chapter 21

Sunday 14th March – 1.30 p.m.

'I'm not sure about this, Nell.' Rav, having agreed to her risky plan, was now having second thoughts.

'It'll be fine,' she said.

They'd planned how they'd do it from the refectory roof walkway, assessing access to Hawke's bedroom. One of his windows was tucked inside an alcove, and aligned with a chimney, reducing the chances of anyone seeing them. So, if they went up to the third floor, out onto the roof, secured the rope around the chimney – and around them, rappel-style – they could lower themselves down to Hawke's concealed window.

Rav had taken some convincing, and he still didn't like the set-up. He definitely didn't want to watch Nell dangling on a rope that was as secure as it *could* be, but not as secure as it *should* be. 'I'll go – you stay here as lookout.'

Nell stared at him. 'As if! Come on, let's get on with it. The police guard changes in ten minutes.'

Rav worried that a guard change meant that one of the officers would check inside the room. But Nell seemed convinced that they'd use the time to gossip about the family, football or colleagues, making it less likely they'd hear any noises in Hawke's room, while he and Nell searched.

A few minutes later, he peered over the edge of the roof while Nell jimmied the window, dangling on the rope. His guilty eyes flicked over the garden. No movement. But anyone could be lurking anywhere. *Maybe the window would be locked and they could give up on this crazy plan.* Their vulnerability, on top of illegally entering the cordoned-off room, only added to the danger of not being able to use proper safety equipment (Nell had protested they could hardly run around in harnesses). Sweat slithered down Rav's back. *Too late now.* Nell had got the window open, and was crawling in. *Oh, bloody hell.*

He looped the ropes around his back and through his legs, then eased his way down, wincing at the friction around his waist and thighs. Especially after eating nearly his own body weight in crispy-skinned, fluffy-centred, rosemary-seasoned roast potatoes at lunch. He passed the third-floor window and continued down, until his foot reached the next sill. He wiggled through the window and unwound the brown ropes, concealing them in the thick wisteria stems.

Relief at the safe descent hit him, just as the dread of an officer poking his head round the door set in. He practically heard Nell chastising him – *get a move on, then* – as he checked his surgical gloves taken from the stash in his car; staple kit for an ecologist.

Already, a be-gloved Nell was scouring the drawers of the writing desk. Nothing was on the top, in front of the chair. The cleared space suggested that Hawke's laptop had sat there and had been taken by the police. But there was nothing else of note.

Rav checked in the huge dressing room – pushing clothes aside, then moving them back to look undisturbed – and looked under the bed. Nothing.

Nell was searching the bedside cabinets, gingerly rummaging through a pile of boxers, looking as exasperated as he felt.

A sudden noise in the corridor made them jump.

They stared at each other in dread, eyes widening as they heard a key in the lock. Nell fell to the floor and slid under the bed, closely followed by Rav, just as the door opened and then shut quietly.

Holding their breath, they squashed together, hearts thudding.

Rav's lungs ached to gasp for air, but he forced himself to breathe slowly, trying to calm his heart rate.

Smart men's shoes, too dark to discern any details, passed the bed. The intruder moved methodically around the room, rifling through the desk, opening drawers, and then approached the bed. Nell gripped Rav's hand and his heart rate went through the roof. He squeezed back, gently, thumb rubbing her hand soothingly. Her beautiful, wide eyes gazed into his, full of fear and . . . trust? But then, beyond her, he saw a gloved hand reach down. And the intruder kneeled on the floor.

Three mugs of coffee and a brisk walk around the garden later, James sat back in what was now Hamish's hotel room. Hamish was slurring less, standing steadier. The alcohol might be leaving his system, but he was clearly still stooped under the burden of emotional pain.

'So you *were* at Finchmere on Saturday evening.' James checked the statement from the security team. Hamish had been spotted in the formal gardens, below the woodland.

'I saw Percy arrive for the ceremony,' Hamish said. 'I couldn't bear to watch, so I headed towards the wood. I saw a few security types coming for me, so I hotfooted it towards the footpath. But when I came to the loggia – where I'd spent time alone with Percy – it seemed the right place to leave what I'd brought.'

'What was that?'

Hamish shrugged. 'Doesn't matter now.'

'OK.' That could wait, perhaps. 'And then what did you do?'

'Then I carried on to the footpath. But I lost my way a bit; I knew the path followed the river, but I came too close to the house. I heard shouting, saw a couple more guys dressed in black running towards me, and I bolted. Got right down to this place, actually. But there was a bar here, and that was enough.'

'So you were downstairs? Until when?'

'Until last orders. Probably a bit longer. The hotel was booked out for the wedding guests, so the bar was empty. Merl ... was kind. He let me stay, let me blather on.' Hamish rubbed his face. 'Oh God, it's all a total mess.'

'OK, look Hamish, I'm going to level with you,' said James. 'You clearly came here either to win Percy back or to have it out with her. But the problem we have is that someone who either loves Percy or hated Hawke killed him last night.' He paused. 'And you fit at least one, if not both, of those categories.'

Rav forced himself to breathe steadily as he gripped Nell and watched the intruder from under the bed.

The gloved hand opened each drawer of the bedside cabinet, one by one, searching thoroughly. The pair of hands closed the bottom drawer, and Rav dared to hope that the person would get up and leave.

But the hands moved to the floor, as if the person was about to peer under the bed. Rav tensed, taking a sharp breath full of Nell's warm, citrussy scent, dreading the next move.

He wanted to squeeze his eyes shut. But he stared over Nell's shoulder, ready for whatever was coming.

She just continued to gaze at him, stock-still, not giving them away by twisting round, however desperate she must have been to see what he was looking at.

The hands pressed against the floor, and the person eased themselves to their feet, crept to the door and slipped out.

In the silence, Nell and Rav remained motionless, holding their breath, Nell's hand still gripping his. With a self-conscious grin, she glanced down, uncurled her fingers from around his, then scrambled out.

Rav's relieved exhale sounded as loud as an explosion. Sliding out, he stood and saw Nell vaulting onto the windowsill, wrapping the ropes around herself and leaning back.

As he imagined noises in the hallway, outside the room, Rav's legs threatened to give way. Silently, he urged Nell to hurry. But she'd paused, staring at the wall. Wondering what she was staring at, he peered over.

An A4 document wallet, inside a clear plastic bag, had been wedged between the wall of the house and the stout wisteria branches. Nell stared at Rav. 'Can you take it?'

He nodded, grabbing the bag and gripping it with his teeth. On the window ledge, he wound the ropes around himself and then arranged the handle so that when he closed the window and gave it a thump, it locked. In case the noise alerted anyone, he scrambled up as quickly as he could. Nell was already on the roof, checking the grounds as she looped her rope up.

He followed her grim stare and saw a gaggle of photographers at the far gate. She gazed at the dark clouds overhead. 'Good job we're in for a downpour.'

He felt too wobbly to grin. He hauled his rope up and packed it away, then sagged against the chimney. 'Bloody hell. That was close. Who do you think it was?'

'My guess is either Crispin or Theo.' Nell frowned. 'Raising the question of how they got hold of a key.'

'Why either of them?'

'Male shoes, light tread. Douggie and Angus are big men, heavy on their feet,' Nell said, bundling her rope into Rav's bag. She rubbed her side, where the rope had dug in, lifting her T-shirt to check the red-streaked indent. 'Are you sore, too?'

'Yes, but you were the one who said no harnesses. More to the point, why would Crispin or Theo be searching Hawke's room?'

'I don't know.' Nell bit her lip. 'But it proves we're on to something.'

A few minutes later, Nell sat in Rav's room, opening the bag and unzipping the leather document wallet. She shook the contents onto the wide desk.

'Huh, a padlock?' Rav picked it up and examined it. 'Oh, no, it's a USB!' He opened his laptop and plugged it in. 'Ha! All that to avoid someone finding it, and it's not even password-protected!' Rav scanned the screen. 'Looks like folders connected to Hawke's work at the casinos. There're folders for Accounts; HR; Operations; PR; Procurements; Security; Strategy. Any ideas where to start?'

Nell shook her head. 'Just go through them methodically. Hopefully, we'll know when we see it.'

As Rav clicked through each folder and its files, Nell examined the rest of the wallet's contents.

A notepad listed properties with calculated valuations in small, meticulous handwriting. Then she pulled out a large handful of letters, and went through them – all addressed to Hawke, at Glencoille Castle. *He'd made himself at home, then.* Most were replies to Hawke's speculative enquiries for purchase.

She checked the notebook and saw that the list matched the properties. Comparing the values in the notebook with those quoted in the letters, Nell saw that Hawke was a ruthless negotiator.

'Looks like Hawke went old-school with his admin,' Nell said. 'Letters rather than emails. I reckon he wanted to make use of headed paper with a castle as his address.'

Hawke had been busy. Skimming the letters showed more of the same, but one made Nell rock back in her seat. Not addressed to Hawke, but to Percy, bulging with its handwritten pages. The opening along the top was a jagged rip. Turning it over slowly, Nell noted the African postmark. And Hamish's spidery writing.

Returning to the bar, James decided to try a different tack. Hamish wasn't willing to tell him why he'd gone to Percy's wedding, but perhaps the barman he'd unburdened himself to might.

'Couldn't possibly, mate.' Merl grinned. 'More sacred than the confessional are confidences made to a bartender.' He passed James a coffee. 'On the house.'

'Thanks.' James took the drink. 'But you'll have to forgive me if I try that question again.'

'Fine.' Merl held his hands up in surrender. 'I can't bear this interrogation.' He shot James another grin. 'Poor sod's really gone through it. He had a lot to say, and not very much of it was intelligible, but I think the crux of the story is this: he came back from wherever he's been.' He leaned in, 'Was it prison?' He held his hands up again. 'Not judging, just it's a barkeep's duty to gather info.'

James sipped his coffee.

'No.' Merl shrugged. 'Well, I can see that's none of my business. Anyway, he buys himself the first phone he's had in a year or so and checks his good lady's social media. And there he sees that she hasn't waited. She's only gone and got engaged to some other fella.'

Jesus. 'And how did he seem?'

'Heartbroken. Devastated.' Merl paused. 'But something else. Remorseful? He said he'd done something stupid. *Ruined everything.* Kept muttering there was no way back.'

James raised his eyebrows, but Merl shrugged. 'No idea what he was banging on about. But I *do* know that's the thing about love, innit? Makes you do daft things.'

* * *

After she'd brought coffees up to Rav's room, and Rav had worked through the first five folders, but not found anything incriminating, Nell picked up Hamish's letter again.

Was this Hamish's break-up letter to Percy? Nell ached to know what it said but didn't want to intrude on Percy's private correspondence. If she gave her the letter, she knew Percy would tell her the contents soon enough. But Percy had enough on her plate: three deaths, a family at war. *Will this just cause her even more heartache when she least needs it?*

Rav stretched, flexed his fingers and turned to Nell. 'What's that?'

Nell held up the envelope. 'A letter to Percy. From Hamish.'

'What was he doing with her post?'

'That's what I'd like to know,' Nell answered grimly. Whatever the contents were, Hawke had obviously read them and very probably kept them secret from Percy.

Hoping she was doing the right thing, Nell guiltily pulled the letter out and read the contents. A heartbreaking letter, then an endearing cartoon of a hapless gangly man approaching a fiery, riotously beautiful woman, offering a flame lily, and rewarded with a kiss.

'Oh, God.'

'What?' Rav asked.

Nell folded the letter and placed it carefully back inside the envelope. 'It sounds like they argued – and broke up – over him staying longer to help treat the Ebola outbreak. He's apologising and begging her to meet up when he gets back. He gave her a time and date, but said if she wasn't there, he'd understand. He explained he'd transferred to Monrovia's clinic in Liberia, but reduced his placement from an extra year to just an extra six months. Which would have been a big deal for him.'

'Big deal for Percy, too,' Rav said.

'Yeah, it sounds like he had agreed to an extra year's posting without discussing it with Percy first, hence her eruption when she found out. From what Hamish said in his apology, she'd told him she'd route his emails to junk, that she'd delete his number . . .'

'Whoa. Bit extreme?'

'Well, she'd have been excited about him coming home; they would have had grand plans. If he changed them and didn't even discuss it – or treated her like her opinion didn't matter – well, to Perce that would have been a sign that she wasn't being taken seriously as a partner. And maybe she thought he wasn't as smitten as she was. Classic wounded pride and heartbreak . . .' Nell bit her lip. Percy had been going through that, and she hadn't even known.

'Right.' Rav gestured at the letter. 'So that was that?'

Nell nodded. 'When Hamish got here, he would have just returned from Africa. Planning to meet Percy to make amends.' Nell slumped back against her seat, her face pale. 'Oh *no*,' she whispered. 'If he came *here*, with a flame lily, then he knew about the wedding. So he'd have found out . . . how? Press? Percy's social media? Jesus, how would that have *felt*?'

Rav pushed his chair away from the computer and looked at Nell in disbelief. 'Oh, that would have been . . . Jesus.'

Nell's heart ached. *Had Hamish come down here to stop the wedding? Or just leave a message? He knew Percy would walk out to the loggia at some point. That must be why he'd left the symbolic flower there.*

She stared at the letter, at the savage tear along the envelope's seam that had revealed the private contents to prying eyes. 'Hawke made sure Percy didn't know about Hamish's apology. If she didn't get this, she wouldn't have made the first move to make up with Hamish.' Nell folded the letter into her pocket, to give to Percy as soon as she saw her.

'Well, that's on her, isn't it? If she'd swallowed her pride, she could have.'

Nell met Rav's gaze levelly. 'How long did it take you to get over yourself? Six months in India, I seem to recall.' A flash of memory hit her: why Percy had been so unimpressed when she'd first met Rav – that he'd absconded instead of resolving their argument. *Because she thought Hamish had done the same.*

'Hawke was a total conniving bastard, wasn't he?' Rav muttered.

Nell was silent. A cold feeling leached over her heart. A familiar fear for her, when it came to relationships: Hawke hadn't been interested in Percy, only in what she had. He'd just wanted her for her position and her money.

* * *

The ignored coffee had gone cold, as Rav clicked through the files of video footage and stills.

As one grainy picture loaded, recognition flickered. A well-dressed woman, aristocratic bearing, hair piled up. He zoomed in on the woman's face, with a prickle of apprehension, and shivered. As he clicked on, his heart thumped.

No wonder Greta hated Hawke. 'Holy . . .'

He'd only whispered, but Nell dashed over, so he clicked back to the beginning of the set.

'Look.' Rav pointed at the screen, as she leaned on his shoulder and peered at the black-and-white image from the CCTV camera, showing a woman in a hotel hallway.

'Greta?' Nell said.

Rav nodded.

'Oh.' Nell straightened up. 'That's no big deal. We know she went to his casinos. She held functions there.'

Rav clicked through the next few pictures of Greta's progress down a wide hotel hallway, into a hotel suite, the room name clearly visible.

Nell shrugged. 'Yes, she'd stay at the casino hotel if it was a large function. What's your point?'

Rav kept clicking, cringing at what he knew was coming. The timestamps on the images showed that Greta was followed a few minutes later by a man, who knocked on the door.

'That . . . doesn't look like Douggie to me,' Rav said carefully, as they stared at the slim silhouette.

Nell shook her head. 'It isn't. But that doesn't mean anything. It's easy for images to look damning out of context. It could be entirely innocent. They could be colleagues.'

Rav clicked again. The picture showed the hotel room door open, and Greta greeting the unknown man in the doorway with an unmistakably passionate kiss.

'Oh.' Nell sank into the armchair beside Rav's. 'Oh God.' Her face flushed. 'Greta's been having an *affair*?' She looked at Rav. 'Do you think Douggie knows?'

'Well, Hawke certainly did.'

'My God.' Nell's eyes widened. 'So that's what Angus was referring to, and why Hawke behaved like he had the upper hand. He was blackmailing Greta?'

'Looks like it,' Rav said.

Nell put her head in her hands. 'God, can you imagine? Having an affair, and being blackmailed about it by a guy you hate and who's going to marry your daughter? No wonder she was drinking.'

There was a silence, while they both came to the logical conclusion.

Nell looked at him. 'OK, so Greta had a motive. A pretty big one. But I reckon Angus knew, too. Which means he also had a motive.'

'And if Angus knew, then probably so did Douggie,' said Rav.

Nell frowned. 'So how would that work as blackmail?' Her eyes narrowed. 'They wanted to make sure Percy didn't find out, do you think?' Her face paled. 'I didn't believe any of them could do it, despite how much they wanted to prevent Percy from marrying him. But if this was going on as well . . .' She stared at the far wall, stunned.

Rav sat back in his chair to give her a moment to digest the revelations and looked back at the computer screen.

For thoroughness, he continued clicking through the images. He paused on one, studying it. *Oh God. Would Nell need to see this? Would she want to?*

Yes. Yes, of course she would. She was a scientist through and through. And a nosy one, at that.

'Nell, look at this. It's hazy, but I think I recognise the man with Greta. See what you think.'

Nell leaned over and squinted at the picture. 'Jesus,' she whispered. Then she groaned. 'Well, of course it's Theo.'

Chapter 22

James had stomped back across the fields and woodland. His smart shoes were caked in mud and it turned out that Hamish had an alibi at the bar until about 12.30 a.m., when he was driven home by a waiter who lived in Cookingdean, near the B & B Hamish had been staying at, arriving at about ten past one in the morning.

And now – *yet again* – he couldn't find Nell anywhere. She wasn't even answering her phone. In utter extremis, he found himself knocking on Rav's bedroom door, his heart in his mouth, dreading her being here, dreading what they'd be up to – but also dreading not finding her, that something awful could have happened . . .

Nell answered the door.

Oh, for God's sake. Of course she'd be here.

'James!' Her face flashed with guilt before her usual composure returned. 'Come in – we've found something.'

As he walked in, James's eyes flicked to the bed. At least it was unrumpled.

'We've . . . er . . . found some things of Hawke's.'

'Oh?' He folded his arms. 'How, exactly?'

'Hidden. Outside of his room.' The heavy breath and slight sink of her shoulders revealed relief at delivering . . . what – a lie? A half-lie?

Nell bundled some envelopes and a notepad into a leather wallet, then held it out to James.

'You'll have to tell me exactly how and where you found them.'

'Outside Hawke's window.' Nell's face was red-hot.

What the . . . 'That's like thirty feet from the ground!'

'We were . . . climbing.'

We. Always bloody we. 'Why?'

'To go into Hawke's room. To search. And lucky we did.'

He gaped at Nell. 'What the hell do you think you're doing?' The fact that she'd been stupid enough to breach a crime scene was awful enough. The fact that she'd done it with *him* . . . 'Don't you realise we can't use any of that as evidence, now, Nell? You . . . *idiots*! This isn't a *game*. This is *serious*!'

He could barely keep the fury out of his voice. *They don't even care. This could put his job on the line, and they don't bloody care. They are more interested in being in cahoots. Together.*

'Of course I know this isn't a game. This is my *best friend's* family. Practically *my* family. And your team aren't exactly making much headway, are they? Didn't even find this in their sweep of Hawke's room.' Nell's voice was cold.

'No, well, they're prioritising the post-mortems. Because searches can wait. Because the rooms are guarded.'

Rav hadn't even had the decency to look up and meet his eyes yet. *Not even an apology!* He *had* at least shrunk in his chair, like he was trying to disappear, but kept himself occupied with something on his laptop.

As James stared at him, Rav jerked in his seat, then leaned forward. He expanded the recording on the screen and hit mute. Without turning round, he said, 'Nell, please tell me this is a deepfake.'

His senses tingling, James knew what Rav was watching before he could make out what was on the screen: Nell's sex tape, with her dressed as a devil, then not dressed at all, leaked by a creep of an ex-boyfriend, who Nell had dragged through the courts and hammered with an injunction and serious damages. Nell crept closer to the screen, her face blotching with crimson. When Rav turned and saw her ferocious blush, he shook his head.

'God, Nell.' He ran his hand through his hair. 'This is . . . This is . . .' He sighed. 'All I've ever asked of you is for you to be open with me. So I wouldn't have to discover crap like this.' He looked at her like she'd ripped his heart out.

Bristling at Rav's proprietary tone, James answered for Nell. 'To be fair, no one should know about this, Rav, not with the injunction on it. So how the hell did Hawke get his hands on it?'

Rav stood, gaping. 'You *knew*?' He turned wounded eyes to Nell. '*He* knows?'

Nell's arms dropped to her sides as she sighed. 'Yes.'

Rav pursed his lips, nodding. 'OK, I get it. You can share things with some people, just not with others. Fair enough. It's just, after everything we've been through, I really thought we trusted each other. I thought we . . . cared about each other.' He shoved his chair in and strode to the door.

Nell ran after him. 'I do care! You *know* I care!'

But Rav ignored her, and stormed out of the room and down the hall. Nell sagged against the wall, groaning.

'Yes, Nell, that's all too clear,' James said.

She turned to him. 'What do you mean?'

'You know what I mean. Let's stop pretending, shall we? All of us.' He shoved the chair out of his path and strode into the hall. Nell tugged his arm. 'James? James, I'm sorry—'

'What for? Stringing me along when you've been after him the whole time? *With* him, for all I know. God knows, you don't get as upset as he just did unless there's something going on.' He snatched his arm from Nell's grip. 'I'm done with being someone's second choice, Nell. I'm done with us.'

He needed to keep moving, to vent all the fury coursing through his veins.

Heading down the back stairs, he stomped into the banqueting hall, pushing open the double doors. Rain sleeted down, and he groaned, turned and paced. Restless feet took him towards the great room, hoping for peace . . .

But everyone had assembled. As he walked in, Douggie beckoned him, and the family walked towards the morning room with a man in a grey suit. Theo and Angus tagged along, leaving Deborah leafing through a magazine by the fire – her brogue-shod foot tapping on the parquet the only giveaway that she wasn't as relaxed as she tried to seem – while Crispin, opposite, played a game on his phone.

Oh, God. I'd totally forgotten. The will reading. Bloody perfect.

James took a deep breath and, ignoring his inner turmoil, tried to put his best professional face on by drawing from deep experience of dealing with all sorts of awful situations. None had been quite so personal, though . . .

Douggie sat beside Greta, who smiled at him as he took her hand. Douggie raised his other hand expansively. 'Well, we're all here.' He smiled around the room. 'We're all ready to hear it. Officially.'

The family solicitor arranged a thick file on the table, opened it, de-capped a fountain pen, set it down, shuffled his papers, cleared his throat. He glanced around the room and swallowed. Then he reshuffled his papers, studying one and placing it on top of the pile.

Douggie's smile faded. 'Well? We're ready for confirmation.' He half-turned to Greta with forced geniality. 'And the sky-high death duties.'

The solicitor shifted in his seat and stared at his page, blinking.

Greta placed her other hand on Douggie's, while Angus shot sidelong looks at them.

Shannon leaned forward, a little too eagerly, while across the table, Percy sunk in her chair, and picked at her fingers.

The solicitor cleared his throat.

As everyone sat to attention, Shannon's narrowed eyes scanned the family – reading hope, expectation – a derisive half-smile on her lips.

Douggie frowned at the solicitor. 'Come on, man!'

Peering up over his glasses, the solicitor nodded. 'Very well. I'll . . . I'll cut to the chase. As you'll expect, there is one sole inheritor of the estate . . .'

'Obviously,' Douggie filled in the pause. 'And?'

'And Lord MacKenzie's named heir is – well, I suppose I should say heiress . . .'

Douggie's head snapped round to Greta.

'. . . is Lady Persephone.'

Douggie gaped. He blinked rapidly, then shook his head. 'No, man. That'll be a mistake. Pa would have left her something, that I'm sure of. But the estate'll be coming to me.' He waggled his finger at the stack of papers. 'Check again.'

'There's no mistake.' The solicitor handed Douggie the will. 'See for yourself.'

Douggie snatched the page and scanned it, frowning. He shook his head, reread it, then stared at the solicitor. 'This is legit? Signed and sealed? It was only last *week*. Was he in his right mind?' James heard desperate straws being clutched.

'Yes, yes and yes.'

Douggie breathed heavily, his barrel chest heaving. He gripped the table like the room was whirling around him. 'But . . . But . . .' His gaze swung to Percy. 'Did you know about this?'

All eyes turned to Percy. She squirmed, red-faced.

'Percy?' Greta rose. 'You knew? After everything . . .' She let out a shuddering breath. 'And you *knew*?'

'I cannae believe this,' Douggie growled. 'I knew Pa had me dancing to his tune.' Greta placed a warning hand on his arm. He shrugged it off. 'But being betrayed by your own daughter is summat else.'

Percy's chest heaved as she stared up at her parents.

'There is a codicil. To permit you to live in Glencoille Castle until death,' the solicitor murmured to Douggie.

'Permit? *Permit?*' Douggie pounded the table with both fists and then leaped to his feet, spittle on his rusty beard, chair skidding out behind him. 'It's my bloody *home*! And it's *my* estate by rights! I'm not living there on someone else's favour, daughter or no. He's gone too far this time. I'm not letting the old bastard get away wi' this.' He pointed at the solicitor. 'You can take this as notice that I'll challenge this.' His eyes burned. 'I don't care what it takes.'

Chapter 23

Sunday 14th March – 4.30 p.m.

As Nell had watched James storm off down the hall, indignation bubbled. *Bloody nerve! As if I'd cheat! How could he* think *that?* Even alone, she blushed. She may not have acted on them, but she couldn't deny her feelings for Rav. How had James seen that, though, when she'd barely admitted it to herself?

God, is it obvious to everybody? Percy had even commented on it. So, does Rav know?

Nell dredged over conversations for any signs that people realised. The scene from the library blazed into her mind: when Theo had teased her about finding love, her gaze had unconsciously locked with Rav's. She'd known then.

Not that it made any difference. Rav had done exactly *the same thing as the last time they'd argued.* No opportunity to explain; didn't want to understand her reasons for secrecy, accusing her of not caring enough to trust him. It wasn't as if he'd given her a rundown of every intimate moment he'd ever had. When the hell did he think it was *appropriate* to bring up the fact that an ex had filmed her without consent? And it had happened over a decade ago: she had a right to leave some things in the past.

She'd been kidding herself that they could be more than friends.

Full of restless energy, she prowled around the room. Percy's letter sat on the desk. She should return it. Percy should know. Then she'd go out. A brisk run was just what she needed. She didn't care about the rain.

Tucking the letter into her pocket, she hurried to Percy's room. But the knock on the door wasn't answered. Checking the time, Nell groaned. Of course. The will. Using the back stairs, she headed to the morning room. As she passed through the great room, Deborah and Crispin nodded from their sofas, pretending not to have ringside seats for any fallout. There was no sign of Rav.

The door ripped open and Douggie stormed in from the direction of the morning room, Greta hurrying behind him, their faces grim, battle-ready. Angus and Theo followed, shaking their heads, in deep discussion. No Percy.

What the hell's happened?

James walked out next, looking preoccupied, then started at the sight of Nell. As they stared at each other in frosty silence, she waited for an apology, for some sign of remorse for his accusation, but he made no move to speak, so she walked past him. She needed to find Percy.

Shannon was loitering just inside the ballroom, watching Nell. She looked deliciously scandalised, yet burning with envy, needing her fix of gossip even though it was killing her.

In the morning room, Percy sat at the table with the solicitor, signing paperwork. Nell frowned.

'What's going on?'

Percy pushed the last sheet of paper back to the solicitor and grimaced. 'I'll tell you later.'

Nell nodded, even though curiosity itched. Shannon, unable to hold out any longer, slipped back into the room and sidled up to the solicitor. 'Was there . . . any mention of any gifts?'

The solicitor nodded and opened the file.

Percy looked at Nell and jerked her head towards the door. Nell noticed her pallor, her eyes red and heavily shadowed. 'Have you slept at all, Perce?'

'A bit. A chunk of hours together which has made me feel a bit less . . . swimmy.' Percy swallowed. 'I still feel sick . . . over Hamish . . .' Her chin trembled and she pressed her lips together.

With sudden certainty, Nell took out the letter. 'Perce, did you know Hamish wrote to you?'

Percy's eyebrows drew together in incomprehension. 'What?'

She handed the envelope to Percy, pointing at the October postmark. 'Did you ever get this? Have you read it?'

Percy stared at the envelope, her lips tugging downwards at the familiar writing. She traced the jagged tear, shot a hard look at Nell.

'Hawke opened it. It might have been delivered while he stayed with you as a guest, in November, before you started dating. Your post is left out at breakfast, like ours is, so it would have been easy for him to take it without you knowing.'

'How . . . ?' The question died on her lips, as Percy turned the letter over in her hands, gingerly, like it might spontaneously combust, then pulled the folded pages out and started to read. Nell moved away but cast surreptitious glances as Percy hungrily scanned the lines, turned pages, held her breath. But then Percy gave a strangled sob. Her tears splashed onto the paper, blurring the ink. She wiped her face quickly, eyes darting as she read on. Nell saw her turn to the last page and waited. After a short pause, she sat beside Percy, took her hand.

'I can't believe it,' Percy said. Her eyes were fixed on the letter. 'Hawke knew how upset I was afterwards, when . . . when . . .'

Nell squeezed Percy's hand.

Percy looked up, her face set. 'God, what an idiot I am.' She gave a bitter laugh. 'Took me long enough to see it. But still, I never dreamed Hawke would stop me from knowing Hamish was trying . . . trying to . . .'

Nell nodded. A long pause stretched out between them. Nell leaned forward. 'Would this have made a difference?'

Percy shrugged. But regret flickered across her face.

'If Hamish had tried to come back sooner, I mean . . .'

Percy frowned at Nell. 'How do you know Hamish was coming back sooner?' Her eyes widened. 'You read my letter? My *private letter*!' She gaped as realisation struck, but she still had the sense to whisper, 'You would have found this in his *room*? You've been snooping in *there*! My *God*! Who the hell do you think you are!'

No denying it now. 'If I hadn't, it would've become police property, and you wouldn't even have known about it.'

Percy still glowered, like she owned the moral high ground. Nell shook her head. 'Don't give me all this, Percy, when you were clearly spilling my darkest secrets to Hawke.'

'What?' Percy's face flamed.

'At least admit it. Who else would he have heard about my tape from?'

'What are you talking about?' Her voice was full of indignation.

'Oh, get off your high horse. It's not just the tape – you've been lying to me about your whole wedding, just to manipulate me into you having your own way.'

Shannon walked in and, clearly catching the whiff of acrimony, her mouth twitched. 'More trouble in paradise?'

Nell and Percy both glared at her.

'Well, this is novel. The two of you cat-fighting, while little old me is turning down a rather lucrative tell-all exposé in a Sunday supplement – *My brush with death and tragedy in murder manor* – in the name of family loyalty.'

'Oh, shut up, Shannon,' Nell and Percy said in unison.

Hoping Shannon would have more sense than to give an interview, Nell walked into the great room. Everyone was still assembled, sitting in clusters. As Percy and Shannon followed her in, Nell came face to face with Rav.

'I've been waiting for you,' he said, holding out a small square of plastic. 'Here.'

Nell took it. 'The SD card? From the camera in the barn?'

'I replaced it with a new one, don't worry. But since the owls have shown an interest in the nest box, I thought it'd be nice to download the recording.'

'Oh.' Nell slipped the card into the pocket of her leggings.

'But I'll leave that to you, now. *If* you can be bothered to care about *that*.' His tone was petulant. But he looked like he regretted the comment.

'Oh, for God's sake,' Nell hissed under her breath, shooting sideways glances to the others in the room, listening in. 'Don't—'

'Look, it's clear I was wrong about things. You act like we're . . . *friends*, but actually it's not real, is it? And it hurts. I can't keep coming back for more of this. I'm out, Nell.'

Nell felt the burning stares of the company. Turning, she tried to skulk from the room. But Shannon, smelling blood, slinked up and whispered, 'Goodness, Nell. I told Hawke you were no angel. Now we all know it.'

Of course. Shannon was the one who'd given Hawke the tape. Not Percy. Blinding red fury ignited and, as she rounded on Shannon, she slapped her. Half-horrified, half-satisfied at what she'd done, Nell gasped. But she gave Shannon a hard look. 'And you're pure spite, Shannon. And we all know *that.*' The urge to escape overwhelmed Nell. And, since she was dressed for it, maybe a run was a good idea.

Striding from the room, Nell headed to the kitchen, reached into a cupboard for her water bottle, filled it, and then headed to the hall. She left it on the table while she used the lift to go upstairs for her earbuds. Shoving them in her ears on the lift's descent, she chose some angry music, cranked the volume, grabbed her water bottle and ran outside, into the downpour.

The miserable weather matched her miserable mood. Her top quickly became sodden and clung to her body; her trainers collected clay along the path to the river, heavier with each stride, mud slapping up the backs of her legs, but she pressed on.

Bloody Shannon. Boiling anger propelled Nell up the hill's narrow footpath. Percy might be hot-headed, but she was fiercely loyal. *I should have known better.*

Reaching the top of the hill, Nell felt a wave of defeat. Percy, James and now Rav – she'd managed to alienate them all, and none of them was talking to her. Her mud-caked shoes squelched and slipped and she slowed to a jog.

Rain was mixing with the sweat on her face – and her hot, stinging tears.

Sunday 14th March – 5 p.m.

Rav didn't know what to do with himself. He'd wanted to make a point over giving Nell the SD card, wondering if it would provoke ... well, *something* from her. But now he just felt like an idiot. *And I've done the same thing all over again, haven't I?*

He groaned. It always, always came back to the same thing. He just wanted to feel like she trusted him. *We are close enough for that, surely?* So why did he always have to uncover things about her? The deep things. Why couldn't she be open with him?

His heart ached.

Restlessly, he paced. Her water bottle was on the hall table. *She can't be going out for a run in this weather, surely?*

Unease crept through him. Trusting his instinct, he ignored the cordon to dash upstairs to his room, looking for waterproofs but settling for a hoodie, and rushed down again. Nell's bottle was gone, and so was she. Bracing himself, he zipped up his hoodie, and the pocket that contained his iPhone, and headed into the rain, guessing she'd run her usual route, to the weir.

He sprinted across the garden and caught sight of Nell, running up the hill to the loggia. He followed as she disappeared in the forest. Running into the woods, squelching heavy clay mud stuck to his thin Converse, making him slip and stumble as he headed towards the river path. His pace slowed, his legs heavy, and he slicked his dripping hair out of his eyes.

What the hell am I doing? She's out here, in this, because she wants space.

Coming to a halt, his hoodie clinging to his body, Rav took a few heaving breaths. Shaking his head, he began to turn back, but then stopped. A slow creeping dread crawled across his stomach. As if magnetically drawn, he walked, jogged and then sprinted after Nell again. As the hill towards the river grew steeper, he scanned ahead for any sight of her, before he stumbled heavily, turning his ankle. Grimacing, he rotated his foot, then after a few seconds he limped on cautiously, trying to pick up his pace. The path became steeper still; on the edge of the hill, the swollen torrent of the fast-flowing river charged over the stones and rocks in the riverbed, swirling relentlessly seawards. From upstream, he heard the rushing of the weir.

To his relief, Rav spotted Nell in the far distance, and he put on a burst of speed until pain flamed through his ankle. Pausing, he flexed his foot, watching Nell jog further away, approaching the bridge just above the weir.

The attack happened so quickly, Rav could barely register what was going on.

Chapter 24

Rav tried to make sense of it. A dark figure burst out of the bushes, following Nell, and gained pace on her as she slowed, jogging up the incline and onto the bridge. The figure caught up and, with both arms outstretched, shoved Nell hard, sending her over the bridge railings, then ran on, out of sight.

Rav watched in frozen disbelief as Nell pitched over. His stomach knotted as he heard her shocked shriek; then his gut twisted, sickeningly, when her scream was cut off abruptly as her head struck the stone footings of the bridge. Her body fell, limp, snatched up in the powerful, fast-moving current.

JESUS. Rav's heart thundered in his ears. He watched Nell's body flop over the crest of the weir, shuddering down the laddering waterfalls, thrown around in the roiling torrent.

Rav's mind raced. Nell was being carried swiftly towards him on the churning water. He had – what, ten seconds? – to catch her. And he'd have just one chance. If it wasn't already too late.

He ripped off his hoodie and threw it aside. He sprinted to where they'd seen the otter. It was the best way in, and he might be able to brace himself against those rocks. Flicking his gaze back to Nell, he forced himself to step carefully down the muddy bank, stabilised with snaking tree roots, into the waterway.

His eyes fixed on Nell, as she was dashed along the merciless current. She looked like a bundle of rags, not a living person.

Oh God . . .

He focused. The rocks might give him something to brace against, but the current was dangerously fast.

Trying to find his footing, Rav kept his eyes on Nell. The slackness of her body made him feel sick and he slipped. Pain flashed through his ankle, and the intense cold shock of icy water snatched his breath as he was submerged and swept up, dragged under the deeper water and rolled around with the eddying force.

He choked, spluttered, fought for air. He tried to grab hold of something, anything, clutching blindly at stones and brambles as he was torn along with the overwhelming current. His body was battered, arms sliced by wickedly jagged flint. In his tumbling vision, Rav saw a large rock obstructing the river and threw himself against it.

As he surfaced, Rav looked frantically for Nell, through the frothing water that obscured his view as he scanned downstream, and then up, in a panic. Had she been swept past him?

Where was she?!

The water buffeted him, before swirling around each side of the huge rock. With a surge of strength, he pushed his back against it and battled to stand in the chest-high river. His T-shirt, plastered against his skin, had been ripped by the rocks, and patches of pink were blooming across the white fabric. He saw her. *Close.* Heading towards him.

Thank God.

He braced himself. He'd only have one chance to catch her . . .

As the current bore Nell's unresponsive body towards him, he was relieved to see she was face up, though her body crashed over stones and tremored as the water eddied underneath her. Holding the boulder with his fingertips, and thanking the strength of his climber's grip, Rav stretched out his arm as far as he could to reach her. But Nell's hand slithered through his grasp and her body flashed past him.

Rav smashed himself up against the rock and reached out again, wildly, just catching hold of her foot by the toe of her trainer. But it wasn't a good enough grip to haul her back to him, against the current. With panic, Rav realised the shoe he gripped was slipping off her foot. But, worse, the swirling water was pummelling Nell's head, pushing her face below the surface. He had no choice: he had to sacrifice his grip on the boulder to reach with his other hand and pull her in. He wedged his right shoulder against the rock and jammed his right foot into a crevice at its base. He reached out to grab Nell's ankle with one, then both hands. Hauling her towards him with all his might, he pressed his bracing shoulder into the rock. The water battered Nell's body. The force dragging her downstream was relentless.

The tension to hold Nell from being swept away felt like it would rip him in two. His biceps and forearms tremored; he felt his tendons straining in his neck. Her head sunk under the water again. Summoning all his strength, Rav hauled her body, inch . . . by . . . precious . . . inch towards him, pulling her close enough to reach for her running top. He grabbed the thin fabric, lifting her head above the water. He squeezed the material desperately in his clenched fist, his nails driving into his palm. His shoulder strained at its socket. He refused to let her go.

Finally, with his muscles screaming, Rav pulled Nell into his arms, panting hard. He braced and turned into the shelter of the rock, slamming his back against it, holding her against him, facing the oncoming flood of water. The swirling river pounded against them unremittingly. Rav locked his arms, wrapping them around Nell, protecting her prone upper body from the onslaught. He cradled her head in the crook of his arm, his broad forearm a barrier against the assault of the current. Her legs flailed against him.

Rav's chest heaved as he took long, steadying breaths. He looked grimly at the narrow stretch of river he had to cross to get Nell safely on the bank. If he could manage a long stride to the next rock, he could brace himself against it. Another long stride would take him into a shallow section, and two more steps would get him to the bank.

Using his left hand to support her head, Rav checked that Nell was secure in his arms, her neck in line. He tensed his quads and pushed himself away from the rock, lifting Nell. She was heavier than expected, waterlogged and unresponsive, and he nearly staggered downstream with the buffeting current.

Swallowing back the bile of rising panic, trying to steady his breathing and keep calm, Rav determinedly strode out. His foot landed heavily. The current crushed his ankle against the rock. Shifting his weight, Rav checked his footing, then took another stride into the shallows. The clay bed was slippery. He tested his weight again and moved carefully. His shoes slipped and he pressed his weight down to steady himself.

He breathed and looked at the bank. Two more steps. The stones, rolling underfoot, made his next footing insecure but he moved with precision until, finally, he reached the bank. Slowly, he exhaled hard through gritted teeth and used his already strained muscles to lift Nell's body up and onto the grass.

Then he reached up, pressed his hands on the bank and clambered out, his shoulder flaming.

He stared at Nell. She was white-faced, blue-lipped . . . She looked . . . lifeless.

Rav sank to his knees and checked her airway. It was clear. He felt for a pulse while he tried to tell if she was breathing. Her chest was barely moving.

No pulse . . . *Christ*. Wait . . . it was feeble, slow . . . but it was there – just. And – perhaps – shallow breathing. *Thank God.* He squinted, looking along the bank for his hoodie, and ran to collect it, taking his phone from its pocket to call an ambulance on the way back to Nell. He put the call on speakerphone as he reached her and wrapped his hoodie tenderly around her.

'Ambulance please! A woman is unconscious after falling into the river and hitting her head on the weir. She's breathing but has a weak pulse . . . I'm at Finchmere, near Cookingdean.' He waited as he heard the operator tapping their keyboard. 'I'm on a private footpath . . . along the Nye River, near Nye weir.'

The operator replied crisply, establishing the precise location and both their names, then asked, 'Is there room for an air ambulance?'

Rav looked around at the woodland. 'No,' he said miserably, and heard more tapping.

'OK,' the operator said. 'You must keep her neck straight and head supported.'

'Right.' Rav looked at Nell like she was made of glass. 'But she's already been battered several metres down some water rapids.'

'If she's hit her head, are there any external signs of the injury?'

'She's got grazes on her face.' Rav leaned over to gingerly feel the sides, then back, of Nell's head, trying not to tilt her neck. As his fingers crept to the base of Nell's skull, they suddenly found a warm, sticky patch. His stomach heaved. He gently pulled his hands away and looked in horror at his bloody fingertips. He swallowed hard.

'Yes,' he said, his voice sounding detached, like it belonged to someone else. 'She's got an injury to the base of the back of her head. It's bleeding.'

'Can you apply anything to the wound to stop the bleeding?'

'Um . . .' Rav looked around. He didn't want to remove the hoodie that was keeping Nell warm. He ripped off his ragged, wet T-shirt, bundled it into a soft pad and gently manoeuvred it under Nell's head.

'Any fluids coming from her ears or nose?' the operator asked.

Rav checked carefully. 'No, but she's soaking wet, so it's hard to be sure. She's freezing.'

'Have you got anything to keep her warm?'

'Yes, I've already wrapped my hoodie around her, but that's all I have.' Rav felt desperate.

'Is there any bruising or swelling around her eyes or ears?' the operator asked.

He checked. His stomach churned at what that could mean. 'No.'

'OK, can you open her eyes and see if her pupils are the same size?'

Rav gulped. His hands were shaking with adrenaline. He could barely control his fingers. He took a breath to steady himself and gently pulled Nell's left eyelid up. The pupil seemed normal. He lifted her other eyelid. The pupil was the same size.

'Yes, her pupils are the same size.' Rav was amazed at how calm his voice sounded. *What did that mean?* Seconds were agony. 'How are you going to collect her?' he asked. 'Please be quick.'

'The ambulance will park at the bottom of the Nye footpath, and the team will carry a stretcher up and across the bridge.'

Oh God. That will take ages. Too long . . . Rav made a decision.

'Are there any other signs you need me to check?' Rav asked.

'No. Stay on the line. Keep an eye on those signs and tell us if anything changes.'

Rav agreed and balanced the phone on Nell's torso.

Carefully keeping Nell's head in line with her neck, he slid one arm under her bent knees and gently wrapped his other arm around her shoulders. He tipped his left elbow upwards so that her head was supported and remained straight. Inside its socket, his shoulder burned. He ignored it, focusing on tucking his folded, bloody T-shirt between her head and his arm to keep pressure on the wound. Gritting his teeth, he pushed himself to standing. The pain that seared through his ankle and up his leg made him catch his breath, sweating despite the shivering. He pressed on. If he walked carefully, Nell would keep steady in his arms.

His eyes flicked between checking the uneven path and watching Nell's face for any change in the symptoms the operator had mentioned. He couldn't open her eyelids as he walked to check her pupils. *What did uneven pupils mean?* But every step was one step nearer to help. He continued steadily, reaching the bridge and stepping with care.

The wooden bridge was treacherous. His shoes, squelching with waterlogged clay, threatened to skid underneath him. *Them.*

As he reached the other side of the bridge, he heard the ambulance's distant siren. He checked his pace, resisting the urge to speed up, knowing it was more important to make steady progress. *Don't fall, don't fall.*

The path towards the village was stony and steep, forcing him to slow. Nell was a dead weight in his arms. He just kept putting one foot carefully in front of the other. Eventually, the steepness levelled, and he saw the swoop of the ambulance's flashing lights. He heard voices as the crew approached.

'Here!' he called out.

He heard the crew speed up in response. Within seconds, they had set a stretcher on the ground, helped Rav to ease Nell onto it, and then braced her neck and strapped her unresponsive body securely. He followed them down the rest of the path to the road. The pain in his ankle throbbed unbearably, but nothing like the desolation gnawing in his chest.

In a practised, slick operation, the two paramedics slid the stretcher into the ambulance and wrapped Nell in a foil blanket. The male paramedic jumped in the cab to drive, while the female stayed with

Nell. She checked Nell's head injury, placing a wadded dressing under her head and discarding Rav's stained T-shirt in a yellow, lidded container.

Rav watched in silent agony, not wanting to be in the way of the help Nell needed, but unable to leave her. He barely noticed the medic wrap a foil blanket around his shoulders and sit him down inside the ambulance. The siren started and the vehicle sped along the narrow, twisting roads.

The female paramedic sat directly behind Nell's head, listening to her breathing through a stethoscope. Removing the earpieces, she called out, 'Lungs sound clear but risk of aspiration. Intubating with ETT.'

Rav looked on in mesmerised horror as she took a metal ... *lever?* And she eased it into Nell's mouth, then pushed a thin plastic rod gently down her throat. Exhaling softly, she threaded a tube over the rod and held it steady while she pulled the rod out, fixing a plastic balloon to the tube and squeezing rhythmically. Popping the stethoscope earpieces back in, she listened to Nell's lungs again, then called out, 'Clear left, clear right.'

Reaching over, she attached Nell to a heart monitor. It bleeped ... then a long pause ... and eventually bleeped again. Nell's heart rate seemed frighteningly slow to Rav. Next, the medic inserted a cannula into Nell's arm and attached an IV. She continued to palpate the ventilator, supporting Nell's breathing. The plastic balloon seemed to sigh sadly, in time with the bleeps from the monitor.

Suddenly, Rav began shivering, his teeth chattering uncontrollably. Turning to him, the medic asked, 'Is she on any medication?'

'I don't think so.' Rav shook his head. 'But I don't know for sure.'

'Could she be pregnant? Have allergies? Taken any recreational drugs or had any alcohol?'

Rav gasped, 'No,' to those, as he stared at Nell's ghostly face with wide, worried eyes.

'Can you describe what happened?'

'She ... she hit her head on the bridge footings when someone pushed her in the river.'

'How far did she fall?'

Rav frowned. 'About . . . three metres from the bridge into the river, I guess. And then she was swept over the weir.' He swallowed against that awful vision.

'Are you next of kin?'

Rav shook his head.

'Can you contact them?'

Rav frowned, then opened his work emails on his phone and found a message about a site risk assessment, with next-of-kin details for his colleagues. Nell's father was listed. Rav dialled the number, but he didn't answer. Rav took a breath and then left a brief, factual message.

The paramedic checked Nell's eyes, tried to get her to speak and checked various pressure points for her responses. As she assessed her, the paramedic called out the medical findings, updating the hospital. 'Patient unresponsive, contusions to face and head. No fluids. Risk of aspiration. Need emergency care at Neuro with CT scan. Traumatic brain injury.'

Chapter 25

Sunday 14th March – 5 p.m.

James had ached to escape the tensions of the family. With Nell in conference with Percy – having had not so much of a twitch of regret on her face about breaching the scene, doing things behind his back and being with *Rav* – he'd just wanted to be alone.

Well, let her derail the investigation. It's not my case. I don't need to protect them. I'm not even on duty. The drawing room was blessedly quiet, the fire cracking, the drinks cabinet open. He sloshed a generous, rebellious slug of whisky into a crystal tumbler and knocked it back, grateful for the distracting burn in his throat.

Pouring a second drink, he sighed, then paced the room, staring at the family photos. He took another long drink. He'd soaked up all these things about Nell, wanting to know everything about her: her life, her estate, the things that were important to her . . . Well . . . that didn't include him. He downed the drink and poured another.

Reaching the wingback armchair facing the fire, he sank down, nursing the glass, swirling the liquid and growing morose. As he finished his third drink, the door opened. James slouched, hidden by the back of the chair. He didn't want to see Nell. Or anyone.

Whoever had come in was clattering at the drinks cabinet. James shrank into his chair, hoping they'd mix a drink and go.

'Bloody Nell.' The mutter was Shannon's voice. 'Makes out she's so perfect.' Ice cubes clinked. 'Moralising over everyone.' A sloshing of drink. 'Total *hypocrite*!' The popping of the olive jar. 'All the time she's got two men on the g—'

'One,' James corrected her, punctuating this by raising the hand that was holding his empty glass above his head.

Seconds crackled, as James imagined Shannon realising she wasn't alone, working out who had overheard her. Suddenly, a drink was passed over the back of the chair. She'd guessed correctly. Neat whisky. He took it with a half-smile and, before he knew it, she was sliding onto the arm of the chair, facing him, ice clinking in her glass. Her violet silk dress rode up impossibly long, lean legs. Tantalising scents of amber, ambergris and honey, and the warmth of her body rolled towards him.

'Just worked it out, then, Detective?' Shannon asked. As she rested her hand on the opposite arm, she leaned across him, her shimmering dark hair tickling his neck.

Gulping, James asked, 'What makes you say that?' Her cleavage was at eye level, her hip tilting over the edge of the chair, her waist dipping towards his . . . areas . . . He had to lift his head to maintain eye contact. And he wasn't going to look anywhere else.

'Looks like you're drowning your sorrows. Why is that? Because you won't get your hands on Nell anymore? Or because you won't get your hands on her *estate*?'

James shifted, making Shannon sit up. 'Oh, come—'

'Don't bother denying it.' She flicked her hair over her shoulder. 'We both know Nell doesn't really appreciate what she has. Whereas me,' she rested a manicured hand on her chest, 'and you . . .' She placed her other hand lightly on his chest, trailing fingers. 'We're both outsiders here. We can see the advantages that Nell refuses to acknowledge, can't we, Detective Inspector?'

James wanted to defend Nell's honour. He knew she never disclosed her title to avoid unfair advantage – or unwanted detractors. And so what if Trent wanted to affirm connections in Nell's circle? *I'm a damn good detective. I deserved that promotion. Not my fault that I happened to be dating Nell.* Still, that voice in his head needled, and Ashley's words haunted him. *Not everyone gets what they deserve. Well, I didn't deserve Nell cheating on me, for one.* He sat back, staring at his drink.

Leaning across him, Shannon murmured, 'Shall we drown our sorrows together, Detective?' The smile over her cocktail glass held wickedness. She bit a scarlet, glossy lip.

'No. We're not in the same boat, Shannon. You're the cheater. I'm the . . . the *cheatee*.'

'I am not!' Shannon drew herself up again. '*Hawke* was the cheater. I wasn't in a relationship with anyone! That's typical, though, isn't it? Blaming the man's lack of morals on the woman. *Hello?* He was a grown man, and *he* could take responsibility for what he did.'

'But you knew you'd hurt your cousin. And you did it anyway.'

Shannon threw back her head and gave a hollow laugh. 'Have you met us? Every single day I have to live with my beloved cousin lording it over me. Literally. My mother's older than Douggie. The title should be mine. The estate should be mine. And I'd be better at managing all of it than Percy ever would. She's happier out on the highlands, rolling around in the mud. She should be a bloody gillie. Whereas I'm a natural. Yet my parents gave it up. So I'm left with nothing.'

'Not exactly nothing. I imagine you have a swanky place somewhere exclusive.' James thought about the small flat his salary had bought. He hadn't spent much time there recently. His ideas had migrated too easily towards what type of place he and Nell could get together. His Rightmove habit had become increasingly ambitious. The thought of returning to meals for one in his cramped, third-floor place, with a view of Pendlebury's industrial estate, made a dark depression roll over him. He took a long draught of his drink, glad again for its fire.

'Darling,' Shannon leaned in again, her tone breathy, her low-cut dress draping to increase the glimpse of cleavage. 'It's all relative. Look at the circles I move in. I'm literally the poor relation. You might think a Thames-side penthouse is luxurious. But it's basic. It's embarrassing. And it's not. Bloody. Fair.' She stirred the olive in her drink and stripped it from the cocktail stick with bared teeth.

James couldn't agree. 'You should think yourself lucky. You live somewhere amazing; you're well off. You can do anything you like. You should appreciate what you have.'

'Mmmhmm. Like Nell?' Shannon arched an eyebrow. 'Because

I sense trouble there.' She slid closer, speaking softly. 'And *I* think Nell doesn't appreciate what she has, either.'

James bristled at the invasion of privacy. Yet his hurt pride responded to someone being in his corner. So he didn't move away, as Shannon murmured, 'I always thought Nell was a fool. She never has known how to take care of the things that matter.' She fixed her cat eyes on him, gleaming in the firelight.

Mesmerised, James couldn't drag his eyes from hers.

'That fire gives out a lot of heat, doesn't it?' Holding his gaze, she slid one of the thin straps of her dress slowly off her shoulder.

Sunday 14th March – 5.40 p.m.

Rav hung back, feeling desperately powerless as the team of medical staff in scrubs clustered around Nell, monitoring her vitals. He felt like his whole world had caved in in the past few minutes.

'GCS seven,' the paramedic called to the team.

The doctor's head jerked up. 'Right, get a CT scan now.' The team sprinted off, pushing Nell's trolley through the door to the neurosurgery wing.

Rav's stomach dropped as he watched Nell disappear through the swinging doors, refusing to accept what was happening. He shook his head and sank onto a plastic chair, folded forward, and held his head in his hands. His body shuddered.

The young male paramedic crouched beside him. 'Rav?'

Slowly, he raised his head and looked at him.

'Looks like you've sustained a few injuries yourself. We need to get you checked.'

Rav shook his head. 'No . . . No, I'll wait here for Nell. Please.'

'She's in the best hands now. For the next couple of hours, you can't do anything for her. Let's get you patched up.' The medic nodded at Rav's chest, zigzagged with lacerations; a deep one along his side brimmed with syrupy claret clots. His arms were a mess of dried, blackening blood; his trousers shredded; his left leg bleeding into his sock; his ankle throbbing in time with his heartbeat.

Rav looked at the paramedic. 'What does GCS mean? What do the numbers mean?'

The paramedic looked at him frankly, then sat next to him. 'It's Glasgow Coma Scale. We use it to measure someone's level of consciousness after a head injury.'

Rav felt sick at the word 'coma'. He swallowed. 'What does seven mean?'

'It means the injury could be severe. But she's unconscious, so that will make her score low, too.'

'Oh God . . .'

The paramedic dropped his gaze to look at Rav's hands, which were clasped in his lap. After a pause, he looked up. 'They'll know more after the CT scan – that will tell them where the injury is, and how extensive it is. And it will also tell the doctors how to treat it.' He looked Rav in the eyes. 'I can tell you that what you did was give her time. Getting her out as quickly as you could, getting help . . . it gave her the very best chance.' He paused to let the words sink in.

All Rav could sense was a wall of shock. He shivered.

'So now you need to let the team take care of you, OK?'

Rav shot a longing glance at the doors through which Nell had disappeared, then nodded. 'OK.'

'Good.' The paramedic stood and nodded at a nurse.

Rav stood up, too. His right ankle collapsed underneath him. The medic grabbed him, his arm shooting reflexively under Rav's, supporting his weight.

'Sorry,' Rav gasped.

'That's OK, mate.' The medic watched Rav's stance carefully. 'Don't put any weight on it. Lean on me; we only have to get you into that bay over there.' The medic pointed at the nearest bed.

Rav winced as he put more pressure on his other foot, but he pressed on until he reached the bed. The medic helped him to sit.

'OK, mate. You're in good hands here.' The medic left Rav with the nurse, closing the curtain around the bed.

'Hi, Rav. I'm Nurse Harris. The paramedic team have briefed me.' She handed him a hot-water bottle in a starched cover.

'Warm up with this while I take a look at that foot and your other injuries.'

Rav hugged the bottle as Nurse Harris unlaced his squelching grey Converse, darkened with blood, and placed them on the floor. Rav's left foot looked OK but his right ankle, already mottled with dark bruising, had puffed up to twice the size of his left one. She explored the swollen joint, each tap of a fingertip shooting searing pain. When she asked Rav to wiggle his toes, he winced.

'I think you've sprained your ankle and possibly fractured some bones in your foot. I'll get you an X-ray and check.'

'No . . . I can't. That'll take ages,' Rav protested. 'I need to see Nell . . . I can't leave here. She won't know where I am—'

'It won't take long. I'll send you straight down there, and you'll come straight back, and I'll see what treatment we need for your foot. Nell will be a little while yet. She's probably having a scan. She may even need surgery, depending on what they find.'

'Why?' Rav gasped. 'What for?'

'I said "may" – it depends what they find. Head injuries are complicated, so it's hard to know.'

Rav's head whirled with questions he didn't dare ask. He barely registered the nurse handing him a hospital gown. 'Can I sort your other injuries out?'

'Uh . . . yeah.'

It took a while for her to clean all the wounds across his back, chest and arms. Rav flinched at the sting of the iodine and liquid stitches needed to hold most of the cuts together.

'You've got one deep laceration on your side which needs proper stiches, and this one.' She pointed to a deep, jagged slice from his left wrist to mid-bicep. 'I'll do it now, if that's OK.'

Rav nodded. Nurse Harris applied a local anaesthetic to the sites and examined him as the medication took effect. Rav winced at each stinging injection, clenching his fists.

He glanced down at the state of himself. The clean red welts criss-crossed his arms and torso like patchwork stitching. The purple stains of bruises seeped along his ribs and sides. He knew as Nurse

Harris touched his shoulder, the sharp pain making him jump, that it was swollen.

'Can you raise your left arm above your head?' she asked.

Rav tried. But he gasped as fire blazed down his neck and back. He could barely lift his arm.

'OK,' Nurse Harris said. She gently probed his shoulder with her fingertips. Rav gasped again, squeezing his eyes shut. 'What do you do for strength and fitness?'

'A lot of climbing. And gym.'

'Right.' Nurse Harris continued manipulating his shoulder, assessing the movement and Rav's winces. 'Your shoulder has been stressed. The strength of your muscles probably saved it from becoming dislocated but there's a lot of inflammation. I'll put some ice on it and give you some anti-inflammatories.'

Within a few minutes, Nurse Harris had stitched the lacerations and dry-dressed them, strapped an ice pack to Rav's shoulder, helped him into the hospital gown, and given him anti-inflammatories to take at regular intervals. His legs, bearing only superficial cuts and grazes, were also cleaned up; his trousers, though ruined and needing to be cut off him, had saved him from any serious wounds.

Then, Nurse Harris beckoned a porter, who whizzed him along the maze of corridors. His foot was arranged in the X-ray machine, which beeped as the image was taken. The radiographer peered at the screen, before the porter zoomed him back.

In the bay, Nurse Harris consulted the computer and nodded. 'You've broken your big toe, and fractured your first and second metatarsals.' She strapped an ice pack around his ankle and taped his broken toe to its neighbour. Rav gritted his teeth through the pain, breathing hard as he gripped the wheelchair armrests.

'Once the ice brings the swelling down, we'll bandage your foot and get a cast boot on to protect it while it heals.' She elevated the footrest, then hesitated. 'And now you'd like to wait and see Nell?'

Rav nodded.

'OK, I'll find out what ward she'll be on and we can get you set up there. What's your relationship to her? Partner?'

Oh God. If he said no, Nell's doctors wouldn't tell him how she was doing and he probably wouldn't be allowed to stay with her. There was no way he'd leave now.

He nodded. 'Yes,' he said. 'I'm Nell's partner.'

Chapter 26

Sunday 14th March – 6 p.m.

James woke up with a start. *Jesus, where am I?* The whirring noise must have woken him. His head pounded; his mouth tasted of stale whisky. He had a very real dread that he'd done something stupid. The sound stopped and he blinked in the dim, unfamiliar room, the last of the gloomy day's light seeping through the gap in the curtains.

The noise started again and he felt a hot blast of air on his cheek.

'So, the beast awakens.' Shannon's unmistakeable purr. 'I *was* hoping for a little more stamina.' She pouted, then blasted him again with the hairdryer, dragging the sheets back and switching the setting to cold.

'Oi!' The icy blast made James leap up. *Ouch.* The thump in his head reminded him he was too old for self-pitying afternoon drinking.

'Have you worked up enough of an appetite for dinner?' Shannon shimmied back into her violet silk dress.

James paused as he pulled on his jeans, side-eying her. 'Why? You got something else in mind?' *What am I doing? That's just asking for trouble!*

'Ha, you wish.' Shannon passed him, as he stood with one leg in his jeans – the other bent like a stork, about to step into the other trouser-leg – and she poked him with her index finger. It was enough to topple him like a skittle, helplessly, onto her bed.

Smirking, she spritzed herself liberally with perfume and took the towel she'd presumably just used after a shower back to her en suite. While she was out of sight, James writhed to get himself into a seated position, and finally pulled his jeans on.

Oh God, oh God, oh God . . . What had he done? He buttoned his shirt quickly, thinking he'd better head down before Shannon. Otherwise, they'd arrive together, and . . .

Bollocks.

'Come along, Romeo.' Shannon was already at the door, crooking her finger.

'Shouldn't we . . .' He splayed his hands.

Shannon laughed. 'Oh, poor darling. This is all part of the *fun.*' She pushed him ahead of her and locked her door.

With every step towards the refectory, dread swelled inside James. It didn't help that Shannon kept squeezing his buttock and chortling when he swatted her hand away. The door loomed and the final footsteps towards it just seemed too much. He could imagine Nell's face at them arriving together. Especially, if Shannon was so determined to be so bloody blatant. *What else did I expect?*

A sea of faces met them and his panicking mind took a while to register that everyone was there – except Nell and Rav.

So they must be together. And, apparently, too busy for dinner. At least he hadn't had to make up an excuse about why he'd arrived with Shannon . . .

Not that I'd need to. I'm not going to feel guilty . . . I don't have anything to feel guilty for.

Sighing, James made a pretence of wanting some of the hearty chicken stew on the sideboard, along with a couple of rolls, still hot from the oven. But his churning stomach made eating impossible. As he sat down, Shannon slid into the seat beside him, a wicked smile on her lips.

Across the table, Crispin shot them both a quizzical look, which immediately became knowing.

'Looks like you've been working up a sweat, Crispin,' Shannon teased.

He ran his hand through his damp hair. 'Been swimming. Just needed something to do – something . . . *active.*'

'Yes, I know what you mean.' Shannon's wicked smile curved again, making Crispin shake his head and raise an eyebrow at James.

He stirred his stew, head down.

'I can't muster the energy.' Deborah missed the subtext. 'But I have just had the longest bath in history.' Her face, scrubbed of make-up, still wore anguish, her eyes red and raw.

Percy looked soaked, too. Her hair dripped down her back. She cast her glower between her family, who didn't seem to be talking to her, and the door. *Is she watching for Nell?*

Percy had certainly riled up her family with the surprise inheritance. Greta and Douggie attacked their food, shooting occasional unsubtle glares at their daughter, while Angus Black was living up to his name: his face like thunder as he stirred his soup and crumbled his bread. Opposite him, Theo – looking dishevelled in a rumpled, damp shirt – seemed agitated. Twitching in his seat, he reached for his cigarettes. Finding the pack empty, Theo crushed it and threw it on the table. He was just rising from his seat, when Mrs Faulkner ran in, looking upset.

'I'm sorry to interrupt, but they insisted . . .' she said, breathlessly, gesturing to Ashley and Ed, who stood behind her.

'What's happened?' James's senses prickled, icy fear gripping him as he got to his feet.

Ashley didn't answer him directly. 'Sorry to call in during dinner.' Her gaze swept the assembled group, before locking eyes with James. 'Even sorrier to bring you bad news.'

As Ashley's eyes dropped, so did James's stomach.

No, no, no. Not Nell.

'There's been an accident,' Ashley said carefully. 'Nell was out running, and she fell into the Nye River and got swept up in the fierce current. She's sustained a serious head injury.'

James gripped the back of the chair as sickness rolled over him. He had to summon his focus. The way Ed was studying everyone's face, there was more to this. *Had . . . had someone tried to hurt Nell?* He scanned the room, too, looking for any signs. But everyone looked genuinely horrified. Even Percy. Hell, even *Shannon*.

Had it happened while he'd been . . . with Shannon?

His mouth was dry when he tried to ask, 'Is she . . . going to be OK?'

Ashley bit her lip. 'She's been badly hurt. Doctors are assessing her injuries. We don't know much at this stage.'

Greta stood up. 'I'll go over at once. Have you informed Imelda and Hugo?'

'They've been told. They're on their way to the hospital. But Nell can't have any visitors.' Her gaze met James's with an apologetic grimace.

'Nonsense. Nell's like a sister to Percy. I don't need to interfere with anything, but I'm certainly going,' Greta insisted.

'Nell's in the best hands. Doctors aren't letting anyone see her at the moment. She's in the Intensive Care unit. Right now, we don't know if this was just an accident, or something else. So the most helpful thing any of you can do is to tell us your whereabouts this afternoon.'

'Dear God!' Greta's hand flew to her mouth. 'You don't think anyone . . .'

'We don't know,' Ashley said. 'But we are obliged to ask, so we'll want to take statements from each of you.'

Friction crackled around the room. Nervous sidelong glances flickered like arrows.

'Where is Nell?' James asked. 'Which hospital?'

'Nye ward, Pendlebury Hospital,' said Ashley. 'We'll take statements in the . . .' Ashley turned to Mrs Faulkner, 'morning room, was it?'

'Yes, through here.' Mrs Faulkner gestured.

'Thanks.' Ashley nodded at James. 'Come through when you're ready.'

He practically vaulted over the table to follow, falling into step with Ashley and Ed, who'd loitered outside the door, expecting him.

'I'm so sorry, James.' Ashley squeezed his arm. 'We should have told you separately—'

'This was a deliberate attack?' he whispered.

Ashley nodded once. 'The attacker was seen from a distance, but unidentifiable.'

Jesus. 'I'll get going to the hospital.'

'You can't, mate,' Ed muttered. 'Hospital's orders. Strictly no visitors.'

Ashley steered him into the morning room. 'She's in ICU. No one can see her right now. Her parents are on the way, so she will have family there soon. But the best way you can help her is to help us work out who did this. Because until we catch them, she won't be safe.'

Around him, the morning room swayed. He sank into a chair, nausea and guilt burning.

His assessing brain took over. *Why? Why would someone hurt Nell?* Or, worse, want her out of the way. *What did she know?* Another tsunami of guilt. *Was it from when she'd found Linda?* She'd have been so close on the killer's heels. Maybe they thought Nell had seen them, or couldn't risk her remembering something. *And if I'd been guarding the hall, like I was supposed to, none of that would have happened.*

He leaned forward, holding his head in his hands.

Ed shuffled his feet, then took a folder out of his rucksack. 'Here. These are all the case files so far. Not all the reports are in yet, but it's a start.' He pushed them across the table to James.

Ashley looked like she was about to protest at the breach of protocol, but Ed cut in. 'Have a heart, lass. He can't access anything, can he? In his shoes, wouldn't you want the same?' He gave a terse shrug. 'To my mind, the more brains we have on this, the sooner we can solve it.'

James didn't want Ed to risk a disciplinary on his behalf. But he couldn't give up the chance to read all the precious information. He pulled the folder towards him, kept his hand on it. 'Thanks.' He took a breath. 'How are we getting updates about Nell? Should I contact her folks?' He stood up. 'I should really go. I hate the thought of her being alone.'

'She isn't,' Ashley said. 'She'll have a guard soon, and Rav's there—'

'Rav?' James looked up. 'How come?'

'He got her out of the river. God knows how. And he's being treated for his own injuries.'

'So he's a witness?' *And a bloody hero, now, on top of everything else.*

'Yes, but he couldn't make out who it was. But it's good to see you thinking like a detective, considering how you must be feeling.' Ashley's face softened with a smile. She sighed, then lowered her voice. 'Look, I'm sorry I've given you a hard time lately. If I have to come second to anyone, at least it's someone who's, well . . . pretty OK by me. You don't need us at odds while you're worried about Nell.'

'Thanks, Ash.' *Great. Now I'm even more of a fraud.*

'So . . . observed anything helpful here this afternoon?'

'Nothing I can think of . . .' His stomach roiled again and he stared out of the morning room's window, watching the rain thrash the glass. 'But it's been raining solidly for a few hours, so whoever attacked Nell was out in this. Check for muddy shoes. There are some in the boot room, but check guest rooms, too. And get to the bridge, where it happened, in case there are any boot prints. The ground is soft, so you should get something. And check Deborah, Crispin, Theo and Percy especially . . .'

Ashley was making notes in her phone when Shannon glided up to the two of them, and draped a hand over James's arm.

'Given your colleagues our alibi, James?'

As he flushed with embarrassment, Ashley arched an eyebrow and asked, 'Which is?'

James fumbled. 'Just—'

'Let's just say we were *otherwise engaged*,' Shannon cut in. 'Since about five o'clock this afternoon . . .'

Oh, perfect.

'Oh?' As James hid another wince, Ashley turned to him, her bewilderment turning to shocked understanding. 'Right.' She tilted her head, her disappointment in him obvious. 'That tells me everything I need to know.'

Across the room, Ed gave a low, long whistle and continued tapping slowly on the iPad.

Before James could make any excuses, the door burst open and Percy burst in, distress and panic all over her face.

'Is Nell OK?' she said, her face ghost-white. 'Please tell me she hasn't—'

'I'm sorry, I can't answer anything at the moment,' said Ashley. 'Can you tell us anything that will help?'

Percy nodded, gulping. 'Yes, I can,' she said. 'I can tell you that it's all my fault.'

Chapter 27

Sunday 14th March – 6.30 p.m.

'OK, Rav, you're off to Nye ward.' Nurse Harris placed a blanket over Rav's lap. 'Keep yourself warm, and your foot rested and elevated for as long as you can. When you need the ice pack renewed, ask a nurse.'

Rav nodded, trying to smile. 'Thank you.'

She placed a bulky cast boot on top of the blanket and handed him a bottle of water. 'Keep your fluids up and take the anti-inflammatories every four hours. Try to rest, because you need to heal. Don't put any weight on that foot; use the wheelchair while you're here and crutches when you go home. I'll get someone to check you if you're still here tomorrow.' She paused, then added, 'If you do go home, get a GP to check the stitches in a week, and try not to get them wet while they're healing. Easier said than done, I know. And if the swelling on your ankle doesn't subside in a few days, get it checked. Is that all clear?'

'Uh, yes, thanks.' Rav hid his frustration. Of all the times to be incapacitated, it had to be now.

'Right.' Nurse Harris nodded at the porter, who wheeled Rav away as she moved into the next bay. 'Right, Mr Allinson. What *have* you been doing with the Hoover?'

Rav could practically taste disinfectant as he was steered down more sterile corridors, until he reached Nye ward. The duty nurse gestured to a side room. She joined him in there, closing the curtains across the small window.

'Dr Aravindan Kashyap, yes?' At his nod, she said, 'You can wait in here until Nell can come up to the ward.'

'How long will that be?' As the porter parked him beside the bed, Rav let him take the cast boot and balance it on the small lockable cabinet serving as a bedside table. Then he leaned the crutches against the wall, between the sink and two plastic chairs.

'Anyone's guess. She's still in Intensive Care. I'll let you know when we have any news.'

Rav had no idea if that was usual or a terrible sign. As the nurse and porter left, he felt desperately alone.

He tried to work out how long he'd taken to be treated. It must have been an hour, easily. He checked his phone. As the screen unlocked, his heart sank. He habitually kept his phone on silent, so he'd missed two calls and three texts from Nell's father, Hugo. *He must be frantic.* All Rav had been able to say in the voicemail he'd left was that Nell had been in an accident, was unconscious with a head injury and was being rushed to Pendlebury Hospital. He'd left the message at 5.35 p.m. – nearly an hour ago.

Hugo, 17.36: *'Just landed at the airport, taxi booked. Will be there soon.'*

Thank God Nell had called them earlier, and they'd insisted on returning, Rav thought. Otherwise it would have taken them hours to get here, and God knows what . . . He stopped himself from catastrophising. He had to try to be positive.

Hugo, 17.38: *'How is she? ETA 1 hour 15.'*

Hugo, 17.40: *'How is she?'*

Then the phone rang in his hand. Hugo's number, but the voice was female.

'Rav? How is she?' Imelda's voice was tense.

Rav felt sick at having to say the words aloud. 'I don't know. She's . . . she's in Intensive Care.'

He heard Imelda's sharp intake of breath.

'I'm in the room she'll be brought to, on Nye ward.'

'OK.' Nell's mother's voice was crisp. 'We'll be there soon. I'll phone the house and ask someone to deliver some overnight bags—'

'*Please*,' Rav interrupted. 'I need to talk to you both before you speak with anyone else about what's happened.'

'Why? What's happened?' Imelda's tone grew wary.

'It's . . . complicated. Can I explain when I see you?'

'I'd really rather you told me now, please.' It wasn't a suggestion – it was an order.

Rav drew a deep breath. 'Nell fell into the river.'

'Yes, I know—'

'Well, she didn't fall. She was pushed.'

His news was met with silence.

Finally, Imelda asked, 'By whom?'

'I don't know.'

'Right.' There was a short pause, presumably Imelda steeling herself. 'We'll see you soon.'

Imelda rang off and, in the silence of the room, Rav distracted himself with useful thoughts. He turned his mind to the people in the main house who might fit the silhouette of the person who'd pushed Nell, narrowing down body type and trying to think of motives. And it seemed he wasn't the only one looking for some answers: a sharp knock was followed by the door opening, and Val's inquiring gaze scrutinised him.

'How are you, Rav?' she asked, appraising him.

'Been better.'

'We're putting a police guard on duty with Nell.' Over her shoulder, through the doorway, he glimpsed a uniformed officer speaking to a nurse, then walking towards the ICU. 'In the meantime, do you feel up to giving me a statement?'

Rav nodded. The account poured out of him as he tried to recall every detail about Nell's attacker, so he could give the detectives the best chance to catch them.

Once Rav had signed his statement, Val asked, 'So, what's happened to James? Lovers' tiff? Or something more serious?' She held Rav's gaze until he squirmed.

'He and Nell argued earlier today. Right after Nell and I had a . . .' he swallowed, 'disagreement.' *Oh God. That seems so petty now. Will I have a chance to make up with her?*

'Ah.' Val tilted her head. 'So have they broken up?'

Rav shrugged. 'I don't know. When I heard them arguing, I was already halfway down the hall. James thought something was going on. With Nell and me.' He shifted, but the transfer of weight made him wince.

'And was there?' Val arched an eyebrow. 'After all, the nurses tell me you're her partner.'

'If I didn't say that, they wouldn't tell me anything, would they? They'd have made me leave. And what if the person who pushed her into the river tries to hurt her again?'

Val's nod was grim. Her professional agreement made Rav's stomach lurch. 'Keep your wits about you, Rav, because that's a very real danger.'

Sunday 14th March – 6.30 p.m.

'We had the most awful row.' Percy sobbed, guilt pouring out of her. 'So, of course, she would have been too upset to see where she was going.'

'I'm sure it's not your fault,' James said.

'You don't know what I said, James.' Her lips tugged downwards.

'Tell me, then. What were you arguing about?' James was eaten up by his own guilt. *What if our cross words had sent her off into an argument by proxy?*

But Percy shook her head, biting her lip.

'Percy, trust me, I may need to know.'

'Not this. It won't make any difference. It's private.' The chin jut told him nothing would be forthcoming. Frustration piled on top of the lack of information from the hospital, the general hopelessness, the crushing guilt.

He couldn't bear having to sit in the morning room and listen to where everyone had been that afternoon. His eyes kept straying to the clock, ticking achingly slowly on the desk. *Seconds surely had to grind by faster than this.* Ashley kicked him under the desk. He knew he wasn't paying attention to Ed, recapping what they already knew. And, as much as Ashley might want him to help, *he* needed to know how Nell was.

He stood, his chair skidding out behind him. 'I think I'll just call the hospital.' Relief at saying it out loud – having a reason to move, *do* something – rolled off him and he sagged against the doorway, looking up the number. Percy watched him, with an expression of hesitant hope. His phone rang in his hand.

'James? I've got some results for you.' It took him a second to recognise the voice.

'Er . . . er, Doc. Hi.'

'I hope my call will win some brownie points because I've moved heaven and earth to fast-track your forensic results. First, no fingerprints on the hilt of the dagger or on the curio cabinet. Smudges yes, so they were both—'

'Wiped clean, in a hurry.'

'Right. Next, Linda died from her wounds, as expected. Toxicology results showed nothing unusual; she obviously took care of her health – nothing wrong with her apart from a bit of heavy drinking. Same for Hawke.'

'Right, so why the call . . .' James itched to ring off and call the hospital.

'Because I've got three headlines for you. Number one: we've got samples of Deborah's DNA mixed with Hawke's.'

Dr Saunders was silent, as though holding her breath, hoping for a cheer.

James heard his impatience in his reply. 'Yeah, she slipped in his blood and cut herself on broken glass.'

'Or she was covering up the fact that she knew there would be a mix of their DNA.'

'Oh, telling me how to do my job, Doc?'

'No, James. If I was doing that, I'd point out that you were supposed to be preserving the crime scene, not letting people bleed all over it.'

'Right. Good. Thanks. What's the second headline?'

'A bloody fingerprint in the library. Deborah's. Again.'

'Yes, she ran in when Nell found her. But that's interesting, thanks.' *Was it a coincidence that Deborah had contaminated both scenes? With apparently very good reasons?* 'What's the third?'

'That the toxicology tests showed high levels of cocaethylene in Cameron's blood.'

'Meaning?'

'Meaning he'd drunk alcohol, and taken cocaine.'

'What?'

'The drinking looks habitual, judging by the state of his liver. But not the cocaine. No irritation of the oral or nasal cavities, nor any signs of infection in either to suggest previous use. And if we were going to explore all possible methods, just to be sure, there were no track marks and, while his lungs weren't in great shape, that's more likely to be from a pulmonary infection than use of a crack pipe.'

'So what exactly are we saying here?' James struggled to concentrate on the unlikely conversation about Cameron's drug habits.

'Well, given that he wasn't a user, I can't imagine he'd pick his granddaughter's wedding to try some coke. So I ran some tests. And I found traces of the same type of cocaine, cut with the same adulterants – a nice blend of procaine, that's the numbing agent, with laxatives and detergent—'

'Where?'

'In the dregs of his whisky. And you can imagine what that would do to his heart.'

James exhaled. 'So you're saying—'

'Exactly. Cameron MacKenzie was murdered.'

Chapter 28

Sunday 14th March – 6.45 p.m.

Through the open doorway, Rav heard, and then saw, Imelda sweeping in like a charging lioness. 'Where is she?'

The duty nurse ushered her into Nell's room, where Imelda gave Rav a curt nod.

'Still in ICU. She'll be there for a while,' the nurse said.

'Right, where's that?' Imelda moved towards the door.

'You can't see her, I'm afraid. No visitors.'

'I'm her mother.'

'You're welcome to wait here, and I'll give you any update I can.'

Imelda wasn't the kind of woman who was refused things very often, and she looked suitably unimpressed. 'So what update is there?' She folded her arms.

'Nothing for the moment, I'm afraid.'

Rav winced, imagining Imelda making her feelings on that helpful remark known. But Imelda took a deep breath. 'Well, is that usual? Or is she unresponsive?'

Rav marvelled at her grit. In one second she'd asked what he hadn't been able to this whole time.

'Head injuries are so varied, it's not possible to say. I'd suggest you get used to the idea that she'll be there overnight. I promise, if I have any updates, I'll tell you straightaway.'

Hugo sidled in, nodded at Rav, then studied Imelda and the nurse, as if ready to throw himself in harm's way. Their grim expressions were incongruous with their holiday attire: Hugo in a pale-blue suit, with a white fedora hiding slightly receding steel-grey hair; Imelda in a sea-green linen dress, with a golden tan and highlights in her platinum jaw-length waves. But the tension in their faces had deepened their lines and they looked like they'd aged a hundred years on the dash from airport to hospital.

As the nurse left, Imelda's brittle, restless gaze swung around the room. 'Rav, tell us exactly what happened.'

He tried to describe everything in enough detail to satisfy them, but not so much it upset them. Yet, recalling that shove, and Nell falling, revived his panic. He pressed his palms on the blanket across his lap and took a steadying breath.

Seeming to notice, Hugo placed a gentle hand on Rav's uninjured shoulder. 'That river's been in flood after such a wet winter. That was seriously dangerous.' He sat down opposite him, his kind grey eyes full of concern.

Rav, consumed with guilt, apologised for carrying Nell down the path. 'I know it wasn't the wisest move. I was scared about keeping her neck in line. But otherwise the medics would have had to climb the hill, and every second counted.'

'You managed that? With those injuries?' Imelda asked, her eyes wide. 'Oh, Rav.' She looked away again, clamping her lips together. Rav noticed the gesture, identical to Nell's when she composed herself. Imelda was an undiluted, more formidable version of Nell.

If Nell recovers . . .

But before he could spiral into worry again, Imelda swept him along. 'Right. Come on. You look like you need something more comfortable to wear, and something to eat.'

Outside the room, Rav saw Conor Kennedy, Imelda's close protection officer, talking to the police guard. Seeing Rav struggle to wheel and steer, Conor said, 'Good to see you, buddy. Can I help there?'

Rav self-consciously sensed Conor's professional assessment of his elevated boot, the dressings along the length of his arm, the ice pack strapped to his shoulder sticking out above the neckline of the hospital gown. But he nodded, grateful not to have to push with his injured shoulder.

Moments later, Rav was in the accessible bathroom, easing his aching body into oversized pyjamas bought at the hospital shop. The top billowed around his patched-up torso as he rolled the long sleeves up to his wrists. When he joined the family in the cafe, Conor moved a chair so he could wheel Rav up to the table, and Hugo passed him a huge mug of tea and a chicken sandwich.

'Who could have pushed her?' Imelda shook her head in disbelief. 'And what the hell is going on? I mean, two murders and now this.'

'*Three* murders, potentially,' Rav said. At Imelda's shocked stare, he clarified, 'Cameron.'

'Oh. But he was . . . Wasn't it natural causes?'

'Possibly. But the police are treating it as suspicious.'

'Good grief. In our home. How is everyone?' Imelda's face furrowed with concern.

'As you'd expect, really. Wary. Worried.'

'So why on earth would someone push Nell?'

'I don't know. I've been wondering that. Who and why. She didn't have anything covering her head or face, so even with the rain, she couldn't have been mistaken for anyone else.' He shuddered. 'So it *has* to be linked to Hawke's death. Surely?'

Hugo nodded, as Imelda sipped her tea, grimly composed. Conor listened, scanning the room.

'Nell and I *had* been wondering who could have killed Hawke,' Rav admitted. 'And then Linda. And then how Cameron died. Someone could have overheard us debating it. And if they thought we'd guessed anything, or were close to working it out . . .' He winced. 'You know what she's like. She was desperate to help Percy and her folks. She wanted to work it out. And she's not the type to let things go . . .' He trailed off, shooting a wary glance at Conor, remembering the last time he and Nell – and Conor – had interfered in a murder enquiry. Conor returned the look with a level one of his own.

'Marvellous. You've just listed a plethora of reasons why the murderer would want to silence my daughter.' Imelda looked livid. 'And you and Nell, with your PhDs, are supposed to be intelligent.'

Conor leaned forward. 'Does that put yourself in danger, too, then?'

'Well . . .' Rav shrugged. 'Potentially.'

'Perfect,' Conor deadpanned. 'So all you have to do is just watch out for everyone, all the time.'

'Well, I've narrowed down who could have attacked Nell,' Rav said, trying to regain some credit. 'Whoever it was, they wore a dark overcoat, hood up, but they were slim, fast-moving. So, that counts out Greta, Douggie and Angus. It *could* have been Shannon, Crispin, Deborah, Theo . . . or Percy.'

'We can discount Percy,' Imelda said dismissively. 'And who knew Nell would run along that particular path? They'd have to have been in position before she got there, surely? Who had that chance?'

'I've been wondering that. And the answer is: all of them.' Rav looked at Imelda. 'Do you know much about any of them?'

'I haven't met Crispin or Deborah,' Imelda said.

'Well, Crispin was downstairs with Mrs Faulkner when Hawke fell, so we haven't said much about him. But Deborah argued with Linda over Hawke. Linda thought Deborah was glad he was dead. And Deborah's been researching Hawke's casinos, despite saying she has no interest in them.' Rav shot a look at Imelda. 'Then there's Theo. He's . . . very . . . *close* to the family.'

Imelda folded her arms defensively. 'Greta and Theo have been close friends since they met at university.'

Rav conceded, 'OK, so that leaves Shannon. Who was having an affair with Hawke.'

Imelda stared at Rav, open-mouthed for a second. 'Good grief. He was a real piece of . . . *work*, wasn't he?'

Hugo nodded at Imelda. 'No wonder Douggie and Greta were against their marriage.'

'Hawke looked at Percy and saw his fortune, didn't he?' Imelda said. 'But he didn't *value* her at all.'

Hugo took Imelda's hand as they sat in sad, contemplative silence. Rav gazed at his lap, trying not to show how intrigued he was to learn how Nell's parents appraised potential partners. He took a deep breath and continued, 'To be honest, I could see Percy shoving Hawke in anger, and it turning into a horrible accident. But the person who attacked Linda, or who did in Cameron, and then pushed Nell . . . Those *couldn't* be arguments gone wrong.'

'Which means it can't be Percy.' Imelda was steadfast. 'She's feisty, yes. But there's no malice in her. Premeditating something isn't her style. *Shannon*, on the other hand . . . *Well* . . .' Imelda shrugged.

Rav sat back, thinking. 'Why does Shannon describe herself as the poor relation?' he asked.

Imelda eyed Hugo, then said, 'It's an old wound, Rav, and quite a . . . confidence.' She sighed. 'Douggie married Greta around the same time that Shannon's mother, Gavina, married John. He was a socialist academic and Gavina admired his ideals. She renounced her title, causing quite a stir at the time. But while she was independent enough for that, she wasn't *quite* independent enough to forego the financial cushion. Gavina managed to persuade her mother to let her have the ancillary properties – things she might have inherited – early. So she was bequeathed the houses in Kensington and Oxford, a Thames-side penthouse that Shannon now lives in, plus a lump sum for investments, which Gavina and John used to start a restaurant business. What Shannon *doesn't* know – and doesn't *need* to know – is that rents on those properties were propping up Glencoille's running costs. Handing them over to Gavina nearly bankrupted the estate. And Granda Cameron disagreed heartily with the whole thing. His wife was the peacekeeper, and ever since she died, his relationship with Gavina has soured beyond repair.'

Imelda glanced at Hugo again. '*We* only know about the issues with the estate because Greta and Douggie confided in us and asked for ideas to build up a business which could sustain it. We'd been through a similar situation for Finchmere. To their credit, they've been very successful. But it was a bumpy road.'

'Just in time to be walloped with inheritance tax again,' Rav said.

Imelda frowned. 'Yes, of course. And it's awful to lose a parent. But Douggie and Greta made a lot of sacrifices for Cameron's ideas of duty. There will be a few changes, now they have the reins.'

'They don't, though. Percy's inherited everything.'

'*What?*' Imelda looked horrified. 'Oh, God. Did any of them know? In advance?'

'Only Percy, apparently. Douggie and Greta are . . . well, devastated.'

'I'm not surprised, given everything they've gone through.' She shook her head. Hugo laid his hand on hers. 'It'll make things worse for the cousins, too. Without knowing what happened behind the scenes, Shannon's jealous of Percy and feels short-changed. *That's* why she calls herself the poor relation. That jealousy will skyrocket now.'

'Jeez.' Rav couldn't hold back the reaction. 'She lives in a London penthouse and she feels short-changed? She needs a reality check!'

Imelda's look told him she didn't disagree. 'We've watched resentment eat into everything, as the cousins have grown up. Everything Percy's ever had, Shannon feels is hers by rights. From toys, to houses, to income, friends, boyfriends . . .' She paused. 'And now husbands.'

'Losing her father made things worse, I think.' Hugo shook his head. 'Poor John.'

Imelda exhaled. 'Yes, of course. John . . . He killed himself. Once Gavina took what she felt she was due from her own family, he had a hard time matching that up with his own ideology. When they invested the money, they made some bad choices, had some poor advice. They lost hundreds of thousands. Of course, that caused arguments, tension. And fear, I suppose. He insisted he could make a good fist of things. Yet he just kept losing money. He hid how he was feeling. But he believed he was letting his family down . . .' Imelda raised her palms. 'He wasn't, of course. Gavina would have done anything to work through it. But, by then, it was too late.'

'Bloody hell.' Rav couldn't imagine being driven to such desperation.

'Deep down,' Hugo murmured, 'I don't think Shannon really thinks Percy's family owes her a title and a castle. I think Shannon believes they owe her a father.'

Rav stared at the table. You could look at these families and assume they had everything. He'd never have guessed Shannon had a tragedy like this behind her.

After a pause, he asked, 'If Percy and Shannon had such a difficult relationship, why would Percy invite her to her wedding?'

'Most families have a difficult relation, don't they? Can't ignore them. And usually Gavina, or a plus one, are with Shannon, which, you know . . . tends to dilute the effect a bit.'

'So why not on this occasion?' Rav frowned. 'Didn't Percy invite Gavina?'

'She did, but Gavina couldn't make it. Last-minute business crisis, or something.' Imelda pursed her lips. 'As I said, Shannon's always had a difficult relationship with Percy and, by extension, Nell. And she *does* have a conniving side to her. But still, it's hard to believe she'd be capable of *killing* anyone.'

'Even if Shannon thought that Nell had made life very difficult for her?' Rav asked warily. 'She would have heard Nell tell Percy about her affair with Hawke.'

'Well, if he'd treated my daughter like that . . .' Hugo spoke through clenched teeth. 'Or, if *I'd* known he'd treated Percy like that, *I'd* have shoved him down those stairs myself.'

'That's the problem, isn't it?' Imelda sighed. 'That's exactly how Douggie and Greta felt. And probably Angus, too.'

'Same goes for Linda's murder.' Rav grimaced. 'Greta's arguments with her put the family in the frame there, too.'

'Yes, but if any of them pushed Hawke,' Hugo reasoned, 'then someone else pushed Nell for an unrelated reason. And that doesn't make any sense. Even if they were in league with someone fitting the description of whoever pushed Nell, Percy's folks or Angus would never hurt Nell.'

Rav leaned forward, speaking with care. 'What about Theo? Is his friendship with Greta . . . *close* enough that he'd kill Hawke for how he treated Percy?'

Imelda gazed at Rav warily. 'I . . . I couldn't answer that,' she said eventually.

Rav agonised over who had nearly caught them in Hawke's room; or whether Nell had inadvertently said something unguarded when she'd been upset before going on her run. He took a deep breath. 'What about . . . *if* he thought Nell and I . . . suspected . . . *something* about their relationship?'

Imelda's eyes widened.

'Might he be ruthless enough to attack Nell to prevent her . . . poking around in their private . . . *affairs*?'

Her inhale was sharp as she stared at Rav with narrowing eyes. 'Look, Rav, I could see him – and anyone who cares about the family – pushing that . . . *worm* to his death. But not Nell. *Surely*—'

'What about if Hawke had . . . a *reason* to blackmail Theo and

Greta? And if that, and his marriage to Percy, drove Greta to drink again? And . . . if Nell *knew*?' Rav pushed.

Imelda sat back in her seat, lips clamped together.

Seeing that she wasn't going to reply, Conor leaned forward. 'So, where does all this leave us?' he asked quietly.

'If we count out Percy,' Rav summarised, 'it leaves Crispin, Shannon, Deborah or,' he glanced at Imelda, 'Theo. Any of them might have heard us talking and wanted to stop Nell finding out anything else. But it seems only Shannon, and maybe Theo, had reasons to lash out at both Hawke and Nell. Adding in Cameron keeps it within the family – which again points at Shannon, and maybe Theo. But, when you factor in Linda's murder, the only connection seems to be business, which suggests Deborah . . . and, um, Theo. Again.'

Imelda clenched her jaw, her chest heaving. 'Well, whoever did it – whoever hurt Nell, old friends or not – they'd better look out.'

Chapter 29

Sunday 14th March – 7 p.m.

If he heard 'Greensleeves' piped on a tin whistle one more time, James vowed he'd throw the phone at the wall, update or no update. A pause – he held his breath – was someone about to answer? The tune began again and he barely bit back a growl.

A click. 'Hello?' *Finally!* Although the huff of breath warned him that this person was tired, overworked, and had more pressing things to do than answer phones.

'Hello, I'm enquiring about a patient. Nell Ward. She's in a guarded room. I'm her . . . um . . . partner. James Clark.' *Am I?* He'd try anything to get news about her.

'Partner?'

'Yes.' James grimaced. But answering 'no' would have ended the call.

'Under observation, given the severe head injury and risk of secondary drowning.'

It sounded even worse in her matter-of-fact tone.

'But she has come round. She's been very sick; she's light-averse, so we have a few things to watch.'

'When can I see her?'

'Not at the moment. But her parents are in the hospital, waiting to see her. As is, ahem, her *other* partner.'

What the . . . ? James shook his head. *I knew it . . .*

'Can I pass on a message?'

'No.' His voice cracked. He swallowed. 'No message.'

Monday 15th March – 6 a.m.

'Nell has a severe concussion,' Dr Brogan told Rav and Nell's parents in Nell's still-empty hospital room. 'The scans show that she has a badly bruised occiput, but no sign of fracture. Which is seriously lucky. But she's still at risk of secondary drowning over the next thirty hours. We're monitoring her, so ICU is the best place for her. And we can't afford to tax her with visitors. She's had a severe trauma.'

Imelda's face blanched, her cheeks trembling. When she nodded, Hugo squeezed her hand and asked, 'How long before she'll be out of Intensive Care and we can see her?'

'If all goes OK, perhaps this afternoon. But we'll continue to assess her.'

Rav saw Imelda's shoulders stiffen as she gave another curt nod. When Dr Brogan left the room, she crumpled into Hugo's arms. Rav saw that her anguish and frustration were heightened by exhaustion. They'd clearly not slept, despite Hugo insisting they go home last night to try to get some rest.

Imelda had taken some persuading. 'You *have* to be joking,' she'd said. 'The ... the ... *person* who did this is staying under our roof. I can't make a pretence of being nice, knowing someone there tried to kill Nell. And has really hurt her. I'd sooner murder the lot of them with my own bare hands.'

Hugo had nodded. 'And I'd help you in a heartbeat, my love. But we have to keep up appearances, don't we? For Nell. We have to maintain the party line – that she slipped. That way, this *person* won't think Nell, or anyone else, knows what really happened. And they won't be driven to do something else. Our daughter's in enough danger, my love. We're not going to make it worse.'

Imelda had sagged back in the plastic chair. With her argument lanced, fight no longer fuelled her, and she'd looked wrung out.

But Rav had wondered if *he* would let the side down. His mood vacillated between fear and vengeance, and he wasn't sure how well he could hide it. Partly because of that, and because he simply couldn't leave the place where Nell was, he'd refused Hugo's insistence to take him home.

Hugo had kindly pointed out that he needed rest, that his vigil might be more important when Nell was out of ICU. But Rav was rigid in his decision. At 3 a.m., cramped from trying to sleep in the wheelchair and shivering under a thin blanket, he'd felt a bite of regret.

Right now, he felt horrendous. He hadn't washed since falling in the river, and the particular odour of freshwater mixed with his stale adrenaline-spiked sweat made him fuggy-headed and self-conscious. It hadn't seemed to matter while he'd been focused on getting through the night, pinning all his hopes on seeing Nell this morning. But if they were keeping her in Intensive Care . . . He fought back the same desperation that Imelda had battled.

The doctors wouldn't keep her there without good reason. And we wouldn't be prevented from seeing her unless something was wrong. Oh God . . . are the doctors more worried than they're prepared to say?

James hadn't slept. Thoughts whirled on a loop. He couldn't be upset with Nell, not when she'd just nearly died. He couldn't be irritated with Rav, not when he'd just saved her life. Yet he *was*; they'd both lied to his face. But circumstances hadn't only dragged that lie into the open, they'd made it all A-OK, now that Rav had saved her.

He'd had the awkward conversation with Mrs Faulkner, who'd been stoically matter-of-fact, about moving out of Nell's room, and into a spare room. He just didn't feel right being in her space in her family home after . . . everything.

He decided to take a shower to wake himself up, bracing himself for the series of meetings that he knew would be beyond awkward.

He felt sick. Sick at being so weak and giving into temptation with Shannon. He'd been more than a little drunk and she was undeniably gorgeous, but still. It wasn't exactly chivalrous to break up with someone and leap into bed with someone else so quickly. And if he hadn't argued with Nell, been so jealous, then maybe she wouldn't have gone for a run in the rain in the first place. The thought of her in danger, of her being injured so seriously, fighting for her life, lanced pain through him. He hung his head, burning with remorse and shame, then washed his face vigorously, rubbing away the sting of his tears.

As he accelerated as fast as he dared along the winding roads to Pendlebury in the grey morning drizzle, the thoughts still whirled. Yet . . . yet . . . The thought that took all the billowing anger out of his sails bobbed to the surface like a buoy: *Nell isn't in the clear yet. She's still in danger.*

God, please let her be OK. Terror gripped his heart. *How could I have been so stupid? And what the hell does she know that's so dangerous?*

Guilt burned again. It took effort to push it down and engage his detective brain. But he had to. At the hospital, James headed to the ward. Nell's empty room and no police guard alarmed him. For a churningly sick moment, all his worst fears mushroomed inside him, clamouring in his brain. He darted out of the room and asked the duty nurse, 'Where is she? What's happened?'

'She's still in ICU.'

'And the police guard?'

'With her.'

James swallowed. 'And her family?' Well, there was no putting this off.

Rav nursed his third mug of coffee as Imelda and Hugo left the cafe to visit the nearby police station. Wondering if they'd get an update, Rav's thoughts trawled through the conversations he'd had with Nell and details of her attacker's silhouette. He kept coming back to Deborah and Theo.

Pulling his phone from his pocket, he googled McAnstruther Hotels and acquisitions, and then looked up the individual companies. The luxury brand, Chamomilla Spa, had been slaughtered in online reviews in the months before purchase. The manager left and was out of work for about a year before taking a more junior role at a rival establishment. So Hawke would have had to attract staff to a failing establishment. *Why? How could that be lucrative?*

Hospitality Magazine reported: '*McAnstruther Hotels acquires Chamomilla Spa. In a bid to diversify, McAnstruther Hotels, already offering Monaco-style decadence with casinos at some of their luxury hotels, have taken a gamble on Chamomilla Spa. Once a known high-end brand, Chamomilla Spa in recent times would look like a bad bet to most, but Hawke McAnstruther has previously shown that he's not averse to a long shot. Only time will tell if the bet pays off.'*

'Rav?' He jumped at the familiar voice behind him and turned abruptly, whacking his elevated leg against the table and straining his shoulder. A groan escaped him as he winced.

'God, I'm sorry.' James sat at the table. 'Are you OK? You look like you're in a bad way.' Rav saw guilt flit across his face, before a heavy frown set in.

'Nothing compared to how Nell is,' Rav grunted. He felt awkward. James was going to want the low-down on everything. And he could hardly withhold anything.

'How is she?' James asked. 'I've been to her room but she's not out of ICU yet.'

'They're monitoring her.' At James's brittle nod, Rav relented. The guy did care about Nell; he must be worried. He filled James in on the frustratingly little they knew, including what he'd seen at the river.

'Well, that helps narrow things down a bit. We've needed a break like that, Rav.' James swallowed, then said, 'I know you and I have . . . you know. But the fact is, Nell's in danger. And we, well, we all . . .'

Rav let James keep going with his floundering 'we're all on the same team' speech for a minute, before taking pity on him.

'Look, I know what you're saying,' he said. 'I honestly don't know what's going on with you and Nell, but you should know that nothing's happened between us.'

He expected James to look relieved, but instead he rested his forehead against his hands, moaning, 'Oh God.'

He looked so anguished that Rav felt for him. 'Are you sure you've broken up?' He forced himself to ask, even though he didn't want to hear any other answer but '*YES!*'.

James nodded, his face still buried in his palms, mumbling. 'Oh yes, we've broken up. That's for sure.'

For a second, pure elation flooded Rav's heart and he stared at his hands, not trusting his face to hide it. But James wasn't looking at him. He was in his own private misery.

Rav didn't care why James was so certain. Nell was still in

Intensive Care with a serious injury. And if she recovered, she was in danger from a ruthless killer. His stomach churned but his mind sharpened.

'Were you going to say that, with Nell being in danger and us all on the same team, we'd have to . . . what, pool what we know? Work together? No matter how awkward.'

'Something like that.' James still looked tortured.

'For God's sake, James. Whatever personal issue you might be having, this is more important.' Rav pushed his phone across the table, the article still on the screen. When James looked up, he relayed Deborah and Theo's conversation, what he'd overheard between Deborah and Linda, and what he'd found so far.

James read the article as he listened, his frown becoming less furrowed with concern and more with concentration.

'Wouldn't that damage his own business?' Rav asked. 'Even if he was sabotaging the business to drive down the purchase price, the work to repair the reputation would be . . .'

'Well, yeah, costly. But probably not as much as paying the business its rightful value. And if those businesses are absorbed into Hawke's brand, it doesn't matter that their original brand is trashed.'

Rav frowned. 'It must have worked to some degree, because Deborah said he's used that pattern three times. Bad reviews, attrition of key personnel, reduced profits. Yet takeover goes ahead.'

'Looks like his aggressive moves just covered up an inability to manage, and his over-expenditure in decking out the casinos.'

'You'd think that would've killed Linda, wouldn't you?' Rav winced at his choice of words.

'From what you've said, it certainly seemed difficult for Deborah. And you're right, Theo may have investments that might have been affected.'

'That may not be his only motive. There's his affair. With Greta.' He took a deep breath and relayed what they'd seen on Hawke's thumb drive.

'Wow. Blackmail?' James exhaled, nodding. 'That makes some sense of Greta's reaction.'

'Then there's Shannon. Aside from spas, the other two types of businesses he predated were hotels and two Michelin-starred restaurants.' Rav raised his eyebrows pointedly. 'What's Shannon's family's restaurant called? They've had a few false starts, I gather.' He recounted some of the relevant bits of Shannon's background, trying to keep Imelda's confidences. 'What if her affair with Hawke was Shannon's way of getting close to him, after discovering that he had ruined her parents' business?'

But James shook his head. 'It's not her.'

'She was furious with Nell. They argued right before Nell's run.'

'It wasn't her who pushed Nell,' James said again. His voice was so flat, so final, that Rav sat back, staring at him. 'I was . . . with her. At the time.'

'Right, OK.' Rav nodded. 'So we can cross her off the list then.' He stared at James, whose face was etched with anxiety . . . No, *guilt*. Rav felt a prickle of unease as he asked, as casually as he could, 'What were you guys doing?'

'Just . . . having a drink. In the drawing room.' James looked like he was doing everything he could not to writhe around in pain.

'Look, I understand if you feel guilty because you were having a drink with someone who wasn't particularly friendly with Nell, while Nell was being—'

But James's groan cut him off. He was clasping his hands so tightly, his knuckles were white. 'Fine. We slept together. I'm going to tell Nell as soon . . . as soon as . . . I can. And yes, I do feel really bloody guilty.'

'*Seriously?*' Rav was torn between a glimmer of pleasure that James had messed up, and pity for him, when he obviously felt so terrible.

'So, that gives us both an alibi.' James sighed.

'Oh, well, every cloud.' Rav gave a wry shrug. 'Especially as Shannon matches the silhouette of Nell's attacker.' But, as he said the words, concern struck. 'Did you fall asleep at any point, when you were with Shannon?'

'What?' James's head snapped up again.

'Is it possible that Shannon wasn't with you the whole time? That she gave herself an alibi by sleeping with you, but in fact you can't definitely verify her whereabouts, because you were asleep some of the time . . .'

They locked eyes. *Shannon was back in the frame.*

'What a mess.' James's head sank into his hands again.

Chapter 30

Rav had returned to Nell's room after James had left. Wheeling himself along the corridor had made his shoulder scream. He hated feeling weak, and resented the boot on his foot and the broken bones. *Fat lot of good I'll be if the killer tries again.*

Hours dragged. He'd bought a *New Scientist* at the hospital's shop and read it twice, dozed a little bit and trawled his brain for any ideas to investigate. He was dozing when he heard a noise at the door, and bolted upright, tense, fists clenched.

A nurse held the door wide for the trolley bearing Nell. She was asleep.

Rav gasped with relief, his heart leaping. 'Nell?' He pushed himself up in the wheelchair, not caring about the burn in his shoulder, to get a glimpse of her face. *She looked awful.*

Nell's bone-white pallor was mottled with lurid burgundy and purple bruises, and slashed by raw cuts and grazes. Corners of a large dressing on the back of Nell's head stuck out on each side.

But she was alive, and out of ICU.

The nurse helped the porter to transfer Nell onto the bed, then made her comfortable, adjusting IVs, attaching monitors, and checking her nasal tube and ventilating machine. Rhythmic beeps accompanied green lines tracing across the monitor screens, as the nurse hooked Nell's file on the end of her bed.

'How's she doing?' he asked, rolling closer to the bed. His broken foot nudged the mattress and he winced, but tried to ignore the throb of pain. He gazed at Nell, longing for her to open her eyes.

'Still being monitored. But she's stable.'

Stable. Oh, thank God.

He sent a message to Imelda to update her, knowing that she and Hugo would be at the hospital within minutes once she received it. He also texted James, although he resented other people diluting his precious time with Nell.

He stared at her again, held her hand – the one without the cannula – between his. He had to parallel park beside the bed and twist in a way that made his shoulder protest, but he didn't care.

'It's so good to see you,' he whispered, and her eyelids flickered. *Can she hear me?* His heart pounded. 'Everyone's looking forward to seeing you. They've been so worried.' His voice cracked. Her fingers curled round his.

His breath caught as he stared at her hand. He bit back a sob. 'They'll be here soon, now they can see you. So prepare yourself.'

Her eyelids flickered again. 'Mmm?'

'Nell?' He leaned in, willing her eyes to open, willing her to say something, and heard the sound of the door opening behind him. He whipped round to see Nell's mother.

'She's responding,' Rav told her, and sheer relief flooded Imelda's face.

Reluctantly, he reversed away from the bed to make room, letting Imelda take her daughter's hand.

The door opened again, giving him a glimpse of the police guard outside. Dr Brogan walked in, her bright eyes darting around the room, taking in Nell's condition and her company. She checked Nell's chart and studied the monitor. Finally, she swivelled on her heels, her trainers squeaking on the floor, to face Nell's visitors.

'Right, well, Nell is doing well. The CT scan showed she's sustained only a minor injury, with no internal bleeding or swelling.'

'Will she need surgery?' Rav asked. His mouth was dry.

Dr Brogan shook her head. 'No. Under the circumstances, she's been very lucky.'

Imelda reached for Hugo's hand. He gripped it, swallowing.

Clearing his throat, Hugo asked, 'How long will her recovery take?'

'We're optimistic it'll be relatively quick. She's generally in good shape. Fit and healthy, which will help. We'll keep her in for one more day and then, if all seems well, she can go home. We'll update you about her condition, her recovery process, how you can help with her care and what to look out for. In the meantime, if her breathing becomes laboured, you must call the medical staff immediately. The nasal intubation,' she pointed at the ventilating machine, 'supports her breathing. And she's nil by mouth, hence the fluids and medication through the drip. But we can take that out soon.'

'Apart from her breathing, is there anything else we need to watch out for?' Rav asked.

'She'll be nauseous, and have headaches, loss of some motor skills and fatigue. She may be sensitive to light and sound, or experience blurry vision. All these will lessen with time. But if anything worsens, we need to know. Another head injury could potentially be extremely serious. She'd need *immediate* medical attention, however well she may appear.'

Imelda squeezed Hugo's hand again, blinking rapidly.

'Tomorrow, we'll do an MRI to check there are no abnormalities. If not, and if she's improved enough, she can go home. You'll need to keep a close eye on her, but you'll know exactly what to look out for.' She smiled reassuringly. 'More good news,' she nodded at Nell, 'the patient awakes!'

Nell's eyes flickered open. Rav pushed himself up in his seat, aching to see her face.

Imelda bent to kiss her daughter's cheek. 'Oh Nell!' Her voice quavered. Nell turned towards Hugo, squinting against the light. He laid a large hand on Nell's slight shoulder, making her look even more fragile.

Nell suddenly frowned. 'Uhhh . . .'

Groaning with effort, she pushed herself up on an elbow, retching. Imelda grappled for one of the waxed cardboard bags stacked on the bedside table and held it open as Nell heaved. Sweat slicked across Nell's brow and her white face flushed. Imelda wiped Nell's mouth tenderly with a tissue, popped it in the bag, and then folded the top over and placed it in the bin. Falling back against her pillow, Nell looked red-faced and exhausted. 'Mmmff,' she mumbled, then dozed off.

Dr Brogan made a note on Nell's clipboard. 'If she vomits more than three times in one hour, please tell a nurse. If she talks, she'll sound terse – that's to be expected. It's normal after a trauma like this.' She turned to Rav. 'And how are you doing? Are you comfortable?'

Rav nodded.

'Good. If you have any questions at any time, there's always someone around to ask, OK? And good work, Rav. You saved her life.'

Monday 15th March – 3 p.m.

Nell stirred. Her mouth was dry, her head pounded and she felt dizzyingly sick. It seemed like the room or her bed was spinning. The sharp slice of afternoon light made her squint, which caused her head to throb again. She closed her eyes, and the spinning slowed but the throbbing surged.

A noise made her freeze. Her eyes flew open, and she looked around, moving her head. *Owwww.* The dressing on the back of her head rustled like a roll of thunder. A nurse was in the room, murmuring to someone . . . *Rav?*

She forced herself to turn her head, to look at him. *Was that . . . a wheelchair? Jesus. What . . . happened?* The nurse helped him to peel off his pyjama top and Nell blinked blearily, thinking something was wrong with her eyes. His torso was marbled with purple, green and black bruises. The deep gouges, down his side and along his left arm, were crusted with brown blood, stitches zipping the skin together. The scarlet slashes of smaller, sealed cuts zigzagged his body and his shoulder was swollen.

As the nurse re-dressed his stitched lacerations, Rav flinched. She swapped his ice packs and spread some anti-inflammatory gel across his shoulder, helped him to put his top back on, and left quietly.

'What . . .' No sound came out. Nell licked her lips, swallowed. 'What happened?' she croaked.

His shocked gaze swung to her, his astonished wide eyes softening with delight. 'You're awake!'

Manoeuvring quickly, he bashed his foot on the metal bed frame. They both winced. 'God, sorry.' He wheeled back and forth, working hard to turn in the tight space.

'Wheelchair?' Nell found that whispering was easier.

'It's nothing. I've just fractured my foot. How do you feel?'

'Headache.' Nell tried to smile but it was more of a grimace. 'What . . . about . . . you?'

'Oh, just a few scrapes. From getting in the river yesterday.'

Nell frowned. The memory was blotchy, red-black and metallic. 'I . . . don't remember. Tell me.'

Rav swallowed. 'You fell into the river and hit your head. There wasn't time to call anyone. I just had to get in your way as you were swept downstream.' He held up his hands. 'I know you're not supposed to get in rivers, I know it was stupid, but there wasn't time for anything else.'

He tried to smile. 'You should thank your otter. I followed his route into the river. Saved me from dithering about on the bank, wondering how to get in and catch you.'

Fragments of memories streaked through her mind. She fought to hold on to them, but they slipped through, like a torrent, before she could make sense of them. The icy fear of tumbling, falling, being unable to breathe gripped her. Her gasp made her head pound.

'What? Do you need something?' Rav asked.

Nell shook her head and winced as it throbbed. 'That was . . . dangerous.' She gazed at him. 'What if something . . . happened to you?' She bit a trembling lip.

A hazy recollection hit her: something strong and protective, a barrier to the onslaught of the battering current. She remembered her sense of utter helplessness, and utter trust. A sob erupted. 'Thank you.'

'Well, you were unconscious. I thought you were going to die . . .' His voice trailed off and he stared at his lap, then looked up at her. 'I've never been so bloody terrified in my life.' An exhale exploded from him, half-sob, half self-deprecating laugh. He blinked hard. 'Nell, I'm sorr—'

'You don't need . . . to say it.'

Nell reached for him. He grabbed her hand with both of his, gripping it like he'd never let it go.

Monday 15th March – 4 p.m.

At least Rav and her parents weren't here. And Nell was awake. *Thank God.* James had never felt so relieved. He'd hoped to see Nell alone, and felt awkward enough that Percy had insisted on coming with him.

'Nell?' James whispered. She looked so . . . *fragile.* Her face was as white as her starched pillow.

'Nell?' Percy demanded. 'Nell, how are you feeling? Are you OK?'

'Been better.' Nell winced at Percy's volume, but smiled her thanks as her friend put down the overnight bag packed with pyjamas and toiletries.

Percy threw herself at Nell's side, making Nell wince again, but she was crying. 'I'm so sorry. I'm so sorry for everything. If I hadn't rowed with you, you wouldn't have been upset.' She gulped the words through sobs. 'You wouldn't have slipped off the bridge. And . . . and . . .' Percy reached out to hug her best friend, but settled for taking her hand, gripping it with both of hers.

'It's not your fault, Percy,' James said.

Nell squinted at him. 'Not . . . yours either.'

'No.' He glanced at her. 'Even so, I owe you an apology.' He crouched by the bed, afraid of touching it. 'I should have . . . I shouldn't . . .'

'No, I'm sorry.' She winced again. 'You were right.'

About what? Had Rav been lying earlier about nothing having happened between them? He couldn't ask – not while they weren't alone – and his pause gave Percy the chance to barrel in.

'Nell, I owe you an explanation. I've . . . I've been such an idiot.'

A weak smile tugged Nell's mouth. '*Shock*-ing.'

Percy flicked Nell's cannula, making her groan in pain. Percy cringed. 'Oh God, I'm so sorry.'

'Explain.'

Percy took a deep breath. 'I was trying to win a dare . . .'

'Oh, Perce,' Nell croaked.

'Me and some friends went to Hawke's casino. After Ma's gala. We tried our hand at card counting . . .' She grimaced. 'We'd

216

practised in advance. It took ages. Did wonders for my mental arithmetic...'

'Every cloud.' Nell's sarcasm was evident, even through her rasping, dry voice.

'It was only supposed to be a *laugh*. But we ended up winning a fair bit, gathering an audience. Then this burly security chap marches us into Hawke's office. And honestly, I thought we were going to be reported to the police.' She shot a worried glance at James.

'Card counting isn't illegal.' James couldn't care less about it. Not when Nell was speaking. She sounded a bit robotic, like it took time to think of the right word, and she clearly had the mother of all headaches. But she was *speaking*, at least.

'It isn't illegal?' Percy looked aghast. 'Well. Hawke gave us the impression it was... And then he was so *gallant* about it. He said if we didn't repeat it, and if we agreed to him donating our ill-gained winnings to Ma's charity, then he wouldn't make a complaint to the police.'

Percy bit her lip. She looked like she was about to say something, then glanced at James and clamped her lips shut. After a sigh, she said, 'But there was another condition. He asked me to have him and some mates over to stay at Glencoille. As guests.' She twisted her fingers. 'I thought I'd got off lightly. But once he was there, he made a move.'

'Oh, Perce.' Nell blinked at her friend.

'I'd... I'd just had that huge argument with Hamish. I'd been so excited about him coming home. We'd been apart so long and it was so hard to stay in contact. And then he just agreed to stay out there a whole extra *year*! Without even thinking he should talk that over with me! I was *furious*! And then, when I calmed down, I was... *hurt*. I convinced myself he didn't love me, and that I'd made a fool of myself. So when Hawke was all attentive and charming, well, I guess I was... susceptible.'

'Percy, what's wrong with you? You don't just... sleep with someone else because... you're *angry*. Not if you love someone.'

James winced.

Percy sighed. 'I know... And Hawke might even have overheard my argument with Hamish.' She shook herself. 'Either way, he used me.' She looked like she was about to say something else, but stopped and shrugged.

Through his guilt, James recognised Nell's fear in Percy's sad shrug: the need to be valued for herself.

'I convinced myself it was passion that made him so keen to get married. Well, that – and Linda, of course. Poor woman. You'd never have known she had a brain tumour, just weeks to live.'

James frowned and pulled out his phone, checking Linda's report. *No mention of a brain tumour. The doc wouldn't have missed it.*

'I'm sorry to say he was lying about that, Percy. Nothing of the sort was found in Linda's post-mortem.'

Percy stared at him. 'Seriously?'

'Seriously.'

Percy shook her head, dazed. 'But that's why . . . that's why I spoke to Granda.'

'Well, doesn't really matter if you told him Linda was ill, if that's what you really believed. Not now, anyway,' James reasoned.

'No . . . that . . .' Percy sank her head into her hands. 'You know Granda. He wouldn't care about that, would he? He didn't have any empathy for anyone. With Ma and Pa against the marriage, I-I . . . needed him onside. So I told Granda we had to wed, quickly, for the obvious reason for someone of his generation.'

Nell groaned. 'You told him you were pregnant?'

Percy chewed her lip, then nodded.

'You're not . . . are you?'

'Don't be daft.'

'But . . . Wasn't he scandalised by that?' James asked. 'How did you get from that to inheriting everything?'

Nell's eyes were wide when she answered for Percy. 'You said it was a boy.'

Percy gave a short, uncomfortable laugh. 'All Granda wanted was a male heir. He had Da, but he carried on like Da had let him down, having a daughter. You'd never believe Scotland has more enlightened inheritance laws than England, would you? Bloody dinosaur.'

'Don't feel bad about that. You couldn't've used your . . . biology against him if he wasn't such a misogynist.'

Percy shrugged. 'Be fair, Nell. Granda was very equal-opportunities: he had every -ist going.'

Nell gave another weak smile. 'Didn't you see any red flags . . . with Hawke?'

Percy winced. 'Maybe. I guess I ignored them. I was . . . so *unhappy*.' Her lips trembled and she looked at her hands, fingers twisting again.

'Then Hawke stole Hamish's letter?'

'Yes. Hawke was a regular guest at ours. If he was first at breakfast, he'd have seen the post. Not hard to guess who sent a letter with that postmark. I guess his letter would have been delivered in . . . November?' Her words came in gulps again. Nell reached for her hand.

'But Hamish has come here. He obviously wants to see you.'

'Doesn't mean he'll forgive me. How *could* he?' Percy's shoulders shook and a clamped-down sob erupted. 'I've ruined it all.' It was like a dam bursting. 'I've thrown away the love of my life for some . . . *player* who had an affair right under my nose. And now we're all in the frame for . . . well . . .' Her eyes slid towards James. 'Which is . . .' She shook her head, then gestured at Nell. 'And now I've upset *you* so much you nearly *died*!'

'No . . .' Nell shifted in bed, wincing, trying to reach her.

'I should have listened to you. Right from the start. I shouldn't have lied to get you to host the wedding. I should have listened to what people said about him. If I'd done any of that, we wouldn't be in this mess, and you . . . wouldn't be hurt!'

Nell flinched at the volume of Percy's wails.

'Percy, listen to me.' James moved to face her, trying to calm her down before she made Nell even more agitated. 'You aren't to blame for what happened to Nell. She didn't fall. She was pushed.'

Percy choked on a sob.

'*What?*'

It took a second for James to realise that it wasn't Percy who'd spoken. He turned to see Nell, wide-eyed, open-mouthed, frozen with horror. *Oh God. She didn't know?*

Fighting to sit up, Nell grimaced at the exertion, closing her eyes as she tried to prop herself up on one elbow. James hurried to plump up her pillows. She reached for the bell and pressed it.

'What are you doing?' James asked.

'Someone . . . attacked me?' Nell took a breath, as James nodded. 'Bloody . . . *nerve!*' She pressed the bell again. 'I'm not staying here.'

The nurse ran in.

'I need to . . . discharge myself,' Nell croaked. 'Immediately.'

James realised why her parents and Rav hadn't told her yet. His guilt grew by the second, as Nell insisted on her drip being removed, threw aside the pamphlet explaining how serious her condition was and ignored the tuts of Dr Brogan advising against her leaving. 'You still need another scan. We need to ensure you're fit—'

'Can I have it now? Or come back . . . tomorrow?'

Dr Brogan tutted again. 'Now, I suppose. But I really advise against this.'

'Sure. Where . . . do I . . . go?' Nell started to get up, but grabbed the edge of the bed as she woozed. Realising she was on the verge of blacking out, James steadied her. But Nell fought him away and staggered along the bed – although she did grab a waxed bag.

Taking her arm again, James murmured, 'Nell, there's no need for this.'

But apparently there was. Nell battled along the corridor, rigid with indignation, disagreeing with doctors, outraged at being treated like a patient – and forgetting that her hospital gown was backless. James held Nell up with one arm, trying to protect her modesty by keeping her gown as closed as he could with his other hand. But Nell weaved like a drunkard and it was tough enough keeping her upright.

They had to wait until Nell was called through to the MRI suite. He was told to remain outside as she made her way unsteadily through the door. *God, if she goes home now, she'll be a sitting duck.*

But Nell was adamant and, an hour later, he'd told Rav, who was incandescent at James's blunder and what it had meant for Nell. Especially since Dr Brogan had pulled Rav and James aside to issue a warning. 'We've checked her lungs but she's still at risk of secondary drowning, so watch her closely for the next twenty-four hours. If she shows any symptoms – out of breath, coughs, chest pain, lethargy or . . .' she arched an eyebrow, 'moodiness – then you have to bring her back. Immediately. Kicking and screaming, if need be. It can be fatal.'

'I'll look out for her,' Rav had asserted. But as soon as Dr Brogan had gone, he'd turned to James, fuming. 'She's not nearly well enough to be discharged yet. She needs monitoring, probably more tests, and she's groggy and unsteady. So she's even *more* vulnerable to another attack. You're sending her right back into their hands!'

James couldn't even disagree. Rav was right. To make matters worse, Rav had known that Nell would react like this to the news; he'd gauged correctly to wait till she was stronger.

And I didn't.

But now it was too late. They were all in the car. Heading home. To the person who'd tried to kill her.

Chapter 31

Nell pressed her forehead against the cool car window, as James drove her, Percy and Rav home. Her parents were on the phone to Rav. He must have texted them to say she'd discharged herself. Judging by his tense replies, they were giving him a hard time. Grabbing the mobile, Nell reminded them that she didn't need their permission, then stabbed the 'end call' button and handed the phone back. She closed her eyes against the arguing and the oncoming headlights that dazzled.

If only you could hang up on people in real life.

Beside her, Percy was wittering on about the investigation, making Nell's head pound. 'You can't walk through the house without bumping into someone dusting something for prints, photographing walls and balustrade, or taking measurements.' A sigh. 'Now the journos are calling. We've had to notify friends, family and police to use different numbers.' Percy shuddered. 'Then, yesterday evening, Val turned up again to question Theo, Deborah, Shannon and me. It was pretty unpleasant. None of the formal niceties of the first interview. A real interrogation.'

At Nell's lack of response, Percy leaned in. 'Can you imagine the *atmosphere*? Everyone's walking on eggshells. It's awful. And on top of everything, there's Hamish . . .'

'Just . . . go to the hotel. Make up with . . . him.'

Percy looked up sharply and flushed. 'I *want* to see Hamish. But what can I *say*?'

'How about "sorry"?' Nell closed her eyes. She felt Percy shift, as if surprised at the stark answer.

'Hamish is a suspect,' James said firmly.

Nell didn't open her eyes but shrugged anyway, in case he glanced at her through the mirror. Honestly, she just wanted everyone to shut up. She couldn't admit how much her head hurt, how sick and dizzy she felt. They'd all make a big deal of it, and it hardly mattered, not now that she knew she was a target. She'd have to face that head-on. So, as James's Land Rover Discovery pulled up to the floodlit, pillared entrance, she peeled her eyes open and braced herself.

But Nell couldn't march into battle. She could only shuffle slowly. In pyjamas. Every step jarred her head, blackened her vision.

Her mother met her in the hall. 'Let me help you to your room. We can bring a tray up if you want dinner.' She was steered towards the lift with Rav, who was clumsy with his new crutches and groaning occasionally, with effort or pain, or both.

'I'll wash and dress. Then . . . I'll . . . come down.'

'Oh, Nell, really. You need to rest.'

Nell didn't argue, but she did lean against Imelda as they squeezed into the lift beside Rav and his crutches. Her mum hugged her gently, firmly, and Nell bit the insides of her cheeks so she wouldn't cry.

While washing, Nell found a million cuts and grazes. Water and soap stung, and drying was cumbersome with her bruised and aching limbs.

She stared at the sink. Only one toothbrush. And in the bedroom, James's clothes and suitcase had disappeared. *So . . . he's moved rooms.* Now everyone would probably know they'd broken up. Underneath the odd sensation of change and people knowing her personal business, relief settled. At least one tricky thing had been dealt with.

She pulled on a baggy jumper and jeans, and staggered to the door.

Rav was waiting outside, with James. And Imelda. And Hugo.

Though she'd normally be irritated by this overprotectiveness, Nell found herself feeling grateful. She was afraid of being alone, even if she didn't want to admit it.

'Lovely to have you home, darling,' Imelda said. 'You have to let us look after you a bit.' But as she moved close to hug her daughter, her gimlet eyes said, *bloody fool.* Nevertheless, she helped Nell along the hall to the lift.

Everyone else was in the banqueting hall, about to start a roast dinner. A blur of faces turned towards her as she swayed in the doorway.

'Nell? We've been so worried!' Greta exclaimed. She stood, hurried over and drew Nell into a careful hug. Nell let herself be pulled against her, glad that no heavy stench of whisky assaulted her senses, and relieved that Greta was steady, composed, *sober*. But then she felt Greta's hands dig into her arms, her breathing ragged. Greta was scared. *Does she know? How?*

'It's OK, Greta,' Nell whispered. As Greta drew back, she met her eyes, and Nell tried to smile, wincing against the dimmed light of the room. 'It'll be OK.'

Behind her, Nell heard Rav on his crutches. Her father helped him to sit at the table, drawing out a chair and pushing him in close, setting the crutches to one side. Nell sat beside him, looking across at James and Percy.

'Well, laddie.' Angus pointed his fork at Rav. 'Let's hear the courageous tale of how you rescued our Nell.'

Despite the delicious-looking food, Nell's stomach, hollowed out from strong painkillers, churned with nausea. But Rav gave her a gentle smile and recounted the version agreed between him, James, Percy and Nell's parents – omitting that Nell had been pushed. The company looked impressed but concerned at the rescue, not least because of Rav's obvious injuries.

'But how did you end up in the river?' Crispin asked Nell.

'I don't . . . remember.' The shrug jolted her aching body. 'I must've . . . tripped. I hit . . . my head.' She wanted to gauge reactions, work out who pushed her in. But she forced a smile, and tried to make the words casual, unloaded.

'Lucky Rav wasn't far behind you to help,' Deborah said. 'That's an incredible rescue story you have there.'

Nell's tense smile softened. At least she didn't need to fake her feelings about that. As the guests turned back to their food, she squinted around the table. *Who killed Hawke . . . and Linda . . . and Cameron . . . and tried to kill me?* Her stomach dropped and sickness burned again. Rav covered her hand with his. Warm, comforting, steadying.

Shannon noticed the gesture, met Nell's gaze with a sly smile. Irritation flashed through Nell, sending white pain slicing through her head.

Nell's grimace only made Shannon's smile widen, of course. She glanced at James, then tilted her glass at Rav. 'Well, all it took was for you to half-kill yourself to get *Lady* Nell's attention. Now, there's commitment to a cause. *Bravo*.'

While Rav squirmed, trying to cut a roast potato one-handed, James studied his plate, pushing his food around, not seeming to have much of an appetite. When Rav didn't respond, Shannon continued needling, until she got a reaction.

'Better hope you measure up, though, Rav. Because the families talk a good game about marriage, yet *Lady* Percy didn't marry her impoverished doctor, did she? She married a millionaire businessman.'

Losing his fight with the potato, Rav speared it forcefully with his fork, and ate it whole. As he chewed, he met Shannon's narrowed eyes, looking unapologetic at being unable to answer. He took his time, and Shannon's smirk faded. Nell admired his stoic silence.

But Shannon's gaze swung to Nell, then Percy, and became a glower. 'Even then, no one could give Hawke credit for his talents, could they?'

'Talents?' Nell couldn't help herself. Her snorting laugh ricocheted around her tender skull and she gritted her teeth.

'Oh, and there's that, too, Rav. Just to warn you. Nell isn't only an heiress and an ecological saviour, she's also a razor-sharp business guru.'

'Thanks.' Nell reached for a sip of water, reminded of how Hawke had baited her. She rested the cool glass against her forehead. She didn't want Shannon's distractions. She wanted – *needed* – to observe everyone's reactions. To see who had murderous intent.

James was watching Shannon, a strange expression on his face: concern, but possibly, almost sympathy.

Unaware, Shannon continued, 'But your main talent is, of course, your accident of birth.' Her tone was spite-soaked. 'It's all been handed to you on a plate. Neither you nor Percy have any idea what it takes to build up a business from scratch.'

Nell sighed. 'Oh yeah . . . You've got all the experience.'

'I've got more experience than you. Out there, in the real world, I've seen how people struggle. I know what Hawke had to do to build his businesses. The *risks* he had to take and the tough decisions. You've got *no* idea what it takes.'

Deborah put her cutlery down. 'Do you know how Hawke operated? Really? Do you know how he bought companies?'

'Yes, I know he diversified—'

'Do you know how he could afford to acquire them?'

'I know he drove a tough bargain.'

'He drove more than that, honey. He drove companies into the ground. And that ruins lives. And, once he had them, he was incapable of managing them.' Deborah picked up her bourbon. 'I'm sorry, but I'm going to have to take my leave. I can't sit here and listen to this.'

Theo got up with her, flashing a glance at the family. As they always did, Nell's and Percy's parents, along with Angus, were steadfastly ignoring Shannon's outbursts. Crispin was simply staring at his plate. Imelda nodded at Deborah and murmured apologies.

Percy's face reddened as she glared at her cousin.

'You don't have anywhere near the business acumen you think you have, Shannon,' Percy said. 'And you should take a long look at yourself. The way you behave isn't as attractive as you think it is.'

Shannon shrugged, splaying her manicured fingers. 'I don't blame you for being jealous.' She leaned forward. 'And at least when he was in my bed, *I* knew that Hawke was there for *me*, not my *money*.'

Percy snorted. 'But you were there for his. Give it five years, love, and you'll be spending more with your plastic surgeon than you can get out of your . . . your *victims*.' Despite her derisive tone, she glowered, her chest heaving.

With Percy successfully riled, Shannon smirked and turned to Nell. 'Same goes for James.'

James spluttered, mid-swig of water.

Nell's head felt so heavy, fuggy, that Shannon's snide subtext was lost on her. Then Shannon reached out to trace the outline of James's ear. He squirmed away from her touch, glancing at Nell, beetroot-red.

'OK, that's enough, Shannon,' he said.

'What's going on?' Nell rubbed her forehead.

'Oh? He hasn't told you?' Shannon clamped her hand melodramatically over her mouth, while James shot her a daggered look. His breathing grew rapid.

Finally, Nell twigged, and nausea rose in her throat.

'Seriously?' She got unsteadily to her feet, gripping the table to stop the room swaying.

'He got what he needed from you, Nell,' Shannon taunted. 'A tasty promotion. And then he was free to pursue what he really *wanted*.'

'*Shannon!*' James's raised voice made Nell clutch her head.

'Whatever.' She couldn't be bothered with the verbal sparring. The room blotched black. Nell blinked and stared at the tilting door, aiming for it. Her leg wobbled underneath her and Rav grabbed her arm, propping her up awkwardly from his chair.

'Maybe I'll win your hero over, too,' Shannon baited. 'Better watch out there.'

'Oh, give it a rest.' Nell sighed. 'Once you stop predating other people's relationships, you might manage a real one of your own. You're making yourself lonely, Shannon.'

Shannon looked like she'd been slapped. She stalked from the table, to the refectory.

With an apologetic glance at Nell, James rose and followed her.

Grabbing his crutches, Rav headed out towards the great room with Nell. Through her brain fog, she heard him grunting with the effort, until they reached the lift. Inside, she crumpled against him. She felt unable to stand. Only his strong arm around her kept her on her feet.

He couldn't hold her up when he had to limp to her room. She steadied herself with one hand on the wall, then fumbled to unlock her door.

He waited, like he expected her to say goodnight. But she didn't. Instead, she turned, then asked, 'Will you stay with me?'

James hurried through the refectory to the kitchen, following Shannon. A loud *smash* was followed by Shannon swearing, then a sob.

He picked up his pace, dashing in to see a wine bottle broken on the floor, the red stain reeking of sour grapes as it leached across the flagstones. Shannon was crouched amongst the broken glass and spilt wine, blood trickling down her wrist. She looked up at James, her eyes puffy and red.

Scanning for a first-aid kit, he spotted one on the near wall. Opening it, he took out a swab and large plaster. Shannon picked her way across the spillage and held her hand out. He wiped it with the antiseptic swab, then stuck the plaster across the cut.

'Better?'

'Don't be kind. I hate it when people are kind.'

'"Thank you" is more traditional.' James gazed at her sadly. 'And you're welcome.' He paused, then said, 'Those comments you made—'

'Ugh. Leave it. I'm not apologising.'

'No, that's not what I was going to say.'

Her eyes narrowed, full of distrust, like a wounded animal expecting to be hurt again.

'Your remarks about people struggling in business. You were talking about your family?'

Shannon sucked in her cheeks, like she was biting them. Her chest shuddered.

'But they had some successes. A Michelin star, for one thing! That's an incredible achievement, Shannon.'

'Huh!' It sounded like an erupting sob. 'But they were a pair of liberal hippies. They couldn't hang on to it, could they?' Her words, lacking their usual sharpness, sounded anguished.

'Well, they'd hardly be alone in that. It's a tough world. You were right about that. Did . . . did they ever sell off a restaurant? Maybe to recoup losses, if it was failing?'

She bit her lip.

'I mean, you couldn't blame them. If they did?'

Shannon wrapped her arms around herself, the plaster rustling against her dress. *Yes, she clearly did blame them.*

'So, having seen that, you *can't possibly* have admired Hawke's methods?'

'At least he got things *done*. And this isn't only about my folks. Percy makes me *sick*.' Shannon's chin jutted in a gesture so similar to

Percy's, it made James's heart ache for the warring cousins. 'Banging on about how she'll take care of people's livelihoods on the estate. She and Nell would *never* be able to make the tough decisions that *he* did. They've had it all handed to them. They'd never be able to start a business from scratch, like his casinos. And then actually *grow* it.'

'Do you know how Hawke managed it?'

Shannon turned away sharply, her shoulders shaking. 'He said he was speeding up the inevitable, putting a business that was doomed to failure out of its misery.' Her voice cracked.

James held the silence, wondering if she'd drop the façade. Hoping she'd trust him.

Shannon's hand dashed across her face. 'Hawke was an outsider, too. But he knew how to get what he wanted. He was ruthless like that.'

'I see plenty of *ruthless* in my day job, Shannon. It's not something to admire. It tears things down; it doesn't build them up. And it destroys people. Not like starting a business, building it up to achieve the highest recognition possible. Like your folks did. *That's* something to be proud of.'

She rocked back against the kitchen counter, like she was seeing him for the first time. Surprise mixed with a hint of respect, and a heartbreaking glimpse of vulnerability.

He suddenly wanted to hug her, but he turned away, walking towards the hall. *Here he was, having feelings for another prime suspect.* One who might have manipulated him into being her alibi. One who might be better at this game than he was.

Chapter 32

Tuesday 16th March – 5 a.m.

Rav hadn't needed asking twice to stay with Nell. He didn't intend to let her out of his sight. Not only because of Dr Brogan's warning. She'd changed in the bathroom and sunk into bed, propped up on pillows and wincing in pain. He'd armed himself with a poker from the fireplace, then settled on the chaise longue. Unable to change out of his clothes, he'd just spread a thick blanket around him. Every noise had shocked him from his dozing, and made him hold his breath, grip the poker, ready to rush – well, hobble – at an attacker.

At 5 a.m. he couldn't lie still any longer and got up to practise with the crutches. His injured shoulder failed, giving way under his weight and sending him flying forward, tripping over the crutch. Staggering forced weight onto his broken foot and he gasped, sweat from the exertion stinging his eyes. He shot a concerned look at Nell, hoping he hadn't woken her.

Her bandage rustled on the pillow. The bruises on her face had grown darker, smudges of purple-black around her eye sockets.

'Mmm . . .' Nell stirred. She drew the covers over her face against the shadowy grey predawn light filtering through the thick curtains. Then her shocked gasp made Rav jump and stare at her. She pushed herself up, squinting into the dim room. 'Who's . . . there?' Her voice was breathy with panic. Her hand fumbled on the dressing table, grabbed the lamp and held it up, the shade clattering off.

'Me! It's me!' Rav assured her. 'Rav.'

'Oh.' She sagged against the pillows, wincing.

He hobbled over, took the lamp and set it on the table, with its shade. Seeing her grimace, he handed her the bottle of painkillers and a glass of water. Then he took his own medication.

'Look at us. In perfect condition to track down a murderer.' His weak joke was an attempt to conceal the clammy, nauseous fear surging through him: neither he nor Nell was in a fit state to deal with what they had to face.

By 7 a.m., Nell felt a little better. She and Rav had tag-teamed on using the shower, both taking ages to wash their broken bodies and change in the bathroom.

The atmosphere between them was charged. Nell didn't dare start up a conversation about how she felt – but she sensed that Rav was holding something back, too. It crackled between them like sparks. Casual words were loaded; glances, caught and held, were electric. Yet there seemed to be an unspoken understanding to wait until they'd dealt with the very real and looming danger. Until then, Nell knew that Rav wasn't going to leave her side.

She felt less groggy and the pounding headache had subsided, even though her bruises looked more alarming as they grew darker. And her appetite was back.

On the way to breakfast, Percy ran towards them, her eyes bright. 'Can't stop, I'm going out to see—'

'I can guess,' Nell said. 'You *are* forgiven, then?'

Percy blushed. 'I don't deserve him to be so kind after I was so stupid. We're going for a walk and a talk. Then, hopefully, lunch.' Percy grinned. 'I'd invite you, but I don't want you to come!'

It was so good to see Percy back to her old self that Nell couldn't help but grin back. 'Have a lovely time. Say hi from me.'

Downstairs, they passed Nell's parents, with Greta, Angus and Douggie, gathered in the great room, discussing how to deal with increasingly persistent press attention.

James was the only one in the refectory. He was ripping open a large brown envelope, but put it down when Nell and Rav walked in. Mrs Faulkner hurried in with a platter of piping-hot drop scones and two large cafetières.

'These are straight from the oven; no one's been in the area. No danger of . . . *tampering*.' Her smile was wobbly and her hands shook as she placed the tray on the table.

'Thanks, Mrs F.' Nell tried to smile. But the reminder of the risk, and their housekeeper's concern, hit home.

Rav and James seemed to have no problem demolishing the cakes and downing the coffee. She couldn't resist either, and felt better for eating. When Rav left to charm Mrs F into baking a second round, Nell glanced at James.

'So, did you move out to the spare room . . . or into Shannon's?' she asked, sipping coffee, her tone innocent.

Gratifyingly, James's blush extended up to his hairline. 'Ah. To the spare room.'

'Uh-huh.'

Nell took another long sip of coffee, regarding him over her cup. He looked agonised.

'I feel terrible, Nell,' he said. 'I thought you and Rav were . . . So I . . .'

'Right. But you were wrong.'

'Yes. I know that now. I'm sorry.'

'Me too.' They exchanged a small, rueful smile. Then Nell teased, 'The lapse of judgement is one thing. But the *timing* of it, James. How are you ever going to make up for that?'

A short laugh escaped and James sat back, exhaling. 'Why is it you can never bloody win with women!' But the tension in his face had relaxed. The sparkle was back in his eyes at the gentle taunt.

Rav joined them, with Mrs F delivering another round of drop scones.

Looking at James, Rav said, 'Right. I shared everything we know with you, so now it's your turn to share what you know with us.'

James frowned, and his tone became officious. 'My information's from a police investigation, though, Rav. It's your duty to share. It's not mine.'

'Bollocks to duty, James! We're facing very real and present danger, here. Someone tried very hard to kill Nell, and now they know it hasn't worked, they'll try again. We have to solve this before they get a second chance! And three brains are better than one. So?'

Nell sat back at Rav's forceful tone.

James pursed his lips in thought, his gaze turning to Nell. His eyes flicked over her face, rested on the dressing. Then he nodded.

He filled them in about the cocaine in Cameron's whisky.

Nell's heart dropped. 'Oh God. I was . . . just *hoping* . . . that was natural causes.' *That had to be Percy's family. Who else would kill him? And, of all of them, with Percy inheriting the estate, she'd look like the obvious bet.*

'Who handled his drink? Do we know?' Rav asked.

'The bartender. Douggie. And Percy, when she and Hawke took him up. And the fingerprints on the glass bear that out.'

Nell winced at Percy's name. *Please no. She didn't like her Granda. But surely . . .*

Taking a gulp of coffee, James pulled the reports out of the envelope. 'I haven't even had a chance to read these. Ed dropped them off this morning. Apparently, one report from Hesha contains all the statements from your entire guest and staff list. Ed said that no one saw anything incriminating. A few mentioned the family arguments, but nothing that we didn't already know. And he got SOCO to see if they could find a boot print at the bridge. There were a lot of prints, all churned up in the mud. Some partial mud prints on the bridge, but nothing descriptive enough. And it looks like everyone in the house had at least one muddy pair of shoes or boots. But they could get into that state from a quick stroll around the grounds at the moment.'

Rav's tense face fell. 'So nothing to indicate who hurt Nell.' He sighed, clenching his jaw.

'No. But, there's also two reports from Dr Saunders, which Ed said were helpful.' He turned the pages, scanning them. 'Here we go. From Hawke's position on the floor, Dr Saunders assessed that he fell backwards over the balustrading, but without any hard force behind the fall.'

James showed Nell. 'See? They can calculate from the injuries what speed he fell at, and hence if he was pushed with force, or if he fell. So, when he toppled over, he rotated around his centre of mass, landing face down, with his head near the stairs and feet near the front door. That's consistent with falling – or *possibly* being pushed, although without much force.'

'So you don't think he was pushed?' Nell asked. 'You think he *fell*?' Her mind raced. Falling was better than pushing. *Was it an accident, after all*?

James shrugged. 'Based on his injuries – broken bones, fractures, ruptured internal organs – Hawke could have fallen from the second floor, where the guest rooms are, which would mean a falling height of about nine-and-a-half metres. Or, he could have fallen twelve metres, from the third floor that's used for storage.'

'You can't distinguish which floor he fell from, based on his injuries?' Rav asked.

James checked the report. 'No, not between those distances. They're too close. The doc can't narrow it down any further.'

Rav sat back. 'That's a shame.'

'Yes.' James read on and raised his eyebrows. '*But* she found three things that stood out.'

Nell nodded encouragingly. 'Go on.'

'Hawke sustained a contrecoup traumatic brain injury, so, basically, his brain ricocheted inside his skull, causing contusions on the *opposite* side from the point of impact.' He looked at Nell and Rav. 'But the contusions are at the *front* of his brain.'

Nell leaned forward. 'So his injury was to the back of his head?'

Rav frowned. 'But he landed on his front.'

'Exactly,' James said. 'Forensics checked to see if he could have hit his head as he rotated in the fall, maybe on the balustrade or the underside of the stairs. But nothing like that was possible.'

He turned the pages towards Nell, showing computer-generated diagrams of the stairwell, and trajectory calculations of vertical height, horizontal distance travelled, centre of mass of the falling body, launch speed and launch angle. Nell followed the equations with fascination, although she read more slowly than usual.

James reclaimed the pages. 'There's plenty of maths to demonstrate the physics. But, essentially, he couldn't have hit the back of his head when he fell. Plus, SOCO didn't find anything on the staircase or anything else in the hall.'

'What does that mean?' Nell asked. 'Someone whacked him on the back of the head and then let him fall over?'

'No,' James said. 'It looks like he was punched – a right-handed punch, which counts Greta out because we can see the print of her left-handed slap clearly – then fell backwards and hit his head on something hard with force. It might not have killed him immediately, or at all. It could have made him woozy; he could have staggered about and fallen over the balustrade on his own. In which case, someone may not *realise* they killed him. Or, he could have been knocked unconscious and the murderer let him fall backwards, or dropped him, over the balustrade.'

'Did you get anything from the DNA evidence?' Nell asked.

'Only Deborah's DNA was mixed up with Hawke's at the crime scene. She did break her glass there, but that could be a cover. And she has gone to a lot of trouble to investigate Hawke.' James leaned back, folding his arms, gazing into the middle distance.

'Would she really have hurt Linda, though?' Nell asked.

'They argued; she could have wanted to inherit,' James reasoned. 'Wouldn't want her business name sullied, and if Linda wouldn't listen . . . And she was first in the library, after Nell found Linda, when the murderer couldn't have got far. If Deborah was creeping away from the scene, as Nell disturbed the whole house yelling for help, it would have been easiest for Deborah to double back, like she'd just arrived. It conveniently explains her fingerprint in Linda's blood in there.'

Nell sat back. She hadn't been taking stock of departures or arrivals, once she'd seen Linda. 'So if the murderer was right-handed, then they attacked Linda from the front?' Nell drew the line of the knife, remembering the wound. 'God, they'd have been a mess. You should search for bloody clothes.'

'Mmmm . . .' James's agreement made her sigh.

'Of course. You've already searched. Found anything?'

'No. We didn't, nor did Mrs F.'

'Mrs F?' At hearing of her involvement, Nell's eyebrows flashed up, making her wince.

'So if Greta's left-handed, who else is? We could count them out,' Rav said. 'James, did you notice when people signed their statements?'

He frowned. 'Hamish. Angus. Crispin. That's quite a high percentage. Anyway, now we know there was a scuffle, we'll look for evidence. So, SOCO are coming in this morning to look again for evidence on the landings.'

'A *scuffle*?' Nell echoed. She frowned, then stared at Rav with wide eyes, as inspiration struck.

Rav looked at her, puzzled. Then his face brightened. 'Of course!'

Nell turned to James. 'Have the SOCO team only looked inside the house?'

'So far,' James answered. 'They've had a cursory look around the grounds, I believe, but their attention has been focused on the stairwell.'

Rav and Nell leaned forward. Nell whispered, 'They need to look in the barn.'

James stared at Nell, then Rav. Since Rav didn't need to ask, James was determined he wouldn't. *Must be something ecological.* He racked his brains, hoping something would occur to him while he emailed the SOCO team.

Nell waited for him to finish, then asked, 'What was the other report from the pathologist? You said there were two.'

'Oh, yes.' James flicked through the pages. 'Here we are. Two findings on Hawke's body. One is a series of four tiny puncture marks on Hawke's mid-thigh. In a line . . . looks like it could be . . .'

Despite her intermittent brain-fog, the memory jolted into Nell's mind.

'A fork,' she said. '*My* fork. I stabbed him when he felt up my thigh at dinner.'

'You *stabbed* him? You absolute *goddess*!' Rav looked delighted. 'You're bloody *brilliant*! I was just going to punch him!'

James glanced from Nell to Rav. 'And did you?'

Rav coughed. 'Er . . . No.' He shrugged at Nell. 'I couldn't find him.'

'So that graze, on your knuckles?' James pressed.

Rav huffed. 'I punched the next best thing: a wall. OK? I was angry with Hawke for assaulting Nell and I wanted to punch the smug bastard's face in. But I didn't find him. So I punched the wall, and I came off worst. It bloody hurt.'

'Idiot.' Nell rolled her eyes at him, biting back a smile. 'Lucky I could take care of it myself, then.'

'Right. I'll update Dr Saunders that we can account for the, er . . . stabbing on Hawke's thigh, then,' James said. 'And I *am* trying to play down your murderous motives, by the way. It would be great if you could get on board with that particular programme.'

'And the other?' Nell insisted.

'What?' James asked.

'The other finding in the report? What was it?'

'Oh. A red mark on his back. A faint horizontal red line. Maybe his belt was too tight? Looks like it's a bit high for that. And far too thin.'

James turned to the post-mortem report. He turned his phone towards Nell. With scientific interest, she peered curiously at the graphic series of pictures, showing the line on Hawke's body, then a close-up with a micrometre measuring the two-millimetre width of the red indentation. Nell handed the phone back, frowning, as James took it from her and emailed Dr Saunders.

Something about that mark was strangely familiar.

Tuesday 16th March – 8 a.m.

Rav tried to act relaxed, as the refectory filled up with people coming in for breakfast. Both sets of parents sat with Angus, Theo and Deborah.

At the other end of the table, Crispin sat with Shannon, looking at her in concern. Rav realised he was staring and looked away.

Nell's dark bruises stood out on her pale skin like a bad makeup job of a Halloween skull. She stood up. 'I need some more coffee. Do you want some?' Rav nodded. So did James.

As she waited by the gurgling coffee machine, Mrs Faulkner brought in the post, piled on a salver, leaving it on the sideboard. Nell glanced at it and took the top envelope.

Opening it, she pulled out a card. Something fell out from inside it, clattering on the parquet floor in the quiet room. It skittered beside Crispin's feet, as everyone craned to see what it was.

'Allow me,' Crispin said.

'Thank you!' Nell said. He stared at it for a second, then gave Nell the SD card as he stood up.

Nell scanned the card and looked at Rav. 'A thank-you note. Sounds like Mum and Dad made a donation to the hospital. The staff found this SD card in the pocket of my leggings, which they had to dispose of.'

Apprehension prickled the back of Rav's neck. *Is that why Nell had been pushed in the river? Is there something on the SD card?*

'Oh?' He kept his tone casual. 'It'll be no good. With all the water damage and being battered around so much. May as well write it off; I'll bin it.' He held out his hand and Nell gave it to him. He nearly sagged with relief to have taken it from her. But he forced a smile.

James stared at the card in Rav's fingers. 'Tech these days is indestructible,' he said. 'Put it in a bag of rice; it should be fine.'

Managing not to scowl in exasperation, Rav made a show of examining it. 'Nah. The casing's cracked. Water will have got into the chip. I trashed one in a similar way, on that building site. Do you remember, Nell?' He didn't look at her or wait for her answer. 'So there's no chance of recovering whatever's on there.'

The only other post addressed to Nell was a small, padded envelope. She opened it to find that the card reader for the owl box's SD cards had finally arrived, so she could plug it – and the card – into her phone. Easier than finding a laptop each time they wanted to check the footage. She held it out to Rav.

'Hey, we could check it now, see if it works—'

Rav knocked his mug of coffee over. 'Oh crap. Sorry.' He mopped up the table, and Nell shoved the card reader in her pocket and passed him a refill.

Quick reactions were still a challenge. Her head throbbed. 'I think I need some air.'

James nodded, scrambling to his feet, but Rav struggled to stand and retrieve his crutches. James paused to help him, as Nell walked ahead of them to the courtyard.

Outside, Nell took deep, cleansing breaths. Rapid steps behind her made her turn sharply. She winced and rubbed her pounding head.

Theo's angular face looked stern as he strode towards her, seizing her elbow, steering her forcefully from the French windows at a brisk pace.

She flinched at his manhandling, pulling away. 'Hey, careful.'

He let go and turned to face her, but he didn't exactly look contrite.

'Nell, you are running around like you think you are invincible,' he hissed. 'You are *wrong*. You will get hurt – *again* – if you continue like this. You can't just blunder around and think people don't notice. Or don't care. They *do*. And more than one person has already paid the price for it. *Think* about that.' Glancing over his shoulder again, seeing James heading towards them, Theo glared at her, then strode inside.

Shocked, Nell watched him disappear through the doorway. She held her arm where his fingers had gipped her. *Did Theo just threaten me?*

Behind James, Rav limped out on his crutches, hurrying, grimacing. 'Are you OK?' James asked.

'Not really,' Nell said, looking at him, and then Rav, as he joined them. 'I think . . . I think Theo just warned me off.'

'Does he know that we know about the affair?' Rav asked. 'We haven't discussed it inside the house. How could he know?'

'Oh, no!' Nell gasped. 'When we were in Hawke's room.' She avoided looking at James, who was sighing. 'Someone came in.'

'What?' James's head jerked round. 'Now you tell me!'

'We were both in there,' Rav reasoned. 'So if Theo also came in, and realised he wasn't alone, why are you the one being shoved off a bridge and threatened? Why not me?'

'Because I was wearing perfume,' Nell said.

Chapter 33

Hearing vehicles across the courtyard, James nodded towards the barn. 'That'll be SOCO. Shall we . . . ?'

Their progress was slow. Rav was clearly in pain, so James tried to saunter casually. But Nell was keen to get to the barn before SOCO did. She tried to hurry but, despite not moving very fast, her hand still cradled her temple.

Rav nudged him. 'James, I was lying about the SD card being damaged. Can you give it to your forensic team? If there was a fight in the barn, it could be recorded on there.'

Fear curled around James's heart. He appreciated Rav's discretion and didn't break stride as he palmed the card.

Nell stood guard at the barn's entrance, squinting against the morning sunlight, as the SOCO team crunched across the gravel towards her. As the team assembled, suited and booted, they looked at James, awaiting orders while he pulled on his forensic suit and shoe covers.

'Thanks for coming out. I'm going to ask Nell to explain what we're looking for.'

Dr Saunders handed Nell a suit. She unfolded it, pulled it on gingerly over her clothes and bruised body, and then donned the booties and gloves.

'This barn is strictly out of bounds,' Nell said. 'All the staff know that, and so do all the guests. Hence the sign.' She pointed at the chain across the open doorway, the No Entry sign clear, as a SOCO team member took photos. 'The reason it's out of bounds is because we had barn owls perching, and now – hopefully – nesting in here.'

James saw the row of blank faces and leaned forward. 'Schedule

One bird,' he said, gratified to see Nell's surprise, then approval. He'd looked it up after he'd found her and Rav installing the box. 'Protected against disturbance.'

'Exactly. So no one could come in here. Yet, there are signs someone has. You might even consider them to be signs of a scuffle.'

She unclipped the chain and the team filtered in, the photographer taking photos of the barn as they progressed.

Inside the barn, James subtly handed the SD card to Dr Saunders. 'Can you bag this as evidence and send to the tech team?' he said quietly. 'It's from the cameras in here.'

Nodding, she bagged it and labelled it. The team around them frowned as they scanned the clean barn.

'No signs of any disturbance. You might have to give us a clue, Nell,' Dr Saunders said.

Blinking in the dim light, Nell pointed at the chunky cross-beam running down the centre of the barn. The barn floor was completely clear, except for a couple of pellets directly below the beam.

'There's about eleven signs of disturbance in here.' Nell pointed at the clear floor. 'All along here, under this beam, is where all the owl pellets *should* be. But they're not. This is an ideal perch for the barn owls to regurgitate them. So you should see them all directly below the beam, like these are.'

The photographer obliged with more pictures of context, beam and pellets.

She pointed at the clusters of pellets along the walls and in the corner. 'But the pellets are here. Too far from the cross-beam for them to have been regurgitated. And there's nothing above the pellets for the owls to perch on while they bring them up.'

Turning to the team, she added, 'So the only way they can be there, against the wall like that, is if there was a disturbance. Something – like a scuffle – to kick them all aside. And we saw them under the beam on the day of the wedding, when Rav and I installed the box. But the morning *after* – the wedding *and* Hawke's murder – they weren't. So I think Hawke and whoever murdered him had a fight in here. Maybe they thought it would be private, and they wouldn't be interrupted?'

Nell's gaze slowly scanned the barn, then stopped as she looked at a rickety shelf. She pointed at it. 'And that twine, on the shelf? It wasn't there the morning after the murder. I knocked that shelf off the wall. It was empty. But the twine was there the day before, and it's there again now.' She frowned.

The photographer took photos, and his colleague bagged the twine wound around two wooden pegs.

James glanced at her. 'I've seen that used in the kitchen garden. Wouldn't people just use that if they needed it? It's not like getting some twine will disturb the owls.'

'No . . . Not from in here. I'm sure of that.' Her hesitation and expression suggested there was more to this. And he knew enough about Nell to trust her instincts, even when she didn't.

Nell saw that Rav was struggling on his crutches. He winced with every step, and even standing still meant he had to lean on his injured shoulder.

She felt guilty for making him rush about to the barn and wait. Even though she was fizzing with curiosity, she didn't need to watch the SOCO team examine the barn, or listen in to their findings. James waited with them, but craned his head to see as much as he could.

'Shall we go inside, take the weight off?' She made the offer to Rav, even though she hoped he would say no.

'*What?* After your genius idea and getting the team to check it out? *No* way!'

Nell grinned at him.

'Sir?' A member of the SOCO team called from inside the barn. James hurried forward. 'Yes?'

As he followed the SOCO inside, Nell and Rav moved closer, but the SOCO put up a hand. 'Sorry.'

'But—' Nell protested. *Bloody hell. How infuriating!*

'Sorry. This is a crime scene now.'

'What have you found?' Nell inched forward, craning to see past the SOCO's restraining hand. Inside the barn, she saw an ultraviolet light flashing. 'You've found blood?'

'Please, madam. I know this was your suggestion. But you have to leave, or you'll compromise our process. Then we won't be able to use this evidence.'

Nell agreed instantly. 'I'm sorry. Of course.'

She turned, as if heading back to the house. But when the SOCOs were all busy again, she steered Rav gently towards the summer house.

'Great minds.' Rav shot her a conspiratorial grin.

'I'm just thinking of you. It's the nearest place for you to sit down.'

As he tried to get comfortable, Nell mused, 'So someone fought with Hawke in the barn. And then, what . . . Hawke followed them? Or headed to bed, and fell from the landing?'

'I know you want to think this was misadventure, but surely someone would have spoken up?'

'Well, you wanted to punch him. If you'd found him and had a fight, would you tell the police?'

Rav exhaled. 'Well, I'd have punched him into next week. If I'd have found him. So I'd be right in the frame. And no, I wouldn't have wanted to tell the police.'

'I hope you would have had the sense to. They'd only find out, and you'd look more suspicious keeping it from them,' Nell protested.

'Well, I'll never know, will I? More to the point, why would anyone think that if they'd punched Hawke in the barn and then he fell to his death somewhere else, the two things were related?' He gazed at her. 'I do know I'd like to smash in the face of whoever pushed you off the bridge.'

Nell shuddered. 'OK, let's not dwell on that. Why kill Linda? Or Cameron?'

'Maybe Linda saw? Maybe Linda was involved, if it was linked to the business?'

'And Cameron?'

Rav shrugged. 'I don't see a link there for anyone but maybe Theo or Shannon, if this is related to the family. Even then, I don't see a motive. Because Percy benefits, rather than Douggie and Greta.'

'Yeah, but no one *knew* that.'

'Except Percy.' He shook his head at Nell's glance. 'No, I know it can't be her.'

'Do you think it was the same murderer? For all three?' Nell asked.

An idea unfolded as she thought about the three different murders. *Who would have had cocaine?*

'Oh God. We're idiots.' She stared at Rav. 'If Cameron's drink was spiked with coke, there's only one person who would have done that.'

'Who?' Rav asked. 'I mean, it's a pretty mixed crowd. Deborah's from that fast-paced New York lifestyle. Theo's very high-life. Percy and Shannon are both hedonists . . .'

'Sure, but only Percy would have gained something, and she wouldn't have done it.'

'Then who?'

'Our murder victim's a murderer. Hawke.'

Tuesday 16th March – 9.30 a.m.

Rav watched from inside the summer house as the SOCO team filed back and forth like army ants, with cases, equipment and plates to stand on.

Beside him, Nell mused on motives for Linda's murder, not finding anything that felt strong enough. 'We don't even know for sure that Hawke's murder was linked to Linda's.'

James ducked under the blue-and-white police tape, searching for them as he squirmed out of his protective suit and nodded at the uniformed officer standing guard. Shielding his eyes from the low sun, he glanced up to the seats on the terrace. Then scanned the garden. His eyes rested on the summer house, and he headed over.

Opening the door, he shook his head. 'Subtle.'

'They found blood, then,' Nell said. It wasn't a question and James sighed.

'Yes. On a staddle stone in there. It'll take at least twenty-four hours to process, so don't nag me until tomorrow.'

'Right. Well, I've got more questions,' Nell said.

'Of course you have.' He perched awkwardly. Despite the effort at civility, Rav noted the distance Nell and James kept from one another.

'Can I see the evidence from Linda's death?'

James took out his phone and scrolled through his photos of the case files. 'What are you looking for?' He passed Nell the phone, a photographed page on the screen.

Nell shrugged. 'Something to connect her murder with Hawke's. At the moment, we don't know if we're dealing with two murderers . . . or three?' She took his phone and looked at the information, scrolling through the pages.

'Not one murderer?' James asked.

'Oh no. We've a hypothesis there,' Rav said. 'And you can help us test it.'

James looked at him. 'Go on.'

'Have you found any cocaine in Hawke's blood?'

'No.' James frowned. 'You think he killed Cameron?'

'Yes. So, OK, did you find coke on Hawke's person?'

James shook his head.

'How about in his room?' Rav asked.

'No.'

'Try again,' Nell said, without looking up. 'And this time check the secret compartments in the furniture. Percy will have known about them. Hawke's a right snoop. He may have found one by accident.'

'Can you tell me where those places are?'

'Yes, or I can show you.'

'Fine. I'll ask the team to check before they leave.'

'Thanks.' Nell enlarged the picture of Linda. 'Hang on. What's this?' She pointed at a grey, pointed item attached to the tartan around the hilt of the dagger.

Rav recoiled from the gory close-up of Linda's gaping wound. *Jesus. Nell had tried to close that wound, while blood was pumping out of it.*

'I don't know,' James shrugged. 'Some oddment from your curio cabinet, isn't it?'

'No.' She raised the phone, pushing the image towards Rav. He stopped resisting and stared at it. A small greyish L-shaped item that was maybe . . . what, one centimetre long? The inside of the long side was serrated like a saw, the blades red-tipped.

He frowned, recognition flickering. The saw-blades were tiny, jagged teeth. 'That's a jawbone. Of a common shrew? Or maybe a pygmy shrew?'

'Exactly.' Nell grinned. 'Not something I've ever had in my, *ahem*, cabinet of oddments.'

James winced but looked expectant. 'So where *is* it from?'

'An owl pellet.' Nell's eyebrows flashed up, like that should be significant.

'Right . . . that's not convincing me that you haven't put it on display. I mean, it *should*. Yet it doesn't.'

'I can assure you, I know everything in that cabinet, and *this* wasn't there. No possibility of it finding its way there, or of me being mistaken.'

'So how did it find its way on to the dagger?'

'It was taken there by the murderer. Although they probably didn't know.'

'So how do you know?'

'Because the murderer could *only* have picked this up when they brawled with Hawke in the barn, where we know they disturbed the owl pellets. If they stumbled and fell over, or if they moved Hawke's body from the floor in there, any tiny remnants of a crushed owl pellet could have stuck to their clothes. Maybe transferring from the floor to Hawke to the killer, or directly from the floor to the killer.'

Rav nodded. 'And then to the tartan.'

James peered at the zoomed-in image. 'So this little bone is our key evidence.' His smile at Nell was grimly triumphant. 'Now we have proof that whoever killed Hawke also killed Linda.'

Tuesday 16th March – 10 a.m.

Nell showed the SOCO team to Hawke's room. Re-garbed in suit, booties and gloves, she pointed out the secret compartment in the writing desk. It was empty. The conscientious team duly took photos anyway.

Then she popped the hidden drawer in the bedside table and saw them. *Bloody hell.* Two small, sealed, plastic bags containing white powder.

Dr Saunders saw her reaction and leaned in. 'Two five-gram bags.' She nodded at her colleagues and Nell stepped back, as photographs were taken and an officer opened a case, removing a tub of powder and a fine, splaying brush.

'I'll test these at the lab,' Dr Saunders called to James, who stood in the doorway. 'If they have the same adulterants as the traces found in Cameron's glass, we'll know it's a match.'

Nell tried to look pleased. Hawke may have found these secret compartments on his own. He had a sneaky enough mind to look for things like that. But what if Percy had told him? What if she knew he had something to hide? *She's the one who inherited, after all.*

Nell jerked her head at James, and they walked outside. As Nell removed her protective gear, Rav joined them. 'Any luck?'

She nodded, but the walls seemed to be crowding in on her. The crushing pressure to work out what the hell had happened was overwhelming. She beckoned them along the hall and downstairs in the lift, to her room. 'We're missing something. We need to work this out.'

Both men stared at her, looking concerned.

But Rav nodded. 'OK, let's go through what we know.'

Nell shot him a smile.

The men sank into the chairs flanking her bedroom's fireplace, researching on their phones as Nell paced, dredging through her fractured memory, trying to recall any sense of the person who pushed her.

'Right.' Rav made her jump as he read from his phone. 'On the business side, Hawke poached the chef – ha! – from two Michelin-starred restaurants, Aigle De Mer and Peregrine's.' He glanced at James and Nell. 'Were either of those Shannon's parents' place?'

Nell shook her head. 'But it doesn't mean there isn't a connection.'

'OK. Also Chamomilla Spa.' He looked at them again. 'Nothing Theo or Deborah had backed?'

'No,' James said. 'I've got a list of announcements of venture capital from the two investors, and those places aren't on there. But Deborah's invested in a few hotels. What was the name of the chain Hawke bought?'

Rav googled. 'Prestige Hotel Group.'

'What did you say?' Nell's face drained of colour. She gripped the window ledge.

'What?' James leaned forward.

'Let me . . . let me check.' Nell took Rav's phone, typed in a search with shaking fingers. A few seconds later, she gasped. 'Oh, God.'

She turned the phone towards them. James grabbed it, reading aloud:

'An inquest has recorded a verdict of suicide for Lord Arthur Peale, Earl of Tercelford, 63, from Oxfordshire, who died on 8th October last year. Lord Peale, husband of Lady Felicity Peale, committed suicide by shooting himself in his study, where he was discovered by his wife some hours later. Lord Peale became depressed due to the failure of his company, Prestige Hotel Group, resulting in numerous redundancies. Lady Peale, giving evidence at the inquest, spoke of the pride Lord Peale had taken in his company, and how he had intended to pass it on as a successful family business to his children. In a statement, Lady Peale said she was "shocked that the company could have been so badly mismanaged, and she couldn't believe [her] husband could have conducted business this way". She ended by sending her apologies to all those affected.'

Rav checked the date of the article. Five years ago. 'Who's Felicity Peale? Is she . . . ?'

'No. Not her.'

Rav looked at Nell. 'Peale? *Crispin* Peale?'

Chapter 34

James stared at Nell as she swallowed. 'Crispin's father killed himself five years ago. Poor Crispin. Well, I mean . . .' She shook her head. 'I can't imagine him murdering Hawke. He *admired* him.' She looked at Rav. 'Do you think he planned it? Before he even came here?'

Rav frowned. He ploughed his hand through his hair. 'No.' He looked up. 'No, I don't think he knew until at least after dinner. He seemed happy for Hawke. I don't see him being that good an actor.'

Nell nodded. 'He must have known Hawke's company bought the business. What he *can't* have known was that Hawke ran it down first. So the ruin Crispin's father blamed himself for wasn't his fault at all. Jesus. Imagine learning that.' She chewed her lip as her thoughts raced over the night of the dinner. 'So how did he find out?'

'Oh, no.' James had the epiphany, even though he didn't want to say it out loud. '*Shannon* knew. She knew how Hawke operated. If she mentioned it to Crispin, as he took her up to bed . . .'

Rav nodded. 'Yes, that makes sense. I didn't see any change in Crispin's mood over the evening, and I don't think he could have hidden a revelation like that. But that was the last we saw of him.'

'And Shannon's words would have turned Crispin's world upside down,' Nell said. 'All this time, he'd seen Hawke as a saviour, buying his dad's failing business—'

'And he'd have realised that Hawke ran it into the ground . . .' Rav raised his eyebrows. 'Jeez . . .'

'And knowing that his dad had committed suicide – for failing the business and his employees . . . Imagine finding out that, actually, he *didn't* fail. That Hawke *deliberately* drove it into ruin. For *profit*.' Nell chewed her lip. 'Crispin even said that Hawke was a rock to him when his dad died. And all along, he'd orchestrated his destruction.'

'Bloody hell.' Rav glanced at James. 'How must Crispin have felt?'

'Murderous.' James took his phone out of his pocket and started looking through documents. He looked up. 'But Crispin was downstairs as Hawke fell. He was with Mrs Faulkner.' He gazed into the middle distance, wondering how he had managed it.

'If Crispin punched him in the barn, could Hawke have got upstairs on his own and been light-headed, and just fallen?' Rav asked.

James frowned. 'He *might* have got to his feet. He *might* have staggered a small distance. But honestly, I don't see him floundering up a flight or two of stairs, totally unnoticed. Do you?'

They sat in silence. James practically saw the seed of an idea take root in Nell's mind as she sat up. 'Of course. That line . . . I know how Crispin did it.'

Rav frowned at her, then his face cleared. 'Ah! Yes!'

As she moved towards the door, Rav heaved himself up, aligned his crutches, and then he and James followed.

On the landing, Nell called the lift, glancing around. On their ascent, she whispered, 'Hawke could have fallen from the second floor or the third.'

James agreed. 'Yes, according to the calculations.'

As the lift doors opened, Rav hung back. 'I'll take the third floor.'

Nell nodded. 'OK, we'll check this floor.' James looked quizzically at Nell. He couldn't help noticing that now she was on the trail, colour had returned to her cheeks, around the gruesome blotches and grazes, and a sparkle was back in her eyes.

She scrutinised the gleaming mahogany balustrade, starting from one end and working along the length of the gallery. She crouched stiffly, then slowly checked each side, and in between every single spindle, methodically. At the end of the landing, she stood and looked over the balustrade, then walked back to where she started.

There, she kneeled awkwardly, and covered the entire width of the hall with a slow fingertip search, groaning occasionally as she moved inch by inch. James watched her curiously.

'Think you're a SOCO now, do you?'

Nell gave a relieved smile as she took a breather. 'No different to an amphibian search or looking for mammal hairs. You could help!'

James pushed the sleeves of his hoodie up. 'You'll have to tell me what we're looking for, first.'

Tuesday 16th March – 11 a.m.

Upstairs, Rav mirrored Nell's actions, but more awkwardly, with his inflexible foot and stiff shoulder.

He'd worked from the end of the hall, back towards the lift, leaning against one of the disused tables that lined the wall and squinting at the wall lighting sconce. His crutches got in the way, so he'd set them aside soon after he'd started the detailed search. Near the lift doors, something caught his eye on the ornate wrought-iron curls of the sconce. He stepped closer, standing on tiptoe as best he could.

He reached out a hand and, with his finger, lightly brushed a small knot of green twine, feathered at the ends where they'd been cut. He turned to look at the balustrade, a few feet away, and peered down to the hall.

'Got it,' he whispered.

He heard footsteps behind him.

'I've found it. Proof of how Crispin did it,' Rav said, turning towards Nell.

He froze. It wasn't Nell.

Crispin stood in front of him, the lift doors beyond silently closing. His face was flushed and he stared at Rav with wide, shocked eyes under a creased brow. Suddenly, Crispin's expression twisted into desperate rage. He gave an anguished cry as he flew at Rav, smashing into him.

Rav tried to sidestep, limping, putting his hands out to push back against Crispin's attack. But Crispin's momentum slammed them both against the iron-and-wood balustrade. Rav teetered and slipped on the polished banister, his back to a void of emptiness that plummeted into the vast stairwell. With his shoulders overhanging the three-storey drop, he gripped the banister with both hands, using all his strength to push back against Crispin's explosive force.

Rav's top-heavy physique worked against him as he tried to gain enough leverage to not . . . fall . . . backwards. Crispin stretched one hand up, then the other, to press against Rav's throat, closing off his airway. Rav realised that if he let go of the banister, he'd fall. He couldn't push Crispin off. He couldn't even kick him. And if he headbutted him, they'd both fall over the balustrade.

He gripped tightly but, as Crispin squeezed, Rav's vision swam, blurring with black spots. He dimly heard running steps pounding up the stairs, as he blacked out.

A ferocious, feral scream was followed by Crispin's grip going slack. Rav suddenly felt light, tipping forward as the forceful weight he had pushed so hard against was lifted. He gasped, as his windpipe was free of pressure, wheezing as he took grateful gulps of air. Panting, he pulled himself to standing.

Rav's blotched vision was clearing, but . . . was he hallucinating? It looked like Nell, as some sort of warrior-angel, was pulling Crispin back by his neck, her fingernails gouging his windpipe. Crispin's arms flailed, but Nell's face was hard with resolve, her fingers rigid as talons, drawing blood. This was taking every molecule of her strength. Rav desperately wanted to help her, but he could barely stand.

And then, as if from nowhere, James rushed in, and Nell was safe to release Crispin, who backed away, cowering.

James stopped dead and stretched out his hands, his palms upwards. His tone was calming, reassuring, as he addressed Crispin.

'All right, take it easy,' he said. 'We understand what happened. It'll be OK. Let's sort this out.'

Crispin's hunted gaze darted wildly between the three of them. His hair was slick with sweat, his face sickly white. Blood trickled from punctures down each side of his neck into his collar. The air was sharp with sweat and panic. Crispin glanced at the balustrade—

Nell's voice was breathless. 'No, no, Crispin . . . No one could blame you.'

He shook his head, an anguished whimper escaping from him. Before anyone could react, with another explosive burst of energy, Crispin bolted towards the balustrade and vaulted over.

'No!' Nell flung herself against the side, leaning over to grab him, her hand outstretched as he fell. Her scream echoed around the stairwell.

They heard the sickening crunch of Crispin's body hitting the floor below. Nell swallowed hard and sank to the ground, shaking.

James dashed to her side, looking down at the hall. 'Oh God.' He glanced at Nell and then – pausing only to pull a dust sheet off one of the tables – sprinted downstairs.

Nell turned to Rav, who held his reddened throat, gasping for air through his battered, tender trachea. She gingerly helped him to a seat and kneeled beside him, then checked his throat with soft fingers, holding his gaze.

'Are you OK?' she whispered.

Her eyes on him scorched with longing. He drank her in, traced the outline of her cheek, his touch feathering down her neck with tenderness and urgency.

'I am now.'

He pulled her against him and, finally, thoroughly kissed her.

Chapter 35

Nell's scream had summoned a petrified gathering. After she'd made sure Rav was OK, they joined the shocked company in the drawing room. James corralled then all with gentle authority, having covered Crispin with a sheet.

With awful déjà vu, Mrs F supplied endless tea and coffee, but gave Deborah special treatment, serving her a bourbon; then Val arrived to take statements and SOCO processed the scene.

No one had been able to face lunch. So Mrs Faulkner occasionally added biscuits or cakes to the trays. A comforting fire still roared in the grate; the room's sofas and chairs had been pulled towards its warmth, with soft lights from lamps chasing out the shadows in the corners. And now the shock was subsiding, curiosity was setting in.

But the company seemed to be hyper-aware of Deborah's feelings. The first questions had to come from her. Finally, she raised her head and asked James, 'Why Linda? I see why he went after Hawke. But why my Lindy?'

James took a deep breath. 'I think because she openly defended her son. After we'd all given our statements. Not just him, but his *work*. Saying she worked alongside him. We all heard her. So Crispin would have known she was complicit or, possibly, actively involved in his father's ruin. And his family's.'

Deborah nodded, uncomfortable. Her eyes slid to Theo, and Nell recalled Deborah telling him about her row with Linda: that she hadn't been surprised about her son's unscrupulous business practice.

Now, Deborah sighed and stared down at her lap. 'To be honest with you, I keep thinking of Crispin's poor mother. Losing the family business, then her husband, now her son.'

Imelda nodded. 'James phoned Crispin's mother, Felicity, today. She wants to come here . . . I suppose to put things to rest in her own mind. I said she could, of course.'

Deborah, nodded, looking completely drained. 'I'm leaving in the morning. I've ordered an early taxi to the airport, to fly back to New York. So thank you for your hospitality. And I hope you'll forgive me if I turn in early. I need to pack and I might actually sleep tonight, now that I'm not listening out for every squeaking floorboard outside my bedroom door.'

She got up and walked across the room to kiss Theo on both cheeks. He squeezed her hand, then released her. Greta rose to clasp Deborah's hands before she left the room.

As Greta squashed herself back into the love seat with Douggie, Percy shot worried glances at them. She was curled up on the sofa next to Nell, both tucking their feet underneath themselves. Rav sat beside Nell, his crutches leaning against the wall.

Across from them, in the armchair, Shannon looked stunned. She glanced at James. 'Are you sure no one else told Crispin about Hawke's business methods?'

'No one else knew, except Theo and Deborah. And they didn't say anything to Crispin.'

Shannon blinked rapidly. A look dangerously close to guilt or remorse flickered over her face. Nell stared at her, wondering if, for the first time ever, she was witnessing Shannon having some empathy.

Beside her, Percy gazed at her lap, her cheeks reddening in acute embarrassment, her fingers gripping a cushion. Nell nudged her. 'You didn't know?' she whispered.

Percy's lips tugged downwards. She looked sideways at Nell and whispered, 'I suppose I didn't *want* to know. I presumed the casinos were successful, not that he had to prop them up . . . like *that*.'

'Aye, we know Hawke was an arsewipe,' Angus announced, winning an approving glance from Douggie. 'But Crispin was downstairs when Hawke fell. So how did he do it?'

James nodded at Nell and Rav. 'These two worked it out.'

Nell leaned forward. 'We reckon Crispin wanted to confront Hawke. He'd just learned from Shannon what had really happened to his family business and why his dad killed himself. I think he wanted answers. The last time Crispin had seen Hawke, he'd been heading out to the terrace, so it makes sense Crispin would have looked there first. Deborah and Linda had also gone out there with Hawke, but then Percy had wanted to talk to him. So I think Deborah and Linda left the newlyweds to it. Knowing Percy,' Nell slid her a sidelong look, 'she gave Hawke a rapid-fire talking-to before storming off?'

Percy blushed.

'So when Crispin found him, Hawke would have been alone. Crispin wouldn't have wanted to risk interruption. The nearby barn would've been the perfect spot to talk. But once Crispin had it out with him, I can't exactly see Hawke apologising, can you? So a fight was inevitable. If Crispin punched him, and maybe knocked him out, he'd have thought he had a body to get rid of.'

'I can definitely imagine that,' Rav asserted. 'I was surprised at his strength.'

'But the punch was right-handed, and Crispin was left-handed,' James added. 'Hence he attacked Linda from behind the sofa, and wouldn't have had any bloody clothes to dispose of.'

'Ah, of course. He was a polo player,' Nell said. At James's and Rav's blank stares, she added, 'You have to play polo right-handed, otherwise you can have a dangerous collision. So he probably had a stronger swing with that arm.'

'Aaaand, bingo!' James held up his phone. 'Ed's told me that the SOCO report has just come in. They fast-tracked the samples to close the case. Traces of Hawke's blood were found on the wall. Just small patches were left after Crispin cleaned them up, but there's enough.'

'And if their brawl knocked that shonky shelf down, that could have given Crispin the idea to get rid of a body out in the open.'

Rav leaned forward. 'He'd had your tour of the place, Nell, so he knew about the nearside door through to the hall, the lift and the unused third floor.'

'Crispin could have hauled Hawke upstairs, via the lift. He would have unwound the twine, with the gardening pegs at each end. If he passed the twine around Crispin's back, and trapped the pegs in the closed lift doors, Hawke's body would have stayed balanced against the balustrade until the doors opened. Then the pegs would fly out, the twine would no longer hold Hawke up, and he'd tip over and fall to the floor in the hall.'

'But the twine would fall with him, surely?' Theo said.

'That's why he tied a mid-section of it around the heavy lighting sconce,' Rav said. 'So the twine and pegs would whip free, but stay *in situ* on the third floor. Then he went into the lift and let the lift doors close on the pegs, knowing Hawke would stay balanced there until someone called the lift on that floor. Which wasn't going to happen, since it wasn't used. All he had to do then was clean up in the barn – easily done, using things from the bathroom – and nip through the boot room, and *then* make his presence known—'

'Hold on, we're talking about twine,' Greta said. '*Garden* twine. To hold up a body? That's a bit risky, isn't it? Wouldn't it have snapped? Or given way?'

Rav shook his head. He shot Nell a small smile. They used twine on site to hold up plenty of heavy things, including Nell's barn owl box. 'It's surprising how much it can hold.'

'The twine has been matched to the thin red indentation the pathologist found around his back and sides,' James said.

'Yes, when I saw the photo, it looked familiar,' Nell said. 'Though it took me a while to place it. I've caught my fingers in garden twine enough times when we put up my owl box. The indents I got were exactly the same as the one photographed on Hawke's body. And when I thought about the marks I got from climbing . . .' she trailed off. James didn't need reminding of her and Rav stealing into Hawke's room, using a rope without a harness.

Mrs Faulkner cleared her throat. She was perching on an armchair. 'So how did . . . Crispin . . . manage to have a conversation with me – even get a drink! – when he was doing all this?'

'Once Crispin was downstairs, he purposefully attracted attention so he'd have an alibi,' James said. 'You happened to be there, I guess. Asking for a drink from you was perfect – while you were busy pouring it, all he had to do was go into the hall, open the lift doors and press the button for the third floor. You would have found Crispin in the hall just as the lift arrived on the third floor: the doors opened and released the pegs, so Hawke's body fell while Crispin was right beside you.'

Mrs Faulkner folded her arms, her face pale and stern.

'Then, later, Crispin went back to cut the twine off the sconce,' Rav said. 'Which is why I found a little bit still tied on. Presumably, he had too little time to undo the tight knot before the police arrived and searched.'

Nell nodded. 'I think he did that when he said he felt sick and went to the bathroom. He could have got the scissors from the first-aid kit in there, gone to the lift, straight up to the third floor, cut the twine and been back downstairs within minutes.'

Theo stared at Nell. 'This was a gamble, *non*? With everyone right there!'

'True,' Rav said. 'But that lift is totally silent. Once he came down, and the doors were open, he could have picked the moment to come out.'

'And Crispin disguised his grazed knuckles from the punch by leaning on them on the wall when he was out there heaving and looking grief-stricken,' Nell said. 'The next day, Crispin only had to retie the cut twine and return it to the barn. But he did that *after* Rav and I had been in there and seen that the shelf was empty.'

'Both situations were totally opportunistic, weren't they?' Rav said. 'He saw the twine, saw how to use it, then found Linda, presumably dozing, right next to a dagger, while he was in a complete state of . . . I don't know . . . rage, despair? Both?'

The room fell silent.

Percy leaned over to Nell and squeezed her hand. 'But why did he push you in the river?'

Nell frowned.

Rav nudged her. 'The SD card.'

Nell looked at him sharply. 'Oh God! Of course!' She looked back at Percy. 'He thought his fight with Crispin had been recorded on the SD card because of the camera set up for the owls. You changed it before I went running and it was in my pocket.' She chewed her lip. 'God, what a bastard. He could have just asked for it or said he wanted to look. He didn't need to shove me off the bloody bridge.'

'I think he was desperate,' Rav said. 'His whole world was upside down. His supposed best friend had destroyed his family. He can't have been thinking straight. I almost feel sorry for him.'

His dark-eyed gaze studied Nell's face. Nell looked back, remembering Crispin's desperate expression as he leaped to his death. Then she recalled him using all his strength to try to push Rav's already injured body over the balustrade.

She gripped Rav's hand until her fingers whitened.

Chapter 36

Wednesday 17th March – 8 a.m.

As Nell, James and Percy saw Deborah off, they turned and saw Shannon struggling with her luggage. James went over to help.

'I can manage.'

'I know.' James still took the largest case, which couldn't be wheeled across the gravel to Shannon's white convertible E-Class Mercedes parked near the door. 'Where to next, then, outsider? To the slums of your Thames penthouse? Some ghastly gallery opening?'

Nell was surprised when Shannon shot him a smile. 'Funny you should say that. Granda left me a gift. So I've got a bit of an idea there.'

Percy kicked Shannon's low-profile tyre. 'Does that mean you're keeping your mitts off my place then? And maybe even my next fiancé?'

But Shannon didn't respond to the bait. She didn't come back with a smart answer. She smiled at James, who tilted his head, inviting details. 'It's all your fault. So, if my idea doesn't work out, I'll know who to blame.'

'Better have my number, then.' James smiled as he reached into his pocket.

Nell averted her eyes, feeling like a gooseberry, as James handed Shannon his card. James really *liked* her? He really liked *her*?

As Shannon drove off – roof down, shades on, spraying gravel – Percy waved, muttering, 'Good riddance.'

'Right, um . . . so I'm going to hit the road,' James said.

Percy dashed over and hugged him. 'Thanks for everything, James.'

'Well, a lot of it was Nell.' His phone buzzed but he glanced at

Nell, then walked over to her. 'Nice work.' He lightly punched her arm. 'Mate.'

Nell just looked at him, at her arm and back at him. '*Mate?*' His phone buzzing again saved him from meeting her enquiring gaze. He fumbled with it.

'Oh, this is too awks for words. I'm going to find my folks.' Percy shot Nell a comedic grimace and left them to it.

James's phone buzzed for a third time. He glanced at it and jammed it in his pocket.

'You'd better hurry, James. Shannon won't wait at the gate for long.' Nell tilted her head in the direction of the long tree-lined avenue, the faint, idling engine, and a brake-light beaming like a laser through the boundary hedge.

Walking to his car, James's footsteps crunched over gravel. 'I don't know what Shannon's up to . . .'

'No, well, who can ever claim that?'

'But *I'm* heading into the office to get the reports tied up.'

Nell arched an eyebrow. 'Sure, James. And I promise not to check with the staff at the Orangery if you stopped off for a brunch date on the way.'

'Good, and likewise I won't ask you any questions about Rav.'

'Seems fair.' Nell knew she was blushing, but she managed to smile.

'Right. Bye then.'

'Bye.' She watched for a moment as James drove away.

Back inside, she closed the door and heaved a huge sigh of relief. Percy poked her. 'I was just cringing myself inside out over that!'

'Weren't you going to see your folks?'

'Ugh. Yes.'

'Right, so let's see how you style out *your* awkward conversations.'

As Percy joined her parents, with Theo and Angus, Nell took the next table and pretended to read something on her phone.

'Just so you know,' Percy said, 'I've revoked Granda's will. I'll go up tomorrow to sign the paperwork. But Glencoille's yours. As it should be.'

Greta stared at her. 'Aye . . .' She glanced at Douggie. 'Thank you. That means a lot.'

Percy let out the breath she'd been holding. 'I never intended to hold on to it. Hawke lied to me about Linda. I thought she was dying. I didn't know it, but he was forcing me to rush the wedding. It meant I had to make up a convincing lie to Granda to get things moving.'

Greta stared at her, guessed Percy's lie, then exploded with laughter. 'Oh, the stupid old duffer!'

Douggie shook his head. 'I don't know why you fell for that Hawke . . . You're smarter than that.'

Percy took the compliment, but she shoved her dad's arm. 'You still haven't told me why you threatened to disinherit me. You didn't know about his affair with Shannon then. So what was it?'

Puffing out a long exhale, Douggie stared at Greta, as Nell slid down in her seat. She wished she didn't know.

Greta poured herself a coffee. 'Because Hawke was blackmailing me, my love.' She added milk and sipped her drink. 'With a . . . compromising tape.'

Percy stared at her mother and shot a sidelong glance at her father, who was uncharacteristically unruffled. Her nosiness won out and she leaned forward. 'You mean . . . of you and . . . *Who*?'

Greta rested her hand on Theo's.

Percy's eyes widened. She stared at her parents. 'But . . . you . . . I thought you were happy together.'

'We are. But we're also grown adults with our own arrangements.'

'But you always talk about being such a good match.'

'Yes, to understand each other so well. To like and respect each other. We're great friends. Best friends. But we didn't have a choice in the matter, did we?'

'So you would have chosen Theo, given the choice?'

'Maybe. In another life.'

'But . . . if you knew,' she turned a quizzical gaze to her father, 'then how could the blackmail work?'

Douggie sighed. 'Same reason we couldn't divorce, petal. Not that we wanted to. Because of me. Because of my bigot of a father. Because he wouldn't accept the person I loved. And he threatened to take Glencoille away from me, away from *you*, if I . . . *disobeyed* him.'

Percy stared at her father. 'So you're having an affair, too? Who with?'

But Douggie shook his head. 'It's not just me I'll affect by telling you, petal. But I think you've got the gist.'

Angus leaned forward. 'May as well tell her, Douggie. She's too canny, this lass.' At Douggie's nod, Angus turned to Percy. 'Douggie wasn't only protecting his birthright, and yours. He was protecting me, too, Percy.'

Percy looked stunned. 'Hang on . . . *What*?'

'Relationships like ours were illegal until 1980. And I'm the Sheriff of Glencoille. Up until then, it was part of my duty to arrest people like us.' He sat back, shaking his head. 'Can you imagine, lass? I . . . I'd turn a blind eye where I could, but I was walking a tightrope of people asking awkward questions. And if I was sacked, or even arrested, well . . . the next sheriff might never've turned a blind eye. Even so, there were a few . . . incidents . . . which I still lose sleep over.'

'But that's decades ago—'

'Aye, but folk have long memories. And I cannae blame 'em, can I?'

'God.'

As Percy stared at her family, Nell saw her absorbing the shift.

'Right.' She blinked, then nodded a couple of times. 'Right.' She smiled. 'Any coffee going spare?'

Angus poured, Douggie added milk and Theo passed it to her.

'Thanks.' Percy took a sip. 'And I thought *my* love life was complicated.'

Her mother laughed. 'Oh, my sweet young daughter, you're a novice.' At Percy's indignant look, her mother winked. 'Give it time.'

Rav spotted Nell on the terrace and limped out to join her. As he did, a gangly man rushed past and paused to hold the door open, despite fizzing with energy to bolt outside.

'Hamish?'

Hamish frowned, and Rav realised they hadn't been properly introduced. 'I'm Nell's . . . um, well, I'm Nell's.'

'Ah.' Hamish clasped Rav's arm. 'Well, don't make my mistake.' As they stepped outside, he dropped the morning's newspapers onto an empty table, and dashed over to Percy.

Ducking the effusive hugs from her parents, Hamish grabbed Percy's hand and strode across the garden to the lake. Halfway across the stone bridge, arching over the mirror-smooth water, he dropped to one knee in front of Percy, patting his hips and then his jacket pocket, and finally producing what Rav assumed was a ring. He held it out towards Percy. As she pulled him to his feet, he stumbled. He looked at the ground, then into the water.

'Oh no . . .' Nell held her head in her hands, peeping between her fingers. 'He's dropped the bloody ring!'

Percy joined him at the side of the bridge, looking over the stone balustrade, then at Hamish. Nell could see she had started to laugh. Hamish was shrugging off his jacket, as if about to dive in, but Percy stopped him, dragging him towards the house, galloping back to share the news.

Greta and Douggie stood up, whooping and clapping. Percy held out her un-beringed hand, while Hamish was hugged by Greta and blackslapped by Douggie. With timing suggesting prearrangement, Mrs Faulkner, joined by Angus and Theo, appeared with champagne. Percy poured Mrs F a glass, as Greta took her tumbler of sparkling water and raised it to toast her daughter.

Spotting Nell and Rav, Greta brought them over two glasses of champagne. 'Oh, Nell.' She shook her head, her face trembling. 'Thank you. This has been such an awful time. I got myself into such a state over Percy wedding that waster. And I could picture shoving him down those stairs, and I could imagine fighting with Linda. But not . . . not what happened to her. I didn't know what was real or not. I was terrified. But now we know the truth. Well . . .' she glanced back at Percy, hugging Douggie. '*All* of the truths. And I've got my girl back.'

Greta beamed at Percy's radiant face, Hamish beside her looking amazed and smitten. 'And he's *good* for her. Not some slimy enabler who'll take delight in leading her into trouble. Hamish is a total sweetheart.'

'Let's congratulate them,' Nell said, but before they reached Percy, Theo nudged her.

'I am sorry for my clumsy warning. But I knew you were in Hawke's room.'

'My perfume?'

Theo nodded. 'Greta and I were never worried about Hawke blackmailing us. But we were scared for Angus, if Hawke kept digging. So I, let's say, *borrowed* the key from Madame Faulkner, while Greta engaged the guard, and took the chance to look in his room to see if there were any signs he'd found anything else. When I knew you were taking such risks, I was afraid for you.'

'Needn't have worried.'

'*Vraiment.* And how *is* your head today, eh?' He sighed, but smiled fondly. 'And you know very well that this is an unconventional family we are part of. But, where there is love, there is always worry. It is just human nature. And here, there is a lot of love.' With a kind smile, he gave her a one-armed hug, keeping his champagne safe from spillage.

Douggie attempted a speech. For once he was lost for words and instead just raised a toast. As glasses were clinked to the chorus of, 'To Percy and Hamish,' Rav whispered, 'Wow, doesn't it make life easier when they're onside?'

'Yes, OK, you're right,' Nell said. 'But who wouldn't be happy for them when they're such a good match?' Nell's impish smile was back. Like she was inferring that they were an equally good match. He felt that pull towards her and leaned in to kiss her.

'Oh, it's gonna be your turn next!' Percy squealed.

Rav looked at Nell, saw her enticing half-smile make her eyes gleam. 'At least we'll be OK if I chuck the ring in the lake, with all the waders we have between us.'

'Oh. Does that mean you have a plan?'

'I have lots of plans.' He bent to kiss her again, inhaling her warm scent. 'Number one, how about we don't waste any more time?' He smiled into her gleaming eyes. 'Let's go for a walk. Have a moment to ourselves?' As they walked towards the garden, with him limping on his crutches, Nell paused at the table to glance at the newspapers that Hamish had brought.

Leaning over her shoulder, he caught the headline: '*Murder mansion claims third victim*'.

Oh, great. It was a national paper. And the press still had another death to catch up with. Another front page featured a close-up of Hamish and Percy. '*Black widow heiress in clinch with ex*'.

As Nell scanned the articles, Rav imagined her huffs were punctuating the liberal mentions of Finchmere and her own name. But she just turned to him and said, 'You're doing better on those. Can you manage some off-roading?'

'I'll give it a go.' As they walked across the terrace, despite wanting to turn their conversation to romance, he couldn't help asking, 'Aren't you worried? About those headlines?'

'Yes, of course. It's a nightmare.' She glanced at him. 'Especially with the Finchmere Cup next month.'

'Oh yes, your classic-car event? What's the problem?'

'Just sponsors grumbling about the press association. Mum and Dad are off speaking to Montague's, the classic-car auction house, to persuade them not to drop out. The slightest dent in our reputation can mean a massive dent in our income. But it goes with the territory.'

As she helped him down the terrace steps, her shrug infuriated him.

'But . . . but . . . this isn't only about *business*. They're talking about your home, your friends, your family. Don't you care?'

'Yes, of course! But it was inevitable, to a certain extent.'

'I thought you had . . . people. To make sure this doesn't happen.'

'Well, sure – ideally, we'd contain anything. But I've been in hospital, there was a police investigation . . . People talk.' She chewed her lip. 'But you're right, you know. In the last case, I was terrified. But only because I feared people knowing about me. Or finding out about that tape. But now *you* know, I'm not worried.' A smile started to spread across her face. 'Huh. Look at that. I don't care what other people think. I was only ever worried what you'd think.'

'Yeah, but you're not the only one with family, Nell.' *How the hell can I explain all this to my parents? There's no way they'll miss it, splashed all over every paper like that.* 'My family are private, Nell. Quiet, conservative. And they haven't even *met* you yet. This is going to be the first time they hear your name. And I can tell you, this isn't how I planned it.'

'More plans?' She was grinning as they wended their way to the barn.

For God's sake! Why won't she take this seriously?

Her phone rang. 'Hi, James.' As she listened, she put it on speakerphone so Rav could hear him, too.

'. . . SD card wasn't too damaged, so we've got clear footage of Hawke fighting with Crispin. Thanks to that low-light camera for the owls, we know that Hawke falls and hits his head on that stone, knocking down the shelf. Crispin checks Hawke, then backs away, looking horrified. He replaces the shelf, stares at the twine for a second, then pockets it and hauls Hawke into a fireman's carry, over his shoulder. Looking at how he picks Hawke up from the ground, it would be feasible for the jawbone from the owl pellet to transfer from Hawke, who'd been on the ground, to Crispin's sleeve, and then to the material on the dagger.'

Nell raised her eyebrows at Rav.

'And that's not all. We've fast-tracked the examination of that shrew jawbone. And there were bits of fabric and hairs attached to it. One of those hairs was Crispin's.'

Nell gripped Rav's forearm.

'So that's clinched it. No room for reasonable doubt. No investigation hanging over any of your heads. Thought you'd like to know.'

'Thanks, James.' Nell hung up and unclipped the chain across the barn's doorway. She pulled the card reader out of her pocket. 'We can see how they're doing a little more easily now. Imagine if this had arrived a day or two earlier . . .' She grimaced.

'I'm not sure if that would have wrapped the case earlier or made things a whole lot more dangerous,' Rav said, as Nell slid the SD card out of the recorder and into the reader.

A black-and-white image of the two owls inside the box, preening one another, filled the screen of her phone.

'Oh, that's a great sign!' Rav glanced up at the box, its silence giving nothing away.

'Look!' Nell pointed at the screen. As the female shifted, a small round shape was detectable. 'Is that an egg?'

'No way!' Rav beamed. 'There's a couple, look!' They shared a moment of sheer delight; this pair had overcome their ousting and were still flourishing.

As they left the barn, Nell whispered, 'See? We make a good team. In a lot of ways. Percy's folks saw that about her and Hamish. Won't your family think that about us?'

'Oh, Nell. You're going to be a shock. You're not what they'll expect. Mum wants me to marry someone whose family she already knows. But she always picks a type. Quiet, conservative, family-orientated and Hindu.'

Nell stared at him. 'You've never told her what you really think, have you? You tell *me* you know it's up to you to choose, but all the time you're still going on those dates your mum sets up. When are you going to tell her?'

He shrugged. 'I was hoping to have time to get her used to the idea. Bring her around to it gently.'

'Right, OK. Well, those characteristics your mum chooses – are they important to you? Because that would make us pretty fundamentally incompatible—'

'Nope.' He rested on one crutch to reach out and stroke her defiant face. 'I think you know what's important to me.'

'Well, your mum doesn't. And that would be a start, wouldn't it? Telling her that much?'

He sighed but he couldn't deny it. 'Fine. You're right. You should meet my parents.' He thumbed in the direction of the newspapers on the table. 'How about at your Finchmere Cup?'

Nell arched an eyebrow. 'I'll call your bluff. With VIP tickets.'

'I'm not bluffing.' *Aren't I? Jesus. Would it be OK?*

Nell gazed at him, reading his reticence. 'Oh, come on, it can't be *this* hard a task to win them over? I'll make sure they have a great time.' She grinned. 'I promise they'll love me by the end of the weekend.'

Her confidence was infectious. He had to smile. He couldn't resist her when she looked at him like that. As she leaned over to kiss him softly, he wrapped her up in his arms and kissed her back.

Acknowledgements

Family is a strong theme in this book, and I count myself incredibly lucky that writing this series has introduced me to a whole new family: the always-fabulous Katie Fulford and Sarah McDonnell at Bell Lomax Moreton, and the incredible team at Embla books in the talented and imaginative Hannah Smith, Jen Porter, Jane Snelgrove and Emilie Marneur, plus the wonderful Emily Thomas, eagle-eyed Daniela Nava, and Nicola Lovick. Most definitely included in this are Lisa Horton, whose delicious cover designs capture such personality in her characters, and Laura Marlow, her brilliant audio team, and the magnificent acting talents of Kristin Atherton who have produced such enchanting audio books. You have all brought my manuscript to life beyond my wildest dreams.

It's also been a total joy to expand my writing family. The publication of *A Murder of Crows* enabled me to realise the ambition of joining the Crime Writers Association – and their support with articles in the Crime Readers Newsletter and Red Herrings was a genuine and unexpected delight. And Graham Bartlett has helped to keep my police procedural side of things on the straight and narrow – although DI James Clark has definitely crossed a few lines in this book, and I'm sure there will be consequences!

My own family is a small one, but a mighty one. Mum and Dad, thank you for the continued support and excitement at this adventure. I love that you keep reading my drafts, yet received book one like it was a brand-new treasure. And I know you'll do just the same with this one. You have the very kindest hearts of anyone I know, and deep wells of encouragement and generosity. Angel, of course, provides unending, unconditional love (just as long as I feed her, and fuss her on demand). Ian, thank you for making all this possible, for taking the leap with me, and for being my co-adventurer.

We are very lucky to have an extended family of extraordinarily caring friends. A certain W. A. Gang: Janet, Alan, Pam M, Paul, David, Jo, Sheila, Mary, Nigel, Jane, Alan B, Joyce, Martin, Elaine, along with Sue, Helen, John W, Denise, John, Trish, Andy and Pam, have all been towers of strength, optimism and cake, whenever needed.

Matt and Lauren, you are of course very cherished members of my wider family. And, along with Esther, Mark, Sabrina, Jo and Rachel, Alan, Bruce, Julie, Brenda, Bob, Jen and Dan, I'm immensely grateful for your support. Although we should really do something about having more cocktails.

And I've discovered a whole new family through these books – I'm so thankful to readers who were kind enough to read, or even review, *A Murder of Crows* and throw themselves into Nell's adventures. I sincerely hope you'll enjoy this one, too.

The Nature of Crime

The obliging signs that barn owls leave for ecologists to find – such as those Nell observed in her barn – make them one of the easier birds to spot.

I've run some delightful school workshops dissecting pellets to discover the diets of owls. Being regurgitated fur and bone of their prey, the pellets don't smell, and they can contain up to six small mammals (voles, mice and shrews). You can have hours of fun identifying who was eaten by finding its skull and measuring its jawbone.

All three British species of shrew share the unique feature of red-tipped teeth, due to the iron content on the outer layer of the enamel, thought to make the tooth more hard-wearing. For Nell and Rav, the red-tipped teeth enabled an immediate ID – leaving no doubt that their wayward jawbone, found on the murder victim, was itself from a victim of the owls.

The Barn Owl Trust (www.barnowltrust.org.uk) has a wealth of resources, dissection ID kits, barn owl box instructions (including some nifty cameras, like the ones Nell and Rav set up) and habitat management advice. It's also a repository for any records of sightings to help monitor barn owl populations, which have declined from loss of the rough grassland habitat owls hunt in, as well as pesticide use.

Another key species in the book has also been blighted by pesticides. The otter, a charismatic character of our waterways, may be rare and elusive, but its signs are as obvious as the owls'. Because otter spraint is intended to be found, as a way of communicating with other otters, it's routinely left on landmarks such as large rocks, tree stumps or bridge footings. This is very helpful for ecologists, as it was for Nell and Rav when they searched along Nye River. Otter spraint is equally revealing of favoured prey: fish scales, bones and signs of flayed frogs are common. And otter pawprints are usually found where otters haul themselves out of the water, hence why our resident otter could be so helpful to Rav in Nell's time of need by identifying a safe spot to enter the river. While otters can live up to twelve years, they typically only survive for four in the wild, just like barn owls.

Working with an ornithologist to replace roosts for barn owls and pipistrelle bats, which were being lost due to a barn conversion, turned out to be a perfect example of ecology being the branch of biology that deals with the relations of organisms to one another and to their physical surroundings. With replacement roosts in the form of barn owl boxes and bat boxes, the ornithologist warned: it might look tidy to put the boxes on the same wall, but don't; you'll just create a bat buffet for the barn owls – more fly-through than drive-though, but still fast food.

Amongst ecologists, ornithologists are a breed apart; able to identify several hundred species by eye, through flight pattern, or plumage – both adult and juvenile, with variations depending on sex and season – then also by ear, whether from song or warning calls. It's a lifetime study and I'm only too well aware that my own capabilities in this field are highly rudimentary. But I have had the privilege of joining some renowned experts, and highlights include dawn surveys for black redstarts, trekking heathland for elusive nightjars, and dusk surveys for barn owls at a sewage works (such glamour!).

Nesting season is the perfect time to observe just how birds relate to each other. Another ornithologist enlightened me that the melodic dawn chorus that sounds so glorious to us is, to a bird, less Ed Sheeran and more Eminem: threats and warnings to stay out of claimed territories – or else. The extreme measures in the book, of a kestrel ousting barn owls from their nest, is the kind of documented behaviour that underlines this competitiveness. As is the revenge attack by the evicted barn owl. And I can promise some astounding minutes on YouTube if you choose to look it up.

The ruthless competition of those raptors is almost matched by Hawke, as he cuckoos his way into Percy's family – and the fierce protection of human family relationships is just as red in tooth and claw as nature herself.

Author Bio

After spending sixteen years as an ecologist, crawling through undergrowth and studying nocturnal habits of animals (and people), Dr Sarah Yarwood-Lovett naturally turned her mind to murder. She may have swapped badgers for bears when she emigrated from a quaint village in the South Downs to the wild mountains of the Pacific Northwest, but her books remain firmly rooted in the rolling downland she grew up in.

Forensically studying clues for animal activity has seen Sarah surveying sites all over the UK and around the world. She's re-discovered a British species thought to be extinct during her PhD, with her record held in London's Natural History Museum; debated that important question – do bats wee on their faces? – at school workshops; survived a hurricane on a coral atoll whilst scuba diving to conduct marine surveys; and given evidence as an expert witness.

Along the way, she's discovered a noose in an abandoned warehouse and had a survey de-railed by the bomb squad. Her unusual career has provided the perfect inspiration for a series of murder mysteries with an ecological twist – so, these days, Sarah's research includes consulting detectives, lawyers, judges and attending murder trials.

About Embla Books

Embla Books is a digital-first publisher of standout commercial adult fiction. Passionate about storytelling, the team at Embla publish books that will make you 'laugh, love, look over your shoulder and lose sleep'. Launched by Bonnier Books UK in 2021, the imprint is named after the first woman from the creation myth in Norse mythology, who was carved by the gods from a tree trunk found on the seashore – an image of the kind of creative work and crafting that writers do, and a symbol of how stories shape our lives.

Find out about some of our other books and stay in touch:

Twitter, Facebook, Instagram: @emblabooks
Newsletter: https://bit.ly/emblanewsletter